RICHES TO RAGS

casey l. bond

RICHES TO RAGS

BOOK COVER DESIGNED BY

Melissa Stevens / The Illustrated Author Design Services

FORMATTED AND PROFESSIONALLY ILLUSTRATED BY

Melissa Stevens / The Illustrated Author Design Services

PROFESSIONALLY EDITED BY

The Girl with the Red Pen/ Stacy Sanford

Published in the United States of America

ISBN-13: 978-1977662897

ISBN-10: 1977662897

ALSO BY CASEY L. BOND

The Frenzy Series
The Keeper of Crows Duology
The Harvest Saga

DEDICATION

To everyone who's ever bravely fought for something their heart wanted.

WAVERLY

AELAWYN

THE SOUTHERN
ISLE

GRITHIM

RINGSTED

LUNA'S
COTTAGE

VIROSA

BROOKHAVEN

CHAPTER ONE

Once upon a time, in a land far away, there was a kingdom ruled by a heavy-handed king. He was stubborn, refusing to budge from deep-seated and long-held beliefs, and his people paid the price. He never thought about the decrees that fell from his mouth until after the repercussions became evident, and even then, refused to apologize. Foolish pride prevented him from making amends, and he was prideful to a fault—cruel and unforgiving.

His word was law. And he was never at a loss for words.

Because of his harshness, many of the surrounding kingdoms, all of which had been great allies with the King's father, now refused to trade with the Kingdom of Aelawyn. But Aelawyn could not supply itself with all the things necessary to thrive, *and the royalty and nobility could no longer live the life to which they had grown accustomed.*

The King grew desperate. But more than that, he felt he and his kingdom had been wronged. His rage and indignation fell upon everyone who dared cross his path, even the innocent.

The King authorized raids on trade routes and ordered his armies to steal and plunder from his neighbors in the name of survival, in the name of what he thought was right and justified. The neighboring kingdoms' rulers sent warning after warning to the King, each and every one of which went unheeded; the parchments sizzling at the corners as he tossed them into the hungry fire, one after another. Until one day, a different type of message arrived. This was not another parchment with a warning scrawled in slanted ink, sealed with a stamp in melted wax. No. This message was written in blood.

ONE WEEK EARLIER ...

The castle yard was full of people from the village, everyone eager to receive their share of the rations Father would share with them. The sound of laughter and friendly chatter made me smile. Yesterday, the people were probably starving, but today, a heavy burden would be lifted. They would have full stomachs tonight.

Curled up in the window seat, I watched the soldiers uncover the wagons and begin to distribute what they held, a thick shawl drawn around my shoulders to guard against the frigid wind.

Soldiers paced atop the walls surrounding our castle, armed with swords, bows, and daggers. They wore the color of Aelawyn, her King, and his ancestors: a shade of crimson, the color of freshly drawn blood. Their eyes were alert, searching the crowd for any sign of disturbance.

Villagers formed a line that already stretched toward the back of the castle yard alongside the wall. The gate was raised for the villagers to pass in and out of the yard. Men, women, and children, old and young, from every walk of life needed help these days, and there were some things only Father could provide for them. I didn't know how long he would provide for them, since trade had ceased between our kingdom and many of the ones that surrounded us.

I leaned over, listening to their conversations. Children petted the animals as they fed on hay and scraps. Times may have been hard, but the people were resilient. They brought items to trade among themselves: dyed wool, scarves, candles made from the wax of bees, and carved flutes for the children.

The villagers brought a vibrancy to the castle that was missing when the gate closed and the yard was empty. It had been a long winter, but my favorite season was almost here. In the spring, villagers set up booths in the castle yard. Last year, a woman sold bouquets of flowers below my window, their cloying scents wafting up to me from where I perched on my window seat. I'd watch the people, the women wearing dresses in every color of the rainbow and the men tossing their little ones into the air, making them giggle.

When spring came, food wouldn't be so scarce. The people would be busy and happy. They would forget the harshness of winter and enjoy the sunshine.

My lady-in-waiting suddenly burst through my door, looking frazzled. Her gray hair shot out in all directions. "You must hurry, Princess." She waved me forward.

"What's the matter?" I smiled, but as she grabbed my hairbrush and all but jerked me by the arm off of my bench, I knew something was wrong.

"Your father wishes to speak with you. He's waiting." I didn't miss the flash of fear in her dark eyes. Father hated to be kept waiting. He was probably counting how many minutes it would take me to get to the Throne Room.

"Do you know what my father wishes to speak with me about?" I asked, swallowing the thick knot forming in my throat as she quickly brushed the tangles out of my dark hair and placed the small, but heavy crown of gold and diamonds on my head.

"No, milady, but we mustn't keep him waiting."

Father's temper scared Hetty. Father's temper scared me.

Rushing across the room, I stepped into the pair of golden slippers she pulled from my wardrobe. They were a gift from my parents and one that he would appreciate seeing used. Or so I hoped.

Following Hetty down the hallway, my emerald skirts billowed behind me despite the thicker fabric that winter required. We made our way down the main staircase, past servants scurrying this way and that, to the throne room. Hetty waved me on as two guards swept open the enormous double doors. I kept my eyes dutifully averted as I entered.

The throne room—floors, walls, and ceiling—was gold. It was decorated with fine paintings and intricately woven tapestries, and towering columns lined the great hall on either side. Father sat on his dark throne tapping his fingers impatiently. I flinched as his voice echoed harshly through the hollow space.

"Come, Carina."

I walked across the room quickly but carefully. I'd once made the mistake of tripping on the fabric of my gown in front of him. I refused to make it again. Father's punishments were infamous. My fists knotted the thick material on each side, lifting it enough so I could step easily and fast.

Mother stood to the left behind Father and my sister stood to his right, several steps away. Her green eyes flashed in warning.

I stopped at the bottom of the four stone steps that separated me from my family. "Father?"

"I have decided you will marry Prince Yurak of Galder."

My eyelids fluttered in surprise. Marriage? They'd only just announced Ivy's betrothal to Prince Enik of Halron, but at least Ivy was seventeen, while I was three years younger. I opened my mouth, careful to avoid the protestation that sat readily on my tongue. My heart thundered in my chest. "When shall we be wed?"

My mother's face was emotionless, but her grasp on the back of the throne was severe. Her knuckles were white and strained. Ivy looked at me and then back to her feet.

"You and Ivy shall be wed on the same day. Won't that be grand?" He stroked his dark beard and watched me with his hawk-like eyes, searching for a single sign of defiance.

Ivy knew the storm building beneath my skin, on my tongue, and she shook her head sharply. For her sake and mine, I played along. "Yes, Father. When shall I meet my betrothed?"

The Kingdom of Galder lay to the south, positioned along the edge of the great sea. Surely we would have a long engagement.

"You'll meet him on the day you're wed. You've no need to get acquainted with your future husband before the day of your wedding, and you *will* marry Yurak. This will help repair the alliance between our kingdoms. That is the end of the discussion."

"Yes, Father." My fingers clawed the fabric of my skirt. I knew he didn't care about relationships or alliances. He'd severed them all without a second thought, and now his people were paying the price. This was about riches— the only thing he loved and coveted. What price had Yurak of Galder paid for me? And why didn't he want me to see him before our wedding day? Ivy's wedding was already being planned. It would take place in three weeks, as would mine.

"Return to your chamber," he said dismissively. He turned and told my mother to have the seamstress prepare a proper dress for me.

Mother inclined her head in response. How long had it been since I heard her voice?

When he was finished speaking, his eyes flashed in anger to see me still standing in front of him.

"Father?"

His beady eyes hardened and then glinted, daring me to begin an argument. Beneath the warning was a hope I'd take him up on it. It had been a long time since I'd been stupid enough to try his patience.

"I was wondering if I might walk the grounds for a little while."

He blew out a breath of frustration. "No. The gates are open. It's not safe until they're sealed. Return to your chamber immediately. You too, Ivy."

Ivy's shoulders slumped slightly as she walked down the steps toward me, strands of her light brown hair streaming behind her. We walked out of the throne room side by side. When the guards closed the doors behind us, we rushed upstairs. Outside our rooms, Ivy hugged me tight, sobs wracking her body. "I'm so sorry. I begged Mother to talk him out of this."

"When Father's mind is made up, there is no use to argue." We both knew that. It was why Mother didn't even try.

"I understand why he's pushing me to wed. I'm seventeen. But you're only fourteen, Carina!" She blinked away tears, staring toward the ceiling and inhaling deeply. I swallowed the knot in my throat. Soon, I wouldn't be able to hug her, wouldn't be able to talk to her. The stone wall between our chambers might as well have been an ocean while we were locked inside our rooms, but after we married and moved away, I might never see her again.

"Yurak of Galder must have made quite an offer," I said. "That's all he cares about."

She nodded. "I know."

For as long as I could remember, Father had damned us both for not being born male. If he'd had a male heir to follow in his footsteps, things would be different, he said. He was right. Things *would* be different. He'd teach his son to be a tyrant as well, the kingdom would continue down the path to ruin, and my brother would ultimately pay the price for our father's sins. Maybe that was why God only saw fit for Mother to conceive females.

"I wish we could run away," Ivy whispered, her soft brown hair brushing my cheek. She seemed *off* somehow, desperate and frantic in her words.

Clinging to her, I told her I wished we could, too. "Where would we go?"

"Anywhere but here." She squeezed me tighter. She only wanted what every girl wanted: to marry for love.

I'd decided long ago that there was really no point in wishing for things that would never come true. A princess couldn't marry for love. As Ivy's fingers trembled on my back, a foreboding shiver crawled up my spine.

"I thought you were excited to be married," I said softly.

17

She pulled out of my arms. "I was excited to leave *this* God-forsaken place; that was all!" she cried, angrily swiping tears from her face. "But it's all too much. I've heard awful things about Enik, things that make me think our Father is a saint! This isn't the life I want, Carina. If I marry Enik, I'll only be trading one cage for another. I just can't..." She paused. "But you're strong, Carina. You'll be fine."

"Everything will be fine," I said with false enthusiasm. "Don't listen to the rumors. People love to tell lies for no other reason than to make their mundane lives interesting and to hear themselves speak. I love you, Ivy, and I am sure that Enik will instantly love you as well."

She gave me a watery smile. "I love you too, Carina, and I'm sorry," she answered, tears streaming down her cheeks. She studied my face a long moment as we stood in the hall outside our doors, her palm on my cheek.

I held her free hand as long as I could, until we heard footsteps on a nearby staircase. The tips of our fingers remained hooked together until space and sadness finally parted us, each stepping into our rooms. We shared a wall, but had no way to penetrate it with sound or paper. I had so much more to say to her. I should have told her that she was strong, too. Everything was going to be okay. She'd see.

On days like this, the castle served more as a prison than as our home. It was a gilded cage.

Pretty.

Confining.

And inescapable.

18

CHAPTER TWO

CARINA

I was in my chamber one week later, lost in my own worries, when the world as I knew it was torn to shreds.

My room was large, and with only a bed and wardrobe inside, it was far too spacious for what I needed. But it was also my sanctuary. It had to be. Father didn't allow me to leave this space without an escort, and only then when he gave me permission, which wasn't often. Until that day, I'd always considered myself lucky to have a window.

The horrors I saw from that window would stay with me forever.

Sitting quietly in the alcove, people-watching, was how I learned the ever-changing styles in fashion, how gentlemen and ladies were supposed to act, and how some acted very improperly when they thought no one was watching.

The day the Kingdom of Aelawyn fell, I was watching and envying the lives of the servants and staff. It wasn't ration day, but supplies sometimes came unannounced.

Nothing seemed amiss as three large, covered wagons approached the castle gate. The man driving the horses that pulled the lead wagon shouted to the guard atop the gate, announcing that they carried supplies, taken from another forest raid. They were granted immediate entry, Father's guard raising the portcullis for them.

One by one, the wagons crept into the yard. As soon as the gate slammed back to the ground behind the third and final wagon, a loud whoop sounded. The guards were stunned, so much so that it took far too long for them to spring into action and defend the castle. The wagon canvases were sliced to ribbons as a small army, clad in armor and donning swords, shields, and all manner of weaponry, unfolded from the wagons and began to slash their way across the yard. They didn't take time to discern servant from soldier, male from female, innocent from guilty.

A river of blood flowed in their wake, draining between the cobblestones. They were so skilled and efficient in battle, that they entered the castle before any alarm could be raised to stop them. In no time, they'd taken the castle itself.

My heart thundered as I watched the army split apart, some of the brutes staying outside to slay anyone the first wave of attacks had missed. Swords slashed and plunged into the bodies of people – my people – and I could do nothing but watch. I screamed for Ivy to hide, praying she could hear me, but knowing she probably couldn't. The Kingdom guard scrambled to combat the force, but the soldiers they faced were well-trained, a surging tide unafraid of death.

I banged on the weathered wood of my door and pulled on the locked handle until it warmed from the heat of my skin, screaming until I was hoarse for someone, anyone to open the door. I wanted to get to my sister and make sure Mother was hidden and safe. Footsteps flew down the hall, but no one stopped to set me free.

Palm flat against the wood, I beat on it. "Let me out! Please!" I begged.

The footsteps disappeared as quickly as they came.

"Please!" I screamed.

It was no use. Everyone was either running toward the danger in an attempt to defend the castle and King, or they were running from the enemy in a feeble attempt to survive. Several long minutes later, all the screaming stopped. I ran to the window.

The cobbled streets were littered with the slain, stained with the blood of those who'd fought and fallen. Years later, it was the fallen who still haunted me through memories of their eyes staring into the heavens, blank and empty. I didn't know until that moment how much life could be seen in a person's eyes, and how horrific it was to see them devoid of it.

The only thing moving below my window was a handful of goats chewing on a pile of hay, oblivious to the horrors around them. It was quiet. So quiet. Only the occasional sound of their bleating filled the air. No birds took flight in the winter sky. Above, there were only cold, gray clouds and a frigid wind to match.

I watched over the dead, pulling the shawl around my shoulders to combat the chill.

My father's knights must have slaughtered the attackers, I tried to convince myself. His guard was the best in the land.

Someone would come for me soon. Probably Hetty, with her wild hair and harried look. And when they let me out of here, I would help bury the dead or carry them to the pyre. Tears streamed down my face. I would wait. Hetty would be here soon to let me out.

But Hetty never came.

Minutes turned into hours, and finally, heavy footsteps stopped outside my door. Someone put a key in the lock and turned it. My door swung open. I was too numb to stand, or do anything more than stare blankly at the person entering my chamber. With the way they fumbled with the lock, I knew it wasn't Hetty.

A man with a long beard, dressed in blood and silver chain mail stepped into the room.

"Princess Carina," he addressed me formally.

He was going to kill me. I crouched, easing closer to the narrow slit in the stone wall where the wind blew and the sun shone and the people lay dead. I waited for him to draw his sword and end me, too. Instead, he extended his hand. "Come down from there."

"No," I gritted. The emotion of the last hours hit me with full force. Sadness mixed with anger and bitterness with resolve. Hot tears carved pathways down my cheeks. He was not a knight of Aelawyn, and I wasn't going anywhere with him.

"You must come with me now," he said again, his voice firmer.

I shook my head, my feet pushing my body further into the wall as he approached. When he grabbed me, I let out a keening shriek that made him step away. More footsteps pounded down the hall and several of his countrymen filed into the room, all wearing the same colors of black and silver. Some bled from wounds on their heads and faces.

22

One man's hand was haphazardly bandaged; blood was seeping through the fabric tied around it.

"Having trouble?" one barked.

The soldier backed away from me, raking a blood-covered hand through his graying hair. "She's frightened," he replied.

"Of you? Of course she is," one laughed. The other men relaxed and chuckled along with him.

"Where is my father?" I asked.

Only one of the dozen men standing in my room would meet my eyes. From the back, he stepped through the crowd of soldiers. His hair was dark and slickened with sweat, and his skin was speckled with blood. The man gave me a stern look and I shook when he rasped, "Your father is dead. Your mother and sister joined him in death, and if you don't want to meet them in the afterlife as well, you'll stop fussing about and come with me now."

Cupping my hand over my mouth, tears flooded my eyes.

They were dead? All of them?

I couldn't breathe.

Aelawyn had no king, no queen, and no princess, save for me.

They killed Ivy? My beautiful Ivy? Tears streamed down my face.

Why would they kill her and spare me? It made no sense. Her green eyes, the ones that matched mine exactly, would be blank and empty now, just like the people outside. Death consumed all of life, hungry for something it would never have, and it consumed my sister as well. The tightness in my chest spread through my limbs.

"Come," he barked. "Come away from the window."

"Where am I to go?" I croaked.

"Tierney."

23

Tierney. Our closest neighbor. "Why did you do this?" I asked as the man stared at me. My voice quivered uncontrollably, just like my knees.

"Your Father has robbed and smothered our people, as well as those from the other kingdoms, for long enough. We had to stop him. Now, quickly gather the things you need. Take only what you can carry."

He gave me a look that said he'd carry me out of here himself if I didn't do as he said. I rose and walked stiffly to my wardrobe, yanking two dresses into my arms. Taking my crown, I turned to face my captor, asking, "Can I get something from my sister's room? It's just next door."

With careful words, he said, "I don't think that's a good idea, Princess."

Hesitantly, he walked toward me, glancing at his men uneasily but with warning flashing in his eyes. A warning for what?

"Please?" I cried, desperate for something to remember her by. My entire body started to tremble. "Please?"

"Calm down." His eyes hardened. "She's in her room and she is dead. Do you understand what you will see if I allow you to go in there?"

Fighting the panic and fear and the hot tears that welled, I nodded. The soldiers filed out of the room as the man led me to Ivy's door. The dark-haired leader asked again, "Are you sure you want to do this?"

"Yes," I rasped, easing her door open. However, when I saw her, I understood why he didn't want me to go. Ivy didn't die by a soldier's hand; she'd taken her own life. Her body was near the window, her skin pale, with lips a sickening shade of blue. Strands of her hair were caught in her lashes, but someone had mercifully closed her eyes. A white sheet was wound tightly around her neck. My eyes followed the trail of fabric to the bedpost.

My sister hanged herself. *My sister hanged herself.*

I made my way over to her body, dropping to my knees at her side. Her hand was cold as ice.

"Did you find her?" I asked the leader among them.

He kept his distance, averting his eyes as he spoke. "No, my men did, but it was too late to save her. Her neck broke when she jumped from the window." I saw the sharp turn in her spine, the way her head was bent at an unnatural angle.

Other than that, she looked like she was sleeping. She couldn't really be dead. "Ivy?" I cried. I brushed a strand of hair from her forehead. She was so cold. "Ivy?" I said, louder this time.

The man gently but firmly told me, "She's gone, Princess. Please get what you wanted. We have to leave."

"Just leave me," I begged, feeling a bubble of saliva form between my lips. "Leave me here."

He shook his head. "The village will be out for blood, and they'll blame you for your father's failure to protect them."

Although his words made sense, what would happen to me in Tierney? No one could protect me now. I kissed Ivy's cool cheek and placed her hands over her stomach.

I had no choice but to go with them. On trembling legs, I stood and moved to Ivy's wardrobe, opening the doors. In a bag of black velvet were the shoes my mother gave her to wear on her wedding day. I clutched the bag to my chest and followed the man outside, too afraid to look back at my sister.

"You'll need a cloak," he said, pausing outside my door.

I shook my head. "I don't have one. Father wouldn't let us go outside." *Why would we need one?*

25

With a frustrated tick in his jaw, he growled angrily and told me to follow him. Then he barked for his men to find something warm for me to wear.

CHAPTER THREE

CARINA

Two soldiers led me to the main staircase. At the bottom, the rest of their small army moved around the room, the metal of their armor clanking with each step. Gingerly stepping around bodies, warriors and peasants alike, I watched as the gruff group of men paid respects to each of their fallen countrymen as we passed them by. They gently closed eyelids and muttered soft words, placing a silver coin on each of their eyes. The stench of blood and death was overwhelming, but I breathed it in and committed it to memory in honor of my people.

This was my father's fault.

I searched for Hetty among the dead, knowing they'd left no one within the castle walls alive—which meant many of the villagers who worked here had also been slain. Bile stung the back of my throat.

One of the giant men rushed to my side, holding out a thick, red cloak. "Put this on, Princess." His words were soft, shrouded in kindness and understanding. I wondered where those qualities had gone while they slaughtered all of these innocent people. I took the cloak and fastened it around my neck, the fabric draping heavily around my shoulders.

The dark-haired and undisputed leader walked ahead, avoiding the dead where they lay. His eyes found me when he reached the castle door. "My name is Piers." There was scuffling and moaning from somewhere, but the way the sound echoed through the room made it difficult to discern where it was coming from, or from whom. "Once we leave this castle, you are the property of the Kingdom of Tierney. I am responsible for protecting the assets of the kingdom. You will do as you're told, and I will make sure you follow my instructions to the letter. Understood?"

I simply nodded. All the fight had been beaten from me a long time ago by my own flesh and blood. Besides, what else could I do? I was one girl among a small army of skilled fighters.

He returned the nod. To his men, he said, "We'll travel in the wagons. We need to move quickly, men. We'll camp by the river tonight."

His men followed his footsteps through the castle yard. Piers commanded respect, but also gave it. That was more than I'd expected after seeing the savagery with which they attacked. I pulled the cloak tightly around my body.

The frigid wind whipped around me as I stepped outside, squinting from the brightness of the day. More tears fell.

I couldn't stop them. Piers watched as his men helped me into the back of one of the three wagons and surrounded me. With arms propped on their knees or hands hanging in their laps, the men huddled together to keep warm. They were dirty, bloody, and utterly exhausted. They smelled of sweat and weariness.

"What of the dead?" one man yelled from the next wagon.

"We leave them," Piers responded coolly. His expression left no room for argument, but the tense tick of his jaw indicated that the decision hadn't been made lightly.

The horses began to pull us forward as some of the men lifted the gate and ran to catch back up, jumping into the backs of the wagons, their comrades helping haul them inside. Piers sat beside the driver in the lead wagon, my wagon. Occasionally, he glanced back at me. I wondered if he regretted what he'd done now that he saw how broken I was, or if he was proud.

I didn't know what would happen to me once we reached Tierney. I had nothing to offer anyone save a couple of dresses and my sister's shoes, which I clung to beneath the cloak.

The horses drove until daylight was gone. Darkness turned the forest roads blue, and though we hadn't reached the river he'd spoken of, Piers decided we'd come far enough. Most of the men chose to huddle near the fires that were hastily built, but I stayed in the wagon with my things while Piers guarded me from the wagon's bench.

The same routine continued for five more days; the driver of the wagons guided the horses that pulled us over the land, up and down, around and through streams and valleys, until our bodies were sore and our lips and skin was chapped and peeling from the cold, unrelenting wind. On the sixth day, the men's spirits lifted. Their bodies were rested and healing, and we were near Tierney, according to their chatter. Some spoke of seeing their wives and children, others of work they'd left undone. But everyone had a plan, something they needed to do or someone they wanted to see.

I had nothing.

Beside me sat the man who'd given me the cloak. He was quiet, his dark eyes kind, as we travelled. He made sure I was given an equal portion of food at each meal. Over the past few days, I noticed that the deep gashes on his arms were healing.

He nudged my arm. "These are Tierney lands, now, Princess."

Princess? I was princess of nothing.

"Where's the castle?" My voice was hoarse and foreign to my ears.

"Still a ways off. Tierney's lands are extensive." He wasn't boasting, but simply informing me of the fact. None of the men had been so inconsiderate as to celebrate their victory in front of me. I knew that would all change the moment we reached the castle, and wasn't looking forward to being paraded in front of their people, a trophy taken—nothing more than one of the spoils of war.

Hours later, the forest thinned. The land turned into rolling hills of dry hay that bent in the wind like copper waves crashing over the countryside. Small houses of waddle and daub appeared. People waved from their doors and windows as we passed. Children ran alongside us through the tall, dry hay.

Piers puffed his chest out, waving back to them, and for the first time since we met, I hated him.

We drove into a town where the houses were built closer together. The dirt trail we'd been on for so long turned into a stone road, which intersected others like it. An imposing castle, three times the size of the one my father's ancestors built, loomed in the distance. It would have been beautiful if a different rock had been chosen. If it were a light granite, it would have gleamed and glittered in the sun. But the stone was dark, like it was made of the stuff of shadows. The very sight of it made my skin crawl.

Unlike my home, the castle of Tierney was perched on a small hill. At the bottom of the hill, a frozen moat surrounded the castle. The spires and turrets stabbed the darkening sky, deadly as the swords of their soldiers.

When the bridge was lowered and we rolled onto the castle grounds, the drivers called for the horses to stop and everyone began to file out of the wagons. The man beside me nudged my arm, but I didn't look at him. I looked to Piers, who ticked his head, indicating that I should follow him. Standing and swallowing my fear, I accepted the hands of two men who offered to help me down, the velvet bag dangling from my arm. Another soldier handed my dresses down to me.

I followed Piers inside, the castle swallowing me whole. A woman, tall and thin with white hair neatly knotted at the nape of her neck, fretted and worried over the men as they poured in and around us. She was motherly and loving; not terrified like the servants at the castle of Aelawyn, afraid of any misstep. I half expected her to swat the men for dirtying her floor.

"Just look at the likes of you! Tell me, were you victorious..." Her words faded as she took me in, and though I was trying to hold my head high, my spine sank against the cold stone behind it. A warm tear slid down my cheek. "Oh, child. What do we have here?"

She looked to Piers, who introduced us. "Madelyn, may I present Princess Carina of Aelawyn."

The woman opened her mouth and closed it back. Then she gently wrapped an arm around my shoulders, her warmth seeping into my frozen flesh. "Let's get you clean and fed, Princess."

The woman was insane if she thought food and false kindness would bring my family and people back from the dead. She was lucky I didn't have a knife to slit her throat with.

CHAPTER FOUR

CARINA

I almost regretted my thoughts about killing her. Madelyn was actually very kind. She was the most motherly person I'd met. Neither my own mother nor my lady-in-waiting had ever taken such good care of me. I rarely saw my mother, and Hetty only spoke when necessary. Hetty didn't like working in the castle, but she had no choice when she was assigned to me, and it ended up costing her life.

Madelyn loved what she did and took pride in making others comfortable—even those who didn't belong, even as my fingers shook with fear and another emotion I couldn't name.

She took my cloak. "I'll see that this is washed and all the stains removed, Princess."

"Carina," I corrected. "You can call me Carina. I suppose I'm no longer a princess," my voice cracked. Madelyn probably assumed it was because I had lost my status, but it wasn't that. It wasn't the loss of Aelawyn or my parents that kept haunting me, it was Ivy. When she decided she'd rather die than be a bird in a beautiful cage… she broke my heart. She was the only person I'd ever loved, and now she was gone. I couldn't get the memory of her lying on her floor, dead, out of my mind. It was all I could see when I closed my eyes, so I hadn't slept in days.

I clutched the velvet bag close to my chest, a warm tear sliding down my face. Followed by another. And another.

"What's in the bag, Carina?" Madelyn asked softly.

Ivy should be here with me.

"My sister's shoes. And my crown," I cried. My lips trembled violently, so I closed them as best I could.

She nodded. "If I promise you can watch your things, will you please lay them down to take a bath?"

Pursing my lips together, I uncurled my fingers from the strings and set the bag on the floor beside me. She stretched my fingers out, staring at the red indentations left by the bag's string. Madelyn smiled gently and glanced over her shoulder toward the door where something banged just outside the room.

"I hear them now. Your tub and water are here. I'm sure you'll feel better once you're all cleaned up."

Sure enough, a crowd entered the room single file; two carrying a large, wooden tub, while the others carried buckets of steaming hot water.

When the last bucket of water was dumped into the tub, Madelyn waited by the door while the servants exited the

34

room. "Now you'll have some privacy. Do you need help bathing or washing your hair?"

"I can do it."

"Very well." She smiled, placing a bar of soap in my hand. "I'll find something for you to eat."

She left me, locking the door from the outside. I should've been used to the sound, but it startled me. The lock sounded different. Warm steam rose into the air from the tub and I peeled the dress from my body. I sank into the water, holding my breath, wondering if I should do as Ivy had done. Simply let go, breathe in the water, and escape my cage...

Would the King and Queen of Tierney kill me? Hold me as a prisoner of war? Would I wish for death soon anyway?

I gasped for air when I surfaced. I didn't want to die. The people of Aelawyn didn't have a chance to fight, but maybe I still did. Taking hold of the soap, I cleaned my skin from head to toe. Then I spent time on my hair. It was matted and greasy, but soon the lavender soap and warm water took all the dirt away, leaving only the soft, floral scent behind.

I sat in the tub until the water cooled and was stepping out and tying my robe when Madelyn returned. "Carina, I was going to bring supper, but the King has asked that you dine with him tonight."

I nodded. I could tell she didn't agree with his decision.

"How old are you?" she asked softly as she laid a thin, white chemise on the bed.

"Fourteen."

"And when will you be fifteen?"

"Why? Is the King planning to give me away in marriage at the first opportunity?" I tried but couldn't keep the venom out of my voice. "Or is he just wondering whether his conscience can handle the death of *another* child?"

Her eyes widened, but she quickly schooled her features. "I don't know what the King has planned for you, but I do know that by Tierney's standards, you're a little too young to be married, and Piers wouldn't have brought you all this way if he thought King Stefan wanted you dead."

"I *am* betrothed, or at least I was... I was to be wed in three weeks." Madelyn inhaled sharply. "To Prince Yurak of Galder," I finished.

"Galder? But Yurak is old enough to be your father!"

The thought made my skin crawl. I figured I'd better not give the King a reason to kill me. I wanted to live, and if I didn't tell him about Galder, he might think I was more trouble than I was worth. Of course, he might decide I was anyway. "I'll tell the King tonight. It could cause problems for him and Tierney if Galder learns where I am."

She winked at me. "Only if anyone knows you've survived." The thought hit me like a stone. No one knew. No one but the knights and Madelyn and the King. The world would assume that I lay dead in the castle with the rest of my family.

Stefan could throw me in the dungeon. He could send me away to Yurak. He could do anything he wanted. Why was he inviting me to dine with him?

She helped me into the chemise. "I'm sorry about your family. Piers told me everything."

She brought a dress over, a purple so deep it was nearly black, the thick fabric pillowing in her hands. "I'll have your clothing washed immediately."

Madelyn laced the corset of my gown. "There we go. You are a vision, Carina. May I plait your hair?"

"Yes," I answered softly. While Madelyn styled my dark hair, I kept an eye on my bag. She must have noticed. "Would you like to wear your crown? Or your sister's shoes?"

36

"No, but would you look after them, please? They are very dear to me."

"I will," she promised. "The King is waiting, dear. He is stern, but fair. He wasn't expecting Piers to bring you to the castle, but he wouldn't hurt you. You'll be eating with the same men you traveled here with and their families. A feast will be held for the entire Kingdom to celebrate tomorrow, but I'm not sure whether you'll be invited to attend that."

The chamber I was staying in wasn't cold like I expected. Even with the dark, imposing walls and matching furnishings, it was warmer than my own had been. There were rich fabrics on the bed and matching curtains over the windows, and cozy paintings of fields with vibrantly colored trees. The fire in the hearth filled the room with warmth and light. My eyes settled on my bag as Madelyn gathered it into her arms. "I'll take care of your things. I promise, Carina."

I prayed I could trust her.

CHAPTER FIVE

CARINA

I was escorted from my room and led down a tight spiral staircase to the ground floor where the Great Hall was located. Inside, Tierney's knights would celebrate the death of everything I knew, and I would sup and drink wine with them as they did. My stomach turned somersaults.

Piers met me outside an imposing set of dark, wooden doors. "I'll escort you to the King. He would like you to dine on the dais with him tonight." I inclined my head, afraid my voice would crack if I spoke.

Piers had never been cruel to me, and neither had his men. There was something to be said for that.

If my father would have sent his knights to invade a neighboring castle and kingdom, no one would have been left alive, least of all a fourteen-year-old girl. That would have been one more mouth to feed, and he wouldn't have cared whether the children of his enemy starved to death. Mercy was a language he never learned to speak, because he believed mercy was a weakness and he couldn't afford to be seen as weak. He even slaughtered his own father and brother in order to claim the throne for himself. Father valued power and riches. Never mercy.

Piers walked beside me through the doors, and I saw the room was filled with long tables that stretched the entire length of the room. The tables were covered with white cloths, candles, and boughs of pine stretched down their middles, filling the air with their earthy, fresh scent. Dark columns held up the ceilings, extending at the top to form arches overhead.

Men I recognized, and women and children I didn't, took their seats. At the far end of the room was a raised platform with a long table that sat horizontally. Two large chairs sat in the center, facing everyone in the room. Those were flanked with smaller, less ornately carved chairs.

"Piers?" I asked quietly. "What will happen to me?" I felt like a lamb being led to slaughter.

"This is only dinner, Princess. I'll show you to your seat."

He led me to the dais and held my chair, scooting it in for me. Then he settled into the chair beside me. "My wife will be along any moment," he said conversationally. "This is a celebration before the celebration, so to speak. However, this meal won't be an easy one for you to stomach."

At least he was honest. Piers rose when a woman his age approached.

"Princess Carina, may I present my wife, Emma."

40

I rose to curtsey. "It is a pleasure to meet you, Emma."

"I'm very sorry for all you have lost." *Even if it was at my husband's hands*, her eyes seemed to say as they found him beside her.

"Thank you," I whispered, my throat clogged with emotion.

I kept my head down until a servant announced the arrival of the royal family.

The King was young and fit. He strode confidently through the room, congratulating the nearest of his knights on their victory. "King Stefan, Queen Grace, and the crown Princes: Carden and William," Piers whispered. The crowd stood as the royal family took their seats. When King Stefan's cool eyes fell on me, I had to suppress a shudder.

The crown atop his head was thick and made of dark metal, studded with rubies and emeralds. "Princess Carina," he greeted.

"Your Highness," I replied.

Queen Grace offered a small smile and then turned her attention to her sons; one seemed a few years older than me, and the other a few years younger. While both looked at me quizzically at first, the two boys each lost interest quickly. Servants filled goblets and delivered steaming platters of food to the table.

After the servants stepped away, and in the midst of the steaming plumes rising from the fresh food, the King stood and raised his goblet high. "A toast," his voice boomed through the hall. "To the end of tyranny. You men fought bravely. Many lives were lost, but their sacrifice will be remembered through the generations because we will tell our children how they stormed the castle of Aelawyn and removed the head of their tyrant King!"

I was going to be sick. It was one thing to know they'd killed my father, and quite another to envision the soldiers

41

of Tierney removing his head. A cold sweat arose on my brow.

For the second time today, I considered slitting someone's throat. Did Stefan put his best knight between us for a reason?

A great roar arose. The women clinked goblets and the knights pounded their fists on the tables. The King reached over and tore a leg off the turkey, taking a large bite. His apparent speech was over, thank God, and once the King began to eat, everyone in the room began to fill their plates. Piers scooped some lentils onto my plate and carved the bird, placing a piece of meat on my plate as well.

"I'm not hungry," I told him. He ignored me and served his wife, while servants came around to serve Queen Grace and her sons.

King Stefan turned his attention back to me as he chewed his food sloppily. I refused to touch my plate. "Princess Carina, I apologize for not greeting you when you arrived. I wasn't expecting you." He gave Piers a levelling stare, which his knight returned with ease. Anger sparked between the two men. "Piers tells me that you were recently betrothed."

Piers leaned close and whispered, "Madelyn thought you might rather have me tell him."

I looked to Stefan. "Yes, Highness."

"Would you like me to honor that agreement?" King Stefan stared at me, awaiting my answer.

I shook my head.

He smiled softly, an expression I didn't expect to see from him. "I'll take that as a no."

I muttered a thank you.

"Don't thank me yet. The way I see it, there are two options. If I let you stay here, I would risk war with Galder. They might figure out that you're here and think I'm keeping you from honoring your betrothal. The first option, and frankly the best for my kingdom, is that I send you to them. You would marry Yurak – as your father had negotiated – and the gesture might ease tensions between our kingdoms."

"And the second?" I asked.

"The second option might be the best one for *you*. If you don't want to marry Yurak, you can stay in Tierney, but not in the castle. Since we are responsible for rendering you homeless, we will provide you with another."

Queen Grace smiled. "Where would she live, if not in the castle?"

Stefan took a sip of his wine. "There are peasants who would take her in," he said, drawing a gasp from the Queen.

"But, Stefan!" she protested.

"You may choose, Carina."

"I'd like to stay here." I didn't think living with peasants would be as awful as Grace thought, but marrying someone three times my age would.

"You'd have to stay hidden. You'd have to forget your former life. If anyone finds out who you are, I'll have no choice but to send you to Yurak. Do you understand?"

"I do."

Stefan turned to Piers. "Would Hayden take her in?"

Piers' sharp eyes met mine. "I believe so."

While I wondered who Hayden was and considered the terms of what I'd just agreed to, the King spoke again. "Then it's settled. Discreetly take her into the village before sunrise tomorrow. Pay him well and tell him what will happen if he fails to keep her identity a secret."

"Yes, sire," Piers said quietly. He turned his goblet up and drained the wine from it. For the remainder of the evening, he refused to meet my eyes.

CHAPTER SIX

CARINA

While the sky was still inky, Madelyn woke me and quickly helped me dress. The dress I'd left home in was ruined, stained with blood and dirt and who knew what else.

Piers had told her everything.

Madelyn smiled warmly, wrinkles forming around her mouth and at the corners of her eyes. "This'll be too nice to roam around the village in, Carina. But perhaps your family will be able to buy a more suitable dress for you. King Stefan will reward the family who is taking you in, so don't feel like you're a burden them."

"Do you know the family?" I slid my feet into my golden slippers.

"I don't know them personally, but I asked Piers about them and he said they're good people. They're farmers. Piers has known Hayden Farmer since childhood, and though they took different paths, they're still friends."

I didn't know anything about farming.

She smoothed my hair to try and comfort me. "I know you're scared, but don't be. King Stefan only means to protect you. We've had trouble with Galder lately. Maybe one day things between our kingdoms will be better, but for now, I'm glad you're staying in Tierney. You made the right decision."

I hoped she was right.

"You're young, and young people adapt to new situations very quickly. You'll be fine in just a few weeks' time."

She took my more formal gown and gently folded it, tucking it into a large burlap sack. She added my velvet bag and tied the opening shut with twine.

"Now," she said, holding the bag out for me to take. "I think that's everything. Piers is waiting for you downstairs."

I followed her out of the room, watching her skirts swish back and forth. "Madelyn?"

"Yes?"

"Thank you…for being so kind, when I'm sure my father's sins didn't make you want to be."

She clucked her tongue. "The sins of the father are not those of the child. I can see the good in you. And no matter what anyone says or how sad you feel, just remember," she patted her chest. "It's better to be a princess in here, than to wear a crown on your head."

Piers was standing at the door, his body taut as a bowstring. "She's ready," Madelyn told him, patting my back. "Well, almost ready. Let me grab your cloak, Carina."

As she ran off to fetch the cloak that wasn't really mine, I met Piers' eyes. "We'll travel through the village, but Hayden lives in the countryside," he said by way of greeting. "Have you ridden on horseback before?"

I shook my head.

"Then you'll ride with me. It's a bitter cold morning, but we need to ride fast."

The traumatic events of late hadn't killed me. I would survive a horse ride, despite the temperature. "Does he know about me?"

"Not yet," Piers said matter-of-factly.

"Do you think he'll turn me away?" Did Hayden have a family? Children? Was I going to be a burden? Another mouth for him to feed?

"Not with the purse the King is sending him."

He patted a bulging pouch tied to his belt. The coin rattled inside. Was Hayden Farmer the sort who only cared about money?

Madelyn reappeared with the bright red cloak in hand. She fastened it around my neck and gave me a quick hug. "I will think of you often, Princess," she said.

I forced a smile and walked out of the castle.

Two stable boys, their hair messy from sleep, waited for us outside, holding the reins of an enormous horse whose hair was the color of midnight. Piers mounted first and then offered me a hand. One of the boys held my bag. "You'll have to sit side saddle because of your gown," he said. I nodded and let him pull me up. The stable boy tied my bag to the saddle horn, but I wrapped the strings around my fingers as an extra precaution.

He looked at the boys, saying, "I'll return within the hour."

"Yes, sir," they said in unison.

We rode through town so fast, I couldn't read the signs on any of the buildings. It was larger than I'd expected, with several little criss-crossing streets. I held my bag and my cloak closed as best as I could. The wind froze my fingers, ears, and feet. My slippers threatened to fall off with every gallop.

Outside of town the trail thinned, and the houses were built much farther apart. Deer foraged in the frosted fields. Hints of the rising sun painted the eastern sky. *I bet it was beautiful in the spring.*

Across from a great piece of rolling land that was sectioned into rectangular fields by waist-high stone fences, was a modest house with a single upstairs window. Piers helped me to the ground and then dismounted.

The scent of mud and dung wafted through the air from the animal pens I could see on the hillside around back. I clutched my bag as he lashed the horse to a post and walked to the door. It swung open before he could knock, even though his hand was poised to. A man with bright orange, shaggy hair and shoulders the width of a carriage stepped outside, buttoning the top of his shirt.

"Piers?" he asked, giving him a large smile. "I wasn't expecting you." His eyes flitted to me, confusion wrinkling his face.

"I apologize for the early hour, but it couldn't be helped. King Stefan needs your help."

"Does he, now? Well, I suppose you, and this young lady, will want to come inside where it's warm. No use freezing out here." The wooden door was weathered and creaked when he pushed it open wide enough for us to enter.

The interior was warm and homey, just how I imagined it would look from the outside, with blankets draped over the modest furniture, dried flowers hanging on the wall, and a warm candlelit glow. The entire house smelled of cinnamon and something sugary sweet. A woman raised up from where she was cooking at the fireplace. Her dark hair, peppered with a few strands of gray, was pulled back from her face. Her smile was as sweet as the scent in the air.

"Well, hello!" she said. "What have we here? Piers, it's been too long!" She hugged his neck and Piers smiled brightly at her. Then she approached me. I took a small step backward. With an understanding smile, she stopped and folded her hands in front of her. She looked at me for a long moment. Could she see all the broken pieces?

Piers spoke up, drawing her attention away. "As I said outside, the King needs your help." He placed the large pouch of coin in Hayden's hand.

Hayden's mouth gaped open as he tested the weight of it. "What sort of favor requires this much coin?"

"Her sort," Piers replied, nodding toward me.

CHAPTER SEVEN

CARINA

ayden and his wife exchanged glances. "He wants *us* to house her? Why, and for how long?" Hayden asked.

Piers shifted his weight. "Until she's wed, and because her presence in the castle could spell trouble for Tierney." The answer was evasive and vague, and if it were me, I would've asked him to elaborate.

Hayden's wife tsked the large soldier. "What trouble could a teenager possibly cause?"

Hayden looked at her and slowly raised one brow. "Honestly?"

"For now," Piers warned, "she should stay close to the house. She stayed at the castle last night, but only my men, their families, Madelyn, and the royal family know who she is. The castle servants saw her, so rumors will probably spread—some correct. It's best she stay hidden until they die down.""

"Who exactly are you, dear?" Hayden's wife asked sympathetically.

My throat clogged with emotion and my eyes filled with tears. *I was nobody.* Certainly no one Galder should come to arms over, and no one Tierney should defend. I couldn't bring myself to answer her.

"She," Piers spoke for me, "is Princess Carina of Aelawyn, the only survivor from our attack on the castle, and the only living daughter of King Berius."

Hayden's wife gasped, splaying her hand over her heart. "But weren't there two daughters? Are you the eldest?" She shot a look at Piers that was equal parts threatening and worried.

"I'm the youngest. My sister is dead," I croaked.

Hayden's wife shot a withering glare at Piers.

"Not by our hand, but by her own," he said hastily. "We wouldn't harm a child. Look, I need to get back to the castle. You have to keep her identity secret. You know what Stefan will do if you don't. If she goes into the village, people will be curious about her. You should tell them that she is your relative come to live with you after her parents passed away, or make up some other such story. Carina," he said, turning to me. "You might want to shorten your name or choose another."

"Why is she in hiding?" Hayden asked.

"She was betrothed to Prince Yurak," Piers continued to explain. "Stefan gave her the option of either being sent to

Galder to honor their arrangement, or hiding in Tierney. She chose to hide. And you need to make sure she *stays* hidden. If Galder finds out she survived, it could mean war."

"Galder," Hayden muttered like a curse.

"She's a child, not a pawn in a game of kings! How old are you?" the woman asked, crossing her arms. I wished I were as strong as she, because with one look, Jewel could make two grown men wither before her.

"Fourteen, madam."

The woman's face screwed up in disgust. "Your father wanted you to marry so young?"

She obviously didn't understand my father.

"Yes." It was more common than most people thought, especially among royalty. I'd heard of younger girls marrying, although I never thought I'd be one of them.

"She'll be safe here," Piers said, "as long as King Stefan believes she isn't more useful as a bargaining tool."

My stomach dropped. What if he felt that way in the future?

I held tight to my bag as Piers turned to me. "You'll be safe and happy here. In time, you'll be able to go into the village. But for now, stay close to your new home."

Nothing felt safe right now. My life was no longer mine. And happiness? Happiness was not meant for me. If I was meant to have a life of happiness, I wouldn't have been born to such a father as mine. I wouldn't have been taken from my home and forced upon a family of strangers.

Piers slipped out the door with a nod, Hayden on his heels. When the door shut behind them, the woman looked me up and down.

"We'll have to get you a few dresses, and they won't be anywhere near as lovely as the one you're wearing." She winced as she took in the fine stitching and embroidery on my gown. Her overdress was clean, but worn. The hem was frayed and the fabric thin in spots. The last thing I wanted was for her to feel uncomfortable because of me. This was her home, and she was taking me in against her will.

"I just need something functional." I didn't care what I wore as long as I wouldn't freeze to death.

Her apprehension melted away and she smiled sweetly. "My name is Jewel. Hayden and I are happy to have you stay with us."

"I'm sorry for the imposition," I said sincerely, unable to prevent the tears that clogged my throat.

She hugged me tight to her, my entire body tensing from the gesture. "Nonsense. If you feel up to it, I'd like to introduce you to our children."

"Sure."

The bottom floor where we stood held a modest kitchen with a small sitting room. There were twin hearths, one in each room, and both containing roaring fires. The air was warm and comforting after such a cold ride this morning. My fingers were still frozen. I unclipped my cloak and draped it over the arm that clutched the only things I had left.

"You can leave your things on the table, dear. We'll make a bed for you soon."

I didn't want to part from the bag, but gingerly laid it on the table like she asked me to and followed her up a small set of steps that sagged in the middle and led to a second floor with sloped ceilings. "Matthew, Millie, wake up. We have a surprise."

The siblings shared the main space, a small curtain on a length of twine dividing their room. "Millicent is your age," Jewel chatted. "We call her Millie. Matthew is eleven and a half. The 'half' is very important to him, dear," Jewel said with a wink. Millie forced an eye open and then closed it

54

again, letting out a groan. Matthew was much more eager to wake.

"Who are you?" he asked, his sleep-bleary eyes taking me in. His hair was bent at all angles.

Jewel waited for me to answer. "My name is... Ella." It wasn't a lie. Born Ella Carina, Ivy had taken to calling me the latter and everyone else followed suit. Holding on to a portion of my given name was a small comfort.

"Millie isn't a morning person," Jewel whispered. The children's fiery hair obviously came from Hayden, but their eyes, dark as burnt bread, came from their mother. She muttered to herself about making room in the corner and moving Millie's things over.

"I don't have enough room as it is, Mum," Millie said gruffly. "Put her on Matthew's side."

"I don't think so. It's not appropriate to have a female on the same side as a male. Not because of you, dear," she assured me with a pat on the arm.

Millie finally sat up, looking completely put out. "How long is she staying?"

"It'll be a long visit. Right, Ella?" Jewel smiled warmly.

I nodded, trying to play the part, and smiled like I was happy to be with them. Millie simply groaned and flopped backward on the bed, pulling the covers over her head. *She isn't nearly as nice as her mother*, I thought to myself.

"All right, lazy bones. Get up. Make your beds and get down the steps! Breakfast is almost ready, and you both have chores to do," Jewel bellowed. She lowered her voice and added, "We'll see about getting those dresses today."

It didn't feel right having them use the coin the King gave them just to clothe me. As Jewel and I made our way downstairs, I asked, "Jewel, do you think you could sell one of my gowns to pay for dresses that would be more suitable?"

"Oh, I'd hate to do that," she hedged.

"I insist. I know what a sacrifice this is, and I don't want to be a burden." Not anymore than I already was.

"We have plenty of coin," she replied.

"I won't be able to wear the gowns anyway." I lowered my voice further. "If I wore them, people might ask questions."

She pursed her lips together. "Very well. You have another in the bag?"

"Yes."

"Which would you like to keep?" she asked. "I insist that you keep *one* of them."

At the table, I untied the burlap and removed the velvet pouch, handing her the bag with my dress in it. "I'd like to keep the one I'm wearing, but this gown and these slippers can be sold." I wiggled my toes, lifting my skirt so she could see them.

Jewel brushed a strand of hair out of her face and gave me a nod. "I'll tell Hayden."

As if he'd been summoned, Hayden stepped back inside, shivering from cold. He moved to the hearth in the sitting room. Jewel sat beside him, whispering for him to call me Ella, and that the children hadn't asked for an explanation as to who I was. She asked him to make up a story. "They'll be down any time now."

He nodded and turned to wink at me. "I'm a master storyteller."

I hoped so.

"Oh," Jewel said, clapping her hands together. "Ella would like to sell one of her gowns to pay for a few dresses and boots that would fare better around the mud than the ones she has."

Hayden nodded vehemently. "That's wise."

Jewel smiled. "I'll take you into the village this afternoon. You can borrow one of Millie's dresses in the meantime."

I nodded my thanks, and then we looked up to the sound of a creaking step and an angry Millicent.

"It's been a year since *I* had a new dress, or even shoes!" she fumed.

"Maybe we'll have enough to get Millie one as well?" I asked Jewel loudly, adding in a whisper that my gown should be worth several.

"We'll need to get you a pair of boots and a few underthings, too. The cobbler's expensive, but sometimes the seamstress sells worn boots from her shop. Let's hope we can find you something there." She frowned at her daughter. "But, we might be able to get you something, Millie."

Matthew pushed around his sister on the steps and made his way to the table. "What's for breakfast? Cinnamon bread?" He sniffed the air.

"Yes. I know how you love it." Jewel ruffled his hair as she walked into the kitchen and removed a pan that sat on an iron grate over the fire. "They're perfect," she crooned. "I forgot all about them with the surprise this morning." She winked at me and set the pan on a cloth in the middle of the thick, wooden table. "Who's hungry?" she asked.

My stomach was gnawing on itself. I moved my things from the table and placed them in the sitting room on a chair as Jewel turned to her daughter.

"Millie, would you pour milk for everyone, please?"

"It's probably frozen," she grumbled. At her mother's insistence, she groaned, tugged a pair of boots on, and went outside. The milk was fresh. Hayden must have milked the cows very early, because we'd been busy since my arrival.

He nudged my arm. "I milked them while Piers and I spoke at the barn. He explained everything."

They only had four chairs around the table, and despite Jewel's insistence that I take her seat, I sat in the sitting room alone, just happy to taste the warm, gooey bread. It was delicious. At home, we ate gruel. Every morning, every evening. The occasional dinner that Ivy and I were allowed to attend was the only meal that varied, and that was a rarity.

I moaned from the taste of it, louder than I realized. Every member of the Farmer family looked at me. My face heated, and immediately a rock lodged in my stomach. I was mortified and scared of the reaction my poor table manners would cause. I put the piece of cinnamon bread I'd been eating on the plate in my lap and waited to see if I would be punished. "I'm so sorry." I was waiting for Hayden to yell or raise his hand at me. "I didn't mean to…"

Jewel smiled brightly. She seemed happy that I liked the food she'd made.

"What do you think of Jewel's cooking?" Hayden asked, patting his wife's hand.

"It's the best thing I've ever tasted in my life," I answered honestly.

Jewel's face lit up as Hayden continued to boast about his wife's skills in the kitchen. Matthew licked his sticky fingers while Millie sat in her seat with her arms crossed over her chest, refusing to eat what her mother's hands had made.

I felt like I was still watching the peasants from my window sill; only now I was close enough to touch and talk with those I envied. Seeing the dynamics of a family who loved each other was both a blessing and a curse.

This. *This* was what I loved watching from my perch. This was what a family should be.

The Farmers loved one another. Even though they weren't expecting to receive, clothe, or house me, they welcomed me. And after breaking their fast, they went about their day and tasks as if I wasn't there in the midst of them, and that was more than fine with me.

Hayden brought an old feather bed in from the barn and then fashioned a stand from four pieces of sawed logs and long, flat pieces of wood. "This'll do for now," he said, testing it with his weight. He took his tools downstairs, leaving me to get settled.

As I lay in the small bed waiting to see what I was expected to do, I could hear Jewel and Hayden speaking quietly downstairs. "She's very quiet," Jewel said. "Do you think she likes it here?"

"I'm sure in time, she'll fit right in and be just as loud as the rest of us. It must be hard for her. I can't even imagine." Hayden's voice, normally gruff and ornery, had softened.

What did I know about farming, or work, or being part of a family?

A tear escaped my eye, sliding into my hair. I wasn't sure I would ever fit in here. I wasn't sure I'd ever fit in anywhere. I simply didn't belong.

CHAPTER EIGHT

ELLA

As first days go, mine with the Farmers was good. When the morning chores were finished, Millie reluctantly loaned me one of her dresses, reminding me that her mother would likely buy *her* a new overdress as well.

The three of us walked toward the village, my feet unable to fill out Millie's old boots. They were worn through on the bottom, and the soles of my feet were frozen pieces of leather by the time we got to the seamstress's shop.

"I used to spin my own wool, but we've sheep right now," Jewel chatted as we walked. "They took ill and died last summer. We didn't have money to buy more, so..."

"I'm sorry for your misfortune," I replied earnestly. Our footsteps were quick and we kept our hands covered to keep them from turning to ice, occasionally blowing into them to warm them up again. Puffs of steam came from our mouths with each breath and word we spoke.

Millie grumbled beneath her breath, "Misfortune? More like a turn of bad luck that apparently has no end." She gave me a pointed look.

I narrowed my eyes at her and she glanced away.

"The seamstress usually has a few dresses for sale that'll be good for farm work, and they fit anybody because they lace up on the sides. Hopefully, she'll have skirts, which might be even better. We'll just have to see," said Jewel, taking quick steps to keep up with mine and Millie's gait, my dress draped over her arm and my golden shoes in her hand. She'd been careful to keep the fabric from touching the frozen mud along the way.

I hadn't mentioned it yet, but I planned to trade the cloak I wore for something less conspicuous as well. Red was too eye-catching, the fabric too fine to fit in here, and it wasn't really mine anyway.

"So, who is *she* again?" Millie asked, eyeballing me and speaking to her mother as if I wasn't standing a foot away.

"*She* is your cousin," her mother explained for the fifteenth time. If I had to hear the story of the fake familial ties again, I was going to strangle Millicent.

Contempt rolled off her in waves. She obviously didn't like sharing her family, clothing, or room with a stranger—distant relative or not. And something in her sensed that I, indeed, was not. Madelyn from the castle had said that the young adapted quickly to change; however, something in Millie's eyes said I was a change she wouldn't easily accept.

Maybe it was for the best. Circumstances might change. *I might not be staying with them for very long anyway.* I overheard the King whisper to Piers to keep an eye on me, telling him I may be more useful than he'd first realized. *Whatever that meant.*

Jewel pointed out the various shops in town as we passed them. Most had weathered wooden signs, badly in need of a fresh coat of paint. They swung in the wind, the chains that held them squeaking. There was a bakery, milliner, seamstress, cheese shop, cobbler, and butcher shop, all lined up on the main street.

The Farmers were named after their occupation, as many paupers were, per my tutor. I wondered if the other villagers were similarly named. Perhaps the weaver was named Mr. Weaver, and the cobbler Mr. Cobbler. I couldn't help but smile at the thought.

The wind grew stronger, whistling between the buildings. My cheeks stung and my eyes watered against the cold air. Blinking the moisture away, I didn't realize I'd come close to running into someone until I was right in front of him.

A young man with dark hair and a frown too intense for his age stared at me as he stepped aside to let me pass, his hands in the pockets of a dark woolen coat, stretched tight over his arms and open too wide across his chest. His eyes raked over my bright red cloak and his frown deepened.

This time I blinked my eyes against his harsh reaction instead of the brutal weather.

"Asher, how nice to see you," Jewel said sweetly, smiling at him and patting him on the arm as he passed her. "Give my best to your father."

"Yes, ma'am. I will," he replied, inclining his head to both her and Millie before glancing at me again. When he did, the sliver of a smile fell away and his face turned back into stone as walked away.

"Mum," Millie squeaked, nearly climbing her mother's side. "He spoke to you!"

What was so special about the young man speaking? Wasn't it the polite thing to do? I watched him walk away. He glanced back, his eyes meeting mine.

"Who was that?" I asked quietly. The muscles of his back were rigid, like his bones were made of iron, his skin formed from sheets of metal. *Why did he need to protect himself with such armor?* I wondered idly.

"That," Millie beamed, "is Asher Smith, the blacksmith's son. He's by far the most handsome boy in all the kingdom."

He certainly was handsome, I had to admit. The 'smith' of his name confirmed what my tutor had taught me; fitting, since he was a blacksmith's son. He turned the corner, never reacting to Millie's shrill praise. She was so loud, the entire village must've heard her glowing opinion of Asher Smith. I was certain it was intentional. I didn't know her well, but from what I could already tell, I doubted Millie did anything without premeditation.

Besides, whether he was the *most* handsome in the kingdom, let alone the village, remained to be seen. Had Millie seen Tierney's two princes lately? Because they were quite handsome as well. *Not as handsome as Asher, in my opinion, but she might think so.*

Before I could ask any other questions, we'd arrived at the seamstress's shop. Asher was gone, but I could still imagine the ghost of him taking long strides away from me, the lapels of his coat flapping wildly in the wind.

A small bell dinged overhead as Jewel opened the door.

I followed my new "cousin" inside. Jewel introduced me to the shopkeeper and I showed the woman what I had to offer for trade. The seamstress was fair. In exchange for my gown and shoes, I was able to pick out a skirt and three overdresses that were functional on a farm, undergarments, and a worn pair of boots that fit my feet. The soles were thin, but intact.

I traded my red cloak for a simple brown one. Jewel bought a new pair of trousers for Matthew—and plenty of fabric to sew shirts for both Matthew and Hayden. Millie got a new dress and smiled as she carried the yellow linen in her arms.

How would that dress, the color of the midday sun, look after it was coated in mud? If the road here was any indication of the soil we'd soon be working in, it would be stained brown soon enough.

I'd hoped to stay home and let Jewel take care of business, but she'd insisted I come with her in case I needed to try on anything. Now, I was glad she made me come. While it was a frightfully cold walk to town, it was nice to get out and see the village; my new home. Piers had rushed us through it so fast, and it was dark besides, so I didn't have time to really study the buildings or general layout of the streets.

When we left the shop, Jewel lingered to speak with the baker for a moment, waving us on. "I'll catch up with you!" she shouted.

Millie nudged me as we walked. She stepped closer as if to tell me a secret, quietly lending me a piece of 'sisterly' advice. "Don't so much as *look* at Asher Smith. I already know he would hate you."

My spine straightened, knob by knob. "And why is that?" I questioned, instead of telling her I wasn't interested. The last thing I needed was to worry about chasing a boy, or having one chase me. But Millie didn't need to know that.

"He had his heart trampled on by a royal who fed him lies last year. If he spares you a second glance, it's only because he wants revenge. He hates your kind."

"*My* kind? I'm hardly royalty." Bile rose in my throat. Did she overhear my conversation with her parents?

She gave an unladylike snort. "You aren't a peasant, either. He saw the fine cloak you wore. Asher swore when she left that he'd never let another woman like that have a chance to break his heart."

"Was the girl from Tierney?" I asked casually.

"She visited from Roane. She led him on for weeks, toying with him, twisting him into knots. The village girls—myself included—have been trying to persuade him to notice us ever since." To no avail, she left out, but I didn't goad her. This relationship was already starting off on the wrong foot.

True to her word, Jewel caught up with us as we reached the outskirts of town and started down the trail that led to their home.

"So," Millie asked with a fake, bright smile. "Mum said we're the same age. When is your fifteenth birthday, Cousin Ella?"

I tried to smile back at her, watching the way her eyes did not crinkle at the corners. But I wasn't as good at lying and playing games as Millicent was. "My birthday is in the spring. May the first, to be exact."

Millie's smile dropped as Jewel gasped. "May Day? Why, that's Millie's birthday, as well! How strange!"

"How strange, indeed," Millie muttered, shooting daggers at me with her eyes. Not only did she have to share her family and space, but she also had to share a birthday. If I'd had any idea, I would've chosen another.

"I don't celebrate my birthday, so please don't worry, Millie," I whispered so that only she could hear me. She didn't respond; she just strode ahead of me and her mother.

When she was out of earshot, Jewel told me, "She'll settle soon."

"I'd understand if she didn't, madam."

She smiled. "You mustn't call me 'madam', Ella. Please call me Aunt or Jewel."

"I'm sorry. This is all so..."

"New?" she supplied.

"Yes. It's very new." I took a deep breath, feeling the way the new dress's fabric scratched against my arms.

We walked in the grass along the road, trying to avoid the mud that had been thawed just enough by the morning sun to make a mess. When Jewel and I reached the farm, Millie was already storming out of the house carrying a wooden bucket. "Afternoon chores," Jewel explained.

The farm came to life as the earth began to warm. Even though the wind was still whipping the leaves and branches, it had become warmer during our trip to the village and back. It was still cold, but I no longer felt like an icicle.

Behind the house was a small barn with a chicken coop beside it. "I'd like to help, but I'm afraid I don't know what to do," I said sheepishly.

Jewel nodded toward Matthew. "He's only eleven, but he's helped his father since the day he could walk. He's seen animals be born and die, seen crops thrive and rot in the ground. There isn't much he couldn't teach you about working on a farm, and he's very patient. I'm sure he'd appreciate an extra pair of hands."

She held out her arms for my dresses and told me she'd situate my things.

I walked toward Matthew. "Hello," I said. "Aunt Jewel said you might like an extra pair of hands."

Matthew's eyes lit up. "Of course! I feed the animals," he boasted, puffing out his thin chest.

I almost reached out to ruffle his bright red hair but refrained. "That's a very important job. Do you think you could show me how to do it?"

"Sure. I already fed the goats and pigs." He pointed to a pile of scraps and hay he'd thrown into their pen. "But we still need to feed the hens and gather the eggs."

"Very well." I smiled. "Lead the way."

Matthew jogged to the barn and then pointed to a large leather bag filled with corn kernels. "Mice get into it, but the hens don't mind. They eat worms and bugs and...well, everything." He shoved the handle of a wooden pail into my hands. "So, just fill your bucket. We have a lot of hens and they eat a ton. Oh, and watch out for the rooster. He'll try to spur you."

Spur me? "How will I keep him from it?"

"You can't. He's just awful! But if you knock him good with the bucket, he'll think twice about doing it again tomorrow."

Tomorrow?

Inside the chicken enclosure that was made of twisted metal and wooden boards that were hammered askew, the rooster attacked me. I screamed and ran, unable to muster the courage to hit the evil creature. But Matthew was as patient and brave as his mother said. He chased the devil bird away with a broom, giving it a sound knock on the head for good measure.

With a satisfied grin, he turned to me. "There. Now, where were we? Ah, the eggs. Most of the hens are eating. All have laid by this time of day, but the stubborn ones sit on their eggs, so you just reach under them and take the egg and put it in your bucket. And don't worry, the hens won't hurt you. They're good ladies," he cooed at them.

I blinked twice. "You expect me to stick my hand under a chicken's backside?"

Matthew smiled. "Do you like to eat eggs, Ella?"

"Of course," I replied.

"Then I suppose my answer is yes, cousin. I do."

ASHER

My feet carried me away from the Farmers and the girl who walked with them. I could tell right away that she didn't belong. She was far too beautiful to fit into this place, too soft. And without a sharp edge to be found, she wouldn't last long in Tierney...much less in Millicent's house.

There was something strange about her. Not the fine, red cloak that would cost a year of wages. Not the way her hair was braided and curled around her head like a crown. It wasn't the way she walked with her back ramrod straight taking small, even steps. The strangest thing was the haunted look in her eyes.

For someone attempting to project boldness, her eyes gleamed with pain, a color of gray that would rival the most intense storms this country had seen. There was a tempest in their depths.

What caused it?

The forge was already warm when I finally made it to the shop. I stopped near the fire to warm my hands, still thinking about her.

"Somethin' wrong?" Father asked as I shrugged my coat off. I'd outgrown it, but didn't have the heart to ask for another.

His eyes watched as I hung it up. He knew.

Business had been slow this winter, and unless it picked up, neither of us could do anything about it.

"Nothing's wrong," I answered plainly.

"Are you ready to learn how to shoe a horse?" Father asked.

"I am."

I was always ready to learn, but this afternoon especially, I'd welcome the distraction. Flashes of red, the color of fresh blood, filled my mind.

Steely eyes in a strong, but soft face. She stared, and I stared back. Tendrils of dark hair whipped in the cold wind. Her face was as pale as frost, her lips pink as a summer rose...

"Are you alright?" Father asked again.

"I'm fine. I just saw Jewel in town. She said hello." I sat my tools down next to his on the work table.

Father smiled knowingly. "And was Millicent with her?"

Since Isabel had returned to Roane to marry her betrothed, the Farmers and my father teamed up to push me toward the Farmers' daughter. Millie wasn't homely; she was pretty enough, but she was bold and her tongue never stopped wagging. I wasn't sure I could endure that for an hour, let alone a lifetime.

"There was someone else with them. A girl," I said, straightening my things.

When I turned back toward him, Father's arms were crossed and his brows lifted high. "You didn't recognize her? Was she a friend of Millicent's?"

"I've never seen her before." I didn't think Millie would keep friends who had finer things than she. "She was dressed like a noblewoman," I added.

Father's head ticked back and his hand fell on my shoulder. A familiar and infuriating sliver of pity shone in his eyes. "We'll have to visit 'em soon. Maybe they have a guest. But for now, let's focus on learnin', okay?"

"Yes, Father."

He smiled, but it was a smile of caution and concern.

Both feelings were warranted, given that I had been a complete and utter fool over the last noblewoman I'd met. When Isabel waltzed into the village, I all but fell at her feet. She told me from the beginning that she was betrothed, but I told her I didn't care. For weeks, I didn't.

For weeks, we spent any time we could together. We pretended like nothing could come between us, that we would run away together and start our own lives. She would giggle when I suggested it. Now, I knew it was because she thought the notion was ridiculous. I was nothing more than a distraction, a toy.

To her, I was just an amusing story to return to home with. Nothing more.

To me, she was the world.

For five weeks, she was the sun in my sky by day, and the moon in my life by night. Until she left without as much as a goodbye, taking our story and my heart away with her.

I wouldn't make the mistake of giving it away again.

Pushing the thoughts of Millie's friend from my mind, I focused on what Father showed me. How to heat the metal, how to know when it was ready to be shaped, and how to form the arch of the shoe itself. For weeks, I worked on making horseshoes that matched the example he gave me until I got them right every time. But I wasn't finished, Father said. The ability to shape a shoe was a great skill, but only if it fit the horse. He taught me to measure and make shoes to fit the horse who would wear it. He taught me that hard work paid off.

I didn't see the girl again, not even when the Farmers stopped by before Church. Father never asked about her, and I didn't bring her up. She was best left a curiosity. If she wasn't already, soon she'd be gone. Distance between us was what I needed, because if one mere sighting of her elicited such a response, speaking with her might ruin me altogether.

CHAPTER NINE

ELLA

THREE YEARS LATER ...

Up before dawn, I feverishly worked through my list of chores. The cows were milked. The horses, pigs, chickens, goats, sheep, and new lambs were fed. My list for the morning was almost through. Matthew was tending the horse because it had been sick. Today was a momentous day. Jewel wanted me to try to sell some eggs and Hayden needed someone to pick up an order from the blacksmith, so they decided it was finally my turn to go into the village. It would be the first time I'd been allowed to take a turn running errands by myself.

"You have the eggs?" Aunt Jewel asked for the third time.

I raised the full basket with a smile. The hens were much happier to lay now that spring was here. "You know what to buy with what you sell," she said. "Now, off you go."

It was warm outside. The bees were buzzing around the freshly bloomed flowers and clovers. The birds were chirping; babies in their nests. I walked down the path with a spring in my step while Millie scowled from the nearest field as I waved goodbye. Matthew called out from the barn, "The next trip into town is mine!"

I rolled my eyes with a smile. "How could we forget?" I shouted back. Matthew and Millie never forgot who was next in the rotation. They never let anyone else forget, either. It surprised me when Jewel asked if I wanted to take a turn. She said it had been years since I'd shown my face there; surely, people would have forgotten all about me by now. I'd never wanted to go before, didn't want to put the Farmer family in danger, but now? *I think Jewel is right,* I convinced myself.

I walked in the grass beside the worn road wearing a smile, careful to avoid the thick, loamy mud. Wildflowers had darted up in the fields. May Day was only three days away. Not only was it my and Millie's birthday, but the town would celebrate spring with a great festival.

Even on the outskirts of the village, preparations were well underway. Men on tall ladders hung strands of flowery garland from one window to another, linking the shops and houses in an intricate, colorful web. It was beautiful now, but on May Day, Jewel said the village would shine.

I'd never gone to the festival with the family, despite their attempts to persuade me. But this year, I was determined to go.

The scent of freshly baked bread wafted through the air and I wondered if I might have just enough coin left over to buy a loaf for everyone to share at dinner. Aunt Jewel liked to bake, but her body ached from the workload that spring brought with its arrival. It would be a treat and give Jewel a break.

I went to the baker first, just in case he needed eggs. I explained who I was, that I had eggs to sell, and wondered if he needed any for his baking. It turned out that he had a large number of cakes to bake for the festival and took the whole basket.

"I'll take more tomorrow if your family can spare them," he added happily, giving me more than enough coin to cover the cost of ribbon *and* bread. The smell of yeast, flour, and perfectly baked bread filled the air. I peeked at the loaves in the oven.

"I would love a fresh loaf, sir. How much for one?"

He grinned, his cheeks ruddy from the heat of the oven. "Tell you what, Ella. It was very nice talking to you. If you *promise* to save this old man a dance, I'll *give* you a loaf."

I laughed. "Of course I will, but I insist on paying you for the bread."

"Nonsense. It's my bread and if I want to give it away, I can. Now," he said, wrapping it in paper and tying a piece of twine around it. "Tell your aunt and uncle I said hello." He wiped his hands on his apron and turned around to take more golden loaves from the oven.

"Thank you!" I chirped, walking outside and across the street to the milliner's shop. We had hats at home, woven of straw with wide brims that shielded us from the sun as we worked… But that wasn't what I needed today. For her birthday, Millie had asked for ribbon. Ribbon in every color of the rainbow, to be exact. She wanted Aunt Jewel to weave them into her hair for the festival and her birthday.

As I stepped into the shop, I remembered the woman who bought my dress when I first came to live with the

Farmers, standing behind a long counter with her husband.
I must have interrupted them, because the two looked like
they'd bitten into something sour as I entered their shop.
"What do you need?" the old man barked.

"Ribbon, sir."

"Ah, over there," he said, his trembling finger pointing to
the far wall.

"How much will this buy?" I asked, walking to him and
laying the rest of my coin on the counter.

"As much as ye need. Now hurry along."

I smiled, turned on my heel, and raided the selection,
clipping strands of every color. With my hand nearly full, I
showed him what I'd cut and he mumbled something about
coin and time with silly hairstyles that were only fashionable
one day in the year before waving me on and settling back
onto his seat

The last stop was the blacksmith. I walked down the
narrow alley beside the milliner's shop, turned right,
and followed the scent of smoke and the sound of metal
pounding metal. The acrid tang of burning coal burned my
nose as I came closer. The workshop had three walls, but the
fourth was open.

It had been three years, but I never forgot the blacksmith's
son or the way Millie swooned over him. Not that I *could*
forget. It had become her mission in life to make Asher
Smith marry her. I heard about every attempt she made
when it was her turn to go to town.

His name alone reminded me of our strange encounter.
I'd lain in bed so many nights thinking about it. The look in
his eyes as he glanced back at me wasn't cold or indifferent,
but angry and burning; as hot as the coals glowing orange
in the forge just ahead. Millie said that he'd had his heart
broken by a royal, and in that red cloak I must have looked

the part. I wondered what he would think of me in the rags I wore now.

Not that it mattered.

In separate corners of the shop, two men with their backs to me pounded away at metal so hot, it glowed orange-red. They didn't know I was there, and I hated to bother them when they were working, but I needed to get back to the farm. I was about to loudly clear my throat when one of the men turned around.

Well, he wasn't a man – he was closer to my age – though he was certainly muscled like one. Could this be the boy Millie swooned over? His hair was the same dark shade. It was longer now; short on the sides, but strands brushed his long eyelashes.

He shoved the metal he'd been pounding into the fire, peeled the thick leather gloves from his hands one at a time, and stalked toward me. His narrowed eyes were a dark blue so deep, I worried about drowning. I noticed he was frowning. It *was* him.

The boy who gave his heart to a royal, only to have her tear it apart and throw the pieces back at him.

I took a step back, but he closed the distance anyway.

We stood in front of one another, both staring until he finally spoke. "Can I help you?"

I blinked and answered, "Oh, yes. I hate to interrupt your work, but my uncle asked me to pick up an order for him."

He waited a long minute and then braced his hands on his hips. "Does your uncle have a name?" he asked dryly, squinting up at the sun above us. It was midday.

"Of course he does." What a silly question.

"May I have it? We have more than one order waiting to be picked up." His face was stunning, strong and masculine, but he was cold and indifferent. If I were a bird, my feathers would have ruffled at his tone.

"Hayden Farmer," I said, squaring my shoulders.

He blinked rapidly. "Of course. Let me get Hayden's horseshoes," he answered, turning to head into the shop. At least he seemed to like my uncle.

The older gentleman eased his work into the fire as well and walked over, extending his hand. His demeanor was warm and welcoming. "Well, hello. You're Hayden's cousin…er, niece, right?"

I shook his hand. "I'm his niece, sir."

"Well, I'm Nathaniel. Hayden was one of my best friends as a child. Still is, to tell the truth," he said with a broad smile. His hair was gray and thin on top, but he and the younger man shared the same sapphire eyes. "We've heard a lot about you, but haven't had the pleasure of meetin' you 'til today. Will you all be attending the May Day festival?"

"Yes, sir."

"Have you ever been to the festival?" He looked like he was sifting through his memories for my presence. He wouldn't find me there.

"I don't like large groups, so I usually stay home." It was true. It was also true that I valued my neck, firmly attached to my body.

"You should come to dinner the next time we have them over," Nathaniel added. "We'd love to have you join us, too."

I smiled. I'd heard about their dinners from Millie. More like I heard about Asher from Millie. How he held his fork and about his long lashes and what he wore and how he looked at her like she was the only girl on earth…

Before I came along, the Smiths and Farmers regularly got together for dinner a couple times a month, alternating

78

houses. When I refused to go, Jewel often suggested that they all eat at the Farmer's. She bribed them with food, of course, but it worked. I wondered what I'd gotten myself into, and if I'd be able to avoid them now. Though with spring here, we'd be up to our necks in work.

Nathanial continued, seemingly unaffected by my lack of response. "I don't know when we'll get a chance to meet up next. Hayden and Jewel must be busy with spring coming early." He looked into my basket. "Ah, I see you've bought ribbon. Is that for your hair?"

"It's mostly for Millie's, but I might use a strand or two."

He turned to the boy who was walking back to us. "Won't she look lovely with ribbon in her hair, ay, Asher?"

Asher, with our horseshoes in hand, approached. "Yes, Father. She will." His eyes bore into me in a way that was equal parts warming and unsettling. Asher was intense and intimidating, and I wasn't sure if he meant the compliment or was merely being polite in front of his father.

Either way, he was handsome. I understood Millie's infatuation.

Nathaniel clapped Asher on the shoulder. "Fine work you did on those horseshoes."

"*You* made them?" I asked.

"I did."

Nathaniel boasted, "And right perfect shoes you've made. He measured Hayden's horse's hooves, came back here, and went straight to work."

"You were at our farm?" How did I miss that? How did *Millie* miss that?

"Hayden stopped in while he was in town last week. Would you like me to carry them home for you? They're a bit heavy," Asher offered.

"I'm sure I can manage, but thank you." I held my hands out and took the horse shoes, which *were* a bit heavy, but nothing I couldn't carry.

"Hayden also wanted me to ask if either of you would consider teaching Matthew how to use a sword—if you have some spare time," I added, glancing between father and son.

Nathaniel clapped Asher on the back. "Well, I think that's a fine thing for one young man to teach another. Besides," he held a hand at his low back, "not sure I'm as agile as I used to be."

Asher laughed. "You're definitely not." He turned to me, saying, "After the festival is over, I'd be happy to come out. Maybe we can meet a couple of evenings a week."

"He'd love that. Thank you again. I'm sure we'll see you at the festival."

Asher nodded his head once, while Nathaniel chuckled and said, "We'll look forward to it, Miss..."

I smiled. "Ella."

"Miss Ella," he finished.

I walked away, feeling the weight of Asher's eyes on my back. My cheeks caught fire from the short conversation. I could definitely see why Millie was smitten.

ASHER

I was in the process of heating iron for a small gate, bending and stretching the metal into long, thin rails and curving some pieces for decorative aspects, when I saw her standing outside. How long did she stand there before I noticed her?

She was more beautiful than I remembered. Having turned into a young woman in the three years since I'd seen her last, her face was thinner but her jaw was more angular, and her body was curvy beneath the ragged dress she wore.

Although years had passed since I last saw her, I never got the image of her out of my mind. I remembered pieces of her dark hair escaping her circlet braid and fluttering in the wind. My fingers had itched to push them out of her eyes.

Hayden told us she was staying with them back then, but since I hadn't seen her since, I assumed she'd left Tierney.

But she was here.

She was still here.

When those steely eyes locked onto mine, my breath caught.

Father asked me if she'd look lovely with ribbon in her hair, and I numbly agreed. She would. She'd be the most beautiful creature I'd ever seen. She was, even without ribbon.

Father inspected the iron I'd been stretching. "This looks wonderful, son."

"Thank you."

He lifted his brows as he sat the piece back down on the table. "She'll be at the festival," he said knowingly.

"Who?" I pretended I didn't know who he was talking about. I held tight to the work table, because my feet wanted to do nothing more than follow her. I was filled with an insatiable need to know why she never came to town with her family, why it had been so long since I'd seen her, and what she'd been doing all this time. Alone.

How could she still have such an effect on me? The pull between the two of us had gotten stronger. Did she feel it, too?

Father wasn't a fool, even with my numb protest. He took one look at my white knuckled grip, gave me a knowing look, and then shook his head. Chuckling under his breath, he returned to his work.

Three days. I had three long days before I could see her again.

CHAPTER TEN

ELLA

On the first day of May, we were rushing around to finish our chores. Matthew and I collided along one of the paths that led to the fields where the animals were grazing. "Sorry!" he yelled, running around me. If we hadn't been going to the festival, I would have balled up a clump of mud and thrown it at his back. He laughed as if he knew what I was thinking.

Millie had a smile pasted on her face all morning. I couldn't remember the last time she'd been so happy. It was a welcome relief from her constant sourness. "Ella?" she asked carefully as we dumped buckets full of water into the troughs for the horses.

Uh, oh. She wanted something from me. It was the only time she was nice. "Yes?"

"Would you braid the ribbons into my hair? Mother can do it, but her fingers ache and I want them to look perfect."

I knew it... "Of course. We can help each other dress."

She shot me a beaming smile. "Thank you!"

With the last of our chores finished, we washed quickly at the well and then ran inside to get ready.

"Take off your shoes!" Aunt Jewel shouted, smoothing her hair back as she blew out a frustrated breath. She rushed around the kitchen in a flurry, icing the cakes she'd baked for the celebration.

We unlaced our boots and ran up the steps, giggling all the way. Millie and I still shared her side of the upstairs room. She grabbed the ribbon and her brush, pulling a small stool toward me. I sat on her mattress and combed out her long, red hair.

"Your hair is beautiful, Millie."

She sighed, her shoulders slumping. "I wish it wasn't the color of fire."

"I don't know. Some men like fire. Asher, perhaps," I suggested with a grin, knowing she liked him very much. "He works in it often enough."

"I doubt there'll be a single girl attending tonight who *doesn't* want Asher Smith." Tenacious Millie was gone, replaced by self-doubting Millie.

"But *I* will capture his attention first," she stated resolutely. And... tenacious Millie was back.

"There's at least one," I told her with a smile. I truly didn't want his attention. Whenever he looked at me, it made me feel like I was burning from the inside. "If he likes you, you'll know. Love should be the easiest thing in the world. It should be fluid between two people, a gentle pull and

84

tug." Not a scorching inferno with an intensely serious young man.

Like I should be giving advice about love...

"You'll find someone, Ella." Her tone was part placating and part uninterested. Of course, any time the topic wasn't about Millie, she didn't care.

"I don't know anyone here, so I doubt that." Millie had always told me how the boys would think I was snobbish, and how the girls would hate me because of my fine manners.

"One day you will," she insisted. "You'll just have to leave Tierney to find it." It was a backhanded compliment. Millie had hated me from the morning I arrived. She still did, despite me plaiting her hair and her half-attempt at being civil. And no matter how I acted, she would still hate me this evening at the festival. She couldn't stay pleasant for very long. It just wasn't in her nature.

The thought of Millie and her pack of friends surrounding me made my stomach twist on itself. She talked often about how cruelly they treated those outside their circle, and I wasn't even anywhere near the perimeter—not that I wanted to be.

Maybe it would be like she said. The boys would think I was a snob and the girls would hate me. That would be fine by me, because if friends like Millie were all Tierney had to offer, I was better off without them.

I just want to stay home.

When her hair was finished, I tilted her head left, right, and up, and then told her she was ready. Over a month ago, I'd asked Aunt Jewel to sell the other gown I'd arrived here with in order to buy me and Millie simple, but pretty dresses for May Day. She hesitated, but finally agreed after I argued that I'd never be able to fit into it again, and that it would become moth's food and good for absolutely nothing if I continued to hold onto it.

It worked. Jewel hated waste.

It seemed like forever ago since I was the lanky fourteen-year-old delivered to their doorstep. I'd filled out over the years and now had the body of a woman, complete with curves and breasts that the gown I'd taken from Aelawyn could never hope to contain. It was time to let it go.

The last few growing seasons were good to the Farmers, and with one more able body, the crops had flourished like they hadn't in years. The harvests yielded more than ever. Even after Lord Windmeyer, who owned the land we farmed, took his share, Uncle Hayden and Aunt Jewel still received a handsome (and well-deserved) amount of money for our hard work.

Millie's voice startled me. "Would you like me to weave ribbon into *your* hair?" She held up the few strings that were left, although she clutched them tightly as if she couldn't bear to part with them.

"Can I just have one to tie at the bottom of my braid?"

"Are you sure? Yours will be *very* plain compared to mine." Her fingers brushed over her head, finding the delicate strands of fabric woven into her beautifully plaited hair.

Millie would love it if I looked plainer than she did, and to tell the truth, so would I. "I'm positive. Save the rest of the ribbon for another time."

She squealed and ran to get her dress. "Would you help me dress?"

"Sure."

Her dress was the color of a beet: red-purple and beautifully dramatic. It would certainly draw attention. After twirling around a few times in front of me, she squealed again and ran downstairs to show her mother, where they fawned over her hair and dress together.

I plaited my hair and dressed quickly. My dress was made of simple white lace, beautifully cut to hug my waist and flaring to the ground. I was happy with how I looked. Not that it would matter. Other than Mr. Baker and Matthew, I doubted anyone would want to come near me, let alone get close enough to ask for a dance.

Today was my birthday, and I wanted to live my life in the happiest way I could, in honor of my sister. Now that it was safe to show my face in town, I could take the opportunity to do what I did best: watch the people of Tierney, the way I watched those of Aelawyn from my window so long ago—safely, and from a distance.

I grabbed the thin lavender ribbon Millie had thrown in my direction and headed downstairs as well, tying it around the bottom of my braid as I stepped onto the landing. Millie was chatting away with Aunt Jewel when I stepped into the room. Jewel stopped mid-sentence and gasped, clutching her chest.

"Oh, Ella. You are a vision, just like Millie!"

A bright flash of white-hot anger flared in Millie's eyes before she was able to tamp it down. She was a childish brat and I was sick of it, but Jewel had worked so hard baking for the festival. If I bloodied Millie's nose now, we'd all have to stay home and it would ruin the evening Jewel was looking forward to.

Offering a small, forced smile, I replied, "Thank you, Aunt."

Uncle Hayden stepped inside with Matthew on his heels. He could undoubtedly sense the tension in the room. "What's wrong?"

"Nothing at all," Jewel replied, giving Millie a needle-sharp glance of warning. "The girls are ready for the festival, and now I need to clean up and change as well." She removed her apron and headed toward their bedroom at the back of the house. "Matthew!" she yelled. "Wash well, then get upstairs and dress in your best!"

"Yes, Mum!" he yelled in reply as he jogged up the steps. At fourteen, his voice had begun to waver between boy and man, and his lanky frame was filling out a little.

"Can Ella and I walk ahead, Mother?" Millie called out.

"Not today," Jewel proudly replied. "Today, we're taking the wagon!"

"Wonderful! It'll be so much better than walking home in the darkness, especially with the road being so muddy," Millie said, her eyes lighting back up.

Hayden laughed and hugged Millie to his side. "I can't have my ladies walking in the mud to such a grand event, now can I? And certainly not on their birthdays." He kissed her head. "You look beautiful. Maybe I should take my knife, in case a boy gets any smooth ideas?"

"Father, no!" she cried.

He simply laughed. "I was joking."

When she took a deep breath, he added, "Mostly."

CHAPTER ELEVEN

ELLA

ncle Hayden and Aunt Jewel sat on the bench of the old wagon together; his grip loose on the reins as he drove the horse forward. They chatted happily the whole ride, talking under their breath about things they didn't think were appropriate for us to hear as we drove toward the village.

Millie sat up straight and held onto the sides for dear life, excitement and anxiety brimming barely beneath the surface. Somehow the dress and ribbons had robbed her of common sense. She'd never fallen from the wagon before, and certainly wouldn't today. Her nerves were getting the best of her. She fussed over her hair as we rode toward town, worried that the wind was messing it up.

"It looks fine, Millie," I commented for the tenth time since we left home.

She scowled at me. "I don't want it to look *fine*. I want it to look stunning."

"You look beautiful," I reassured her. Millie threw me a look that said she didn't care about *my* opinion.

Matthew pretended to make over his own hair, laughing at her. She hit him in the arm, but he still chuckled.

Hayden guided the horse toward a post on the outskirts of town and then turned to us. "A word, please."

We climbed out of the wagon after he secured the horse and waited as he helped Jewel to the ground.

"No fighting. No name-calling. No *meanness* of any sort," he said, aiming the words at Millie. "Stay at the festival. No running off," he said to Matthew. "And please, try to enjoy yourself," he said, with his eyes directed at me.

His children muttered, "Yes, Father," at the same time I said, "Yes, Uncle," and then we were told to run along.

Millie and Matthew ran toward the crowd, while I lingered by the wagon. There was a large, grassy field in the shape of a square, right in the middle of town, where most of the May Day festivities would take place. I offered to carry two of Jewel's cakes to the square where long tables were set up. She'd baked six, and each one smelled and looked delicious. My mouth was watering, just knowing how good they were.

The late afternoon sun warmed my skin. I found the almost-full cake table, easing one cake and then the other into the small spaces I could find. In the center of the grassy square was a tall pole, and affixed to the top of the pole were strands of ribbons in every color, hanging down to the

90

ground. Some of the silken fabric strands matched those in Millie's hair. I knew that as she danced today, Millie would look lovely.

"It's a maypole," Jewel said as she stepped up beside me, following my gaze. "You didn't celebrate May Day?"

I shook my head. Ever gracious and understanding, Jewel didn't pry into the shadows of my past. Maybe she just thought Aelawyn had different traditions.

"It's tall," I said, staring up at the top of it.

"Maidens will grab a ribbon and dance 'round the pole in just a little while. The ribbons weave a pattern down the length of the wood. I hope to see you join the fun," she said, nudging my arm gently.

I hated to see the briefest moment of disappointment in her eyes, but I knew I wouldn't be dancing this evening.

Jewel and I cleared two spaces for the cakes Hayden carried and I watched as his eyes found Mr. Baker. Hayden and Jewel, a pair still so obviously in love, held hands as they walked over to him, and the trio chatted happily about life in general.

Matthew found some boys his age and they stood together with their hands in the pockets of their trousers, sharing glances with a group of girls just across the square. He was fourteen, and as every young person eventually does, he'd discovered the opposite sex.

Millie was surrounded by her group of friends. 'The pack', as Matthew and I affectionately called them, was comprised of both genders. I'd heard enough stories from her trips to town that though I'd never spoken with them, I knew each one's name from her descriptions.

Millie was certainly in contention for the position of leader among them. The girls marveled at her new dress, fingering the fabric and telling her that the color looked beautiful with her hair and skin tone. Her eyes locked with mine and hardened as she looked quickly away and smiled, saying something that made them all laugh.

Near the maypole, a group of musicians began to play and dancing started in the grassy square. Everyone looked happy. The bitter strain of winter was over, and sweet relief was in the warmer air.

"Tis May Day, May Day," someone began to sing. The crowd joined in, singing with them. I helped Jewel and some other ladies serve slices of pie and cake as a line of people passed by, taking their favorite. A couple of hours later, the once-full dishes and platters held nothing but crumbs, icing, and filling.

Millie and her friends walked by, snickering about how I'd ruined my dress with the messy desserts. I glanced down. I hadn't spilt anything on me.

"Don't worry. There's nothing on your dress," Jewel said apologetically. "I'll talk to her."

I shook my head. "She doesn't bother me." I knew it wouldn't do any good. I'd lived with her for three years and was well aware that she refused to be civil most of the time. Any time Jewel asked her to be nice, she'd turn the conversation around and whine that I was ruining her life.

Millie's bad behavior wasn't worth fighting over. She and I were both seventeen, which meant that soon, one or both of us would marry and move out of the house. Millie couldn't wait. Since we got here, I saw her speaking with more than one young man, but she still hadn't spoken with Asher. I hadn't seen him at all.

"I saved you a piece," Jewel whispered, holding up a small plate with a beautiful slice of vanilla cake.

"Oh, thank you! I love vanilla."

"I know. I made it just for your birthday. Now, go enjoy it before someone steals it from you." She shooed me away and walked over to where Hayden was in deep conversation with the cobbler.

I walked to a large oak tree and leaned against the bark, enjoying my first bite of moist cake.

"Looks delicious," came a deep voice from behind me, causing me to jump out of my skin.

I whirled around to see Asher Smith standing there, smirking at me.

The tree we stood beneath was close enough that we could see the festivities and hear the music, but the crowd and noise weren't loud here. It was why I chose the spot. Maybe I wasn't the only one who liked the quiet. "I'm sorry. I didn't see anyone here," I stammered.

A smile tugged at his lips. "That's because no one *was* here when you walked over."

Oh.

"The village looks beautiful," he said admiringly. "May Day is my favorite celebration of the year," he said. The wistfulness of his words conflicted with his stoic expression; staring at the villagers who danced, at the musicians, and then turning his deep blue eyes on me, his brow quirking in question. Right. He'd said something…

I cleared my throat. "It's really nice," I said awkwardly. I set my fork down on my plate, my palms suddenly too sweaty to keep hold of it.

"You should've come to the festival before. Your uncle, aunt, and cousins always make it a point to attend."

I bristled at his accusatory tone. It was none of his business whether I came to the festival or not. "I don't like crowds," I said pointedly. I'd told his father the same thing, and I was pretty sure he heard me say it. The years I spent isolated in my room tended to make me anxious around a lot of people.

The last three years, I refused to attend because I told myself I should heed Piers' warning to stay at the Farmers' home until things quieted down, but the truth was that the village never seemed quiet enough.

Besides, there were always rumors swirling through town, and I didn't want to be the subject of any of them.

"We should both be happy that looks can't kill," he said into my ear, making my skin prickle.

"What do you mean?" I asked, and then followed his eyes to Millie, who wore a look of pure rage.

A deep sigh spilled from my lips. Millie had claimed Asher years ago, as far as I was concerned, rightful or not. I guess that meant I couldn't even talk to him. "It isn't you," I said, exasperated. "I should go," I said.

His arm shot out and gently grabbed mine, stopping my retreat. "Stay."

"Why?" I asked, looking at him.

His dark blue eyes twinkled with mischief and I wondered what lay beneath the hard exterior he tried so hard to project. "Share your cake with me," he requested boldly.

Ah – so *that* was why he approached me in the first place. He just wanted something.

"You can have it," I answered quickly. "I lost my appetite." I handed him the plate and left him standing beneath the tree. *So much for my slice of birthday cake.*

ASHER

What just happened?

One minute she was fine, and the next she was upset and running away. Millie had made a spectacle of herself all night. I'd managed to avoid her thus far, but knew she was searching me out every time she searched the faces in the square.

Her silly crush was driving me crazy.

I blew out a frustrated breath, holding the small plate in my hands. I didn't even *want* the cake; I just wanted her to stay and talk for a few minutes. Now she was gone, and the vanilla cake would go to waste.

That was when I saw her at the edge of the square, Millie and her friends closing in. Ella's back straightened and she held her hands out defensively. I crossed the yard faster than should've been possible, just in time to hear the hateful words spew from her cousin's mouth.

But I was too far away to shield Ella from them.

CHAPTER TWELVE

ELLA

I didn't get far before Millie and her friends found me.

"Why were you talking to Asher?" Millie demanded angrily.

"It was nothing, Millie. He just wanted a piece of cake," I replied.

"So you thought you'd give him yours to lure him in? Well, it won't work! You're just a prissy little nobody," she spat. "I bet your parents killed themselves just to get away from you!"

I blinked, clutching my throat and gasping for air as the memory of seeing Ivy rushed back.

"She can't even come up with something to say back to you, Millie!" a girl laughed. The rest of the group chuckled with her.

But I couldn't see them; I could only see Ivy. Her neck. Her pale skin, the blue veins dark beneath the surface, her mouth slightly agape, and her tongue dry and shriveling in her mouth. The twisted, knotted sheet. Her chest lying still, where it should have risen and fallen. A swarm of dark wasps overtook my vision, but even they couldn't block the memory of her.

Her neck. Oh, God. Her neck.

A sheen of cold sweat broke out over my body.

The whole world was spinning.

"You shouldn't have said that to her," a loud voice boomed. "She's your flesh and blood, and you treat her like that? I'd hate to see how you'd treat a stranger." Strong hands clamped down protectively on my arms and steered me away from the beet-colored blur I knew was Millie. "Come on," the voice softened. My feet felt heavy and wooden, but they followed him. Away from her.

When the swarm receded, I saw Millie staring angrily at me from across the lawn. "Don't worry about them," Asher said, removing his hands from my arms. The warmth of his skin on mine suddenly disappeared and I couldn't help but shiver.

"That's easy for you to say. By reacting that way, I just let her know where to cut me next time; where I'll bleed. I'm so stupid!" Looking away from her, I pressed the heels of my palms to my eyes to staunch the tears. *Stupid girl. I should have ripped those pretty ribbons out of her hair.*

"You aren't stupid. You lost your family, Ella. I understand that loss more than most." He was quiet for a moment before he began to speak again. "My father is alive, but my mother passed away. I understand the feeling of a wound that never heals. It re-opens every time I think of her, and about what she's missed, what she should've been here to see. And you aren't stupid to hurt, Ella. You're better off for it. It's the ones without a heart that I pity." He shot a glare at Millie and the pack to reinforce his point as I took a moment to compose myself, straightening my spine and my dress.

He was right. I was fortunate enough to love Ivy while she was on this earth. Though the loss of her hurt, loving her was worth the pain.

Asher shoved his hands in his pockets and cleared his throat. "The maypole dance is about to start. Do you want to join the others?" he asked.

"No, I don't." I stood up straight, thankful that the terrible spell had passed and embarrassed that he, of all people, had to witness it. "Thanks for helping me, but I'm fine. I don't want to ruin your evening. You should go find your friends."

I suddenly heard the strains of a sprightly tune, and all eyes fastened on the center of attention, the maypole. Millie and her friends, along with several other maidens from the village, each took a ribbon. As the musicians played, the young women danced, weaving an intricate braid in every shade of the rainbow down the length of the pole. It was as beautiful as Jewel said it would be.

Millie's eyes kept finding Asher every time she spun around the maypole. She watched him with the same single-minded ferocity as a kestrel sighted its prey.

Asher's father called out to him, raising a hand to get his attention, from where he was speaking with Uncle Hayden and Aunt Jewel. When they saw that we were talking, they waved me over as well.

"Why aren't you dancing, Ella?" Jewel asked. I shrugged noncommittally. After the maypole was finished being turned into a work of art, the entire village made their way to the square. Women, men, and children alike spun and twirled to the music, with partners or alone. They were happy to simply dance and be carefree for an evening.

"I'm afraid I'm to blame," Asher intervened. "Ella had to share her slice of cake with me."

"How nice of you," Jewel said, nudging my arm before a sly grin stretched over her lips. Her eyes glittered as she turned to Asher. "Perhaps you can find a way to make it up to her, Asher."

Kill me now, Lord, so Millie won't smother me in my sleep, thanks to her meddling mother.

A smile tugged at the corner of his lips. "And how would I do that, ma'am?"

"By dancing the next song with her, of course." I felt like sinking into the spongy earth.

"Asher doesn't look like the dancing sort," I said with a smile. I silently hoped that I'd guessed right, that Asher either couldn't or didn't like to dance, or that he'd take the hint that I didn't feel like dancing.

But apparently Asher wasn't one to back down from a dare—that, or he actually liked dancing—because he fixed his eyes on me determinedly. "Ah, but you're wrong. And I'll enjoy proving it to you."

He bent down to my ear, his warm breath fanning over my skin and making it pebble. "Are you feeling better now?"

I nodded, afraid to speak as he laced his warm, calloused fingers through mine.

The sun set beyond the hills, and with the change in lighting came a change in music, from a whimsical harmony to a daring, upbeat tune. "Try to keep up," Asher teased, grabbing my hand and pulling me into the crowd of dancing couples.

100

It had been more than three years since I'd danced, but even then, I never danced like this. Asher wrapped his large hand around mine, flashed a wicked grin, and pulled my body flush with his. I sucked in a shocked breath, which earned a brilliant, roguish smile. With his hand splayed across the small of my back and our bodies pressed tightly against each other, we took off.

I'd never laughed so hard in my life.

For the first time, Asher dazzled me with his wide, brilliant smile. It was as beautiful as the sunrise, but much rarer. When the song was over, he paused so we could catch our breath. Then he stood up with a wicked gleam in his eyes. "Still feeling okay?" he asked.

"Yes."

"Good," he said with a grin. "Let's go again."

Large iron baskets attached to the tops of posts were filled with firewood and lit, providing a warm glow. Tiny embers of fire leaked from the popping wood. Asher and I had danced for the better part of an hour when we finally stopped to find something to drink. A table to the side held goblets, mugs, and a large tub of water. I drew a drink for each of us and we gulped the cool water down greedily, pausing to laugh as our chests heaved from exertion.

I felt a small tap on my shoulder and turned to find Matthew standing beside me. "Matthew! Are you having fun?"

He scuffed his shoe on the ground. "I was hoping you might dance one song with me." He looked from me to Asher and back, eyes hopeful—like he was asking for permission to cut in.

I smiled, giving an apologetic glance to Asher. "Of course, I will." When the music started again, Matthew took my hand and stood several feet away, his arm stretched to the point that his hand barely reached my waist. My cousin was young, but almost as tall as I was.

"You dance well," he said, attempting to make conversation.

"You're making me look good."

He paused, and I could tell he had something he wanted to say. "I'm sorry about Millie, about what she said and how she upset you." He cast his eyes down to our feet. I ignored it when he stepped on my toes.

"I'm sorry you had to see that, Matthew. I didn't realize you were close by."

"I wasn't close," he said. "She was very loud."

Of course she was. Swallowing, I gritted my teeth and nodded. "Well, enough about that. Let's just have a good time."

He grinned and kept moving his feet around in a square. I followed his lead, and when the dance was over, thanked him for the dance. Looking around, I noticed Asher was gone.

The baker, whose name was Jack, came around to ask for his dance and we took our turn around the square. I told him how much the family had enjoyed his bread, and he told me to stop in any time to take another loaf home with me.

When the song ended, Asher still wasn't anywhere to be found. How silly of me to think I'd finally made a friend. Squashing my disappointment, I went to get another drink. Millie walked over to the table, a haughty look on her face and her arms crossed over her chest.

"He's gone," she said acidly.

"Who's gone?" I asked in a lilting voice, pretending not to know or care of whom she spoke.

"Asher Smith. He left when you started dancing with Matthew. Maybe he spent enough time with you to know what kind of person you are."

"And what kind is that?" I asked, feeling my fists tighten into balls.

"The kind who lies," she spat.

"I'm not a liar, Millie, and I've had enough of your games for one day." I tried to step around her, but she wasn't having it.

"You said you didn't want anything to do with him! You *know* what he means to me," she said beneath her breath, grabbing my arm and holding me in place before her.

"What, Millie?" I tore my arm away from her. "What could he *possibly* mean to you?"

She bared her teeth. "I love him! You're just trying to ruin the only chance I have of getting away from here."

What was so wrong with her life that made her feel so desperate to escape? If she became anyone's wife—even Asher's—she would still have the same chores she did now. Beyond her daily chores and planting, very little was expected from her. She didn't go without food or clothing. Everyone put up with her awful attitude, and her parents even made sure she had special gifts from time to time. They loved her. Her brother worshipped her. Yet, she was unhappy and ungrateful, in spite of it all.

"I feel sorry for you," I finally said, leaving her behind me.

"For what?" she yelled.

"You can't see how lucky you are, Millie, and it's incredibly sad."

She tried to reignite the argument, but I was finished. I shook my head and went to find Jewel. She was chatting with a friend near one of the torches. When she noticed me walking toward her, the smile she wore fell away. "Ella? Is everything alright?"

"I'm fine. I'm just very tired and have a headache. Would you mind if I walked home?"

She looked me over. "I'm sure Hayden would take you. Let me find him real quick..." Her head swiveled left and then right as her eyes scanned the crowd for her husband. "Now, where did that man run off to?"

"I'd rather walk, if you don't mind. The fresh air might help." Truly, my head was fine. It was the pain in my neck that I wanted to escape.

She hesitated. "If you're sure and promise to be careful, I guess that's okay. You aren't a child anymore."

I wasn't a child when I came to live with you, I thought, but I simply said, "Thank you."

"I'll check on you when we get home," she promised.

I walked away from the flickering light and into the darkness, away from the music and Millie.

CHAPTER THIRTEEN

ELLA

A branch snapped behind me, but when I turned around to look, nothing was there. Swallowing my fear, I walked a little faster through the grass, my heart racing. *It's probably just an animal, a deer foraging for food*, I told myself. But then a familiar voice came from behind.

"Don't be frightened."

Goosebumps pebbled my skin. "What are *you* doing out here, Asher?"

He jogged to catch up to me. "Making sure you get home safely."

"Why?" I turned around, exasperated. Why did he disappear during the festival? Where did he go? I thought we were having fun, that we were becoming friends, and then he disappeared. Why was he following me home and acting like a shadow?

He started to tick the reasons off on his fingers. "Well, it's midnight. You're a young woman. You shouldn't be walking home alone in the dark. And, it's dangerous."

The only real danger was his fickleness. "I'm perfectly safe to walk this road alone." There was nothing along this road that would hurt me. Most animals were more afraid of humans than we were of them, and most of the people who lived out here were still in the square. The houses I passed had no candles lit in the windows.

"You're angry I left," he said softly.

"I don't understand why you did," I admitted, keeping my eyes trained on the ground in front of my feet.

"While you were dancing with Matthew, my father wanted me to dance with Millie. I refused, and then walked away because I knew if I returned, he would make me."

"Why would he care if you danced with her?" Realization set in and my heart stopped for a brief moment. So did my feet. I could feel my lips part, speechless at last.

"My father and your uncle and aunt thought it would be wonderful if Millie and I married. I think it's why Millie has a crush on me, even though we don't really know each other. We see each other from time to time at a distance, but we've never had a meaningful conversation. She doesn't even know who I am."

"Who are you?" I asked. "What would she learn from such a conversation?"

He glanced over shyly. "For starters, she'd learn that I'm not a man who would ever marry a woman like Millie." I let out a pent-up breath. *Thank goodness.*

He fell into step beside me and we walked through the darkness. The need to apologize welled up inside me.

"I'm sorry you've been put in such a position."

Asher shrugged. "There's nothing to apologize for. My father knows how I feel about Millie, but Hayden is his best friend and he doesn't want to hurt his feelings or Jewel's."

Honestly, I wasn't sure that Jewel would be too upset. It felt like she'd nudged me toward him this evening, but I could be wrong. Maybe she was just trying to be nice and make sure I was included. "Better to disappoint them now than marry someone you don't love. At least you *can* marry for love. Think of the royals. They get no say in the matter."

He stopped for a second.

"What?" I asked, and then wanted to slap myself. With that careless statement, I'd probably dredged up unhappy memories of his first love.

"You're right," he said, walking again. "I am lucky. And so are you."

I knew it. I counted my blessings every day. Just the memory of the name *Yurak of Galder* made my skin crawl.

"So, tell me your story," he said conversationally. "How did you come to live with the Farmers?"

I fed him the same lie I'd told everyone else: "My family lived in Paruth, along the Northern Sea…"

It was an easy lie to tell because of Paruth's well-known history. I remember when my tutor told me the news. About six months before Aelawyn fell, almost every citizen in Paruth fell ill from plague and died. The few that survived the plague fled, traveling to other kingdoms to rebuild their lives. Now, I pretended to be one of them.

"I managed to find Uncle Hayden through the kindness of several people who offered me food, let me ride in their wagons, or pointed me in the direction of Tierney so that I could travel on foot."

For three years, the lie felt safe to tell. I was protecting Tierney, the family who let me become one of them, and myself. But now... It felt wrong to lie to Asher. I couldn't tell him the truth. I could never tell him the truth. But the lie tasted bitter, like poison on my tongue.

"That's awful. You lost both your parents?"

"My parents and a sister, as well. We didn't know it was the plague until it was too late. It swept through the kingdom like wildfire, and the healers couldn't do anything to stop it. The Farmers are distant cousins. We'd visited them once, when I was really small. It was the only reason I remembered them. I didn't know of any other family, so I came to them for help. You can imagine how surprised they were when I showed up on their doorstep."

"That must have been difficult," he said softly. I wondered if his searching eyes, as dark blue as the midnight sky above us, could see the truth between the lies. "The fact that you're from Paruth explains a lot."

"What do you mean?" I asked.

"You speak differently, more properly than most. And you hold yourself more confidently than any other girl in the village."

I sighed and inwardly cringed.

He stopped walking and his hand gently clasped my upper arm, sending tingles and goosebumps over me like a wave. Butterflies took flight in my belly and I couldn't help but stare back at him with the same intensity with which he was looking at me.

"I like that you've stayed true to yourself. It takes more courage to be yourself than it does to conform."

I wished everyone felt that way. Offering him a small smile, I thanked him.

We began walking again, his hand hovering over the small of my back. All too soon, the Farmer's house appeared just around the next bend. "Thank you for seeing me home."

"Thank you for letting me."

I laughed. "You didn't really give me a choice."

We stared at each other in peaceful silence until he broke it. "I'll see you again one evening this week."

"You will?"

He nodded. "I'll be bringing practice swords to teach Matthew the basics of sword fighting. It'll be nice to see you again, too."

I let out a pent-up breath and smiled. He walked me to the porch and waited until I fastened the door behind me. I hurriedly lit the wick of a taper and waved at him through the window. He waved back and grinned.

Having a friend would be nice.

I wondered how he would feel about teaching me how to use a sword, too. If anything bad ever happened, if Piers ever came for me…I could defend myself.

I was outside sitting on my knees in the grass beside the front door, scrubbing the pots and pans from supper in our large washtub. Matthew had just brought out the dishes when he squinted, shielding his eyes from the western sun. "Asher's here!" he said excitedly, rushing away to meet him.

There was a commotion in the house, rushed footfalls on the steps. Millie must have heard Matthew's announcement.

Asher and Matthew walked together to the front yard, Matthew testing the weight of the wooden practice sword Asher handed to him.

"This is perfect!" Matthew gushed. "I'm so excited to learn. Thank you for coming all the way out here to teach me!"

Asher grinned. "This is the perfect place to practice. Plenty of room to move, and soft grass to break our falls. But don't think I'm going to go easy on you, though. If you want to learn, the best way is if I'm ruthless."

"Ruthless, right." Matthew nodded. Asher could have said the sky was green and Matthew would've agreed. I smiled and rolled my eyes.

"Hello, Ella," Asher greeted.

"Asher." I smiled, but kept to my chore. I wanted to learn, too, but Jewel needed me to help around the house first. I could still watch and absorb, and then maybe jump in later.

Millie burst out of the door a moment later with Hayden and Jewel on her heels. Once she started talking, I thought Hayden would never shut her up.

I was almost finished with the dishes when Hayden finally interrupted her monologue about how wonderful Asher was to spend his time teaching her little brother all there was to know about swordsmanship, how she expected that he might want to be a page at the castle one day, and how this would help him get an edge on all the other young men from the village.

"Imagine that," she said wistfully. "A Farmer. Living in the castle."

Truthfully, Matthew was too old to be a page now. Boys were typically trained until age seven and then served as pages to royalty or knights until they were fourteen, but I kept my mouth shut. Matthew wanted to learn to swing a sword, and that was all that mattered.

When she started to babble again, Hayden chuckled, saying, "We need to leave them to it, dear. Daylight's wastin'."

Millie's emotions flipped lightning fast from excited, to angry, to acceptance, as she sank down onto the grass next to me. Jewel took the clean pots inside. "I'll bring in the rest of the dishes in a few minutes," I called after her.

Asher positioned Matthew a few feet away and gave him a few minutes to get the feel of the sword. "Test the weight when you lift it overhead and bring it down. Swing it side to side. You'll need to work on controlling your actions until your muscles adjust. Metal swords are even heavier than these."

I took the dishes in, drawing Asher's eyes for a moment. Jewel was watching the two from the window. "He's so excited," she commented when I stepped up beside her.

"I don't blame him. Jewel?"

She turned to me. "Yes?"

"Do you care if I also learn?"

Concern furrowed her brow. "Why would you want to?"

I shrugged, picking at a piece of lint on my sleeve. "It just looks like fun."

She looked back at Matthew. "I imagine it does. You're older, and would probably catch on fast. And it *would* help if Matthew had a sparring partner. Asher can't come every day."

Smiling at her back, I rushed back to the yard and watched.

Asher was instructing Matthew. "Left foot forward, hips pointed straight ahead. That's your power position. Don't shift your hips away or it might throw you off balance, and you don't want that. It could mean life or death if you were actually fighting someone."

Matthew followed along, concentration furrowing his brow.

"Sword on your right shoulder," Asher coached.

Matthew looked at Asher on his left side and changed his grip on the hilt to match his instructor's. "Now," Asher continued, "we're going to bring the sword forward and down in a slicing motion."

The muscles beneath Asher's shirt rippled as they brought their swords down in a high arc, right and high to the left, and low to the ground. They stepped forward with their right feet as they sliced.

I could do that.

Asher caught me watching and his next words were directed at me. "The blade should protect your head, hand, and body at all times. You want to try it, Ella?"

Millie made a strangled noise. "She's a woman!" she sputtered incredulously. "Why would she need to learn to wield a sword?"

"I would," I said, ignoring her.

Asher smiled. "Very well. Take my sword, and you and Matthew try to follow the motions of the overhead attack."

I caught the sword he tossed to me.

Asher moved to stand in front of us. With sweaty palms, I held tight to the sword's hilt, leaning it over my right shoulder. At the same time, Matthew and I stepped forward, bringing the blades down in an arcing motion.

Asher smiled. "Good. You can keep those swords and practice together when I can't be here. I have other practice swords at home. Ready to learn to defend the move I just taught you?"

Matthew was in heaven. Together, Asher taught us how to quickly lean or back away from a blade, and how to bring our own blade across the attacker's and put counter pressure on it to stop the sword from finding its mark. Matthew had been holding his own against Asher, when suddenly Asher broke free and lunged forward, the tip of his sword closing in on Matthew's throat.

"Now, what are you going to do?" Asher asked him.

"Put your blade in his belly!" I yelled.

Asher smiled and stepped away. "He could, but he also might die if I keep moving forward. We want him to win, not lose or draw. One thing he could do is use his feet to stop my forward momentum." He looked at Matthew. "Kick me away, and when I lose my balance, you'll have an opportunity to attack again."

With a determined look on his face, they repeated the motions slowly until Asher's blade was gliding toward Matthew's neck again. This time, my cousin didn't hesitate. He kicked Asher hard in the stomach, and when Asher stumbled, Matthew brought his sword down hard, stopping just shy of Asher's shoulder.

Asher smiled as he recovered. "Good job! Now it's your turn, Ella."

Matthew stepped aside as I drew my sword and stepped forward to meet him. "Are you ready?" he asked.

I knew the motions in my mind, but making my limbs follow them was another thing. "Yes. I'm ready."

He circled me and I stayed opposite him, our feet moving slowly, step by step. "Ooooh," Matthew teased. "This looks fierce! Mum, Dad, look!"

He caught me by surprise, bringing his sword over his head. I defended myself, my blade catching his and holding it off, but he saw me flinch.

Asher stepped back and smiled at Matthew, who teased me that this sparring session might be over with before it started.

To me, he whispered, "I won't hurt you."

I nodded and tightened my grip.

"Ready?" he asked.

"Yeah."

I can do this, I thought. I needed to know how to defend myself. When Asher gave the command, I brought my sword down in an arc and he met my sword with his own, the impact stinging my palm.

"I can't go easy on you," he warned. His dark hair fell into his eye, but he ticked his head, moving it back. There was a small smirk on his mouth and I had the insatiable urge to forcefully wipe it off his pretty face.

I gritted my teeth, meeting the pressure he was putting on my blade as we kept circling. "I didn't ask you to," I panted.

He lunged, and his blade jabbed at my throat. I panicked inwardly, but still managed to lean back so he couldn't reach me, and then kicked him hard to shove him back. But instead of throwing him off balance, Asher dropped to the ground in a heap.

I dropped my sword. "Are you okay?" I asked, concerned.

He was groaning as he rolled onto his side, but I could make out the words, "Good job," before Millie ran to him and knelt beside him, rubbing his back sympathetically.

She scowled at me. "Why did you do that?" she demanded.

"I didn't mean to hurt him!"

Hayden laughed. "Just landed that kick a little below the belt, cousin. He'll be alright. Give him some space," he aimed at Millie.

My face was on fire, yet Matthew couldn't stop laughing. "That was amazing!" he choked out. "Just… don't do that to me when *we* practice."

When Asher recovered enough to sit up, he smiled at me and nodded. "That was good."

"I'm really sorry."

"Don't be. I told you to do it, and I told you not to hold back."

"I thought you were going to stab me."

"I would never hurt you, Ella."

Matthew scoffed, crossing his arms. "What about me?"

"That's another story," Asher replied with a wink.

"Better watch out," he smarted. "Ella's going to teach me that move when you aren't around." Everyone except Millie laughed at his joke.

Maybe I'd use it on her one day.

Before he left, Asher walked over to me and slipped a folded piece of parchment into my hand. I hid the tiny square, giving him a quizzical look, which he just returned with a grin. I kept his note in my pocket until I had a moment alone in my room. My fingers unfolded the parchment, revealing his scrawled handwriting in black ink.

Dearest Ella,

I'm not sure why, but I felt compelled to write to you. I sit at my desk in the corner of my room, a room that's bare except for a bed and bureau. My father is asleep and I should be, too, but I can't seem to turn my mind off. And I can't get you out of it, either.

I wonder what you do in your spare time, not that you have much of it. But do you like to read? Swim? Play games with Matthew? Do you sew? Do you like to write? Most of your life revolves around the farm. The plants and animals must keep you busy.

You've seen what we do at the forge all day, but at home, I help Father with our chores. Once a month, we fell trees and cut firewood, hauling it back to the house. I set snares in the woods to catch hare, squirrels, and other small game. Father's the cook, though. I burn anything I try to cook.

He won't admit it, but he feels like a failure as a parent. He doesn't feel like he's done a good enough job in raising me, but the truth is that he misses my mother. I miss her, too. Next week I'll be eighteen, which means she'll miss another birthday. It's the things they miss that hurt the most. Those reminders of what life they won't get to see or live. Father would never admit it, but he cries for her sometimes. In the night, in the next room, I hear him. There are some heartaches that never heal, I guess.

But if you asked him if he'd do it all again, he would say yes. He would have courted her, married her, loved her. They would have had me and he would have held her hand while she passed from this world to the next. Because even if her time on earth was short, it was worth it.

I want to live my life like that. I don't want to hold back from fear of being hurt. But maybe this is just a moment of bravery and clarity talking, and tomorrow I'll go back to being how I always am: friendly but aloof, too afraid to be close to anyone for fear of losing them, too. But I hope not. I hope you can help me make that change in me. I don't have many friends because of it, but on May Day, I thought we had a connection. If you'd like a friend, I'd love to hear back from you.

Hopefully,
Asher

CHAPTER FOURTEEN

ELLA

Two evenings later, Asher came with another practice sword for him to use along with us. He even brought an extra one for Millie in case she wanted to join. She declined, but daintily spread a blanket on the grass to watch from the yard. If Asher hadn't been here, she would've just sat on the grass.

Matthew and I practiced during every bit of free time we had in between chores, and it showed.

"You're doing great!" Asher beamed. "At all times, be mindful of where your head and body is in relation to your opponent. Don't give him even an inch to slice you."

What would a slice feel like? What about a mortal wound? I couldn't imagine the pain.

"I brought something to show you," Asher announced.

Grabbing a long, leather bag, he took two metal swords out and handed one to each of us. My breath caught for a moment when the cool metal touched my skin. I remembered the sound of metal clashing with metal, of women screaming and men roaring, and the coppery scent of blood.

I blinked away the memory. If I'd been in the castle yard, holding a sword I knew how to use, or if Aelawyn's people had been better armed and trained, the kingdom wouldn't have fallen. I might never need to use a sword, but if anything happened and I needed to, this lesson could save my life.

Asher stepped close to us. "Do you feel the difference in the weight?"

"I do," Matthew answered as he pretended to swing the sword across someone's belly.

I looked at the edge, polished and slick, and eased my thumb toward it. "It's sharp. It'll cut you," Asher cautioned, coming to stand at my side.

I turned to face him, and in that moment, I felt like I owed it to the blade somehow; just a taste of my blood to atone for all that was spilt the day I survived, when all the people inside the castle gate didn't.

I eased the pad of my thumb down the edge and it sliced cleanly through the skin. It burned for a few seconds, my blood smeared on the edge of the blade.

Asher's brows touched, confusion on his face. "Why'd you do that?"

"I needed to." I didn't care if he understood, but he didn't pry.

"Do you understand now why it's so important to stay away from it?"

I nodded.

He gave me a small smile. "Good."

He placed the real swords back in their bag and we took up our wooden ones again. For the rest of the afternoon, Asher taught us how to deflect blows and how to deliver them. Matthew and I faced off with our practice swords, our arms trembling with the strain. Parry. Strike. Parry. Strike. The pattern repeated itself until nightfall, until I could barely grasp the handle.

As Asher packed his leather bag, he called for me over his shoulder. Millie followed me to him. When he stood and saw her standing there, he gave her a placating smile. "Would you mind if I spoke with Ella for a moment alone? I have a question for her."

"Sure," Millie said sweetly, piercing me with a glare as she walked toward her brother, pretending for a moment to be interested in what he was doing. She was obviously eavesdropping, and from the look Asher shot her, he knew it, too.

"You okay?"

"Yeah. I'm fine."

"Didn't seem fine earlier."

I gave him a small smile, hoping he would drop it. "I was just curious, that's all. It was a silly thing to do."

Asher stared at me a long moment. He didn't believe me, but thankfully he let the matter go.

"I like teaching you," he finally said. "You aren't afraid."

When you had nothing to lose, what was there to fear? "It's only a wooden sword," I teased.

He chuckled. "I doubt you'd fear *any* sword," he said admiringly. "There's a wildness in your eyes when you fight. Don't lose that. Just make sure to use your head."

"Hopefully, I won't ever have to worry about needing that particular piece of advice."

Asher eased the bag's strap over his head and the blades crisscrossed his back, the hilts rising above either shoulder. "I hope you won't, either." He was quiet for a moment. "Why did you think I was going to hurt you?"

"You just moved really fast, and it caught me off guard," I said with a smile, hoping he bought it.

He nodded and let it go.

Before he left, I slid my own folded paper into his hand. Asher smiled brightly and tucked it into his pocket. Then he turned around and waved to the family. "Goodnight, Farmers. I'm not sure when I'll make it back, but I hope it won't be too long."

"Thank you, Asher," Hayden said while Matthew rushed to thank him as well.

Jewel chimed in, "You come early next time, and have supper with us. We'd love to chat a bit before you get to the maiming and slaughtering."

"Yes, ma'am," he laughed.

The hay alongside the road waved in the breeze as he walked away.

Hayden and Jewel were the first inside. "Wash up!" Jewel shouted from within, and the three of us walked to the well.

"You need to stop embarrassing yourself, Ella," Millie hissed. "Asher isn't going to be impressed with a woman who swings a wooden stick."

"I'm not doing it to impress Asher, Millie. I'm doing it because it's fun. You should try it sometime." She would probably have fun if she did.

"You look desperate and pathetic."

Well, she would know the look, wouldn't she?

"And you don't, sister," Matthew said in challenge. "You've been chasing Asher for years and what have you to show for it but desperation?"

"Oh, what do you know about anything," she replied to him.

Matthew gave me an ornery grin and hefted the bucket from the well. "Gotta get these muscles built up. I want to look just like Asher," he muttered.

Millie scoffed. "Asher pounds metal all day. There's no *way* you'll ever look like him. You're too skinny."

"I don't know," I interjected. "I think with all the work he does on the farm, one day he could be even more muscular."

"See?" he said to Millie with his brows raised challengingly. "Farmers are just as strong, if not stronger than smiths. I could throw you into the well," he teased, and went to pick her up. Raising her into the air on his shoulders, he spun her around. She shrieked, furious, and beat his back with her fists.

When he sat her down, she reared back to hit him in the face and I stepped between him. "Not your smartest idea," I warned.

"Oh, what'll you do, slice me with your wooden sword?"

My fingers shook and I fought to control my temper. "Make another move at him like that, and you'll bloody well find out!"

Millie stared at me, likely considering her options and whether I'd actually throttle her if she hit Matthew.

I would. Make no mistake about that. And she must have realized it, because she turned and walked toward the house.

"This is ridiculous," she scoffed angrily over her shoulder.

"*You're* ridiculous!" Matthew yelled at her back. Then he turned to me, hurt lacing his features. "I can handle myself, you know."

"I know, Matthew," I sighed. "I'm just sick of it."

I'm sick of her.

ASHER

She wrote back. Fighting the urge to jog, I walked fast, waiting until I was around the bend in the road before I pulled the note out and unfolded it.

> *Sleepy Asher,*
>
> *Thank you for writing to me when you should've been sleeping. I've lain awake at night thinking about things, too. You've often been one of those things. So have memories from my past. You're right. It's what they won't see and experience with you that makes you feel so alone. It's what they won't be there with you for. Do you feel the constant guilt of having survived? Some days it's like I'm drowning in it. I'm happy to have found a friend in you.*
>
> *When I'm not helping with chores (which I have plenty of) or working in the garden, I do play card games with Matthew. A word to the wise: don't ever play him for coin. He's a very good cheater. Sometimes, I walk in the woods behind our house. It feels good to be alone.*

I like to look at the stars. They remind me that everyone is underneath them, no matter their station in life. And that helps when I don't want to be alone.

Maybe you can look at them and be reminded of that, too. I wish you the happiest of birthdays.

Your Friend,
Ella

Asher and Nathaniel showed up for supper the next Saturday afternoon, both rushing toward the well to wash the soot from their hands and faces. Jewel was positively glowing. She loved having someone new to fuss over and cook for. Dinner was fun; the conversation as light as the sunshine beaming in through the windows. Everyone was full of joy, laughter, and jokes.

Once everyone had eaten the stew Jewel made, Nathaniel and Asher stood to go outside. I stopped them, pleading, "Please. Sit back down. For a few minutes, I mean. We have a surprise."

Jewel nodded toward me; my co-conspirator and helper. I stood up, smoothing my skirts and wiping the sweat from my suddenly clammy palms.

In the kitchen, I uncovered the butter cake and brought it to Asher. "Happy Birthday," I said shyly.

His jaw clenched tightly, and for a moment I thought he was angry. But then he blinked and moisture shone in his eyes. "Thank you," he said, obviously moved.

Nathaniel clapped his son on the back and they shared a glance. Nathaniel choked out his thanks to Jewel.

"This wasn't my doing. This was Ella's," Jewel said proudly.

Millie fumed across the table, crossing her arms over her chest and shooting daggers at me.

The rest of us ate too much cake and listened to Nathaniel's stories about Asher's childhood, much to his chagrin. After everyone was finished, Millie stormed outside.

Matthew promised to regale everyone with a demonstration of his mastery of swordsmanship, and asked me to be his opponent. It was possible that we *may* have practiced something a little theatrical for the event, once Hayden told us we would have company.

Jewel pushed me outside when I hung back to help with the dishes. "Go on with Matthew," she chided. "I'll clean up and be outside in a little while."

I stepped out the back door and hadn't quite acclimated to the brightness of the sunshine before Matthew punched my arm. "Where's Asher?"

"I don't know; I thought he was outside with you."

"He's not inside?" he asked.

"No, Jewel is the only one inside." I saw Hayden and Nathaniel standing in the yard discussing the spring crop and Nathaniel's work in the forge, but I passed them by and went in search of Asher. He was probably getting some sort of surprise ready. Some special sword or something. There was no way I would use a metal blade with Matthew. I didn't want to accidentally hurt him, and on the flip side, I didn't want him to run me through. I just wanted to apologize. If the cake hurt him, I was incredibly sorry. I just knew it had been a long time since his mom passed, and didn't know if Nathaniel made him cakes for his birthday.

I finally heard his voice from inside the barn, and I broke into a jog. But when I got to the open door, I stopped dead in my tracks. Asher and Millie were standing toe to toe, looking at each other, her hand on his chest. My footsteps must have drawn their attention, because both of them swiveled their heads to look in my direction.

"I'm so... sorry," I said awkwardly, rushing away.

Asher yelled after me. "Ella. Stop!"

"Let her go," Millie argued.

Asher caught my elbow. I felt the flush on my cheeks, but that wasn't the only thing I didn't want him to see. I was on the verge of crying, even though I knew it was ridiculous.

Millie was right.

I *was* pathetic.

Somehow, I must have developed a foolish crush on Asher. The feelings that hit me when I saw them together suddenly made me realize how much I liked him. I gave him a wavering smile and pulled my arm away gently.

"I didn't mean to interrupt. Matthew was looking for you, and I heard your voice." My own voice threatened to break on the word.

"It wasn't what it looked like. I promise," he pleaded.

I blew out a breath, staring into the distance. If I looked at him, I knew I would shatter and shards of me would fall at his booted feet. "It doesn't matter what it was or wasn't. I'm just embarrassed. So, if you could give me a minute to collect myself, I'd appreciate it."

His eyes were fixed on me. I could feel the intensity of his gaze, and his voice held traces of disappointment when he agreed to my request. "Anything you need."

ASHER

Millie was way worse than I thought. I'd made makeshift breastplates to surprise Matthew and Ella, and hid them in the barn earlier. They were crude, but I thought Matthew and Ella would enjoy the mechanics of them.

Millie found me when I ran out to get them. The barn was where she cornered me.

"Happy Birthday, Asher."

"Thanks," I replied flatly.

"You made those?" she asked sweetly. She walked into the barn, swaying her hips with each step.

"I did," I answered evenly.

Before I could pick them off the hay bale, she was in front of me. "You seem to enjoy teaching my brother and cousin how to swordfight."

"I do," I answered simply, standing up straight.

"It's so nice of you, taking them under your wing."

"I suppose. You could learn, if you wanted," I offered, trying to be nice, when all I wanted to do was walk away from her. She had a devilish gleam in her eye. She'd had it all evening, and it was making me decidedly uncomfortable.

"Actually, I wanted to talk to you about something, so I'm glad we *finally* have some privacy."

Whatever game she was playing was getting old. "And what's that?"

"Asher," she said, putting her hand on my chest. "I know how Isabel hurt you, how your heart must still ache, but our parents are pushing us together for a reason."

I closed my eyes. "Millie, I don't have those sort of feelings for you."

"They can come in time!" she pleaded.

That was when I heard footsteps. Ella stood staring at the two of us, at Millie's hand on my chest, and I knew. The gleam, the twinkle, in Millie's eyes all evening had been cruelty.

"Ella. Stop!" I shouted.

Millie grabbed my hand, saying, "Let her go," and I wheeled around on her.

"I would *never* marry someone like you, Millicent. *Never.*"

Her mouth gaped open at my harsh words, but I knew she didn't understand subtlety. I had to make sure she knew beyond a shadow of a doubt that she and I would never be together.

I raced to catch up with Ella and managed to catch her elbow before she got back to the house. She gave a weak smile, looked out toward the fields beyond the house, and refused to meet my eyes. I knew in that moment that Millie's plan had hurt her, which was its intended purpose. I just hoped the damage wasn't irreparable.

I tried to explain that what she saw wasn't what it seemed, and that nothing had happened between Millie and me. I didn't even *like* Millie, let alone love her. And I certainly wasn't the type of man to lure a young woman to the barn for selfish purposes.

When she asked for space and a little bit of time to compose herself, I figured it was the least I could give her – that, and the note in my pocket. I'd never been so thankful when she took it and stuck it in the pocket of her overdress. I needed to say so much more. She actually baked me a cake! I hadn't had a cake for my birthday since my mom passed away. No one had ever done something so nice for me. My father tried. He did his best to fill her shoes, but there were only so many hours in the day; only so much time to finish all we had to do to run our business and household. But that cake? It meant the world to me.

I walked back to the barn and took the breast plates, refusing to look at Millie. Anger radiated off her in waves, but I didn't care. I hoped she felt the anger roll off me, too.

Walking up to the front yard, I met Matthew with a forced smile, hoping it looked real. "Try this on for size."

His eyes widened and lit up. "Did you make these?" he asked excitedly.

"Yes," I laughed.

"For us?"

"No, for Jewel. Of course, for you! Do you need help putting it on?"

"Yeah. Please!"

When his plate was fastened around his back, I looked over at Ella where she stood close by. She was trying to smile, but it didn't reach her eyes. "Would you like help putting yours on, Ella?"

She swallowed. "Sure, thanks." Turning her back to me, she held her arms out as I fastened the straps across her back. "It fits well," she said, looking down at the front plate.

"Thank you. Now, are you ready to show them what you've learned?"

She took up her practice sword and finally smiled, a true one. "Absolutely."

As I watched the spectacle, I realized the two of them must have practiced and made a routine of it. They swung their swords, grunted, yelled, and all but clawed at each other as they parried, their swords clashing and striking again. Matthew rolled across the grass at one point, and that was when Ella struck, tackling him and putting her sword to his throat. What I didn't expect was the blunt, wooden dagger that Matthew had hidden in his boot. When he put it to Ella's heart, mine skipped a beat. *She isn't really in danger*, I told myself. But my stomach twisted into knots anyway.

The family erupted in applause. My father especially enjoyed it. He found me after he'd congratulated the two on

128

a job well done, and told me I'd taught them well. He was biased, but it meant a lot to me that he cared.

Hayden and my father told stories until the crickets began to sing and the sky was black as pitch, clouds rolling across the moon in thin strips. Ella studiously avoided eye contact with me, but laughed along with everyone at the tall tales the two men came up with, each one more blustery than the one before it.

Millicent, thankfully, had gone inside after the fake sword fight. Finally, Father thanked Hayden and Jewel for a lovely meal and an even better evening with friends, and we set off down the road. Even though Ella hadn't looked at me after catching me with Millie in the barn, she watched as I left.

I waved at her, but she turned and went inside without a matching wave.

"Father, can I ask you a question?"

It was time to get some advice about women.

ELLA

Beautiful Ella,

My window is open. The sky is clear tonight, and I'm looking at the stars and wondering if you are, too. If you are, then that means we're together. We aren't alone. With this ink, I'm making a promise to you. From this night forward, I will stare up at the sky and remember your words. If you do the same, it'll be our way of saying goodnight to one another.

You're doing well with swordsmanship. I wasn't sure if I told you or not, but you should know.

I look forward to seeing you at dinner. But then again, I always look forward to seeing you.

Your Amazing Instructor,
Asher

Even as I read his words, I worried Asher was never going to write to me again. He probably hated me for making the cake. I've never seen a man fight back tears so hard, let alone two men. With a simple confection, I'd nearly broken both the Smiths; men I thought were made of steel. But steel didn't compose letters like this. There was more to Asher than there seemed at first glance, and now I might never know how much more.

I stared out the window at the clouds streaking across the sky, hoping to see a twinkle, a sign that I hadn't ruined everything. A sign that what he said was true, that he didn't want Millie. And that he might want me.

CHAPTER FIFTEEN

ELLA

For three days straight, it poured rain. Every time we stepped out of the house, it soaked my dress and hair completely within seconds. We hadn't seen Asher, because we couldn't practice. And he couldn't come out here in this deluge.

It was silly, but I missed him.

The evening of the third day, the chores were finished and the dresses I'd soaked earlier were hanging to dry upstairs. Matthew and Millie had fallen asleep early, and Jewel and Hayden sat in front of the fire, talking about this and that, reminiscing about the days when they were first married. I lingered nearby, legs draped lazily over the arm of a chair, a book in my hands.

All three of us jumped when someone softly knocked at the door.

My heart faltered. Was it Piers? Were the knights of Tierney coming for me at last?

Jewel and I glanced at each other, her eyes telling me to hide. Quietly, I got up and made my way to their bedroom. Would hiding even help? If the King of Tierney called on me, I wouldn't let them tear apart the house just to find me.

Just as I was about to close their door, Hayden's voice rang out. "Asher? You're gonna catch your death out there, boy. Come in."

Asher Smith stood on our doorstep in the driving rain, water sluicing off his skin and clothes. His white shirt was translucent, leaving nothing to my imagination. Dark clouds rumbled overhead, matching the thunder of my racing pulse.

His blue eyes were stormy as the sky when they met mine across the room. He nodded his head once in my direction and I returned the gesture, easing out of Hayden and Jewel's room.

"I was wondering if I could speak with you, Hayden. Privately. In the barn."

Hayden straightened. "Of course. I'll be right out."

Asher disappeared and Hayden shut the door behind him, pulled on his boots, and grabbed his coat from the hook. He quickly shrugged it on, placing a hat on his head.

He turned to us. "I'll be back."

When the door closed behind him, I met Jewel's bewildered eyes. "What in the world could have caused that boy to walk all the way here in this storm?"

Was his father okay? Did something happen? Did he find out about me?

Jewel and I stayed up until the sky darkened, and then we lit candles in the windows. She paced and sat, and paced and sat again. Finally, she looked at me. "I think you should go upstairs. There's no sign that he'll be coming in anytime soon, and it's already late. You have to get some rest."

"I won't be able to sleep," I protested.

She pursed her lips. "I know, dear, but you can't stay down here all night. At least go lie down."

Careful of the squeakier steps, I managed to make it upstairs without waking my cousins. If Millie knew he was here, she'd run out to the barn to see what was happening. But Asher didn't want an audience. He'd asked for privacy for a reason.

I dressed quickly for bed and drew the covers around me, fighting off the cool, damp air. It wasn't long before the door opened downstairs and Hayden stepped back inside. "Where's Asher?" Jewel asked in a loud whisper.

Thunder rolled through the sky ominously. "Walking home."

"Well, what in the world was that all about? Is Nathaniel okay?"

He sighed. "Nathaniel's fine, and everything's okay. But right now I need to get out of these wet clothes. We can talk before bed."

That was all I was able to overhear, and it took me a very long time to go to sleep, even knowing that there wasn't an emergency. Asher was walking home in the dark in the middle of a storm. Something serious brought him here and kept him talking into the night. And I couldn't, for the life of me, figure out what it was.

Matthew went to town. It was his turn, but he would've been sent anyway. We were selling a goat and the poor thing thought Matthew was his mother. It followed him everywhere it could. He arrived back home without his goat, but brought coin to Hayden and slipped something into my pocket. "From Asher," he whispered, carefully watching his sister at the well, trying to make sure she didn't hear.

"Thank you," I said gratefully.

He nodded, and I took off to the woods behind the house. As soon as I was alone, I frantically unfolded his parchment.

Thoughtful Ella,

Thank you for making the cake for my birthday. Thank you for caring. I can't tell you how much it meant to me. My mother made a cake for me every year, but those stopped when she died. This year, you made the sting of her absence better just by being there.

So, thank you...and I'm sorry. Those two phrases shouldn't be allowed in the same letter, but they have to be in this one. I'm so sorry about what happened in the barn, but I promise what you saw wasn't what you probably think you saw. Millie has a crush on me, but I don't feel that way about her and never have. It wasn't her hands I would want on my chest, if I could choose.

I'm sorry this apology comes in the form of a letter and not from my lips.

I hope I can see you soon. And when I do, I'll explain my visit the other night, if your uncle hasn't already.

134

Gratefully yours,
Asher

A few days later, we were in the field planting as fast as possible. Uncle Hayden had ten fields plowed and ready, but because of too many days of torrential rain, only three had been planted. Taking advantage of the break in the weather, we'd each taken a section of one of the gardens and were feverishly planting a variety of herbs and vegetables: peas, kale, leeks, lettuce, broccoli and spinach, basil, chives, mint, sage and thyme.

We'd planted garlic cloves the previous fall and the warm spring weather brought them back to life, sending their shoots out of the ground. The green leaves were strong and pointed toward what they wanted most – sunlight. Soon, there would be scapes for eating and selling at market.

My overdress was heavy, caked with mud from the bottom hem to my thighs. I wiped my brow and removed my hat for a moment to let the breeze cool my head. Aunt Jewel was working across from me while Uncle Hayden, Millie, and Matthew were at the far end of the field working their way toward us. We would meet in the middle and cover more ground that way.

"Hayden asked me to speak to you about Asher," Jewel said, her voice low. She covered a seed with a clump of earth. "I haven't had a single free moment alone with you until now."

Just the mention of Asher Smith made my ears perk up. "Is he okay?" I'd wondered non-stop about why he needed to speak to Hayden the night of the storm. In his letter,

Asher said that either he or Hayden would explain, but it seemed Jewel had other plans.

She smiled knowingly. "He's fine, but he won't be able to come and teach you and Matthew this week. Nathaniel is letting Asher make a few new candle holders for us, and they have a few other orders to fill by week's end. That means he'll be busy at the forge until late."

I pictured Asher holding the glowing, orange metal and pounding it into something purposeful with strong blows of his hammer, his brow slick with sweat and soot, and his shirt stretched taut over his arms.

I placed my hat back on to cover my burning cheeks. I'd never cool off with him in mind. I poked another hole into the turned earth and dropped a seed inside. Another hole. Another seed. And so on.

"He asked to call on you," she said in a conspiratorial whisper.

My hands stilled. "Call on me for what?" I whispered back.

Her eyes widened as I looked up at her. "He would like to... get to know you, Ella. Privately."

My fingers tightened on the small burlap sack of seeds.

She smiled. "Hayden told him he wanted to talk with you first, but he asked me to do it so Millie wouldn't overhear. And because he sees you as one of his own, it's hard for him to talk to you about certain things."

"Millie already hates me. This will certainly give her another reason to."

Aunt Jewel's hand laid on mine, stilling me. "Millicent and Asher... don't suit. He was very candid with Hayden the other night about his feelings." She sighed. "I suppose it's our fault she wants him like she does. We've pushed them toward one another since they were children, but even more after the girl from Roane broke his heart. We thought it might help him heal, but nothing helped. Until you, that is."

Shaking her head, Aunt Jewel continued wistfully, "It would be different if they complemented one another, but they don't. You can't force love where there's only friendship, and I want my children to love their spouses and live their own happily ever after." She paused a moment, gathering her thoughts, and then continued. "You're like one of my children, Ella. Asher's made it clear how he feels about you, so if you like him in that way, you more than have our blessing. We'll handle Millie."

Asher wants to call on me. He came to the farm in the middle of a thunderstorm just to talk to Hayden... about me. I couldn't wrap my head around it.

"It'll be hard to find time at first, between his work and yours, but when these fields begin yielding, we'll have to set up at market. That job will require someone to take the produce to town in the wagon on Sundays, sell them, and then return that evening," she said with a wink. "I think you'd be the perfect person for the job. And who knows? You might be able to take a walk together at the end of the day."

I breathed a sigh of relief.

"Until then, maybe meeting in the middle for a short time would be best. I could pack a basket lunch for you both. You both have to eat," she said with a grin.

"It would be wonderful to have a friend."

She smiled. "I know, dear. But I think Asher wants to be more than just your friend."

The butterflies took flight once more. I fervently hoped that was what he wanted. He made it clear that he didn't want Millie; he even told her father that. But his wants wouldn't erase hers. When she found out, there would be war between us. And though I wouldn't declare it, I wouldn't back down from the fight.

CHAPTER SIXTEEN

ELLA

Four more days of planting later, Uncle Hayden announced that he needed something in the village. When he got back, the afternoon would be full of more planting, watering the fields that were already sprouting, and planting again. We'd been planting all morning and were heading inside to eat when Hayden asked me to go with him.

"Would you ride with me and help with a few errands, Ella?" he asked politely.

Millie groaned, bracing herself on the doorway of the house. "Why can't *I* go?" she whined.

"It's not your turn," her father answered as he hitched the horse to the wagon. He and Jewel had the patience of Job when it came to their daughter.

Hayden took a basket from Aunt Jewel and quickly put it in the wagon. "Go wash up as best you can," he said quietly. My skirt was dirty, but I dusted it off as much as I could. There was no time to change clothes, and I knew that when I got home, I'd have to get back to work.

The dirt from my face and hands clouded the fresh water, but I was fractionally cleaner. I scrambled up and sat on the wagon's bench next to Hayden, and then he snapped the reins and the horses tugged us forward. It was hard to tell if I'd left any mud streaks on my skin, but if they were there, I wore them with a smile.

We'd been riding for a few minutes when Hayden commented, "Ella, you've been working hard and keeping up with Jewel in the fields. It's been a difficult year with all the rain, so we appreciate you working so hard." The wagon rocked back and forth along the road, the wheels squeaking as Hayden guided the horses.

"Thank you."

"We'll be done with the last few fields soon enough. Then comes everything else, but planting is the hardest part, I think," he explained. "Hard on the back."

I'd noticed his gait had been stiffer lately. Hayden wasn't old, but each year robbed him of more strength and agility. Fidgeting with my skirt, I noticed the holes and thinning fabric. Hayden smiled and patted my hand.

"Don't worry. Asher's excited to see you."

My nose scrunched.

"What?" Hayden asked. The horse whickered, but Hayden urged him forward.

"It's hard to imagine Asher excited at all," I said dubiously.

140

Hayden laughed heartily. "Well, he was so worked up about talking to me about you, he marched through a thunderstorm and stayed long past my bedtime and his, so I'd definitely say he's excited. He's a tough one; serious on the exterior, but he has a soft spot for you. Everyone can see it."

My shoulders tensed and I sat up straighter. "Does Millie know?"

"She knows Asher asked to call on you, but she doesn't know that you're meeting today."

That must have been why she wouldn't look at me. Not that I cared. Let her pout. She had acted ridiculous and inappropriate, all in an attempt to make me think he wanted her. She would do anything to drive a wedge between the two of us.

He blew out a long breath. "She'll come around. Just give her time. In all honesty, we've let Millie have her way too often. She was spoiled before Matthew was born, and then after he came along, it was just easier to give in to her tantrums to avoid turmoil. She needs to grow up, and maybe this will help her."

Maybe it would, maybe it wouldn't. I wanted to see Asher; I just hated that Hayden, Jewel, and Matthew were caught between me and Millie.

"Sorry you're stuck in the middle of it," I said, ashamed.

He smiled softly, guiding the horse along the road, the scent of wild onions swirling around us. "You're part of our family now, Ella. Jewel and I both hope you know that. I can't imagine it's been easy for you, given the lifestyle you were used to. I mean, I know we don't have much." Hayden scratched his jaw the way he did when he was embarrassed, but he had no reason to be ashamed.

"You've given me so much more than I ever would've had in Aelawyn, Hayden. People look at castles and think the lives they contain are somehow better. Not all of them are."

"Hmm," he said simply, his eyebrows knotted together. "Never thought of that. You've had a foot in both worlds, so I'm sure you know better than anyone."

He'd never asked me to tell him about my upbringing and I'd never offered it. But it was in times like this, in the subtle hints, that showed he understood more than he let on. He was quiet for a few moments. "Ella, I know you probably already know, but you can't tell Asher about your past. No one can know."

I nodded, my conscience eased somewhat. "I won't."

"It's not safe for you or us, but it wouldn't be safe for him, either. I've heard there are visitors staying at the castle... visitors from *Galder*," he added ominously. "All it would take is one slip of the tongue to spell trouble for us all."

"I understand, and I won't say anything, I promise." I bit my lip and watched the land roll alongside us. *Why would visitors from Galder be here?*

Kingdoms hosted neighboring kingdoms all the time, so it probably didn't mean anything. I'd been hiding out here for three years. Even if Galder had looked for me in the past, surely they weren't looking for me now, not after so long.

Suddenly, the mood of the conversation changed. Hayden shifted on the bench, looking uncomfortable and hesitant, and then looked at me from the crinkled corner of his eye. "Er, what you're doing, what I'm allowing, isn't exactly proper for a lady to do, technically speaking. You're supposed to be chaperoned, but the way I figure it, you're almost grown. The only way for you to figure out if you like the boy is to talk to him, and I doubt you'll do much talking if I'm sitting at your side."

"It's just a picnic lunch," I reassured him.

"I know. It's just that..." He spoke on about how things would be if someone did find out, in case it was a risk I

142

didn't want to take. About how he worried because boys could be eager, ready to jump into things that girls maybe weren't ready for.

I stopped listening when I saw an unworked field up ahead, the grass growing as tall as my hips, with a large oak tree growing in the center of it. Under that oak sat Asher Smith, his back against the trunk. Uncle Hayden didn't even have to wave him over; he was up on his feet and striding toward us in an instant, slicing a path through the hay to get to us. To me. And I couldn't help but smile.

In a world where no one wanted me, I may have finally found someone who does—someone I wanted back just as badly.

Hayden tugged on the reins as Asher met us along the road. "Asher," Hayden said sternly, shooting me a wink.

"Hello, Hayden," his deep, raspy voice replied.

"Jewel packed a lunch for you both. I'll be back in an hour. Remember our talk," he said to me, "and mind your manners!" he added for Asher's benefit.

"I will, sir," Asher answered resolutely. Walking around in front of the horse, he gave her neck a pat as he made his way to my side. His shirt must have been old, or he'd grown out of it quickly, because the taut, cream-colored fabric was stretched tightly over his arms and chest, over angular muscles that were usually shielded by the leather vest he wore.

"Can I help you down?" he asked. I nodded. His hands found my waist, gripped it surely but gently, and eased me to the ground in front of him. His eyes stayed glued to mine, even when my body passed so closely to them. The wind toyed with a strand of his hair, and for a moment, I wished it were my hand.

I removed the basket Jewel packed from the back of the wagon. Hayden waved, clucked his tongue at the horse, and rode away toward town.

143

Asher tucked my hand into the warm crook of his arm and took up the basket of food I'd been carrying with the other. "I'm starving," he said with a grin. "Please thank Jewel for the meal."

"I will, but she was happy to make it."

I didn't feel as conscious about my dirty dress when I saw that his clothes had holes burned in them and were streaked with soot. I felt lighter, my nervousness melting away as we retraced his steps back to the tree, trampling a path through the grass.

Lying on top of the basket was a checked cloth, so we each grabbed two corners and spread it out in the shade. The bright green leaves of the oak danced, enjoying the cool breeze blowing across the land, allowing the sunlight to wink through them occasionally. Aunt Jewel had packed a small loaf of rye bread, four boiled eggs—two for each of us— sliced onion, and two chunks of goat cheese wrapped in cloth. In the bottom of the basket was a corked jug of ale for us to share, but Asher laughed when he saw the food.

"Jewel is a very smart woman. She obviously planned the meal with us in mind."

I looked at the basket for a heartbeat, and then it dawned on me. One of those foods would have made our breath smell awful, but the combination of all three? *She doesn't want us to kiss.* I couldn't help but laugh along with him.

"I didn't have the time to write another letter. I came empty handed, so I guess you'll just have to talk to me instead," Asher teased, easing the tense silence that was stretching between us. "How have you been?"

"Busy. We've planted most of the fields already." My muscles reminded me of the fact every time I moved. I rolled my shoulders to alleviate the soreness settling in them.

144

"That's good," he said, pulling the bread apart and giving me half. "I know it's hard work. You must be tired."

I *was* tired, and it *was* very hard work, but it was also rewarding. "It's the most satisfying thing I've ever done," I told him.

"Why is that?"

"I love everything about working in the fields—the fresh scent, the earth, and that there's always something to be done. We take tiny seeds and stick them in the ground, and in a matter of weeks or months, they give us what we need to eat and a way to provide for our family."

"I love that you're passionate about what you do. Most people would hate farming."

"In thirty years I might feel differently," I teased, biting into my egg and chewing with a shrug. "But for now, I enjoy it."

"I'm glad we could meet today. We've been so busy, I haven't been able to get away to continue the lessons. I've missed you," he said, clearing his throat.

I smiled. "We've missed you, too. Matthew and I have been practicing when we can, but it isn't the same."

"That's not what I meant. I mean, I do miss teaching you and Matthew, but I miss *you*," he enunciated. "I like watching your expressions and wondering what you're thinking. I want to get to know you so well, I know what they all mean without having to ask. I miss the sound of your laughter and the ornery glint in your eye."

I don't have an ornery glint! I took a sip and set the jug down between us, licking the ale's froth from my lips. "Can I ask you a question?" I blurted.

"Of course." He sat up straight, giving me his full attention.

"Why me? Why not another girl in the village? Why not one you already know, someone you grew up with? Someone like Millie?"

His lips lifted in half a smile. "I know all the girls in the village, and understand their motivations for wanting to marry a blacksmith, Millie included. But I've never wanted to really get to know any of them. They're all false. It's like they're two people: the one they want me to see, and another they actually are."

Story of my life.

My brows must have scrunched together in confusion, because he further explained, "Smiths are hard workers, and they get paid well for what they do. A smith can provide well for a wife and family. Life would be less of a struggle. If Hayden has a crop that doesn't yield well because of weather or insects, the entire family will suffer. But as long as I can work with iron and steel, I can still provide. There isn't anything out of my control that would affect my work and income. Most women find that stability appealing. Of course, everyone has difficult times, some more than others."

"I understand." I did. Not only would he be an attractive husband, he could provide well for a family.

"And Millie... I've known her since we were toddlers, and maybe that's why I know she isn't who I want. And just so you know, there's never been anything between us. What happened in the barn was all her, not me. I've never been interested in her that way."

"She mentioned once that someone broke your heart," I admitted gently.

He shrugged. "It's no secret, and I'm sure Millie told you all the sordid details. I fell hard for a young woman named Isabel, a duchess from Roane. She stayed at the castle for a summer, and by chance we met and began talking. She snuck away every day after that to come see me. I honestly thought I loved her, but it wasn't love. She was just playing a game, and I was too young and foolish to see it."

146

"What did you think of me when we first bumped into one another?"

"Honestly, you scared me."

"Why?"

"Because you were the most beautiful creature I'd ever seen, wearing that fine, red cloak, and I thought that if Isabel had hurt me as bad as she did, someone like you might crush me. But I know better now. You're different from her; different from the other girls in the village. You're kind, but brave. Not afraid of hard work, either." When he took my hand and looked at the dirt staining my cuticles, I could barely breathe. "You're passionate about even the simplest things in life, but you're well-educated. Not to mention the fact that you're the most beautiful woman I've ever seen in my life. But beyond that, there's something about you that I can't quite explain. You light up the faces of everyone in the village when you step foot in it. When you come around, even though it isn't often, I take notice. Everyone does. It's like… it's like seeing the sun when the sky has been gray for months."

Oh, my.

He put some cheese on a piece of torn-off bread and then added, "Millie and her friends are hateful to you because they see it, too. They're jealous."

"I don't know about that," I said bashfully before taking a bite of egg.

He watched me chew, which was an oddly intimate thing to do. Not necessarily the act of chewing, but the way Asher studied my movements. Learning them. Learning me.

"Can I ask *you* something?" he asked.

"Of course."

"How do you feel about me? There are plenty of young men in the village who don't smell like wood smoke, and don't look like they've been wrestling in a fire pit." He smiled nervously, waiting for my answer.

There *were* other young men, but I didn't see them. Not like I saw Asher. Beyond his ruggedly handsome looks, Asher was a good man. He was exactly what I'd hoped for when I dreamed of finding someone to truly love—back when I thought I'd never find it, or have the chance to take advantage of it if I did. Back when love was a fanciful notion for other girls, but didn't fit into the life of a princess.

This was new, and though I couldn't say I was in love yet, I *did* care for him a great deal. I wanted to see if there could be more between us, so I nodded. "I was so happy when you asked to call on me, Asher, and not just because of the stability you might provide. I can't explain it, but something in you calls to me; and I can tell something in me calls to you. I never thought that would happen."

Asher tilted his head with a smile, and I thought I heard the sun give a sigh of relief at the sight of it. "Good." He grabbed my hand and held it in his until I thought my heart might burst. "I feel it too, by the way."

CHAPTER SEVENTEEN

ELLA

After that heavy conversation, it was easy to talk with him, about anything and everything. The tension between us melted away, leaving us both feeling comfortable enough to open up to one another. His smiles were no longer rare. I couldn't help but smile back, and wondered if I would ever be able to *stop* smiling.

Asher and I finished our lunches and were happily chatting about the most basic of things, when he asked a sobering question. "Does Millie know where you are?"

I shook my head, explaining, "Uncle Hayden spoke with her, so she knows you asked to call on me, but she doesn't know we're meeting today."

Asher nodded. "I think it would be wise to tell her soon and not keep it from her. At the barn, after you saw us, I told her that I didn't and never would want to be with her, so she already knows where my feelings for her stand. But enough about her. I've been thinking…I'd love if you could visit me at the shop on market days, or maybe I could steal away and come see you." He brushed a strand of hair behind my ear and gave a shy, sideways smile. "I don't want to hide this from anyone."

We were officially a *this*, and *this* was so new. This relationship. This beautiful creation toeing the line between friendship and so much more.

"I'd like that," I admitted. "I've never even been to market, so it'll be a learning experience, but one I'm looking forward to. Another chance to see you will make it even better."

"Hayden's crops are always the best of all the farmers, and he always sells out first. We'll have plenty of time to spend together," Asher teased.

"Tell me about *your* father, Asher. You know Hayden, but I don't know much about your father at all."

Asher smiled. "My father is the man I want to be one day. He's strong, steadfast, and loyal, but also kind and patient—which was nice growing up. He loves to laugh because he loves his life. He's the best smith around, but he'd never boast about it. He just lets the work do the talking for him."

"I've heard you're quite a prodigy, as well," I said, following with a sip of ale.

"I hope I can work metal half as well as he can one day, but I'm learning from the best." He shrugged, staring out at the swaying hay beyond us, specks of pollen gliding on the breeze.

Modesty looked good on Asher. Yet another striking difference between this young man and any given royal. A royal would have boasted that he was better than his predecessor, even if he knew he wasn't.

"What happened to your mother?"

His smile fell away and a shadow seemed to fall over him. "She died four years ago. Fell ill, and was dead within a fortnight. It wasn't the plague but might as well have been, because no one knew how to help her and she just lay there in agony until she finally passed. It was the hardest thing I've ever had to watch. But I know you know the feeling of losing someone and being helpless to stop it."

I did know that feeling. And knowing that he understood that part of my past, even if he didn't know the real details, was comforting.

"I'm sorry, Asher."

"You lost both of your parents and your sister," he pointed out.

He obviously loved his mother, so I didn't have the heart to tell him that the death of my parents didn't bother me the way it should have. I didn't think he would understand without an explanation I couldn't give. But the truth about Ivy, the fact that she took her own life... Well, that crushed everything inside me. I squashed the wave of grief threatening to crash over my head and feigned a slight smile. "Well then, we have that unfortunate thing in common."

His thumb brushed the top of my hand in gentle, soothing strokes. He didn't pry or ask questions, he just held my hand until the sound of clomping hooves drew nearer. Hayden drove around the corner, waving his hat to us. We stood and Asher grabbed the basket and jug while I folded the blanket. He walked over to the base of the tree and grabbed a small sack that I hadn't noticed before.

When I finished folding the blanket, I threaded my hand through his arm and looked up to find him smiling down at me. I wondered what the stubble beginning to appear on his jaw felt like beneath my fingers, but Hayden was watching us now and that would be too forward. I didn't want to give him a heart attack, or a reason not to trust me. We walked back toward the road, all smiles.

"I can't wait to spend more time with you," he said hopefully.

"It probably won't be until market," I said wistfully. "We have so much work to do in the fields."

"Then I'll count the days, lovely Ella," he said properly, but with a roguish grin. He placed a chaste kiss on my hand, and I surprised him with a small note slipped into his hand. He helped me into the wagon with a smile. My hand fit perfectly in his, and I tried to memorize the feel of him.

"Please give my thanks to Jewel for the lunch. It was delicious," he said to Hayden, handing him the sack. "Your candle holders."

"Thank you, Asher."

It was awkward to hear them be so formal around one another, but I supposed it couldn't be avoided. I knew what a risk it was for Asher to ask to court me, and again for Hayden to give his blessing. If something went wrong, if this didn't work out, their friendship and a working relationship with the best farmer and smith in town might be strained. So for now, everyone was on their best behavior.

Hayden often told me that he considered me to be one of his children. I had no doubt that if a boy came to call on Millie, he would expect formality and respect. There would be no rule-breaking or even bending, but since he knew Asher, the trust they already shared weighed into the equation of us being together.

As Hayden urged the horse forward and Asher began walking alongside the road in the opposite direction, I turned in my seat to find him looking back over his shoulder at me. I threw a small wave to him, and watched as he waved back.

"Looks like you had a good time," Hayden teased, nudging me with his arm. I couldn't contain my smile.

"I did." An image of Millie's scowl drifted through my mind, but I pushed the thought of her sourness away. Asher was interested in *me*. If our positions were reversed, I would be ecstatic for her. In time, maybe she could find it in her heart to be happy for me, too.

ASHER

I couldn't get her out of my mind. The softness of her hand, how she finally relaxed and opened up to me and I to her... The hour with her was nothing short of amazing. Her soft, clean scent drove me crazy. It lingered on my shirt sleeve and I hated that soon it would be erased by smoke.

She'd lost everything. Everything. And yet she survived. Losing my mother was the worst thing that had ever happened to me, and some days I still wasn't sure I was strong enough to face the world without her. But her death brought me and Father closer, so in that regard, I was lucky.

I couldn't even imagine how hard it would be to lose both parents and my only sibling at once, and then be left completely alone to travel to find a family who might not even be there or want to take me in. I'd bet she was half-starved by the time she made it to Hayden's. Imagining her hungry or hurt along the way made my stomach turn.

Up ahead, the road curved into town and I quickened my pace. I'd have to work into the night to finish my projects, but the time spent with her was worth it. She was worth it.

Father was eating when I entered the forge. He smiled and patted the bench beside him. I sat next to him, elbows on my knees. He took a bite of smoked meat, chewed until it was gone, and then took a drink of water from his mug. "Well, how was it?"

I couldn't help but smile, struggling to find the right words to describe her and the time I'd had.

Father chuckled. "That good, eh?"

"Yes," I breathed.

He clapped me on the shoulder, and with his eyes told me to be careful. He was concerned, not only about my heart, but about his friendship with Hayden. Ella and I would have to tread lightly, take things slow, but it was difficult; reining oneself in and holding back when everything in your heart wanted to sprint forward.

"Father, do we have any scrap iron?"

He took another sip of water and nodded, setting the mug down between us. "We do."

I took her note out of my pocket. It was only a tiny square.

Sweet Asher,

I would bake a thousand cakes to see you happy. Your apology is accepted. Thank you for asking to call on me. It means the world to me.

154

It was my cake.

Yours,
Ella

ELLA

On the way home, Hayden said he would speak with Millie tonight after supper, to try to clear the air and ease the troubles between us. Throughout supper, the tension in the air thickened until it was nearly unbearable. When everyone finished, I took the plates outside to wash. Matthew went with me, climbing the tree beside the well. He kicked his legs playfully and chatted about how he'd given the evil rooster a sound knock with his bucket.

"One day I'll eat him," he vowed. "And the bloody devil will never spur me again."

Smiling up at him, our conversation was interrupted by the loud banging of the front door against the house. I'd expected the conversation between Millie and Hayden to take longer, or maybe I expected too much maturity from Millie. She stormed toward me, her face scarlet and contorted in rage. I almost let go of the rope and dropped the bucket back into the well.

Pointing an accusatory finger in my face, she screamed, "Don't you *ever* send my father to talk to me on your behalf! I can't believe you. You stole Asher away from me and I hate you for it!"

I paused to look at her; cheeks puffing with every exhalation, looking savage and wild with hair escaping from her braid. After a tense moment, I turned my back to her and continued tugging the rope upward, levering the heavy bucket of water to the surface. "I'm getting to know him at *his* request," I finally responded. "I didn't steal anything from you."

Asher didn't want her. He would never want to be with her, and had told her clearly himself. Even if in the end he didn't want me, and we parted as friends—he would never want her.

"You knew how I felt about him," she seethed.

With a deep breath, I steadied the bucket on the stone sides of the well and turned around to face her. "He doesn't feel the same way about you, Millie, and you can't force him to. Whether it's me or another girl, he doesn't want you."

Lightning fast, her hand darted out and she slapped me across the face. The loud crack rang in my ears. With half my face on fire, I stumbled back against the bucket. It fell into the well, clattering along the stone sides and splashing hard into the water. She raised her hand to strike me again, but I moved faster this time. Fist balled, I hit her square in the nose. She stumbled backward as a river of blood trickled down her face. Shocked, she dabbed her fingers at the warm liquid, eyes bulging at the sight.

I stepped toward her, fist raised again. "Don't you *ever* strike me again! I've put up with enough of your nonsense!"

She stepped away from me, her lip trembling in anger as she shouted, "You are the worst thing that ever happened to me! You're the worst thing that ever happened to this family, and I wish you would just leave!" Tears welled in her eyes as she clutched her face, running toward the house.

Matthew, wide-eyed, clambered down from the tree. "Are you okay?"

"I'm fine," I said, slumping against the trunk of the tree he'd been perched in.

"Is she okay?" He lingered, unsure of whether to stay with me or go check on his sister, his feet teetering between us.

"She will be, but you can go see about her if you want."

Uncle Hayden came outside with Aunt Jewel on his heels. "What happened?" he asked, concerned.

"We had a fight," I answered simply. Hayden looked at the side of my face that still stung.

"Long time in the making," Jewel said with a slight laugh.

As Matthew ran toward his father to relay the event second by second, I calmly hoisted the bucket full of water back to the surface again. Punching Millie felt cathartic – it *was* a long time in the making – but I didn't want to have to repeat it.

CHAPTER EIGHTEEN

ELLA

ong weeks had passed since I first met Asher under the tree, but today was the first day of market and I couldn't wait to see him. He'd only sent one other note since Matthew had only gone to town once. Millie had gone twice, but we both knew she wouldn't deliver anything to or from him, so we didn't ask.

His note was as amazing as the others, though.

> *Lovely Ella,*
>
> *I sincerely hope that in the future you have the opportunity to bake a thousand cakes—cakes that we'll enjoy together. I think about you all the time. When*

I'm scrubbing the soot from my shirts, or cleaning my father's boots, when I'm cleaning out the fireplace or replacing a board on our porch.

I think about you when Father is snoring so loud I can't sleep, or when our cat hisses at me. She reminds me of Millie, but since you're her cousin, my thoughts drift to you again. Always you.

I'm counting down to the first day of market. I promise to visit your booth.

Missing you,
Asher

Hayden drove me to town on market day. Long tables filled the back of the wagon, along with baskets of our herbs and vegetables. It was filled to the brim. The village was bustling, an excited energy filling the air. Despite the cool drizzle falling from the sky, everyone wore smiles as they set up their booths and tables, stretching whatever fabric they could spare overhead to keep themselves and their wares dry.

Hayden and I unloaded the vegetables, sitting the baskets on the ground, and then set up our tables. The years of use scratched across their surfaces didn't detract from their sturdy craftsmanship. We positioned them in the shape of an L, and covered their tops with freshly-washed linen and our baskets full of herbs and vegetables. Hayden gave me a small pouch of coin to make change with, and told me what to charge for each item.

"You'll do fine," he said soothingly. "I'll come back to get you before sundown, and will help you load the tables and anything that's left over. But let's pray you sell everything we've brought, and you only have empty baskets to worry about," he said with a wink as he returned to the wagon and drove away. Asher had said Hayden's crops were highly sought after, and I was anxious to prove him right so he'd let me come back next week.

Beside me, a kind woman was arranging a booth of pies and tarts, and the sweet scents made my mouth water. Across the grass was a booth for sewn and knitted goods, a booth with candles and supplies, and a large lad selling firewood. Farther down the lane were the butcher and fishmonger. The baker was assembling a booth laden with palm-sized loaves of bread, as well as loaves so long, they would feed a family for a week. A woman selling pottery and another woman with paintings and hand-woven rugs organized their tables directly across from mine. Booth after booth stretched around the grassy square until it was completely covered.

I didn't know Asher had snuck into my booth until his warm hand grazed my elbow. I looked up to find him smiling at me. "Ella."

"Asher," I breathed, trying to calm my wildly beating heart. "I didn't know you were here."

"You wound me, madam." He clutched his chest dramatically.

"I highly doubt that would be possible, sir."

"You underestimate yourself, Ella. I'm absolutely certain that you have the ability to wound me... perhaps fatally."

The air grew thick with something I couldn't describe, and when his lips drew closer, I inhaled sharply. But at the last moment he turned his head, reached into the basket beside me, and plucked out a cabbage. "This'll do nicely," he said with a mischievous grin. "How much for this head of cabbage?"

I mumbled Uncle Hayden's price and he gave me a coin in that exact amount. "Thank you, Asher," I replied dutifully.

"Hayden's goods will go quickly, and I knew I had to get here first thing this morning to get my father the best there is. He's working on a large project and will need a hearty meal for supper. This'll go nicely with the rabbit Father bought this morning. We'll make a stew." My stomach growled in response. I loved rabbit.

"You were my very first customer," I beamed, happy to have gotten at least one sale for Hayden and Jewel, and even happier that I got to see Asher so early in the morning when I wasn't expecting it.

"Of course I was," he replied with a wink. "Can I see you again before you go home?"

"I hope so. If you can't make it back, I'll try to stop by the forge before we leave the village."

"I'd love that," he answered, and then glanced in the direction of the blacksmith's shop. "I have to run." He lingered like he didn't want to leave. I didn't want him to, either.

Just then, an older woman cleared her throat, breaking the spell between us. "How much for a head of lettuce?" she asked.

I waved at Asher as he walked away, turning back to glance at me with a grin. Once he was out of sight, I regained control of my mind and helped the woman find exactly what she needed. "Thank you for buying from us," I told her.

"I always have, and always will buy from your uncle. He's a good man," she replied tersely. "He and his father... they helped us when we couldn't afford to pay them. John worked off what he owed, but they didn't even want that. They're just kind. His dad said he'd been in a bind when they were young, and knew what it was like to go hungry. I don't know how he could tell, but he was right. And I'll be forever thankful for what they did."

The day passed in a whirlwind. I spoke with more villagers than I knew existed. Asher was right – everyone loved Hayden's herbs and vegetables. The overflowing baskets we'd brought that morning were completely empty just after midday.

"You've done well," the woman with the pies and tarts said, looking at my empty baskets. She had hair like spun gold and freckles all over her face. She wasn't old, but was older than me and married, according to the ring on her finger and swell of her belly.

Her tables were almost cleaned out. "You as well!" I responded happily.

"Thank goodness!" she laughed. "I suppose I'll see you here next week, dear. My name's Ann."

"I'm Ella. And yes, I'll be here."

She nodded behind me. "Is that your fella?"

Sure enough, Asher was walking toward my booth. "It is. If my uncle shows up, could you tell him I'm with Asher and that I'll be right back?"

"Aye. Go have a walk with him. You've nothing left to sell, anyway."

I smiled at her in gratitude and ran to meet Asher. His hands found my waist and he spun me around. "Do you have a few minutes?"

"I sold out of everything, so yes!"

"Good. Let's go." He folded my hand in his. I'd never seen him so excited, but he pulled me in the direction of his shop and I couldn't help but follow. "I want to show you something."

In front of the forge, Nathaniel was talking with two fair-haired men who wore similar tunics the shade of an angry, deep bruise. I knew that particular shade of purple and the fine weave of fabric only meant one thing: royalty. The men turned to face us as we approached, and Asher slowed his steps. The smile fell from his face and his hand tightened around mine protectively. Both men fastened their eyes on me.

"Is everything okay?" I whispered to Asher.

"I'm sure it is," he said, offering me a fake smile that was meant to reassure, but did anything but.

"Oh, good!" Nathaniel bellowed. "Asher, you're just in time. These gentlemen are visiting Tierney from Galder. The castle smith is too busy to fill their order, so they've commissioned us to craft swords for them."

Galder? I wanted to run, but Nathaniel waved us forward. Asher squeezed my hand gently. Did he sense the panic racing through my chest?

"That's wonderful, Father," Asher's deep voice boomed.

Their tunics were embroidered with an intricate royal crest, an eagle situated in the center. *Galderian royalty, no less?* My heart was a caged animal, panting to be unleashed.

"This is my son, Asher, and his friend, Ella," Nathaniel said, introducing us in turn.

The men had to be related. Both had pale blond hair and flecked hazel eyes. Father and son? Hayden's warning about visitors from another kingdom, Galder, ran through my mind. I shouldn't be there, but couldn't run. Leaving abruptly would only draw more attention.

Once the formalities were finished, the men returned to their discussion. They were on their way to visit the three northern kingdoms and wanted to procure something from every kingdom they visited. From Tierney he wanted swords, and Nathaniel had come highly recommended.

"Right," spoke the older Galderian. "So, half a dozen broad swords. If you could do something to the design to make them unique to Tierney, you'll be paid an extra sum."

"We can do that, no problem," Nathaniel promised.

"How soon can you have them finished?" asked the younger man, his eyes still fixed on me for some reason. It made my skin crawl. I looked toward Asher, who was staring as intently at the young man as the stranger was at me.

"At least a fortnight," Nathaniel answered. "Maybe longer, but we'll work day and night on them."

The older Galderian nodded. "Very well. We'll return in a fortnight to check on the progress." Their dialect made the words sound strained and thick.

As they strode away, the younger man glanced back at me over his shoulder. "Why does he keep looking at you like that?" Asher growled. Aggravation rolled off him in waves, threatening to drown us both.

"I'm not sure." I wondered what their names were. It was obvious from their style of dress, their posture, and the expertly groomed horses they mounted that they were royalty.

Royals from Galder.

A foreboding shiver crawled up my spine.

There was no way they could know who I truly was. Yurak had never visited Aelawyn, so he wouldn't know what I looked like. We weren't supposed to meet until our wedding day.

CHAPTER NINETEEN

ELLA

"What did you want to show me?" I asked Asher as he continued to stare after the Galderians.

"What?" he asked, as if coming out of a daze. "Oh!" he remembered. "I'll be right back." He jogged into the shop and rifled around a tabletop in the back.

A proud smile stretched across Nathaniel's face as he looked at his son. "He's been working on it for weeks in his free time. I'm glad he finished it today. We'll be busy from dawn to dusk with an order like this."

Asher stepped out of the shadows holding something behind his back.

"I should get started on the swords," Nathaniel said with a kind smile. "Tell Hayden and Jewel I said hello." I promised I would as he walked away.

From behind his back, Asher produced a beautiful work of art. He held it out and I fought back tears as I accepted his gift; a metal rose with delicately curled petals, the thorns on the stem sharpened to points. He'd poured his heart into it until it wasn't steel at all, but almost alive and breathing.

"It's beautiful! Thank you so much, Asher," I said, my voice cracking a little as I said his name.

He pulled me to his chest and held me there, stroking my hair. His mouth against my temple, he whispered, "You should be given a thousand roses, dear Ella. I wanted to show you how much I care about you. I thought of giving you a real one – they're in bloom, but this was made by my hands and heart. When you're at home and see this, I want you to think of me."

"How could I not?" I said softly. How did he manage to claim my heart in such a short time? It beat for him alone. His arms were made to envelop me. They warmed my skin, wrapping me in comfort. It was a sense of belonging I'd never felt before.

Even my dear sister Ivy and I held each other at a distance, rather than opening up and aching for one another all the time. If I'd known then how short a time we'd have, I would have loved her more fiercely and with every ounce of myself. I wouldn't have held back at all.

If I'd been strong enough to love her the way she needed, she might still be alive. She might be with me now. I wouldn't make that mistake again. Not with Asher.

I blinked rapidly to dry my eyes before pulling away. "This means so much to me, Asher. Thank you for this gift." *How long must this have taken to make?*

He placed the rose in my hand, adding, "I'm glad you like it."

Suddenly, Nathaniel muttered a curse and then apologized over his shoulder. Asher and I laughed, the seriousness of the moment broken. Uncle Hayden would be returning soon to load the tables and baskets.

"You need to get back," he said, as if reading my mind.

"I should. And you need to help your father with that large order." Asher held tight to my hand and the pull between us became stronger in that moment. I didn't want to go.

"It'll be a week before I see you again," I told him. "But I'll look at this every day until then."

He gave a vibrant smile. "Thank you," he said, bringing my hand to his mouth. Warmth flooded through my veins. He tucked a folded note into my hand, told me to be careful, and watched as I walked away.

Uncle Hayden hadn't arrived yet, so I read it while I had the chance.

Sweetest Ella,

I hope your first day at market was a success. I also hope you had fun and met some of the folks from town. Some are crotchety, but they mean well, and most are good people.

I've been keeping my promise to you. Every night, I've stared up at the sky, whether there is clouds or stars and I think of you. I miss you more than you'll ever know. I feel like I can talk to you, tell you things I wouldn't say to anyone else. Not for fear that they wouldn't care, but just because they wouldn't understand. Thank you for understanding me. Thank you for taking a chance on me. I don't deserve it, but I thank God every day for it and you.

I hope you like the rose.

Yours,
Asher

Of course I loved the rose! I set it down just long enough to empty leaves from the baskets, cleaning them out as best I could and stacking them up. While folding the fabric that had covered the tables, someone cleared their throat behind me. I looked up to see the younger Galderian man standing before me.

"Beautiful," he said, staring at me intently.

"What?" I took a step back. He was far too close for my liking.

With his eyes fixed on me, he motioned toward the rose that Asher had made. It lay on one of the tables beside the small coin purse. "The rose. It's beautiful. I assume the young smith crafted it for you."

"He did," I replied, resuming my chores and hoping he would get the message that he needed to leave.

The young man didn't smile. "What is your name?" he asked. "I know we were introduced, but I'm afraid I'm terrible with names and have, much to my embarrassment, forgotten yours. If you give it to me again, I promise I won't forget it."

"And if you do, I won't have to give it to you?" I asked, raising my brow.

His lip upturned on one side. "That would only be fair, milady."

"It's Ella Farmer."

"You're a farmer?" he asked.

Of course, he must have already known I was a farmer since he knew where to find my booth. He looked me over

170

from head to toe, my body heating uncomfortably. Why would a royal concern himself with a peasant? *Unless he knows...*

"I am," I said proudly. He was the embodiment of every self-righteous royal I'd ever known. I loved my life, and no one was going to make me feel like less of a person because I did. I kept my chin up, my shoulders squared, and stared him down, inwardly willing him to leave. If Uncle Hayden drove up now and saw him, he would worry.

The young man's hazel eyes contained every natural color except blue. Varying shades of green, brown, and amber swirled within them. "You're a strange girl, Ella Farmer. Every other peasant I've spoken with in Tierney has barely looked me in the eye, but you seem to be unable to keep from it."

I wondered who I was dealing with, and impulsively asked, "What's *your* name?"

He smiled. "You'll know it soon enough." He bowed and walked quickly away.

Uncle Hayden suddenly appeared with his wagon. He lashed the horse's reins to a nearby post and jumped down from his seat. "Who was that?" he asked, worried eyes darting around after the man who had already disappeared.

"He was just someone looking around the market. He and his father ordered half a dozen broadswords from Nathaniel and Asher."

"He is from Galder," he whispered.

"I know."

Tense silence dampened our spirits as we quickly loaded the tables, cloth, and baskets into the back of the wagon. Hayden and I climbed up onto the wagon seat and he drove us down the road that led home. "What was that young man's name?" Hayden finally asked.

"I didn't catch it. We barely spoke, but Nathaniel would know."

"I'll ask him tomorrow," he vowed, the lines on his face deepening.

"I think it was innocent, Uncle Hayden. He just seemed curious."

"Well, I don't like that he was curious about you."

"He really wasn't. He happened to see me with Asher at the forge, and then he stopped at the market to look around. He said he was looking to buy a few vegetables, and heard that we had the best at market. We were already sold out, so he left to find some elsewhere."

The lie sat heavily on my shoulders. He would know the Galderian didn't want herbs or vegetables. Royals had servants to buy and prepare their food.

The young man didn't want me to know his name… but now he knew mine.

My fingers touched the rose in my pocket, careful of the thorns.

THE YOUNG GALDERIAN

Ella Farmer. When the young smith introduced her, I could see from my father's appraisal of her and the haunted look in his eyes that she was indeed Carina—Ella Carina, Princess of Aelawyn.

I thought the smith was lying, attempting to conceal her; but after I followed her back to the market and saw her booth, as well as the man who came to gather her and the wares, it became apparent that there was no concealment. Ella was truly a farmer, and living the life of a peasant. How very clever of Stefan to keep her just under his nose. When we left the forge, my father—a man who never minced words— only uttered two of them. "It's her."

"How do you know?" I whispered.

"Because she looks exactly like her mother did when she was the same age."

The fact hurt him. The pain lay heavily on his brow and his usually proud shoulders. He told me to learn more about the girl and strode away to gather his wits.

Dark-haired and fair, Ella Farmer was the woman to whom I was betrothed. I came here hoping we wouldn't find her, but after seeing the beauty and strength she possessed, and after hearing her sweet voice, I couldn't help but thank God that we did.

For years I'd been angry with my father for admitting to having loved a woman who was not my mother, even though they'd fallen in love before my parents were wed. But after seeing Ella today, I finally understood how he could have become so bewitched.

A deep, unexplored part of me was jealous to see her with the young smith—a situation I hoped to rectify sooner rather than later.

CHAPTER TWENTY

ELLA

The sun scorched our backs, leaching water from the soil and our bodies. The fields were all planted, but now came the weeding and watering, the constant working of rows to keep the plants healthy. Millie cursed each time she had to move farther down the row. She was at the bottom of the slope working her way toward me and Jewel as we worked our way down. Matthew worked happily by himself in the next field over, whistling as he worked his row.

"These weeds," Jewel cursed. "They're going to ruin the crop if we can't keep up with them."

"We will," I tried to reassure her, working with a renewed enthusiasm.

She wiped her brow, smiling at my newfound burst of energy. "How was Asher yesterday?" she whispered.

"He was my first customer," I said, trying but unable to hide my grin as I tried to focus on the weeds grasped in my hand.

"Was that the only time you saw him?" she asked, using a tool Nathaniel had designed to help us uproot weeds. It had two sharp prongs at the tip and was thick and strong, allowing us to use leverage to remove weeds from their roots.

"Well, we walked to his shop after everything sold at market," I admitted, blushing. I hadn't shown her the rose yet. I didn't want Millie to see it and break or hide it.

"Did you now?" she teased. Jewel saw me struggling with a strongly rooted weed and came to my rescue. "Let me get that one, dear. This tool is amazing. Nathaniel will be making more in his spare time."

"He might not have much of that for a while," I commented.

"Why is that?" Jewel sat back, giving me her full attention.

"The shop was commissioned to make half a dozen broadswords."

"By whom?" she asked.

"A Galderian royal."

"You were there?" Jewel froze, her tool stuck in the dirt.

"I was. There was a man about Hayden's age, and another man about my age. They were talking with Nathaniel when Asher and I walked over to the shop."

"Did they see you?"

"Yes, but they were just talking about the sword order," I said, trying to downplay the encounter.

She removed her hat and fanned herself with the brim. "There could be trouble brewing. There's talk in town; rumors spreading that the Galderians are here for a reason, and that they've been snooping around town. What if they're looking for you?"

"They wouldn't know me if they found me," I said with far more confidence than I felt.

"Probably not, but I'll speak with Hayden. Maybe someone else should tend the booth at market." Too late, I realized that this reaction might be why Hayden didn't tell her about the swords or that the young Galderian man had come to my market booth.

"I promise it was nothing, Aunt Jewel. Please don't take market day from me. It's the only time I get to see Asher," I whispered.

"Hayden and I will discuss it, but in the end, we'll have to do what's best for the family. I hope you understand that we're charged with keeping you safe. If we don't, the whole family will face consequences, Ella."

Consequences from Tierney's King, who forced them take me in the first place, and told them they had to keep my identity secret. Consequences from Galder, should they learn who had hidden me all these years. But why would Galder care what happened to me? Why would they come looking for me after so long? My parents and my Kingdom were dead, as were the betrothal promises they made before dying. It didn't make sense. How would that man even know what I looked like?

Hayden had already driven into town to meet Nathaniel, searching for answers I couldn't give him. Kingdoms often sent parties to visit other Kingdoms, to discuss trade and solidify relationships. It was common. Soon, they would leave Tierney and I wouldn't have to worry about them again. A fortnight wasn't very long. We just had to keep our heads down and our mouths closed, and stick with our everyday routines. We couldn't lose our heads about a series of silly coincidences.

"I heard them say they needed Nathaniel's work in a fortnight," I offered. "They're leaving Tierney then, and moving on to the northern Kingdoms."

Millie groaned in the field's bottom. I noted with irritation that she'd barely made any progress and was moving at the speed of a slug. Matthew worked as hard as a boy of his size and age could, carrying bucket after bucket of water to the rows he'd just tended, soaking the earth again. Hayden spent much of the afternoon away.

Jewel didn't say it, but it worried her that he was gone so long. She kept looking down the road, willing him to appear. When the sun began to sink toward the west, she abruptly stood up. "I'm going to wash up and prepare supper."

Her skirts swished as she walked down the row and pushed against the small, wooden gate that swung in the opening of the stone fence. "Where's Father?" Millie yelled.

"He'll be home shortly. Mind your work, Millie. You've barely moved today," her mother answered hotly.

I kept working long after Matthew and Millie left the field. I needed to see Hayden return home safely, and I needed space and fresh air. What if something happened to him? He had gone to town to speak with Nathaniel, but if someone heard he was asking questions about the Galderians...

Finally, the creaking sound of Hayden's wagon came from just around the bend in the road. Uncle Hayden was finally home, and I wasn't the only one relieved to see him. Aunt Jewel rushed outside to meet him as Matthew unhitched and guided his horse to the barn behind the house, promising to feed and give the exhausted animal some water.

"Where have you been?" Jewel whispered loudly, brushing her hair back into her bun.

"I'll explain everything later," he said tersely, putting an abrupt end to the conversation and explanation we'd all hoped for.

My skin crawled with the tone of his voice and the implication that something was very, very wrong.

CHAPTER TWENTY-ONE

ELLA

After supper, Matthew and Millie were sent straight to bed. Matthew groaned, but Millie went quietly, which was suspicious. She didn't fool her father, either.

"Let's go outside. I know they're listening," Hayden whispered, pointing a finger upward.

We filed out and walked past the house and farther down the road before Uncle Hayden stopped, raking his hands through his hair.

"Piers found me in the village today. But if I hadn't bumped into him, he would've come here to seek me out."

"What for?" Aunt Jewel's words tumbled from her mouth in a rush.

"It seems that a young Galderian noble mentioned Ella Farmer to King Stefan in conversation. The King is very unhappy. He thinks we failed to keep your identity secret."

"But the Galderians *don't* know who I am! He couldn't. I simply met the young man and his father while they were placing an order with Nathaniel. Then he showed back up as I was packing everything up at the end of market day. That was the extent of my dealings with him." There was no way the Galderians could know who I was!

Jewel's mouth widened. She knew I'd omitted the last few details about seeing the boy back at our booth. "I didn't want you to worry," I explained hurriedly. "You were already scared when I mentioned seeing him at Nathaniel's shop."

She opened her mouth, but before she could speak, Hayden did. "No time to worry about that now. We've been invited to a ball Saturday night, and we'll still have to be ready for market on Sunday."

"A ball? Us? Tell them we can't go," Jewel said, wringing her hands.

"I can't. The King insists we attend." Hayden blew out a heavy breath, adding, "Piers would like to see you tomorrow morning at daybreak, Ella. You'll have to walk to town alone. He said he will meet you along the road."

This was such a mess! A feeling of dread crawled its way into my stomach. What if Piers planned to kill me and leave me to the scavengers to rid the Kingdom of me for good? No doubt the King felt I was more trouble than I was worth, but I wasn't worried about me. "What if you're in danger?" I asked, tears clogging my throat.

"I don't think it's come to that, yet," Hayden tried to reassure me and Jewel. "I think you simply happened to catch the young Galderian's eye—purely by coincidence—but it's dangerous because of your history. At the ball, you have to convince him that you're not interested in him in any way."

"That won't be too difficult since I'm *not* interested." Asher's dark hair and midnight blue eyes flashed through my mind.

"*I* know that; you just need to make sure the young man knows," Hayden said with another sigh. I didn't tell him that the Galderian already knew I wasn't interested. He saw me and Asher together, our fingers interlaced, and he saw the rose Asher made me. He even commented on it.

"We should get some rest," Hayden finally said. "You'll leave before daybreak, Ella. Millie and Matthew can't know about this."

"Yes, sir."

"A ball?" Jewel fretted. "But what will we wear?"

Wearing a clean chemise and overdress, I slipped on my boots and was out of the house before the rooster began to crow. Crisp air filled my lungs, but worry gnawed at my stomach.

I didn't have to go all the way to town. Beneath the tree where Asher and I met for a picnic lunch what seemed like a lifetime ago, Piers had lashed his horse to a low branch and patted her back affectionately. As I stepped through the tall hay, following the path his horse had trampled, he called out.

"Ella. Thank you for meeting me," he said formally, his eyes appraising me. He wasn't finding fault; he was casually noting differences since the last time he saw me, or so it seemed. "You've grown up."

"I have." He had aged, too. His hair was silver, and his skin more wrinkled than I remembered. Still, beneath his

183

fine clothes, he was muscular. Still capable of fighting, which was good for him. He was still of use to the King. I wasn't sure what Stefan did with the knights who could no longer serve him. Maybe he wished them well and sent them to live out their lives as they pleased.

My father hadn't been so generous. Any knight who couldn't serve him was a threat, or so he thought. Having been privy to damning information, the knight would be put to death once they were deemed no longer useful. Not publicly, but by one of his own; cloaked in darkness and willing to stab a former friend in the back, all because he'd been given the order and didn't want to die for refusing to comply with the King's decree.

While most men fought for positions of honor within the courts of their kingdoms, the men in my father's favor knew their days were numbered. It was how he kept them honest. It was also what made them ruthless, greedy, and bitter just like him. Was Piers like that now?

"Stefan asked me to meet with you. He knows you've spoken with the Galderians and he wants to know what you've spoken about. He told me to make nice and coax you into answering, but I prefer bluntness and honesty," Piers said, cutting straight to the heart of the matter, exactly as I'd expected him to.

"I don't even know their names, Piers. That's how little I know about them. I only know they are from Galder because of their tunics. I met the young man twice on market day; once at the blacksmith's and once when he stopped by my booth at market. For what it's worth, I don't think he knows, Piers." My true identity was in the past, and I wanted to leave it there. If only it were easy to forget one's history.

Piers smiled ruefully. "The young man's name is Trevor, and his father's is Yurak."

My heart stalled on a breath. *His father?* I was betrothed to Trevor's father? I clapped a hand over my mouth. The man who ordered the swords from Nathaniel was my betrothed?

"I can see by your reaction that you had no idea who they were. Yurak's wife died a year before your betrothal. He was within his rights to take another, but given your age, it would seem more likely that you'd have been betrothed to Trevor."

"Why are they here?" I asked.

"They say it's to repair our relationship with them, to reconsider trade among our kingdoms, and maybe that's truly all they're interested in. They say they're moving on, traveling to the northern kingdoms after this brief stop in Tierney, but they seem to be in no hurry to leave, and my men caught theirs snooping around the castle for something. We thought they might be searching for you."

"Why would they even care? It's been *three years*, Piers. I just want to be left alone." Thick tears welled in my eyes, blurring my vision.

He shifted his weight. "I'm still trying to figure it all out. Yurak mentioned you in conversation with King Stefan, and then asked the King to invite you to the ball so he can get to know you better. Stefan wants you to attend so we can watch the Galderians while in your presence. If they know who you are, it will be apparent."

"The King wants to use me as bait?"

"In essence, yes," Piers said.

I ground my teeth together until the gritting sound filled my ears. "I want my family kept safe. If anything happened to the Farmers, I would never forgive myself. I want your word on that, Piers."

"You have it. Hayden is my friend."

"Even if it means going against the King's orders?" I asked.

He gritted his teeth and didn't answer. I could tell he didn't know what he would do in that situation, but it wouldn't be an easy decision to make.

"Tell Hayden that a royal carriage will arrive Saturday at sunset. My men and I will accompany you to the castle. From there, you will all be guarded. I won't let you out of my sight, Ella. Not even for a second."

He thought I was in danger. I saw it in the fierce darkness of his eyes and the way they blazed with his vow. "Thank you," I told him, his apprehension spilling over onto me and making my fingers tremble. The wind gusted violently as the morning sky turned darker and storm clouds overtook the rising sun, mirroring my mood.

"King Stefan wants you to continue on as you normally do. He doesn't want the Galderians knowing that we suspect them of anything, and truthfully, they haven't done anything overtly threatening. They just keep turning up in parts of the castle they should not be in. If it were anyone else, it wouldn't be an issue. But given that it's Yurak and his son, it's enough to raise suspicion."

"I think we're all just being overly paranoid. This is probably just an innocent misunderstanding," I said.

"I hope you're right. If that's the case, and the Galderians leave, everything can go back to normal."

Before parting ways, Piers restated the plan. His men would come and escort us to the ball in one of the King's carriages. We were to be polite and gracious, but I needed to make it clear to Trevor that I wanted nothing to do with him. Piers and his men would see me and my family home safely afterwards.

After the ball, we should keep our regular routines and go about our days as we always did. I could return to market – where I could see Asher again. The Galderians would leave and everything would go back to normal.

TREVOR

Father mentioned Ella Farmer to King Stefan at dinner. Though the King's grip tightened on the handles of his knife and fork, he only smiled. "The Farmers are a lovely family," the King answered. "Piers knows them well." The King nodded to the knight seated at his right hand. Piers levelled his dark eyes on me, a slight and very fake smile playing on his lips.

"I should like to see her again. Perhaps you could invite them to the ball so that I may dance with her?" I suggested.

Piers looked to Stefan, who nodded slightly and narrowed his eyes. "Perhaps we should."

My stomach dropped. Father only intended to see if there would be a reaction to her name. He'd no doubt noticed the same things I had, and now, I couldn't help but regret mentioning her or suggesting the invitation. In trying to bait the King, we put Ella on our hook. I never thought Stefan would invite peasants to a royal ball, but in Ella's case, he was willing to break with tradition. And that was a very bad thing.

I would speak with Father after dinner, but Saturday, I would push her away in front of Stefan and his men. I would make it seem that I favored another, and that Ella was just a passing fancy of an immature and roguish young prince.

But I also desperately needed to talk to her.

Although this was rapidly turning into a nightmare, I vowed to keep Ella safe from King Stefan.

CHAPTER TWENTY-TWO

ELLA

It had been two days since I met Piers at daybreak. Two days since I stopped in the village to buy candles we didn't need as an excuse to be there, so my cousins wouldn't question where I'd been. Two days since I saw Asher. He and Nathaniel were feverishly working on the sword order for the Galderians that were causing so much trouble in our lives.

I didn't tell Asher about the ball. He would hear from Hayden or gossip soon enough, and right now, he needed to focus on the swords and not worry about me and the Prince of Galder. I was afraid he would ask questions I couldn't answer. I was also afraid he would decide I wasn't worth it and walk away from me.

Millie had been giving me strange looks all morning, like she wanted to ask me something but didn't know what to say or how to say it. Finally, her patience snapped.

"I'll milk the cows for you," she offered solicitously, trying to take the bucket from my hands.

"I can do it," I said, jerking it away from her.

"Why can't you just let me do something for you?" she screeched.

"Because I don't need your help!" My voice rose to meet hers. She wasn't pushing me around. Not today.

Her shoulders slumped. "I want to do it so you'll fix my hair tonight. I'll look wretched if you don't," she said, tears welling in her eyes.

"Millie," I said, but she wouldn't look at me. "All you have to do is ask. I'd be happy to fix your hair tonight. You don't have to do my chores to get me to treat you like a sister."

I saw the flash in her eyes when they met mine. I actually *did* consider her a sister – a hateful one, sure – but to me, Millie was family. She had never felt the same way and never would.

"Thank you," she said bitterly.

"You're welcome."

She stomped away to finish her own chores right as Matthew entered the barn. "What's wrong with her?" he asked, hooking a thumb over his shoulder.

I didn't know what was wrong with Millie; only that she was unhappy with life and blamed me for it. She had all she needed, but I guess in the end, she didn't have what she *wanted*. I didn't think anything would ever be enough to make her happy. Not ribbons, dresses, or a royal ball. Those things didn't last. Happiness was found within, and Millie had no intention of searching herself for it.

Around midday, Aunt Jewel called us inside. Millie dropped her bucket on the ground mid-task and ran toward the house, but Matthew and I finished feeding the chickens before walking back slowly together. He stuffed his hands into his pockets.

"Is something wrong?" I asked, stopping outside the door for a moment.

"Yeah," he drawled. "It's just... We're going to be so out of place – farmers at a ball with nobility – and I don't want to be laughed at."

My heart broke for him. "I understand why you're worried, but try to think of it in a different light. We have an opportunity to act like royals for one night. We'll taste their food, drink their wine, and enjoy their music. We can dance on their sparkling floors and drink from polished goblets. And while we do all of that, we can be proud of what we are; because without us, they wouldn't have food to fill their soft bellies, or the tables of their banquet halls." I winked, nudging him with my arm.

A small sense of peace washed across his features. "Thanks, Ella." At his mother's frustrated call, he smiled. "Better start getting ready before she has a conniption."

Jewel was not herself. By the time I walked in the house, she had already cornered Matthew and was frantically scrubbing his cuticles with a brush. The door squeaked, drawing her attention. Her eyes narrowed on my hands and she waved the scrub brush at me. "You're next, so don't run off. We might not be royalty, but we won't arrive at the castle as filthy as pigs."

From his room, Uncle Hayden gave a dramatic groan. "No sense in pretending we're anything but what we are,

Jewel. Clean hands won't change the fact that we work in the dirt. They won't hide our clothes."

"You'll all mind your manners," Jewel warned. She sighed, finally allowing Matthew to pass her inspection. "There's a tub in our room, Matthew. Get a bath and then get dressed quickly."

The afternoon faded fast into evening. Jewel scrubbed my cuticles and nails and then sent me upstairs, where another tub waited. I washed my hair and bathed quickly.

When Millie came upstairs, I styled her hair in a bouquet of braids and pearls. She looked stunning in her beet-colored dress. Satisfied with her hair, she left me alone to dress and plait my hair. The soft white lace of my dress fell over the soft curve of my hips and down to the floor.

There was only one problem. I hadn't thought about washing my shoes. They were covered in mud, but they were all I had to wear. I walked downstairs, holding them away from my dress. "Jewel?"

"Yeah?" she called from her bedroom.

"Do you have an extra pair of shoes I could borrow?"

Her head popped out of her doorway. "I'm sorry, I don't. Millie?" she yelled.

"I'm wearing my only pair," Millie snapped at her. She turned to me with a disgusted look. "Clean the ones you have."

They were caked with thick mud, and there was no way to get them clean without soiling the dress I'd put on. And if I undressed and went to wash them, I'd be wearing wet, squishy shoes all night.

Not to mention the fact that I was out of time. "I see the carriage!" Hayden shouted from outside.

I couldn't attend the ball in dirty shoes...but there was one other option. Climbing the steps, my fingers shook with

192

anxiety. *Would they even fit?* I hadn't looked at them in years. I pulled the black velvet bag from its hiding spot under my bed and prayed Ivy's shoes would fit me now. A layer of dust coated the bag.

They looked perfect, like Ivy had just taken them off and tucked them away. My feet were an exact fit. The heel didn't slip and my toes weren't pinched. When I stood, the hem of my dress covered them almost entirely. This would work.

As long as Millie didn't notice them.

I held my breath as I walked down the steps, trying not to let the heels click on the boards. Just the sparkling tips of the shoes peeked out, but luckily, my family was already outside. I'd just have to be careful to avoid stairs tonight.

Piers was whispering something to Hayden and Jewel when I stepped out of the house. The two men helped Millie into the carriage, and then Matthew climbed in next. Inside, Millie carried on about how grand the carriage was; the upholstery a luxurious, ruby fabric, and the fine varnish on the wood.

There were four knights, all clad in ebony, with polished swords at their sides.

"Your family will be honored tonight, Hayden," Piers said with a smile, clapping Hayden affectionately on the shoulder. The two helped Jewel into the carriage, and then each man took one of my hands, helping me up the steps as well. Piers flashed a look of warning and I returned it. His eyes caught on my shoes and his lips parted, but I quickly covered them with the hem of my dress.

He slammed the door closed behind me.

Millie glowed, talking incessantly about all we would see and experience. "I've heard all about the balls. They say there are fountains of gold..." she chattered, but I tried to ignore her. Jewel sat between me and Millie – a wise decision on her part – and Uncle Hayden and Matthew sat across from us. Matthew tugged at his collar but seemed to relax when Hayden asked if he liked the horses that pulled the carriage.

The driver maneuvered the carriage around in a careful tangle of movements until we were facing the village.

Would Asher see us? How would I explain this to him?

If he didn't already know about our attendance at the ball, he would soon. I hadn't written him back yet, but didn't know what I'd write if I could.

CHAPTER TWENTY-THREE

ELLA

The carriage rolled through the village streets, drawing people from buildings and homes alike, whispering behind covered mouths. Millie waved out the windows, drawing attention none of us wanted or needed. Jewel told her to stop – repeatedly – but Millie was undeterred. She wanted to be seen; wanted the rumors to swirl about the Farmer family in a royal carriage. It took everything I had not to pull her back inside.

The faint scent of wood smoke filled the carriage. Asher and the forge weren't far away. Jewel sat rigidly beside me. She was quiet, and when she did say something, her smile didn't reach her eyes. Throughout the ride, her hands clutched her skirts and then smoothed the fabric when she caught herself clutching it. Hayden sat stoically across from us, the lines curving around his mouth more pronounced.

Piers rode alongside the carriage, his eyes meeting mine again for an instant before we turned onto the road that led straight to Tierney's castle. He kicked his horse's flanks and rode ahead. *If we failed tonight, if I failed...*

The muddy road disappeared and the carriage wheels bumped along the narrow, cobbled street. Torches were being lit all along the road that led to the castle, and the castle's silhouette was dark against the purple sky. Jewel reached over and squeezed my hand. She needed me, just like I needed her. I had to put an end to this nonsense once and for all.

We passed over the moat's bridge and circled around to the front entrance. Piers dismounted, handing the reins of his horse to a stable boy. His men did the same and then surrounded the carriage, helping us down the carriage steps. I nodded to Piers.

I'll handle this. Keep them safe, I told him with my eyes, and he nodded in return.

Millie gaped at the turrets and spires; the walls were tall, with merlons tipped with dark metal that glistened, even at night. Servants held the doors open and we moved inside as a group. Hayden and Jewel led our family, followed by their children and then me. Millie was dazed, drunk on the finery surrounding her, and Matthew grinned from ear to ear as he took in the castle he'd only ever seen from afar. My heels clicked against the stone with each step, but everyone was too caught up in worry or awe to notice.

Piers plastered a smile on his face and gave us a short tour on the way to the ballroom, recanting the castle's long history along the stroll. The walls had never been breached, he said. *The same was true of Aelawyn's until the day Tierney attacked.*

The ballroom was full. Women in dresses made of rich fabric and the men in fine tunics whirled around the floor as the musicians played. The din of conversation swirled around us. I glanced toward the dais to see King Stefan. His stony gaze met mine, and he raised his glass ever so slightly before bringing it to his lips.

I felt like a mouse, desperately scurrying to get across the floor in a room full of hungry cats. Knights and Dames, Barons and Baronesses, Dukes and Duchesses, the two Princes, King Stefan and Queen Grace. Their eyes openly appraised the family of peasants who strode into the room, surrounded by knights.

"This is the most beautiful thing I've ever seen," Millie said in awe under her breath, her eyes darting across the ceiling and walls to take it all in. Piers told us to make ourselves comfortable, and then pretended to dismiss his men. They relaxed and made their way to various points around the room, one at every exit.

Aunt Jewel suggested that we find a seat together and have something to eat. As she led the way through the crowd, I was the last to follow her, stopping only when a soft hand landed on my elbow.

"Ella Farmer," Trevor said. I was supposed to pretend I didn't know his name. Piers said to play along.

"Hello," I replied. I couldn't fight the stiffening of my muscles, or the way my body pulled away from his instinctually.

"Would you like to dance?" he asked, eyes glittering with mischief.

"Very well," I answered stiffly. "If you give me your name, I'll dance with you."

He smiled, offering a hand with a bow. "By now, you must be very well aware that my name is Trevor, milady."

I didn't deny that I knew. Playing games with the Prince of Galder meant only one thing: I was sure to lose. Having lost years of practice with the fine art of manipulation, the best course of action was the simplest. I wouldn't play at all.

"I've heard rumors, but wanted to make sure they were true," I told him with a smirk.

The musicians played a waltz. Trevor grasped my hand in the air and placed his other hand at my waist, the posture tense and distant, and nothing like dancing with Asher.

Trevor smiled, and we fell into step with the multitude who were also waltzing in circles. My feet knew the steps, my body the rhythm, but I was no longer Princess Carina of Aelawyn. I was Ella Farmer, who would fumble and falter. So I made sure that I did.

His toes will be black and blue tomorrow, I thought with a smile.

Trevor glanced around the room as we spun, his eyes locking on something here and there, but when I tried to follow his gaze, we'd already moved into another position and I couldn't see anything that might interest him.

He drew me in tighter against his body. "I need to speak with you privately," he whispered. It was said so lightly, I wondered if his lips had even moved.

"That's not possible." I tried to pull away from him, but he clasped my hand and waist tighter to keep me in his orbit.

"Because *you* refuse, or because of the hulking knight who's watching us?" His lips curled at the corners.

"Does it matter? I don't want to speak to you privately. About anything," I offered.

"How interesting that the King assigned his best knights to guard simple farmers."

Swallowing, I couldn't think of anything to say in response.

"Ella, I have information you need." The ferocity of his plea was off-putting. I tried to wrench my hand away from him, but he was stronger.

"What information could a simple farm girl like me need?" I scoffed.

I could hear him gritting his teeth at the dismissal, but when the last notes of the song finished, he bowed and I curtseyed. Trevor reached for my hand, kissing it lightly, his eyes meeting mine as if to say that the conversation wasn't over.

"Thank you for the dance, Ella Farmer," Trevor said formally. "It looks like the next has been spoken for." He ticked his head toward the edge of the dance floor where Matthew waited impatiently.

I'd never been more thankful for Matthew than in that moment.

Trevor waved him over, and Matthew and I danced across the floor to a lively song. By the time it was over, beads of sweat had formed on my nose and both of us were laughing so hard, we could barely catch our breath. People stared, but we didn't notice them.

"That was fun!" Matthew said. "Never imagined we'd be dancing at a ball in the castle, but you were right. It's not so bad," he said with a smile.

Leaving the dance floor, we walked to the table where Uncle Hayden and Aunt Jewel were sitting. It was in the corner farthest from Stefan, but no matter where I looked, Piers was there, watching. The conversation with Trevor kept playing through my mind. There was something in his voice; an urgency I didn't understand.

Millie was hovering near the dance floor when Trevor walked up and asked her to dance. He whispered something in her ear, making her giggle.

When dinner was served, we ate chicken, vegetables, pastries, and slices of pie. We sipped wine from polished goblets, just like I'd promised Matthew. He didn't like the taste.

When Trevor asked for another dance, I accepted and let him lead me to the dance floor, determined to put an end to his attention once and for all. That was why I was here. "My cousin Millie loved dancing with you," I said boldly as he whirled me around.

"At least *one* of the Farmer women prefer my company," he retorted with a sly grin.

"True."

He threw his head back laughing, and while still chuckling asked, "And has the young smith managed to capture your attention?"

"He has."

"I would be lying if I said I wasn't jealous."

"Why would you be jealous?" I breathed, half-laughing.

"Getting close to you would be the most difficult thing for a man to do, but also, I imagine, the most rewarding."

I wasn't sure if he'd complimented or insulted me, so I kept quiet, my heart thundering as he pulled me close.

"Your guard watches," he whispered against my ear.

My eyes found Piers for a moment. He was standing solidly against the wall, his stern eyes on me and Trevor.

"He's very good at what he does," Trevor said as the music slowed.

"He is."

Trevor was relentless. "I'll be at the market tomorrow. I must speak with you."

"Trevor, I want to make it plain to you, just so there is no misunderstanding, that I am not interested in you in any way."

"Message received," he said stiffly, pulling away and bowing as the music notes stopped. "Do you think your cousin would like to dance with me again?" he asked loudly, punctuating the sentence with a wink.

"I'm sure she would."

He gave me a smile and went off to find Millie. As I walked off the dance floor, I caught the eye of King Yurak, Trevor's father. His gaze shifted to something behind me, and I turned to find Piers standing there.

"Piers, I didn't see you there," I gasped.

"Did you succeed?" he asked in a clipped tone.

"I did. I believe the young Galderian actually fancies Millie." I nodded to the couple, now gliding happily across the floor, right as Millie threw her head back in laughter. "We've all been paranoid for no reason."

"You've done well," Piers complimented.

"Thank you. So, are we in the clear? No more guards? No trouble? Things can go back to normal?"

"I believe so, though the final decision will rest with the King."

"Of course it will," I added, glancing at Stefan, who was whispering something in Queen Grace's ear.

Someone cleared their throat behind us. "Prince Carden," Piers said with a bow. I turned around quickly and curtseyed to the young man.

"It seems the Galderian prince is taken with the Farmers' daughters. Would you do me the honor of a dance, so that I may enjoy your company as well?"

Piers narrowed his eyes at the young prince, whose hair was dark as midnight and purposely messy. His eyes were bloodshot from drink, but I knew I couldn't refuse him. He was one of the princes. I swallowed back my fear and curtsied. "Of course, Prince Carden."

When the musicians struck up a slow waltz, the prince's hand clasped mine tightly. "My father has been staring at you all night," he said suspiciously.

He certainly didn't beat around the bush.

"We're out of place," I said sheepishly, looking down at my attire and motioning to his. "We were given an invitation, but everyone here knows we don't belong."

"That's a nice lie you've concocted, Ella. My brother doesn't remember you, but I do. I remember when Piers first brought you here."

Would he give us away? I thought with alarm. Drunkenness tended to make one's mind unclear. "It doesn't matter who I once was, Prince Carden; it matters who I am now," I told him, forcing my shoulders to stay squared.

"My father thinks you'll try to take control of Aelawyn when you come of age," he said matter-of-factly.

"Take control of what? Aelawyn is in ruins."

Carden gave me the strangest look before clearing his throat. "If you're lying," he said seriously, "there is nowhere you can hide that my father's men can't find you."

"I know."

The remainder of the song was filled with beautiful notes and uneasy tension. Trevor's hazel eyes found mine several times across the floor from us, and each time my stomach churned. He was still dancing with Millie, but if he didn't stop watching me and Prince Carden, he was going to arouse suspicion. Especially if Stefan was paying as close attention to me as Carden claimed. Right before the number ended, Carden looked at me and said the most curious thing.

"For the most part, we are all bound to our birthrights but you," he mused. "You were given a unique opportunity to be anyone you want. I envy you."

What could I possibly say in response? He was right, although 'unique opportunity' was a generous turn of phrase. "I pray your father feels the same way," I answered lightly. "All night he's looked at me like he'd as soon flay me as deal with my presence."

"That's because he hates it when his plans are in jeopardy of being spoiled, Miss Farmer. And unless you would prefer *being flayed*, as you put it, I would advise you not to stand in his way." With that, Carden gave a quick bow and took his leave.

I stood on the floor for a moment, wondering what had happened and how Carden went from envying me to threatening my life in just a few seconds.

I saw Piers waiting nearby, so I walked to him and asked, "When can we leave?"

Piers watched as Prince Carden carved a path through a sea of people who gladly parted for him. "I'll ask King Stefan. Stay here with Hayden."

I nodded and went to sit with my uncle and aunt. "You danced with the Prince," Jewel said with a nervous expression.

"Yes. He was nice. I believe he danced with Millie earlier."

"Nice?" she asked again.

"He felt obligated to ask. We're invited guests," I lied. She visibly relaxed. "I'm exhausted. Piers is asking the King when we might be able to leave."

"Thank God," she answered gratefully. Squeezing her hand, I felt her tremble. "I feel so out of place here," she said, glancing around the room.

"So do I."

CHAPTER TWENTY-FOUR

ELLA

iers returned from Stefan with good news. We'd been given permission to return home and were quickly ushered out the doors of the ballroom and through the front door of the castle, where the carriage was already waiting. I didn't know what time it was, but I did know that the sun would rise far too soon for any of us to get any real rest tonight.

Hayden rubbed his eyes tiredly once we were safely inside the carriage. "Would you like for me to go to market tomorrow, Ella?"

"No, I'd still like to go."

"You won't get much rest," he argued gently.

"I know, but I'll be fine," I told him.

"All right, Ella, but I'll drive the wagon and help you set up." Hayden was a good man. Jewel patted his free hand and hugged Matthew tight to her as his head bobbed up and down. He was losing the battle with sleep.

The carriage's wheels bumped along the cobbled road toward the village. Beside me, Millie was quiet, a small smile playing on her lips. I recognized that look. She'd enjoyed Trevor's attentions tonight, and even now was imagining herself a Queen.

I watched out the window as we wound through the muddy streets of the village and then into the countryside. The moon was full overhead and stars glittered in the dark sky, trails of thin clouds shrouding them intermittently. The scent of hay and wild onions filled the night air. Deer foraged in the fields, lifting alert eyes as we passed by, their bodies still as statues. The sound of insects hummed from the trees and grass, their singing becoming louder the farther into the countryside we travelled.

Piers and his men were relaxed on the way home. I heard their horses, but didn't see them ride close to the carriage. At home, while the rest of us filed out of the carriage and into the house, Hayden stayed behind to speak with Piers. Meanwhile, Jewel told us to get straight to bed and promised to wake me in the morning in time to leave for market.

The night was over.

Hopefully, Stefan was appeased and the Galderians would stop snooping around the castle—if they really had been in the first place. Tomorrow, Trevor would seek me out to tell me whatever 'important' thing was on his mind. Once that was done, I could steal a few moments with Asher.

Tucking Ivy's shoes back into the velvet bag, I slid it under my bed.

"What are you doing?" Millie whispered from across the room. Her back had been turned while she dressed for bed, so I thought she wouldn't notice if I hid them quickly. I thought wrong.

"Nothing," I lied. "A huge spider just crawled under my bed."

"Did you kill it?"

"He was too fast."

She snorted.

Dawn would be here earlier than I wanted, but I couldn't seem to fall asleep due to the questions whirling incessantly through my head. Why did Trevor need to speak with me so badly? Would I still be able to sneak away and see Asher? Did he hear about our attendance at the ball tonight, and that I danced with not one, but two princes? Inwardly, I groaned. He wasn't going to be happy.

Matthew fell onto his bed with a loud sigh. Millie blew out our candle, and her soft snoring filled the room a few minutes later. I pulled the metal rose from beneath my pillow and held onto the stem as I tried to fall asleep. It was useless. I couldn't force the racing thoughts from my head any sooner than I could make the iron rose become real.

TREVOR

My first dance with Ella was... for lack of a better description, stiff and uncomfortable. She'd trampled my feet – purposely, I was convinced. Her eyes glittered with orneriness. There was a panicked determination in her eyes when I asked her to dance and she accepted. I should've known then that I was in for it.

She all but shoved me toward her cousin, which was my plan to begin with, but I'd be lying if I said it didn't sting.

207

Was it because Stefan was watching and she feared the King, or because she was thinking of the young smith?

Piers was guarding her. He was the King's right hand, and he kept close watch through our first turn about. But by the end of the evening, he and Ella had relaxed somewhat, and I was able to whisper my most urgent message into her ear. I needed to speak with her, but not there. Not while all those eyes and swords were trained on us. We would be safer walking barefoot through a pit of scorpions.

Carden had whispered something, too. If he had threatened one hair on her head... My hand tightened on the goblet of wine I held and I gulped it down. I was sitting and speaking with William, Stefan's youngest son. I laughed at his jests and played the part I was supposed to. Father had held Stefan's ear all evening, and the evening was almost at an end, thankfully.

Tomorrow, I would see her at market.

As I watched her leave with her family, trying not to be obvious, I remembered how my hand felt upon her back, the softness of the lace on her dress beneath my fingers. I remembered the light, clean scent of her hair and the way she tried to control the arch of her brow when I told her I would come to her tomorrow.

She and I were playing a dangerous game against the King of Tierney. But we would be victorious.

I would see to it.

ELLA

Hayden yawned as he urged the horse along the road to the village. It was contagious, and before I knew it, I was yawning, too.

A thick mist shrouded the ground and soaked into the fibers of my overdress. The sun had risen, but hadn't yet burned through it. It was going to be a long day. We arrived at market and began to unload the overflowing baskets of herbs and vegetables. So many things were ripe for the picking.

Hayden dragged a table out and we righted it, and then came the smaller one, which we set into an L shape again. I covered them with tablecloths and we placed the baskets on top. He reminded me again of the prices for each item, handing me a small pouch of coin in case I needed to make change. I already knew the information, but it made him more comfortable to remind me. His eyes darted around the booth and then around the market stalls, searching for any hint of trouble.

Hayden hesitated, running a hand through his thinning hair. "I want you to be careful," he finally said. "I know I don't say it often, but you're like a daughter to me, and I... Just be careful, okay?"

I smiled and gave him a quick hug. "I will. I promise."

He put his cap back on and unlashed the horse. "I'll be back before supper."

"Yes, sir."

Uncle Hayden climbed onto the wagon seat and gathered the reins in his hands, the leather peeling and flaking away. He gave them a flick and Brutus pulled the wagon away. I watched him until he disappeared around the bend.

The cobbler set up his tables to my left, and instructed his unfriendly wife on the prices of the shoes he was selling. Her sour, pursed expression made me want to squirm. Ann, with her pies and tarts, set up on my right and I was thankful to see a familiar, smiling face.

"How was your week, dear?" she asked.

"Long."

"Aye, it was. Seems to stretch a bit once in a while, doesn't it?"

Time *did* stretch. Take today, for instance. Every moment with Asher would fly by, and then time would slow until Trevor showed, which was the time I hoped would rush by. Yes, time was cruel and unflinching in her punishment of men.

Despite the damp mist, people still came to market eager to buy, and fresh food was at the top of their lists. I sold out of three baskets straight away, so I tucked the empty ones under the table.

I had expected Trevor to show up in the evening when things had already settled down for the day. I certainly didn't expect him to step up to my booth in the middle of two women who were getting into a shouting match over who should get the last head of cabbage.

I grinned as he tried to intervene. "Ladies, please. Let's discuss this," he said, trying to calm them when my attempts failed.

"Never you mind," one angrily shouted in his direction, never even glancing at him. They kept arguing, tugging at the head of green leaves clutched in both their hands.

Trevor's deep laugh caught them off guard. "How about you split it?" he suggested.

Their hands stilled. They paused, both still clutching the head of cabbage, neither willing to give up her grasp on it. They turned their focus on Trevor.

"Split it?" one of the woman asked. Both had white hair and neither had teeth. I wasn't sure they weren't related, to be honest. But the question had each considering whether she should indeed split the leafy orb.

"Very well," the other woman said. "I'd be happy to split it with you, and the cost as well. Then we can both have some."

"I haven't a knife," the first one said, looking to me. I shrugged, holding empty hands up.

"Allow me to assist you," Trevor said, producing a small dagger. "Careful, it's sharp," he warned, holding it out to me. I took the cabbage from them and carefully split it into two equal halves. Each woman paid me for their half and thanked both me and Trevor as they walked away in friendly conversation.

I blew out a sigh of relief. "Thank you," I said, handing the dagger back to him.

"Keep it."

The hilt was elaborate, made of gold and inlaid with rubies. I was sure he had ten others just like it. "I can't." When I insisted he take the blade back, he tucked it into his belt and stared me in the eye.

"Can't, or won't?" he challenged.

"Both."

His hazel eyes glanced to the side. "Ah, the young smith, right on cue..."

I followed his gaze and saw Asher fast approaching. Trevor dropped a coin on the table and grabbed a head of broccoli, snapping a piece off and biting into it. "Thank you, milady." He glanced toward the table meaningfully, and I saw that it wasn't just a coin that he'd laid down. There was a scrap of parchment tucked beneath it.

"You're welcome." I tucked the paper into my pocket casually and placed the coin in the pouch with a clink.

For a moment, my eyes were torn between watching Trevor walk away and Asher's arrival. My dilemma ended when Asher pulled me in for a hug, his hands tense on my hips. "What did *he* want?" he asked crossly.

"Broccoli. Apparently, he was hungry."

Asher's cheeks puffed out with each breath. He must have jogged from the shop. Finally, his dark expression lightened and he smiled. "I tried to be your first customer. I'm sorry I wasn't faster. We're still working on their order," Asher explained, ticking his head in the direction Trevor had gone. His head was already lost in the crowd that was easing toward the church. Quickly selling a head of garlic scapes, I turned my attention back to Asher.

"I've missed you," he said, the words rushing from his lips.

"I've missed you, too," I answered truthfully.

He pulled me toward him, his warm breath fanning my lips. "May I?"

"Yes." The words were more whispered than spoken, but the meaning was the same. I wanted this as much as he did. His chest rose and fell quickly under my palms, but I watched as he lowered his lips to mine and pressed against them; softly at first, and then harder. When he began to retreat, I wanted to pull him back to me. His kiss felt and tasted like heaven.

Asher's hands remained on my waist as he took a deep breath and smiled. "I've wanted to do that for a long time."

"How long?" I asked cheekily. Even though I tried to make myself invisible for so many years, in moments like this, when Asher Smith saw me, I never wanted to be invisible again.

"Since you came to live with your uncle and aunt. From the day we almost ran into each other."

My heart skipped a beat. And then, it changed its rhythm and began beating solely for him. I realized then that I loved him. I knew it was fast and that we were young, but I didn't care. Hayden said he'd taken one look at Jewel and knew she was the one. She said the same thing. Sometimes these things just happened.

I was in love with Asher Smith.

212

And if I was right, he loved me back.

An elderly man cleared his throat, and I turned around with hot cheeks to help him gather what he wanted and take his payment. I saw Asher shifting his weight on his feet in my peripheral vision and knew he needed to return to the forge soon. There was work to do, and Nathaniel couldn't fill the large order himself. "Go," I told him. "I'll come to the forge at the end of the day."

"Promise?"

I smiled. "Yes, I promise." The lines marring his forehead disappeared. He planted a peck on my lips and then walked away with a spring in his step. Even though I was busy, the day passed slowly. I ached to see him again. It was all I could think about. Somehow, his kiss made me forget about the note Trevor passed me until I felt it in my apron pocket. Unfolding the small square, I read his scrawled writing.

Meet me at midnight beneath the tree where you met Piers.

How did he know about me meeting Piers? How did he know *where* I met him?

Would my family be in danger if I didn't go?

What if this was a trap?

My stomach churned as I tucked the paper into the sole of my shoe. How was I going to sneak out in the middle of the night without waking anyone? And if I somehow managed to do it, how would I sneak back in without doing the same?

CHAPTER TWENTY-FIVE

ELLA

As day faded into evening, people were still strolling through the market. Ann offered me a strawberry tart when things calmed down. I bit into pure perfection; sweet, with a flaky crust, the scent of strawberries filling my nose and mouth. "This is wonderful!" I exclaimed, my eyes wide.

"I'm glad you like it. They're made from the berries I bought from you last week."

Her smile faded into a scowl as she peered over my shoulder at the old crow in the cobbler booth who was glaring at her, lip curled in distaste. I turned back around. There was no time for ugliness when I had such a beautiful piece of pastry in front of me. For the second week in a row, I'd sold out of everything we brought to market.

"Are you going to go see the smith's son?" Ann asked suddenly.

I looked around for Hayden and his carriage, knowing it was too early for him to arrive. *Thank heavens.* "I think I will," I answered with a smile.

"Well if your uncle comes, I'll let him know where you are. Go on, now. And take him and his father a tart. My treat."

"I can pay for all three," I offered, removing a coin from Hayden's pouch. Surely he wouldn't mind if I bought something so small.

"No, no, I insist!" Ann exclaimed. "I have a high opinion of Nathaniel and his son. They're hard workers, honest and good men. You don't find that nearly as often as you used to. Besides, I need to talk to them about some work I need done, and this might help me negotiate a better price."

I smiled and thanked her, picking up the two tarts and jogging away, heading toward the scent of smoke and the harmony of pounding hammers.

As I approached the shop, I saw Nathaniel lay a hot piece of metal back into the fire right as Asher dipped the metal he was working into a large barrel of water to quench the piece. Steam plumed all around him, and a line of sweat soaked the dark brown fabric of his shirt all the way down the center of his spine. That same sweat and sheer determination shone on his face as he turned around.

His expression melted into something softer when he saw me. Asher hurried to finish what he was doing and then walked over, wiping his face with the sleeve of his shirt. "Sorry. I'm a mess," he said, looking down at me sheepishly.

"No more than I normally am."

"I'd like to see that," he said, grinning mischievously. "Dirt smeared across your pretty cheek..."

I handed a tart to him before he could go further. "Compliments of Ann. She insisted that I bring one for both you and your father."

"Set his on the work table, if you don't mind. What he's doing is difficult, but I'm sure he'll appreciate it when he's finished."

I walked inside the three-walled building and set the tart on the table. Nathaniel shouted his hello, eyeing the confection with glee, and then returned to the metal he'd been pounding with a renewed vigor. Asher waited for me outside in the fresh air. Heat radiated from the forge.

"How do you do this all day without falling to the floor from exhaustion?" I wondered aloud.

"I've collapsed before, especially when I was younger and took on more than I could handle—which was more often than I'll ever admit." He winked.

His stubborn streak could be seen from a mile away. It was in the way he held himself, and the way he wielded a hammer and beat pieces of iron into submission with gritted, bared teeth and sheer will. It was a beautiful sight to behold.

As Asher chewed on a bite of his tart, I noticed that his dominant arm was slightly larger than the other. You wouldn't notice it unless you were looking carefully, but it was another badge, praising his hard work. It couldn't have been easy meeting the expectations that his father and the village itself had for him. They had to have a smith, and he would be the only one after Nathaniel became too old to swing a hammer.

"What are you thinking?" he asked quietly, brushing a strand of hair behind my ear.

"I was thinking about you."

His dark blue eyes bore into mine. "Good." He chuckled. "I was worried the young Galderian gentleman had his sights on you, and that you might prefer his company to mine."

Trevor couldn't hold a candle to Asher. There was no competition. "I've only spoken to him a handful of times. Besides, he's obviously royalty, and I'm just a farmer."

"A beautiful one," Asher breathed, grabbing my hand.

"One who has no interest in royalty."

He smiled, biting into his tart. "Good."

My heart thumped wildly.

For him. Always for him.

"Even royals can take a peasant wife if they aren't heir to the throne, and even then, I'm sure if they were determined to have a woman, there'd be little she could do to avoid their attention. I heard about the ball, by the way."

A shiver ran up my spine when his hand fell into place at the small of my back, but I wasn't completely sure if it was from his touch or by what he just said. He was right. Royalty and nobility had the capacity to pretty much do anything they liked. Attending the ball was a prime example. Trevor wanted me to go, so I did. Stefan wanted to use me as bait, so he did.

"Of course Millie loved it, and even Matthew warmed up to it the longer we were there. But for me, it felt like we were on display, and I hated every second of it."

"Did you dance?"

"Yes."

"I can guess who asked you." His lips thinned.

"Just because he's curious, doesn't mean I am."

The tension bled from his shoulders. "That makes me feel a little better," he breathed.

Just then, the corner of Trevor's note poked the tender sole of my foot, reminding me of one more thing I had to keep from Asher. I had to meet Trevor – tonight – even though I wasn't exactly sure what he wanted. The snowball of lies kept growing, and at the rate I was going, I feared I couldn't keep up with them all.

"I wish I could meet you again this week, but this is our last week to get the sword order filled," he said, disappointed. "I had hoped to fit in another sword lesson for you and Matthew, but it seems that will have to wait."

"I wish I could see you, too, but right now the work in the fields is overwhelming. We're barely keeping up with the weeds."

Suddenly, Nathaniel stopped hammering. Asher looked over his shoulder as his father rolled his neck in a circle while waiting for the metal to heat again.

"I need to get back to work, Ella."

"I know; I just wanted to see you again before Hayden came."

He drew me in, my body pressed flush against his. Our breath mingled in the tight space. "Can I kiss you?" he asked tenderly.

"Of course."

He kissed me like he wanted to imprint it into his memory; embedding the taste of us on his lips and mine. Soft and searching, but hungry, holding back an intensity that threatened to swallow me whole. Too soon it was gone as he pulled away again. I wasn't sure I could kiss him long enough to have my fill. *Was that even possible?*

"Hayden's probably waiting." He nodded toward the market, but refused to take his eyes off mine.

"Until next week, then. I'll miss you."

Asher's lips captured mine again. And then again. When he finally let me go, we were both smiling, both wanting another taste, our mouths slowly moving toward one another again when his father called his name.

I blinked. Hayden... he was probably waiting for me. And worried.

Asher pulled my hand to his lips and kissed the back of it. It was such a small motion, and the back of my hand had been kissed more times than I could count, but this was different. It was reverent and there was a promise carried from his lips to my flesh.

"I count the days, sweet Ella," he replied.

I slipped a note into his pocket, hoping it would explain everything well enough and calm his fears about Trevor. As I turned to walk away, he stuffed his hands into his pockets and watched until I was out of sight. I would count the hours until I could see him, feel his hand in mine, his lips on mine.

Walking back to market, Trevor's note rubbed against my foot. I had to hear him out. I knew he wouldn't leave me alone until I did, but still I was afraid. If he was playing some sort of game, it could cost me everything with Asher. If anyone happened to see us, it would break his trust. And once Asher's trust was broken, there was no getting it back.

My greatest fear?

If Trevor knew who I was, everyone I loved was already in trouble.

ASHER

We had so much work to do, but I needed a minute before I got back to it. I watched her until she was out of sight and then walked back into the forge, but I took out her note, hoping Father wouldn't be angry about it.

220

Handsome Asher,

By now you've heard that our family was invited to a royal ball. It was everything I expected: boring, filled with judgmental people, and worst of all, you weren't there to dance with me. Please don't be upset that I danced. It wasn't something I wanted to do, but Jewel would have had my hide if I'd have declined. She was nervous enough without me adding to her stress, so I danced. But it was stiff and awful because you weren't my partner.

When we danced at May Day, you took my breath away. You showed me how to let loose and have fun. You brought back my smile.

Just like cakes, I hope we have a thousand more dances in our lifetimes together. I just hope you know that you are the only one I ever want to dance with again, and that I'm glad this night is over. I'm looking at the stars. I stared at them the whole ride home, thinking of you.

You might not have been at the ball, but you were in my every thought.

Yours,
Ella

Thank God she had a bad time, as awful as that sounds. I blew out a relieved breath, folded her words, so elegantly written, and went back to work.

CHAPTER TWENTY-SIX

ELLA

When Hayden arrived at the market to pick me up, he was unusually quiet. We silently broke down our booth, loaded the wagon, and left for home. Along the road, the only words he spoke were, "It's about to rain." And he was right. A few minutes later, the sky turned a sickly green.

Thunder crashed overhead, spooking Brutus. The clouds opened up and rain fell in heavy sheets, stinging our skin and eyes. The horse bolted toward home as fast as he could run, spurred on by fear. The road's corners were the worst part, the wagon's wheels straining against the speed and mud.

Hayden drove straight into the barn and jumped down to unhitch Brutus. Lightning split the sky around us, flashing through the slats of wood. He eased the horse into his stall and refilled his bucket of oats. When I held out the pouch of coin for Uncle Hayden, he took it without meeting my eyes.

"Is something wrong?"

"Yes," he said. "Nathaniel and I spoke on my way to town. Asher told him that the Galderian boy visited the booth today. Prince Trevor's going to get us killed!"

"He just bought broccoli," I said lamely. The easy lie had me twisting my hand into my skirts, and I wondered if the smell of my fear and lies swirled through the air.

"Is that all?" Hayden asked, his eyes flashing. "Because the King will not hesitate to chop my head off if you're lying to me. And frankly, you owe me the truth. You owe it to this family, because we are now *your* family, Ella."

"You're right," I choked. "You're absolutely right. I was trying to protect you." I took a breath and continued, "He wants to meet me tonight."

"When and where?" Hayden said, his brows drawing together as a dark expression tightened his face.

"The tree where I met Piers and... Asher. At midnight."

He raked his hands through his wet, stringy hair and draped his forearms across the nearest stall door as he leaned on it. "You'll go." It was more a question than a statement.

"I don't think I have a choice. At this point, he's determined to speak with me, and he's not going to leave me alone until he does. I have no idea what he wants, but if he shows up here or keeps hovering around me while I'm in town, the King will certainly catch wind of it."

"You can take a horse. Brutus will mind you. Just be careful."

224

"I'd rather walk. If it's still storming, I won't be able to control him, and I'm pretty sure he can sense my fear."

"You shouldn't be afraid of him. He'll listen if you're firm," he said. "But walk if you want to. It might help clear your mind. I'll be honest with you, Ella – I'm worried. I don't know what he wants with you." His face softened as he said, "I know you're exhausted. You had little sleep last night, and you won't get much tonight. If I let you to sleep in tomorrow, you'll have to pretend to be sick. Understand?"

That wouldn't be hard since I already felt sick to my stomach. "I can do that."

He stood up straight. "I expect you to tell me everything," he said seriously.

"I will. I'm trying to protect you all, Hayden."

Rain dripped off our clothing, forming puddles at our feet. "We should get inside," he finally said. "Will you be able to stay awake and slip out without waking Matthew and Millie?"

"It would be easier if I stayed downstairs. I can tell them I'm feeling sick and need to stay near the fire."

Hayden nodded gravely. "That'll work. One more thing," he started, reaching into his boot and removing a folded iron knife. "Carry this tonight," he said. "Just in case."

I swallowed, taking the blade from him. Could I really use it if I needed to? It was one thing to use practice swords and play around, but quite another to use a weapon on a human being. Even though Trevor seemed strange when I first met him, he'd always been nice.

"I don't think he would hurt me."

"You never know a man's intentions until he reveals them," Hayden said stoically. "Now, let's get inside and change into something dry before we catch our deaths."

Inside, Millie and Matthew were already upstairs and Jewel was fluttering around the kitchen. "Oh, my. You're dripping wet!" she exclaimed when we stepped inside. I toed off my shoes, careful to grab the note I'd tucked inside before anyone noticed. Jewel slipped a blanket around my shoulders and told me to sit by the fire. I flicked the paper into the flame when she wasn't looking. The flames gobbled it up, erasing all traces of the secret meeting.

Once I was dry enough to go upstairs without leaving a trail of water droplets, I quickly changed clothes. Millie and Matthew were talking to each other in hushed tones, but quieted when they heard the second step from the top creak under my foot. I gathered the only dry overdress and chemise I had left and folded them in my arms.

"You look awful," Millie said snidely.

Well so do you, but at least I have an excuse...

"I think I'm sick," I answered.

"You're pale, and your hair is a stringy mess," she continued, sitting up in bed to get a better look at me.

"Why are you two going to sleep so early?" I asked.

"*Some* of us had to work our fingers to the bone today. Since we got so little sleep last night, we're tired," she explained sourly.

Matthew just smiled and shrugged. "*I* was tired. *She's* just boring," he laughed, hooking a thumb in Millie's direction.

"I'm freezing," I told them. "I'm going to sit by the fire to warm up. I might just sleep downstairs tonight."

"Suit yourself," Millie said, sinking back into her bed.

Ugh. I hated her when she was like this. Which was almost always, at this point.

"I hope you feel better by morning," Matthew said, fighting back a yawn.

Hayden and Jewel were in their bedroom when I got back downstairs, so I told them through the door that I needed to change into dry clothes.

"We'll give you a moment. There's some warm soup over the hearth if you're hungry. It'll warm you right up," Jewel answered.

Soup never sounded so good. I dressed quickly and filled a bowl, settling by the fire to sip it. I really was cold all the way to my bones. Even the hot broth couldn't warm me. Neither could the flickering flames. I threw another log on and hugged my knees to my chest. I had a few hours before I needed to slip away.

I tried to stay awake, but every minute in front of the warmth made it harder and harder to keep my eyes open.

Uncle Hayden cracked the door to their room right as I nodded off, and my head jerked up at the sound. He covered his lips with a finger and motioned toward the front door. It was time.

I grabbed my cloak and quickly laced my boots, easing the door open just enough to squeeze through. Any farther, and the hinges would have squealed. I was glad to see the rain had stopped, and for a moment I considered taking Brutus, but he made me uneasy. I couldn't risk his whinnies waking my cousins, and I didn't have enough time to saddle him anyway.

I set off down the path, walking in the grass, careful to avoid what thick mud I could see. My heart beat faster with each step closer to the meeting spot. All too soon, the silhouette of the oak loomed in the distance. I crossed the road and made my way through the field, my clothes dampening with each step through the hay. A dark figure moved beneath the tree.

"Ella?" he called out apprehensively.

Of course it's me! Who else did he tell to meet him here at midnight? "It's me," I answered, the heft of the knife in the pocket of my dress lending me confidence.

He stood in front of the tree trunk with his hands folded behind his back. "Thank you for meeting me," he said formally.

"You're welcome, but I've been working all day and I'm tired, so can we skip the pleasantries? What was so urgent that I had to meet you in the middle of the night?"

"My father asked me to speak with you. We know who you are, Princess Carina."

I'd expected as much, but hearing it from his lips took my breath away. I couldn't speak. Couldn't move.

With his hands outstretched like he was trying to comfort a scared animal, he approached slowly. "It's not what you think, and you don't have to say anything. Just please hear me out."

My feet tingled with the need to turn and run. Trevor was tall, but was he as fit as me? I was pretty sure I could outrun him, but there was no escaping the strong arm of Galder if they chose to flex their muscles.

"We don't mean you or your family any harm, but there are some things we think you might want to know; a situation that should be brought to your attention," he said, shifting his weight. He shook his head. "I don't even know how to say this."

"Just say it," I growled. "What should I know?"

"Tierney has taken control of Aelawyn. Stefan is about to give *your* kingdom to one of his sons."

"And?"

"And?" he snarled. "Don't you care about your people?"

"Tierney cut its way through Aelawyn three years ago. My Kingdom died that day." *Along with my people*, I didn't add.

228

"But it didn't," he growled, raking his hands through his pale hair. "Aelawyn rebuilt itself. Your people didn't let the attack from three years ago ruin the Kingdom. They appointed a new ruler, a fair one, and rebuilt what Tierney tore apart. He kept the kingdom alive, and it had just begun to thrive again when Tierney caught word of it and had him and every member of his court slaughtered while they slept."

The words hit me like a hammer to the chest. My people had rebuilt? They didn't give up? How could I not have heard? Questions swirled through my mind, but Trevor wasn't finished.

"Stefan had cause to attack your father; he truly did. But he had no right to slaughter these men. It has become apparent that he wants the Kingdom of Aelawyn for himself. He wants your land and all the gold in it, and Carden is going to march into your Kingdom, into your castle, and take the throne for himself."

I pressed a clenched hand to my chest. "What can I do about it?"

"Three years ago, King Stefan took everything from you. He tore your Kingdom to shreds, and butchered your family and hundreds of innocent people—women, children. Now I ask you this: are you going to stay here and let them be hurt all over again?" When he began to pace, I paced with him.

Was it true that Aelawyn had healed itself? Were the people happy again? True, Stefan had no right to march in and remove their leader elect, but why was Galder so intent on helping me?

"Why do you care?" I asked harshly. "Did your father tell you I was betrothed to him? I was only fourteen, Trevor."

He stopped in his tracks, jaw ticking. "You weren't betrothed to *him*. You were betrothed to me."

The air left my lungs in a whoosh. "What?"

"Your mother arranged it. When my grandfather died, Father ascended the throne; however, *I* was the Yurak you were supposed to marry. My name is Yurak Trevor."

That couldn't be possible! My mother was terrified of my father. She would *never* cross him. For as far back as I could remember, she'd stood by his side, cowering and catering to his every whim—even when it came to her children. This made no sense.

"Why would my mother go to the trouble to arrange something like this behind my father's back? If he ever found out she had anything to do with it, he would have removed her head himself."

"That's why it was so secretive and fast. Did you know your mother was from Galder?"

At my shocked expression, Trevor continued.

"Your mother and my father grew up together. Back then, my father loved your mother very much. He was going to ask for her hand, but when your father, Berius arrived on a visit, he took one look at your mother and made her parents an offer they couldn't refuse. The sum of money was astounding, even to Galderian royalty. Your parents were married so quickly there was nothing she or my father could do to stop it, and my father has regretted losing her every moment since."

"But your father was married!" I protested, still not believing what I was hearing, even though I could tell it was hard for him to talk about.

"Yes, eventually he married. And while he did love my mother, that doesn't mean he stopped loving yours."

I struggled to come to terms with this newfound knowledge. My mother must have loved Yurak very much to entrust him with something of this magnitude, which meant she must have loved me, too. All my life, I never knew she cared at all. Always cold. Always stoic... yet she'd been planning and plotting, in spite of the punishment she would face if her plan was discovered.

Trevor continued, "Your mother wrote to Yurak when she first learned of your father's plans to offer your hand in marriage, and he used your father's greed and methods against him. My father wrote to him and offered a sum of money he knew Berius couldn't refuse. My father, in all his correspondences, simply did not specify *which* Yurak you would be marrying, and your father never asked."

My head swam with all the plots and thoughts that had to go into crafting a plan so devious. Even while at court back in my former life, I was never a part of intrigues such as this.

"There's another reason we came to you." He paused for a moment, weighing his words, and I felt the gravity of the situation. "We found secret maps and documents that caused us to believe you were in danger. First, Stefan will forcefully take Aelawyn. Then he wants Galder. He plans to encircle and cut our Kingdoms off from all the others. We would suffocate without trade. It would slowly kill us."

I knew that with the addition of Galder, Stefan would control all of the south...including its many bountiful and wealthy resources.

"Carina, Aelawyn needs you," Trevor implored.

Tears welled in my eyes. I wanted to help – truly, I did – but what could I possibly do?

"I'm not of age yet, Trevor. Even if I wanted to help, I'm not old enough. Besides that, I'm my father's daughter," I said disgustedly. "He was a tyrant in the truest sense of the word, and the people will assume that I am the same."

I paused a moment, shuffling through memories of the castle and its capabilities. Comprehension dawned on me as I said, "Aelawyn's people have no way to defend themselves, do they?"

His features were softened by the moonlight at the same time they sharpened in the shadows. "There is no army," he confirmed sadly. "A few peasants with pitchforks willing to die to protect their families and homes, but nothing that could stand up to Tierney's forces." He was quiet for a second, his hands on his hips. "You are not your father, Carina. From what I've seen, you are kind and fair. You would make sure Aelawyn and her people – her land – prospers. I think the people would accept you as their Queen. And just so we are perfectly clear, if you decide to help us and your people, *I* would stand behind you. As would my father and the army of Galder."

"What?" My mouth gaped at the vow.

"If you choose to reclaim your throne, all of Galder will stand behind you. We will fight and die to defend you and your land."

It was a lot to take in, and I struggled to connect the dots. "How did you find me?" I asked suspiciously.

"Honestly, we weren't expecting to. Father knew Stefan had been sending his men close to our border, looking for something, so we decided to pay him a visit to see if we could figure out what he was doing. That was when Father saw you at the blacksmith's shop. You look so much like your mother, he knew it was you." He paused a moment, looking at the ground before meeting my eyes. "We looked for you after the castle raid, Carina, but you'd already disappeared. We assumed you were dead."

"Stefan is just like my father," I said flatly.

Trevor nodded. "Yes; ruthless and rotten to the core. Believe me when I tell you that he didn't hide you away for your protection. The Kingdom of Galder would have taken you in as one of our own in a heartbeat. The only reason he kept you hidden was in case he needed to use you to extort anything from us."

232

In case he decided I was worth something he wanted...

Trevor pursed his lips. "We can take you to Aelawyn. You can see the Kingdom with your own eyes and make a decision to stand against Tierney or not. If you choose not to, we'll take you somewhere safe."

"What does this mean for my family?"

He sighed, and I knew what he was going to say before he said it. "They would need to leave Tierney. Stefan would use them as leverage against you."

I pressed my eyes tightly closed. *Asher and Nathaniel.* They were in danger, too. "What if I decide to stay where I am? If I decide not to fight?"

"Then we'll respect your wishes and stand down."

"You'll just go back home? Just like that?" I scoffed.

"We would gladly fight for Aelawyn, knowing you would keep the trade routes through your lands open. But if you choose not to fight, we won't be able to stand back and let Stefan suffocate us. War is coming either way, Carina. Your decision will determine where it's fought."

What if Trevor was right? What if my country could thrive again? If Galder stood behind me, and if my people would have me, what if I could restore the Kingdom to its former glory? What if I could make it one of the best in the land?

"I need to talk with my family before I make any decisions," I finally said. "I won't risk their safety until I hear what they have to say first."

He inclined his head. "That's more than fair. I'm sure my father will agree to meet with them if you asked."

I pointed to a low-hanging tree limb, adding, "I'll tie a ribbon around this limb if I decide to go with you and see the kingdom for myself."

Trevor took my hand and kissed it quickly. "May I see you home?" he asked expectantly.

I looked over my shoulder and stared into the darkness in the direction of home, where I knew Hayden and Jewel were lying awake, wondering what was happening. "No," I answered kindly. "I'll be fine on my own."

"Then be careful. And a word of warning: do *not* trust Piers. Never forget that he is Stefan's right hand, paid to do his bidding. Even if he's been kind to you, he would not hesitate to lock you in the dungeon if he had the slightest inkling you knew anything I just told you."

He was right. Piers was Stefan's closest confidant, able to communicate through glances and gestures, and he was loyal to his king. I'd asked him to keep Hayden and his family safe, but deep down I knew that if it came down to choosing between friend or loyalty, Piers would stay loyal.

I just hoped Hayden would understand that he couldn't breathe a word of this to Piers. But what would happen if he did, in order to protect his family? What if he ran to Piers and told him everything, and had me dragged away?

He wouldn't do that.

He wouldn't. But Millie would.

"This is insane!" I exploded. "I almost wish you hadn't found me."

"Fate found you," Trevor gently corrected. "I wish you weren't in this situation. I wish you could have all you want in this life. After living with your father, you more than earned the chance to be happy."

"I was happy," I said.

"You're thinking about the smith?"

"I am."

Trevor pursed his lips together thoughtfully. The tone of my voice told him I'd already made my decision. "Will he understand?"

"I hope so," I answered.

TREVOR

Seeing tears glisten in Carina's — or Ella's, as I thought of her now — eyes was something I never wanted to witness again. Sharper and deadlier than any weapon, they gutted me. Everything I told her, broken apart, would be hard to accept, but altogether, it overwhelmed her. It overwhelmed me. I could tell she'd made her mind up, but wouldn't say the words until she spoke with her adoptive family.

I admired her even more for that.

Like an apparition in the night, she turned from me and disappeared through the tall hay. My feet longed to walk alongside her, to protect and keep her from harm. But my presence, if noticed, could damn her.

I'd pledged my life and the lives of my soldiers to her. Would she understand that I would do anything to right the wrongs Stefan and her father brought down upon her house, her family, and her life?

Father would wage war in the memory of her mother.

I would wage war for Ella.

Father was still awake when I slipped into his chamber, using the passageway behind the walls. "Did you speak with her?" he whispered.

"I did."

"And?"

235

I blew out a breath. I couldn't tell him she was coming with us. "She needs time."

"I'm not sure we have any to give her," he replied quietly.

"Father, I think you should send word to the Earl Marshal. Our soldiers need to leave for Aelawyn as soon as possible. If she decides she doesn't want this, we can send them home; but if she decides she does and we don't dispatch them now, they won't make it there in time to stop Carden."

He took out a piece of parchment, his ink, and a quill and began writing. He sealed the letter with crimson wax, sealing it with the stamp of Galder. Then, I found one of our most trusted men and sent him out with the order that night.

CHAPTER TWENTY-SEVEN

ELLA

The people of Aelawyn couldn't win a war against an army like Tierney's, but the fight was coming to their doorsteps, regardless. *If Galder fought with us, we could win.*

Hayden was sitting by the fire when I squeezed through the door. He held out a mug of something hot. "Tell me it was simple infatuation," he whispered hopefully, handing the mug to me.

Staring into the flames, I shook my head. "I wish I could, Uncle. I wish it was something simple like that. But no matter what I tell you and what we decide, you cannot breathe a word of this to Piers."

Confusion wrinkled his brow. "I give you my word."

"Did you know that over the past three years, Aelawyn rebuilt itself?"

Slowly shaking his head, he answered truthfully. "I didn't."

"Trevor told me they had. They even elected a ruler, but then Stefan had him and his entire court executed." I took a sip of the steaming drink, trying to contain my swirling thoughts. "He's going to put Carden on the throne."

Hayden gasped, "How can we be sure? How can we trust what the Galderians say? What if they're trying to start a war by putting you right in the middle of it?"

I couldn't articulate it, but for some reason I believed Trevor. Even if I had no proof other than the feeling in my gut. "They want me to see it for myself."

He kept his voice low. "They want you to take back the throne?"

"They do."

"What about you? What do *you* want?" he asked, taking a sip of his warm drink.

I paused. "If I leave, you'll be in danger. If I'm not at market, or if Piers shows up unexpectedly and I'm not here…"

"Forget about Piers for a moment, and forget about us. What if it's true? What then? How will you help them, Ella? Tierney's army would decimate—"

"Trevor said the Galderian army would fight and defend Aelawyn."

"My God." That was all he could say.

"And if it's a trap?" he asked.

"Then I'm a fool. But I need to see it, Hayden. I don't know why, but I need to go with them. I want to see my home, and if there's any way I can help, then I have to."

"I'll need to talk it over with Jewel. We either need to hide your absence and hope for the best, or go with you.

And Galder… well, they'll have to move their forces soon if they genuinely want to beat Tierney to the gate. Stefan will want to seat Carden quickly."

I knew what had to be done. "I have to do this, Hayden. If I don't try to help my people, Tierney will keep attacking. They'll slaughter anyone and anything in their path until nothing remains." I'd seen it with my own eyes; the might of their army, the stealth and deadly skill of their knights. "I couldn't help them before. I couldn't fight. But I can now."

He pinched the bridge of his nose. "You're only seventeen," he argued gently.

"I know." That fact alone would make it more difficult for the people of Aelawyn to accept me as their leader.

Thick tension filled the room before he finally spoke. "I believe them."

"The Galderians?"

"Yes. I've heard some disturbing rumors about Stefan, and I believe his greed has gotten out of hand. Piers let it slip at the ball that the King sent an envoy to Paruth to see if the lands were free of plague. If so, he means to take it while the people are still weakened. It would give him a foothold in the north. If he took Aelawyn, he'd have the largest Kingdom that ever existed. If he took Galder, he'd rule all of the southern lands." Hayden shook his head. "Now it makes sense."

"I need to let them know tomorrow."

His mouth clamped together and I heard the sound of his gritting teeth in the quiet space. "I'll wake Jewel and talk to her now, but I want you to know that no matter what *we* decide, you will always be part of this family. And we'll stand behind your decision."

"If you don't come," my throat tightened, "you'll be in danger."

"We have to consider what's best for us, Ella. Sometimes paths converge, and sometimes they diverge again. Either way, we won't betray you." With that vow, he stood up, his back popping at the base. "I'll let you know in the morning."

"I want to tell Asher and Nathaniel too, Uncle. Trevor said that anyone I loved could be used against me."

Hayden stiffened. "Tomorrow." He walked slowly toward his room, leaving me by the fire. My tea was now cold.

They spoke in urgent, hushed tones, and Jewel cried as they discussed whether or not to leave everything they'd ever known behind. It wasn't a decision anyone could make lightly. Their home. Their livelihood. Friends. Neighbors. The village and Kingdom where they'd grown up and raised their children. But the risk of them staying turned my stomach.

What if Stefan learned I left and that they hid it from him? Or what if they decided to protect themselves and go to Piers in the morning? What if they left their home and came with me to Aelawyn, and then Galder didn't follow through on their promise to fight alongside me? What if Galder's army wasn't enough?

When the sun peeked over the hills, just before Millie and Matthew would be waking, Hayden and Jewel finally emerged from their room. Jewel's hands shook as she brought a cloth to her eyes. Her face was swollen and the whites of her eyes were bloodshot.

Before they had a chance to speak, I did. "I'm sorry I put you in this position," I said wretchedly.

"You didn't," Jewel said vehemently. "*They* did." She stabbed an angry finger in the general direction of the castle. "You were only a child."

She hugged me tight and wouldn't let go, and in that moment, I realized she was saying goodbye. "You aren't coming with me."

"Not immediately," Hayden answered. "There are a few things we have to sort out first, but we won't tell anyone you've left. We'll hurry, and when we finish what we need to, we will join you, Ella."

"This is dangerous."

"Staying or leaving?" Hayden said on a thin chuckle. He had a point. "And what you're doing isn't without risk, either. What if Galder is lying, Ella? What if you're walking into a trap?" I unwrapped my arms from Jewel, but she clasped my hand, squeezing it tight.

Sometimes people didn't know they were captive until they tasted freedom, and mine was so close I could almost taste it. My mind was made up.

"I need to leave word for Trevor, and I still need to tell Asher."

"Go ahead and clean yourself up, and then I'll take you in the wagon," Hayden said gently. "But when you get home, you need to rest."

"You're pale," Jewel agreed, softly brushing errant strands of hair from my face. I felt thin as parchment; like a gust of wind could blow me away. But I had to remember that even the thinnest parchment could carry heavy things; written in ink and blood and the strongest of messages.

I needed to see my home, my Kingdom, my people. I needed to do more to help them this time. They needed a leader. Royalty. Someone the other kingdoms would respect and speak with regarding trade and alliances.

I loved the life I'd made with the Farmers. Honestly, when I walked out of my castle, over the bodies of the dead and rode out of Aelawyn, I never thought I'd go back. But now, there was no changing my mind. Just like there was no changing Hayden and Jewel's. They'd spent the night tearing themselves to shreds making their decision, and I knew they would honor it.

It was time to face Asher and tell him who I really was and what I needed to do, and then hope and pray he wouldn't hate me. Could I dream that he would come with me to Aelawyn?

"I'll wash up as well as I can, and then I'll be ready."

Hayden nodded. "I'll meet you at the barn."

"Ella?" Jewel said. Her smile crumbled slowly in a series of twitches at the side of her mouth. "Here's a red ribbon."

The color of my Kingdom.

I took it from her hand and ran my thumb over the scarlet silk. Trevor would see it and know my answer: *Take me there.*

Hayden was waiting outside, the horse already pulling the wagon when I stepped outside. Matthew's face smashed against the glass of the upstairs window next to Millie's, her nose wrinkled. No doubt she would scream at the injustice of me going without her, of having to work while I traipsed off to town.

"Where are they going?" she screeched, her muffled voice still audible through the glass.

And so it begins.

"Millie, calm down. Ella is sick and your father is taking her to the church hospital."

"She isn't *that* sick," she protested snidely. "I saw her last night!" Millie argued, her voice shrill.

"Well she got worse through the night. She needs help, Millie, and we have the means to see that she gets it."

Millie would be glad when I left, and if Hayden and Jewel were serious about the whole family joining me in Aelawyn, she'd hate me even more for uprooting her.

When she finally learned who I was, she was going to come unhinged.

CHAPTER TWENTY-EIGHT

ELLA

When we made it to the tree, Hayden stopped long enough for me to run across the field. I tied the ribbon around the base of the lowest branch where it would easily be seen and then ran back to the wagon. Hayden pulled me up into the seat.

"Thanks," I said gratefully. He flashed a wan smile and urged the horse forward, toward the village and Asher.

How could I possibly explain myself?

Would he understand why I had to lie to him?

Just then, the familiar *bang, bang, bang* of twin hammers rang out in the morning.

"I'll talk to Nathaniel, Ella." That being said, Hayden lashed Brutus to the post and pulled a carrot from his pocket. The horse seemed happy to have a snack, and Hayden patted his head affectionately and told him we would be back soon.

I took a deep breath. It would take every ounce of strength I had to look Asher in the eye and tell him the truth.

One hammer stopped, and Nathaniel wiped his hands on a towel and came out of the shop to meet us. "Hayden! What an unexpected treat to see you out and about this morning."

"Do you have a few minutes to talk? Ella needs to speak with Asher, as well."

The tone of Hayden's voice set the other two men on alert, and in a flash, Asher pulled his gloves off and jogged to me. "Are you sick?" he asked hurriedly. "You're very pale." His hand ghosted over my cheek.

"Is there somewhere we can talk privately?" I asked in a shaky voice. Asher glanced to his father, who nodded his head once.

"I know somewhere we can go," he said, grabbing my hand and leading me away from the shop and village. We walked past rows of homes and into the woods along a wide, well-trodden trail, where birds sang in the treetops all around us. Asher looked around to be sure we were alone and then pulled me into a quick hug. "What's wrong?" he asked apprehensively.

My fingers quivered as I fidgeted with the hem of my sleeve. "I have to tell you something, Asher. This isn't easy for me to say, but you have to swear, no matter how you feel about me afterward, never to repeat what I say."

His gaze never faltered, his sapphire eyes locking onto mine as he agreed. "I swear it."

I steeled my shoulders. "I'm not really from Paruth, and Hayden and Jewel are not my kin. Three years ago, Tierney

246

attacked the Kingdom of Aelawyn and killed the King and Queen."

He blinked rapidly. "I remember. Aelawyn kept attacking the trade routes. But what does that have to do with you? Are you really from Aelawyn?"

My stomach twisted in knots, I answered, "I'm the only surviving member of the Aelawyn royal family. I'm a Princess."

He sucked in a breath. "You're the Princess of Aelawyn?"

"Tierney's knights brought me here as a sort of hostage, and King Stefan decided to hide me with the Farmers."

"As punishment?"

"No; at the time, King Stefan said it was to keep me safe from Galder. You see, I was betrothed to Yurak of Galder."

"Galder?" he whispered. "Is *that* why they're here?" I watched his features darken, disgust curling his lip.

"They're here because their kingdom is in danger, and they happened to find me by accident."

"What happened?" he asked.

I took a deep breath and told him exactly what Trevor told me. When I finished, he shook his head and pinched his lip, deep in thought.

"There's something else I need to tell you, Asher. I'm going home, back to Aelawyn. I have to at least *try* to help my people. And even though I didn't mean to, I've put you and your father in danger just because of your relationship with me. If you stay here and they find out I'm gone, they could use you against me." Saying the words out loud filled me with raw feelings of guilt, and a tear slid down my face with the admission.

"You can't go, Ella," he pleaded, desperate.

"I have to." My voice broke.

He watched another tear slide down my cheek before softly asking, "Ella...is that even your real name?"

247

Stung, although I knew I had no right to be, I answered, "My given name is Ella Carina. Growing up, everyone called me Carina. My older sister, Ivy insisted on it. Asher, parts my story are true. My parents *were* killed, and Ivy... She's dead, but not by the hand of a Tierney knight. She hung herself once the attack began."

She was a coward, I thought bitterly. *I've been a coward, too. Paralyzed by fear, hiding and worrying and waiting for the next shoe to drop, manipulated by those in power. But not anymore.*

He closed his eyes tightly.

"I'm afraid for you," I said, my voice cracking. "I want you to come with me. That's the only way I can protect you and your father."

"How can *you* protect us? Aelawyn doesn't have an army."

"The Galderians have vowed to fight with us. Trevor said he was going to send for their army."

"Of course he did," he said, his eyes darkening. "You were promised to his father once. They probably still want you to make good on the betrothal, right?"

"Actually, I was promised to Trevor. His full name is *Yurak* Trevor..."

Asher let out a curse.

"It's not what you think—"

"I don't know *what* to think, Ella! I just can't believe... I don't know what my father will decide. Are the Farmers leaving with you?"

I shook my head. "They said they'll come, but not right away. Hayden wants to settle a few things first."

"And then what? Do they wait around until the King kills them all? Are you okay with him slaughtering the family who took you in?"

"Of course not!" I said, indignant. "I want them to come with me now, but Hayden and Jewel need a few extra days

248

to get things straightened out. What I *can't* do is wait for Stefan to figure out that the Galderians are talking to me about what happened. He'll throw all of us in the dungeons, where we'll all rot and die; that is, if they don't charge us all with treason and behead us first. Or worse, he'll put Carden on the throne and expand Tierney's land. Think of how that will inflate his ego and make his Kingdom look!" I shook my head, disgusted. "Galder isn't helping me because of the betrothal, Asher. They don't want to be cut completely off by Stefan if he takes control of Aelawyn."

He shook his head, a bitter laugh escaping him. "I can't believe I fell for someone *else* I can't have," he muttered, turning away from me.

I grabbed his arm. "Asher, you haven't lost me! I want you to come with me." The muscle in his jaw ticked. He was overwhelmed. I knew it, because so was I. "You're angry," I said.

"I'm hurt," he corrected gently. "I need time to digest all this." He sighed. "I need to get back and see what my father thinks."

"Please believe me when I say I couldn't tell you, Asher. I promised the King, his men, and my family I wouldn't tell a soul. I hope you can understand."

He nodded, but I knew my actions hurt him worse than Isabel ever did. I wish he could see that she and I were different. I was finally owning up to my past and telling him now, even knowing the disappointment I would face. I didn't just disappear like she did. I wouldn't do that to him.

Back at the forge, Nathaniel and Hayden were in the middle of a heated debate in the back of the shop, although they stilled when they saw us walking toward them. Nathaniel glared at both me and Hayden, then looked at his son.

"We'll go," he answered bitterly. "But we're going to finish the sword order first. We've been paid half the sum already, and will need the other half if we're to start over again, so we have to hurry. We'll take what tools we can without being too conspicuous."

Asher pursed his lips. "Father, you've worked so hard to build all of this."

"And we can build it again, but not if we're taken to the chopping block. Now, Hayden, Ella, if you'll excuse us, we need to get this order finished as quickly as possible. Please keep us informed."

The formality of his voice, combined with the almost palpable anger roiling beneath the calm facade, meant both smiths were furious with me. I was equally furious. I was angry that I had been put in this situation at all. The whole situation – every part of it – was unfair, and that injustice had endangered my loved ones.

As we rode home, I apologized to Hayden again. "I'm so sorry I've put you in danger."

"You didn't do anything, Ella. You're just a pawn in all of this. I'm sick to death of being pushed around, of having to look over my shoulder and yours all the time. Maybe this is for the best."

I *felt* like a pawn. Exposed, vulnerable, knowing an attack was coming, but not when or from what direction.

"What you need to realize before you do anything else, or make any more decisions, Ella, is that deep down, you're *not* a pawn. You were born a princess, but now, you will be Queen—if not in title, then in birthright, and your actions are your own. You have no king to answer to, and your only loyalty should lie with the people you govern, not with petty rulers from other kingdoms who couldn't hold a candle to you if they tried. And don't worry about overcoming your

Father's legacy. Worry about convincing the people that you will make your *own* future with them by your side, not under your thumb. That's how you'll win the hearts of the people. Show them yours."

He was right. It was time I put away childish things like young love and hurt feelings, and began acting like a queen.

ASHER

I pounded the steel into shape, my teeth gritting against the strain and heat. *She was a princess?* She lied to me all this time! Did that make her just as bad as Isabel? She lied, too; but in the end, Isabel didn't come to me in tears, worried about my safety. Shoving the steel back into the fire, I braced my hands against a work table.

"She couldn't tell you, Asher," my father finally said.

I knew it. I just didn't like it.

If she'd slipped and told me, and I happened to mention it to someone else, her family would have been killed. It still hurt that in the end, she didn't trust me enough to share her secret. I wondered how long it would have taken her before she realized I would never hurt her, never betray her like that. Would she have broken down and told me after I asked for her hand?

Father resumed his hammering, and after pausing a moment more, I resumed mine. We had work to get finished. Because if Ella was leaving, so was I.

Trevor wanted her. He was charging in on his white horse to rescue her and acting like he only wanted what was best for her, but I could see right through it. And I wasn't going to stand back and let some sniveling Galderian weasel try to worm his way into her heart. I just had to figure out how to show her I was better for her than he was.

With every strike, I pictured Trevor's face under my hammer, when it occurred to me that I was forging the very weapon he might try to use against me.

I would fight for Ella. He just didn't know it yet.

"Does she know you want to go?"

"She knows we're going," I mumbled.

"That's not what I asked, Asher. Does she know we're going because you want to, because you want *her*, not just to save your skin and mine?" Father finally asked.

I shook my head.

"Then after you finish that blade, you'd better get your arse down there and tell her," he chastised. "If you lose her, you'll regret it for the rest of your life. That girl isn't Isabel, son. She loves you. She loves you when you make her steel roses and when you teach her to strike with a wooden sword, and she loves you when you're harsh and judgmental. And if *you* love her, you'll have to forgive her. Because she was only doing what she thought would keep you safe."

My throat was tight when I knocked on her door. Hayden answered, his voice incredulous when he asked, "Asher?"

"I'm sorry to come so late," I said sheepishly. "Can I talk to Ella for just a moment?"

He gave me a tight smile and called for her. She came down the stairs a moment later, her feet slowing as she came near the landing and saw me. Instead of a smile, she wore a frown. "Asher?"

"He needs to speak with you outside."

She nodded, laced her boots, and together we walked to the barn. Crossing her arms, she waited for me to speak.

"I'm sorry I acted the way I did. I was surprised and hurt, and that hurt bled into anger. I took it out on you, and I was wrong."

"I understand, but you hurt me, too."

I swallowed thickly. "I know, and I'm sorry. I wanted you to know that I *want* to go with you. I want to be with you. I don't particularly want to leave our home, but if it keeps you safe, Ella, I'll follow you to the ends of the earth. None of this changes how I feel about you, and I hope you still feel the same way about me."

Her lips parted and she dropped her arms to her side, exhausted. "Of course I do." She stepped closer, wrapped her arms around me, and I held her tight.

"Sorry if I woke everyone."

"It's fine. I'm just glad you came."

I headed back towards home feeling ten times better than I had when I got there. She had forgiven me. I still felt tension between us, but nothing like the rift I left between us earlier.

CHAPTER TWENTY-NINE

ELLA

The following day, Hayden went to check the tree for any sign that Trevor had received my answer. The ribbon was gone, and tension settled into the muscles of my shoulders and back. Gone were the days where farming the land was a soul-quenching experience. Now, every time I stepped outside, I expected Piers and his men to come riding down the road to round us up and drag us all away.

For days he checked around the tree, finding only bark and branch—no word from Galder. In the meantime, we worked harder than we ever had to harvest anything and everything we could.

Millie repeatedly questioned the sense of urgency and why her father was selling so much of their crop. "Mind your business," Hayden would snap at her. She became quieter, angrier, and more sullen, and I was worried what she would do when she found out they were leaving Tierney behind, all because of me.

Hayden said the Smiths had finished the sword order and were waiting for the word to leave. "They're ready to pack and head out. Nathaniel's been cleaning out the forge, packing a little each night so no one notices."

It was on a Saturday when we finally received word from Trevor; Hayden found a scrap of paper under the rock. It read: *Go to market as usual tomorrow and then tomorrow night, meet us at midnight at the Urgahney River. Bring everyone with you. They are in grave danger. -T*

With those words, Hayden's plans to stay behind for a few days evaporated. Jewel hadn't even begun to pack.

Everything changed when he came home with the message. Hayden rushed through the gardens with Matthew, Millie, and me following behind, picking herbs and vegetables for market tomorrow as usual, while Jewel began packing up the house in earnest.

"Where's mum?" Matthew asked. I looked at Hayden with a questioning look. Had they told Millie and Matthew what was going on yet? When Hayden's cloudy eyes met mine, he gave a slight shake of his head.

They would figure it out as soon as they went inside and saw their mother rushing around, but maybe that was his plan.

"Pick as much as you can," Hayden instructed. "Lord Windmeyer asked us to sell all we can as quickly as possible." His voice was gruff and left no room for argument, even from Millie. His children could sense that something was wrong. Hayden was rarely cross, and then only when he was angry or worried.

So we plucked all we could and filled twice as many baskets as the previous week. When we were finished and had taken all the fields could offer, he told us to wash for supper and strode quickly into the house.

Matthew and Millie washed first and ran to the house as I slowly took my turn. I expected to hear Millie shrieking once they stepped inside, but nothing came from the house but a rare, eerie silence.

Inside, Jewel was cutting slices of cooked meat. I did a mental count of the animals on the farm, wondering which one they had to slaughter for this meal.

"Come and eat. Something killed a lamb, but I found him when he was still alive and the meat was still fresh," Jewel said cheerfully, not able to meet my eyes. "Couldn't let it go to waste."

I took my portion and sat down at the table. Matthew and Millie were arguing about something and not paying attention when Hayden whispered, "They don't know yet. She packed what she could into the wagon, and she'll smoke the rest of the meat for the trip."

It would take days to reach Aelawyn at a steady pace, but something told me we'd be traveling as fast as we could. The devil was at our backs. Nagging doubts continued to assault my mind, like: Had the Galderian army already been dispatched to Aelawyn? What if we beat the army there, and then had no way to defend the Kingdom against the defending Tierney army? What if we didn't make it there at all? Was this a trap?

A cool sheen of sweat prickled across my forehead when Hayden stood up from the table and started out the door. "Uncle?" I said abruptly.

"Yes?" he barked.

I knew every moment was precious and he didn't want to waste time, but I desperately needed to talk to him. "Can I talk to you outside?"

"Of course," he answered distractedly.

I bolted from my chair and threw the door open, letting it clatter against the house carelessly, clutching my chest, unable to catch my breath. There wasn't enough air.

"Are you alright?" he asked carefully.

Tears pricked my eyes. *No, I was not alright! Nothing was alright. Nothing was ever going to be alright. We weren't going to make it out of this alive.* Something deep down in my soul, a warning, settled into my bones. I was scared. I was scared for the people I loved, and I was scared for myself. I didn't want us to die like the villagers had, like my sister had; just erased from the earth and forgotten.

"What if we don't make it, Hayden? Maybe I should run, just leave by myself, and as soon as I have a head start, you go tell Piers. Tell him that I've been sneaking out and you suspect I've been conspiring with the Galderians. He'll believe you!" I whispered tearfully. "Because you came to him first, he'll believe you, and then you can all stay here and be safe." I paced frantically, hoping the steps would calm my beating heart.

He shook his head. "And what kind of life would we have if we stayed, sweet girl? Working our fingers to the bone for the benefit of someone else?"

I threw my hands in the air, frustrated. "It's what you love! This land...you're part of it, and it's a part of you, Hayden."

"I *do* love it, but I want better, and maybe we can find it somewhere else. It's worth the risk, Ella. We've made our decision, and as a family, we go. I need to gather what we

258

need from the barn, but you should take a minute to... get yourself straightened out."

I stayed outside, letting the last heat from the late evening sun warm my face as he walked toward the barn. Taking deep breaths, I thought about what he said. It had never occurred to me that this might actually be a good change for the Farmers. There was fertile farm land in Aelawyn. I would help him find it. It would be his own, to do with as he pleased. If the Farmers had lived in Aelawyn, and if I'd seen them from my window in the castle as they set their booth up on market day in the cobbled streets below, I would've seen a family built on love. I would have envied the simplicity of their lives, not realizing what a struggle it was to work so hard and receive so little in return.

I felt more confident that Galder would help us. We were leaving tomorrow night, and all our lives would be irrevocably changed. I just had to go to market tomorrow morning like normal, come home, help them pack what I could, and then we had to make it to the river.

Failure wasn't an option.

Because failure meant death.

And I couldn't let them die just because they believed in me.

Hayden's heavy hand on my shoulder woke me before the sun was up. It was Sunday, market day. Tonight, we would slip away and meet the Galderians at the river. I scrambled to get dressed quickly and met him outside. Brutus was already hitched to the wagon and pulling us toward the village before I was ready.

"You have to do everything like you usually do," my uncle instructed. "Smile. Thank people when they buy from you.

Talk to Ann about her pastries. Steal away to see Asher in the afternoon, but know that he's coming to see you first thing this morning."

I wasn't ready to face him. He told me his feelings hadn't changed, but would he still feel that way now that we were really leaving? "I'm probably the last person he wants to see," I replied gloomily.

"He's hurt, but time will mend all of this." Hayden's strong hands held the reins far too tightly than was necessary, and I wondered if he was really sure about this decision, or if he was simply trying to persuade himself that he was.

Everything inside me said I was doing the right thing, but I couldn't help but worry. One misstep could punish my whole family. I couldn't begin to imagine my heartache if someone I loved was hurt or captured by Stefan's men. Would Galder help me free them? Would they still march on Tierney, knowing the bloodbath that would ensue? It was one thing to travel to defend a defenseless kingdom, but quite another to attack a larger force on its own soil.

A chilling thought wormed its way into my head… If Stefan had been watching the Galderians' every move, did he already know about Trevor meeting me, or about the notes we passed? Was Trevor the one who left the note beneath the rock, or were we walking into a trap? I wouldn't put it past Piers to orchestrate such an ambush.

Dwelling on the possibilities was a fruitless exercise, and I vowed to focus on the task at hand. We set up the booth at market just like we did every Sunday morning. The routine had to be the same.

Ann quickly moved to set up next to me. Hayden nodded to Ann before he left, making sure to hand me the small pouch of coin before leaving. "I'll be back before sundown," he promised.

I placed the cloth over the tables and arranged the baskets, storing extra baskets that brimmed with herbs beneath them until they were needed. I hoped I would be able to sell everything we brought today. We'd been fortunate enough to sell out every week prior, but this was nearly double the amount of herbs and vegetables I'd brought just last week. I squeezed my eyes closed for a second, praying that no one noticed. My fingers were freezing.

"Are you cold?" Ann asked with a chuckle, her eyes drawn to the motion. "It's summer. Won't get any hotter than this."

"I've had a summer cold," I answered sheepishly.

Glancing in the direction of the forge, I saw a thin tendril of smoke rising in the distance. Would Asher really come to the booth this morning? If Hayden was the one who arranged it, did that mean Asher wouldn't have come on his own to see me?

Knuckles wrapping on wood startled me from my contemplative mood, and I looked up into the cold, calculating eyes of Piers. "Good morning, Ella," he greeted.

I forced a surprised but pleasant smile, even as my legs trembled under my skirts. "Good morning."

"Are you ill? You look very pale," he commented, his eyes cold and calculating.

"Actually, I've been sick this week, but I'm on the mend. Thank you for asking. Can I help you with some herbs? The thyme and rosemary are beautiful this week. We also have a new variety of pepper."

He studied me, crossing his arms. "What would you suggest I buy?"

"The tomatoes are enormous and the best we've had in years."

"I'll take a few, then. My men are escorting the Galderians out of the city within the hour," he said smoothly, seeming to watch for my reaction.

"That's nice of you," I replied calmly. "This will be a nice snack along the way," I said with a smile, choosing the best tomatoes for him. Piers was only there to make sure I wasn't escaping with them.

"How much?"

I eased them into a small burlap sack and handed it to him. "You've done so much for us. A few tomatoes are the least we can give you in return."

The wrinkles along his forehead disappeared, and he finally relaxed his stance as he accepted the bag. "Thank you."

"Have a lovely day, Piers."

"And you as well." He looked to my left and nodded in greeting. "Asher, good day."

"Good day," Asher replied cordially. Smelling of wood smoke, Asher caught hold of my hand and drew it to his lips for a soft kiss. "Ella."

Piers smiled at the small display of affection. "Thank you again," he said. And with those parting words, he strode away.

Asher pulled me into a hug, but I felt the tension in his back when my hands moved over his muscles. "He was making sure you were here," he whispered.

"I know."

We parted and he tugged at the collar of his shirt, acting shy. "Do you have any garlic?"

"Yes, the first of the season," I chirped.

"Five cloves, please," he grinned, handing me a coin. I collected his garlic, choosing the largest and best smelling bulbs, and handed them over. During the transfer of goods, he slid a small sliver of paper into my hand. I slipped it into my pocket and thanked him.

"Will I see you this afternoon?" he asked. Was all forgiven, or was he simply playing a part right now? I couldn't tell.

"I'll try my best to come visit," I promised cheerfully, hoping no one noticed the tremble in my voice.

"Good." He stepped forward and placed a hesitant kiss on my temple. "Until then, Ella."

"Until then," I answered, my voice cracking slightly on the last word.

Asher walked away toward the forge and his work. Watching his departure, I prayed this day passed quickly, that Piers escorted the Galderians from the kingdom and reported back to the King that nothing was amiss.

CHAPTER THIRTY

ELLA

The morning was busy. I sold bundles of herbs, heads of lettuce and cabbage, and every single clove of garlic. One basket of corn was gone and two baskets of tomatoes—of course, those were so huge, the baskets didn't hold many to begin with.

After the sun rose to its highest peak, people flooded the market and began to buy everything that hadn't sold before the church services began. Soon, I was setting new baskets out and placing empty ones beneath the tables that held them. By evening, I'd sold nearly everything. There were only a few ears of corn, some spinach, dill, basil, and two onions left. Ann handed me a coin.

"Will this buy what you've got left?"

I smiled. "Please, keep your coin. Take the rest."

"I insist," she tried, pushing the coin back toward me.

"And I insisted I would pay for the three tarts last week, but you made me take them."

She smiled in response. "Well, if you're sure. I've been staring at those onions all day. They're beautiful."

I placed what was left into a burlap sack and handed it to her, and she thanked me. "Shouldn't you be running off to see the smith's son?" she asked playfully.

Flicking my eyes toward the forge, I smiled. "Would you mind telling my uncle I've gone to see him if he comes early?"

"Of course. Run along, dear. Be young for a few moments. They are fleeting, for sure."

The note Asher gave me that morning made my heart a little lighter. He'd only written two words: *We're ready.*

As I approached the forge, I saw that Nathaniel was moving methodically from table to table. To anyone else, it would simply look like he was cleaning up. After all, they'd had an enormous job to complete over the last fortnight. But I knew better.

Asher was working further inside the forge, pounding a piece of metal, flattening the iron with every angry strike of his hammer. His brows were drawn together and his jaw ticked back and forth. I memorized the way his dark hair fell into his eyes, the way sweat made his skin shimmer, the way his muscles rippled and the smoke smelled.

His stormy eyes met mine and he stared for a moment before starting toward me, wetting his lips as he walked over. He met me with a rigid hug. "Ella."

"I thought I'd stop by for a few moments before Uncle Hayden comes to help me pack up," I said, infusing my voice with excitement.

"I'm glad you did."

My chest tightened into an uncomfortable corset of bone, squeezing my lungs until they couldn't draw breath. This was really happening tonight. Nathaniel stepped up behind Asher and slapped him on the shoulder.

"Hello, Ella. Beautiful day for market. How did you do?"

"I sold everything, and we had even more to sell this week than last week. The crop's been substantial this year."

"Good, good. Well," he cleared his throat. "I'll leave you kids to it."

Asher watched as his father retreated into the forge once more. When he turned back around, I was the first to speak. "I should go. I'm sure you both still have a lot of work to do."

"We do."

"Very well." I turned to leave.

"Ella?" he called out as I walked away, making me stop abruptly.

"Yes?" I asked over my shoulder.

"I'll see you soon."

"And I you," I said.

We both knew what he meant. He would be seeing me *very* soon.

At home, the evening was a blur. I packed quickly, my dresses, overdresses, chemises, stockings—all thrown into a sack. While I was on my knees on the floor reaching for the velvet bag far beneath my cot, footsteps creaked across the floor behind me. Millie stood over me, tears streaming down her face. Her fists were balled and her bottom lip trembled.

I braced my hands on my thighs and waited for the tantrum to unfold. I'd decided I was done playing games or coddling her. I wasn't like her family and half the village who'd put up with her attitude for far too long.

"You're a *princess*?" her voice broke.

Reaching beneath the bed again, I grabbed the bag and dusted it off as best as I could.

"I was," I answered steadily. "And if my people will still have me, I will be again."

That was the true question. Would they want me to rule them? I didn't know anything about being a Queen, but I supposed I knew what *not* to do. My father had given me that lesson, at least. I wondered what we would do if we got to Aelawyn and they wanted nothing to do with me or Galder.

"What's in the bag?" she asked in a quiet voice. Gone was the tempest. Millie was broken. She sank to the floor beside me.

I eased the drawstring and gently removed my crown and Ivy's shoes. Blinking rapidly, Millie reached her trembling fingers toward the glass slippers. "They're beautiful," she whispered.

As she picked one up, I said a silent prayer that she wouldn't try to throw it against the wall in spite. "They were my sister's."

"Where is she?" she asked, her voice breaking as she rubbed her thumbs over the delicate details, clutching the heels for dear life.

"Ivy took her own life right after Tierney attacked the castle. If she had waited just a few hours, my sister would still be alive."

Millie's eyes widened. "I'm sorry. I didn't know," she said sheepishly, looking down, a tear splattering onto her overdress.

"I know," I said quietly. "No one knew."

268

"How were you able to pretend for so long?" she asked, staring at the crown. After so long, I'd forgotten the shape and heft of it until I held it again. "I can't believe these were under your bed all these years."

I smiled. "It wasn't easy."

"I should think not, but you were very good at it. Well, maybe not at first," she finally laughed. "I just wish I'd known."

If she'd known I was a princess, it would have made her hate me more than she already did. And even though I'd finally stopped caring what she thought about me and stopped trying to force a once-sided friendship, I did feel bad she was caught up in this mess. "Millie, I'm sorry you have to leave your home and friends."

She waved me off. "I can make more friends, and my home is with my family. Half the girls in the village want to stab my eyes out with a spoon, anyway."

That made me laugh, and when Millie joined in, neither of us could stop. Jewel poked her head into the room, her eyes darting between the pair of us warily. "Is everything okay?"

"Yes. We're fine," Millie answered with a smile, carefully handing Ivy's shoe back to me.

"Have you cleared out your things?" she asked us.

"I just finished," I told her.

"My bags are waiting by the door," Millie replied.

"Then I'll need you both to help pack up the tools in the barn. Matthew is already outside helping arrange the wagon. I wish we had a larger one, but we'll have to make do with what we have."

"What about the animals?" Millie asked.

"We can't take them, love. They would slow us down and make too much noise, besides. But your father is sending word to Lord Windmeyer about the land, house, and livestock. He'll see they are tended to. Knowing him, he'll probably have a new tenant here by next week," she said. "Now, out you go."

I took my meager things to the wagon and then Millie and I helped Hayden and Matthew load what was essential.

"We're ready," Hayden announced once we had finished.

Millie ran back inside to take one last look at the house in which she was raised. She came back out a few moments later, brushing moisture from her cheeks.

Darkness draped over the land like a soft blanket, and Hayden was as satisfied as he was going to be with what he'd packed and how he'd packed it, so we set off, walking behind the wagon that Brutus pulled. *One horse is easier to feed and care for*, Hayden had said as he packed a sack full of oats for him, but I could tell it hurt Matthew to leave the other animals behind.

"I'm sorry, Matthew," I tried to comfort him as he walked along beside me, Jewel and Millie in front of us.

"It's not your fault. Father explained everything to me." His voice was forced, and his smile seemed tighter than normal.

"Don't worry about moving to Aelawyn," I tried again. "I've heard it's a lovely kingdom now."

"You lived there. Shouldn't you know?" he said with more attitude than I was used to hearing from him.

"It's been a little over three years since I lived there. It was nice then, but I hear it's wonderful now."

"What was it like?"

"My father... made life unpleasant. But the kingdom itself was beautiful. The people were kind."

He swallowed. "I'm sorry. I shouldn't have asked."

"You can ask me anything, Matthew. I'll always answer you honestly."

270

"Except when you're lying about something, like being a princess, right?" he quipped.

I inhaled deeply. He wasn't going to forget that any time soon. "Right."

CHAPTER THIRTY-ONE

ELLA

We heard the rumble of a wagon come from behind ours, and Matthew stepped in front of me protectively. My stomach tightened and my heart beat against its bony cage, straining for release.

"It's just us," Nathaniel's voice called out softly.

The dark swallowed Asher's features until they came closer. "You can ride in our wagon if you're tired," Nathaniel offered to the rest of us. "There's some room in the back."

"We're okay for now," Millie answered after glancing at me to make sure it was true.

"Did anyone see you leave?" Hayden asked anxiously.

"I don't think so," Nathaniel replied.

"Good. We best get to the river," Hayden said, turning back around and urging Brutus forward.

We'd been walking for a couple of hours but it felt like days. I worried about the time, imagining an enormous clock with hands that stretched north toward midnight, and whose chime announced to the world that we were *too late, too late, too late.*

Matthew and Jewel ended up taking Nathaniel up on his offer and rode in the back of his wagon while Millie and I continued to walk through the inky darkness. She was quiet. Unusually so. *What was she thinking about? And why was she taking this in such stride?*

I thought she'd be kicking and screaming as Hayden dragged her away from their home. She was either in shock, or she was actually looking forward to leaving Tierney. She'd always seemed so popular among her friends, but maybe that was all talk, too. She said the girls wanted to gouge her eyes out with a spoon. What had she done to make them feel that way? It sounded like Millie had more adventures than she told the family about, or else there were things she thought she couldn't open up about. I knew where that sort of thinking led.

"Millie?"

"Yes?"

"Are you okay?"

"I think so," she replied in a tired voice.

"If you're not, I'm here for you. I want you to know you can talk to me."

She nodded, her red hair glistening in the moonlight. "I will," she promised.

274

Since she found out who I am, it's been too easy. She's been too nice.

When we finally arrived at the river, Hayden got down from the wagon and stopped to watch the water's current. "Looks about waist deep," he said as Nathaniel pulled their wagon next to ours.

Nathaniel handed the reins to Asher and walked over to stand near Hayden. "Can't see anything. It's too dark." They didn't want to risk damaging a wheel and getting stuck, but the only way across was straight through, and they couldn't see what lay beneath the surface.

After they talked it over, Hayden walked over to me and Millie. "You should get into the wagon while we cross to keep dry, but if something goes wrong, jump out. Understand? If it turns over, you don't want to be on the wagon. There are sharp tools that could hurt you, or worse, you could get pinned under the wagon and drown."

Millie and I climbed into the back. I could feel Asher's eyes on me, so I looked to him, unable to make out his features in the darkness and with the distance between us; the distance I prayed wouldn't grow with each step we took away from Tierney and toward Aelawyn, and a life that would change soon, for better or worse.

Jewel and Matthew were sleeping in the back of Nathaniel's wagon, but they woke as Brutus took his first hesitant steps into the water. I clutched the side of our wagon, watching over the side for signs of us overturning.

"Easy," Hayden called out to Brutus, who whinnied and tossed his head side to side. The water rose with each tug forward, until it covered most of the wheel and lapped at the bottom of the wagon itself. When cold water splashed onto my hand, my body tensed. Millie threw a worried glance my way, her body as rigid as mine. I bit my lip and hoped we were almost out of the deepest part. We were half way across.

And then slowly, laboriously, Brutus pulled us out. The water became shallower, and little by little, the wheels eased out of the water and mud. Safe on the opposite bank, Hayden yelled to Nathaniel, "It's a little deeper than I thought, but if you go slow and steady, you'll make it fine."

Nathaniel's horse crept into the water. We couldn't do anything but watch from the bank as the water swirled around them. They had just made it to the deepest part when the wagon's back wheels slipped and the swift current pushed the back end downstream, askew from the front wheels. Their horse's eyes rolled, only the whites showing, and it began to panic. Nathaniel growled, an awful sound coming from him as he tried to keep control.

Jewel and Matthew screamed and got ready to jump out of the wagon, but Asher beat them to it.

"I can guide her!" he shouted, trudging through the water to the front of the wagon. "Give me the reins," he demanded.

"Watch her. She's wild!" Nathaniel shouted.

He threw the reins and Asher caught them in one hand, taking hold of the bridle with the other. "It's okay, girl," he said gently. "I've got you."

He slowly led the horse out of the water, one step at a time. The wagon righted itself and Asher somehow managed to keep his footing in the swirling water. I was moving toward Asher, within arm's reach, needing to hug him and tell him how amazing he'd been, when a voice called out from the trees ahead of us. "Ella?"

Asher closed his eyes for a second and then opened them, tilting his head back to look at the night sky. He took a deep breath.

Trevor walked up with a broad smile on his face and kissed the back of my hand. Asher's body tensed at the sight of Trevor's lips on my skin, and I pulled my hand away. Their caravan was waiting just ahead, hidden in the forest but in sight of the river crossing and trail.

Where were they when we needed help?

"There is much we need to discuss with you, Princess," Trevor said, urging me to walk along with him.

"Where are your soldiers?" I said, stopping abruptly. "Did you already send for them?"

He pulled the red ribbon from his trouser pocket. "As soon as I had this in my hand, we sent a messenger. Because of the distance and the fact that they must take the forest road to keep out of Tierney's sights, they probably won't beat us to Aelawyn, but they shouldn't be far behind."

Thank goodness. "When King Stefan finds out we're gone, he'll send his army," I told him, praying the King would learn of our disappearance later rather than sooner. My stomach churned at the thought. Lord Windmeyer would have to tell him as soon as he got the message Hayden sent. We wouldn't have long.

"All will be well, Princess. You'll see. My Father would like for you to ride with us," he added, clutching my elbow possessively.

I pulled away. "I appreciate the offer, but I want to stay with my family."

"Are..." he started to say, and then paused, looking around. Millie's arms were crossed over her chest, an angry look on her face. I wasn't sure if she was mad that he hadn't acknowledged her, or if she was just impatient. Knowing her, it was both. Jewel and Matthew stood next to Hayden. Asher was closest to me, drenched from the waist down, and Nathaniel was rearranging the load in the back of his wagon. It had shifted when the wagon almost turned over. "Are you certain?"

"Yes."

Right then, I knew this was going to be a long journey.

TREVOR

"Where is Ella Carina? Did you invite her to ride with us?" Father asked when I returned to the caravan alone.

"I did, but she declined in favor of riding with her family."

His eyes narrowed ever so slightly. "I see."

"She feels comfortable with them, Father."

"Them? Or with the smith's son?"

I feared both, unfortunately, but I wouldn't answer my father's question.

"If you are truly smitten with her," he said quietly, "now is the time to begin your pursuit. Before she and the young man get any closer. When we restore her to the throne, when she's in the castle dressed in fine gowns and wearing her mother's crown, and the boy is back to pounding metal at the forge garbed in ash and sweat… she will see that you are her true match. *If* you wish her to be." Both of his thick brows raised, and he gave me an encouraging smile.

God, did I ever want that.

I hoped he was right. With everything in my heart, I hoped he was right and I still had a chance to win her heart. She had already captured mine.

278

CHAPTER THIRTY-TWO

ELLA

illie walked beside me, closer than she had been before the river crossing. "Are you sure you can trust them?" she whispered.

I followed her gaze to the Galderian wagons in front of us, to their armor-clad men who sat astride enormous horses with bows across their backs, and swords and knives hanging off their belts. "I hope so." I wasn't sure I could trust anyone at this point.

"Prince Trevor seems very... protective of you," she said artfully.

"He assumes I'm like every other princess he's met, compliant and helpless."

Millie smiled. "He's never seen you fight."

We both laughed at that.

After another hour of walking, Millie and I asked Hayden to stop while we climbed into the wagon. She fell asleep almost immediately, laying against the piled wooden handles of Hayden's farming tools and a few of the bags of clothing we'd brought. At some point, I drifted off to sleep with her, clutching my bag in my hands. I woke after dawn with a pounding headache and instantly realized the wagon wasn't moving.

I sat up and saw Matthew crouched on the ground beside our wagon. "Where are we?"

"Stopped to break our fast," he answered. "I can't believe you just now woke up. Lazy princess," he teased.

"I must've been tired."

"Hungry?" he asked with a smile.

"I'm starving, but first... I need to go for a walk."

"You should take Mother or Millie with you. Father said you shouldn't go into the woods alone. He said not to let you out of my sight."

"Why?"

Matthew shrugged. "Doesn't trust the Galderians, I suppose."

Just then, Aunt Jewel came around the wagon. "She's finally awake!" she teased.

"Go with her into the woods, Mother," Matthew said.

Jewel rolled her eyes. "I'll watch her. Now, go eat," she said, shooing him away. We were walking toward the tree line when Jewel whispered her concerns. "There are Galderians everywhere. There are so many people in this entourage, I'm not sure there's much of an army left to travel to Aelawyn."

"That might not be a bad thing. At least we're well guarded. Why doesn't Hayden trust them?" I asked cautiously.

Jewel sighed. "It's his nature. He doesn't trust anyone until they earn it."

When we'd handled our needs, Jewel smiled and threw her arm around my shoulder. "Let's get you something to eat. You must be starving."

When we returned, we saw Hayden, Millie, and Matthew standing around a small fire while Nathaniel poked something in the bottom of a pan. "Eggs?" he asked with a smile on his face.

"I would love some."

Where's Asher? I glanced around but saw only horses, wagons, metal, and the Galderian colors of deep purple and gold.

"He and Trevor are having a little chat," Nathaniel said, answering my silent question.

Gazing throughout the camp, I finally found them. It seemed they were exchanging heated words. "What are they discussing?" I asked, curious.

"The route to Aelawyn, defending the back of the caravan… and you, I'm sure."

My cheeks heated until I thought my skin would melt off my bones.

"Don't fret, sweet Ella. He's just making sure the Prince knows you're already spoken for," he joked.

"I thought he might have changed his mind," I said quietly.

Nathaniel scoffed. "Have you met my son? He doesn't change his mind so easily."

Jewel wrapped her arm around me and chuckled beneath her breath. "That boy is so overwhelmed by his feelings for you, it's a wonder he can stand upright."

ASHER

"We need knights at the back of the caravan," Trevor insisted, tipping his chin up. I wanted to hit him square on that sharp bone and hear him yelp for his father.

"I agree, since that's where Ella's riding. If Tierney attacks, they'll go straight for her. I want her protected."

"We'll split the force," Trevor decided. "Father is well-trained and can largely protect himself." He glanced toward his father, the King of Galder.

"And what about you?" I goaded. "Do you need to stay in the middle, or are you able to fight?"

"I can defend myself well enough." He gave a haughty snort. "You *do* realize that princesses don't marry blacksmiths, right?"

"We'll see. She seems to like me pretty well," I replied with a smirk. His lip twitched in response, and I knew I hit him in the right spot.

ELLA

After we broke our fast, packed our things, and were ready to push forward, King Yurak rode around to speak with our party. He looked regal and splendid in his polished armor, although his stern lips were pressed into a thin line.

"My men will be positioned at the rear of the caravan to ensure safety," he said imperiously. "If Tierney has somehow learned of your departure, their forces will mobilize and move quickly; more quickly than we can, given all the wagons in our group." He looked pointedly at our banged up old wagon and Nathaniel's. "For this reason, I would like you all to move to the front," he said, looking around, "so that Princess Carina is as far away from any threat of attack, and to give her the best chance to flee."

I'd just opened my mouth to protest when a strong hand gripped my elbow. "Thank you for considering her safety. We'll make our way to the front."

Asher Smith.

The infuriating creature turned to face me with a smirk as King Yurak said, "Very well," and galloped away on his horse.

"I can speak for myself," I seethed.

"I know; but I can also see when you're about to do something insane, like tell the King of Galder you refuse his protection." He lowered his voice, tucking a strand of hair behind my ear, the motion both familiar and frustrating, all at once. "There are many things I can tolerate, but you in danger is not one of them, Ella."

And...just like that, he was forgiven. As I raised up on my tippy toes and placed a soft kiss on his lips, he returned it with one of his own. "You don't fight fair," I murmured.

"All's fair in love and war," he quipped.

Asher was the most dangerous man in the whole world as far as my heart was concerned, because it was beautifully and irrevocably his.

"Asher, Ella. Time to go," Nathaniel called out pointedly.

We made our way toward the front, hand in hand.

With a group so large, it *was* slow, but Yurak told us we were making good time. For three days, we stopped at dusk and dawn to eat as fast as we could before moving on again. There'd been no sign of Tierney's forces behind us.

On the fourth morning, Yurak and Trevor rode just ahead of our wagon, while Asher and Nathaniel stayed directly behind us in theirs. Asher's eyes, if made of fire, would have melted the armor Trevor wore. Trevor wasn't a threat, but that didn't keep Asher from hating him.

CHAPTER THIRTY-THREE

ELLA

 lost count of the days. Exhaustion made everyone sluggish and weary. "We must be near Aelawyn by now," I said to no one in particular.

Trevor trotted beside me on horseback as I walked along the road, trying to ease the ache in my legs from riding in the back of the wagon too long.

"We are very close, but we can't camp too near to the village because someone might see the smoke from our fires. We'll camp tonight and ride in just after sunrise," he assured me.

Thank goodness. It had been such a long journey. When I was taken from Aelawyn to Tierney three years ago, I was numb, in shock and afraid. The trip didn't seem as long, but maybe that was because the party was smaller and we traveled faster. Piers had been determined to get as far away from Aelawyn as he could, as quickly as possible.

"What do you plan to tell your people?" Trevor asked, halting his horse and dismounting to walk beside me. He looked at me carefully, the wind teasing his pale hair.

"I'll tell them the truth." They deserved it.

"You will need to change into a clean gown and wear your crown as we ride into the city. You need to start assuming the role of Princess Carina, and quit pretending to be a pauper. If you don't drop the village slang and act like a princess, they won't believe you," he said in challenge. "You may ride with me, if you like." His hazel eyes fastened onto mine expectantly.

"I'll do no such thing!" I retorted quickly, stung by his pompous attitude.

"What, ride with me? Of course not. We wouldn't want to upset the smith, would we?" he said disgustedly, his lip curling up on one side.

I brushed a smear of dirt from the side of my skirt. "I will wear what I wish, speak how I like, and tell the people what I please. And no, I don't want to upset Asher—which is his name, in case you forgot it so quickly."

"And if the people accept you as Princess and one day you become their Queen, will they accept Asher as Prince consort? Your equal in nearly every way? I highly doubt that," he scoffed, showing the hubris of his royal blood.

"Have you and your father discussed the fact that Aelawyn's people might not accept me at all? My father was a tyrant, Trevor. And while I'm nothing like him, they might not want to give me an opportunity to prove it. Or what if they see this army arrive and think another attack is underway?"

"That's why Father, you, and myself will ride ahead with only a handful of knights. A smaller party won't frighten them, and the people will have a chance to see you. That way, we can protect you if things don't go as well as we hope." Trevor looked at me with an intensity I hadn't seen before. "I don't want to see you harmed," he added.

"Why does it matter to you?" I asked, my voice scraping from my throat.

"I've seen people and kingdoms and villages all across the land, from sea to sea, Carina. But I have never met anyone like you," he said sincerely.

I swallowed thickly.

"You are brave when you should be terrified, kind when you should be bitter, humble when you could be prideful, and your spirit, instead of being crushed beneath circumstance, somehow managed to rise above it all and remain joyful. How can I not think about you? How can I get you out of my head, because despite all my efforts, you are still in my every thought?"

He paused, and when he spoke again, there was a tremor in his voice. "I know you and Asher have gotten close, and I hate it. I hate that I didn't meet you first, because I believe you could love me just as you do him, given the chance." Not waiting for me to respond, he mounted his horse and guided the animal forward until he rode next to his father.

I was at a loss for words.

Asher had seen everything I'd been blind to.

287

Trevor called me brave, but I was a coward; too cowardly to even look in Asher's direction, too afraid I would see *I told you so!* on his face.

That evening when we made camp, King Yurak came to speak with us, flanked by two knights. Nodding toward Hayden, Yurak stepped forward. "My son and I would like Princess Carina to ride into Aelawyn with us in the early morning. A few of my men will escort us for protection, just as a precaution. If the people see a large group approaching, they might panic, fearing another invasion. A small party will be less intimidating, and it will give Carina a chance to speak with her people before our army arrives. She'll need to tell them her story and warn them that Tierney may lash out in retaliation."

"What if they don't take kindly to that news?" Hayden asked.

"Tierney has already begun to make preparations for Carden's arrival. At this point, we are already in for a fight."

"You failed to mention that bit of news!" Nathaniel barked. "Didn't he?" he asked Hayden pointedly.

"Aye, he did," Hayden agreed, crossing his arms across his barrel chest. He looked like he wanted to break the man in half for what he'd just said.

"A small group of Tierney knights guard the castle. We will stay out of their sight, but she has to garner their support. She *has* to win the hearts of the people or they won't fight with us," Yurak said, softer. "It's the only way Galder will be able to support this. The people have to *want* her to lead them. They have to fight for their freedom from

Tierney's oppression, or this won't work. We'll fight *with* them, not *for* them," Yurak added.

"May I ride with her?" Asher asked, his father clapping a hand on his shoulder to stop his approach.

"Not this time," King Yurak answered. "She'll ride with either me or Trevor."

If they wanted me to look like a leader, I certainly didn't need to ride in front of a man. "I'll go," I finally said. "But I want my own horse."

Hayden's mouth dropped open. He stepped around Jewel, Millie, and Matthew, whispering, "Are you sure you want to ride alone?" He knew I was afraid of horses, which meant he also knew how much this was costing me.

"I need you and Asher and Nathaniel to protect the family, Hayden. And yes, I'm sure. I'll be careful."

Asher and Nathaniel joined our huddle. "I don't like this," Asher voiced his concern.

"Yurak is right; I have to talk to the people. If Tierney is already guarding the castle, we'll need their help even more now to take it back, or at the very least to help us fight when Tierney does catch up with us." It was the only way.

"I will personally see to the Princess's safety," King Yurak vowed. "No harm will befall her."

"How can you possibly guarantee that?" Jewel spoke up protectively, placing her hands on her hips. "Anything can happen! Someone might attack her, or Tierney's army might just show up in the morning and roll over top of us all."

Yurak looked properly chastened. "Then I vow to give my life to save hers. If Tierney attacks, I will protect her until I can no longer fight."

Jewel gave a harrumph and crossed her arms over her chest defiantly.

"Thank you for your protection," I said, staring down the man my mother once loved, wondering if he saw any of her former flame in my own eyes, and what hers had looked like before my father smothered it.

"Very well. I will send my son to collect you before dawn," King Yurak said, nodding his head toward my uncle and fastening his piercing hazel eyes on mine. "Thank you for your time, Princess."

He and his men strode away, and we stayed quiet until they were far enough away that our conversation couldn't be heard. As soon as they were, Hayden, Jewel, and Nathaniel began to hotly debate the fact that Yurak waited until now to mention the Tierney knights who guarded the castle. While I hadn't expected the news, I wasn't exactly surprised by the information. King Stefan wasn't a fool. If he took a castle and intended to keep it for himself, why would he leave it unguarded for someone else to come along and claim?

I listened to them argue and fret over how dangerous this would be long into the night, until I was falling asleep sitting upright. I laid down on the grass and pulled a thread-bare blanket over my shoulders. Matthew and Millie did the same, and the conversation softened and then stopped altogether as everyone settled in to sleep.

Since we left Tierney, Asher had been staying up at night, watching over us. I slept better knowing he was there. Tomorrow, after I got back from the village, I vowed to watch over him while he slept in the back of his father's wagon. I took a deep breath and drifted off to slumber.

CHAPTER THIRTY-FOUR

ELLA

Someone gently tapped my shoulder. I blinked awake, expecting to see Trevor's face, but found Asher crouching before me instead. "Is everything okay?" I whispered, alarm flaring through me as I glanced around. Nothing seemed to be out of place.

"Everything's fine. I just wanted to talk to you before you left." He stood and offered me a hand, and his fingers wrapped around mine as he tugged me toward the tree line. When we were far enough from prying eyes, he kissed me and whispered against my lips, "It's driving me crazy."

"What is?"

He looked down at our intertwined hands, brushing his thumb over my skin. "The thought of letting you go."

I placed my hand on his stubbly cheek. "I'll be back soon."

The muscle in his jaw ticked. "I'm worried," he admitted.

"So am I." I was terrified that my people would turn me away; terrified that I couldn't do this, even though I kept repeating to myself that I could. "What if they don't want me?" I asked desperately. *What if they did?*

His eyes asked the same thing, but in the end, he wordlessly pulled me into his chest.

"How could they not?" he whispered, brushing his lips over mine, warm and soft and inviting. I melted into him and he kissed me slowly, making me forget the weight of the world on my shoulders.

"When I first told you who I really was, I thought I was going to lose you-"

"Not possible," he said, cutting me off.

"Good. Because despite everything I've lost, the thought of losing you was worse than all of it. I was so scared you'd never look at me the same way again; that you'd hate me for keeping this secret, and when you got to Aelawyn, you'd decide you wanted a fresh start with someone new."

"I understand how you feel, Ella, because I've thought the same things about you. I'm afraid that if you become their Princess again, or one day their Queen, you'll wake up one day and decide you want Trevor because he's more your equal."

I smoothed a hand over his jaw. "That couldn't be farther from the truth, Asher. *You* are my equal. I love *you*."

His eyes widened slightly at my revelation. When his lips parted, he breathed the words back to me and pushed his lips to mine again as if to seal them inside.

292

The sound of footsteps coming closer tore us apart like guilty children. When Trevor cleared his throat and extended his hand, I hugged Asher tightly one more time, my fingers memorizing the feel of him. Leaving him behind was one of the hardest things I'd ever had to do. He watched me leave with Trevor, and I could almost imagine the irritated tick in his jaw.

Trevor was quiet. Most everyone else in the camp was still sleeping, enjoying the first night that we weren't forced to travel.

"Where are our horses?" I whispered.

"My father is waiting on the other side of this field," he answered in a clipped voice. "He'll be disappointed that you aren't wearing your crown."

"Better to disappoint *him* than the villagers. I think it would be too presumptive to wear it, and I'm sure they would have thought the same."

"Have you thought about what you'll say to persuade them?" he asked.

I *had* thought about it. Lost sleep over it. Worried and wondered what I could possibly say to show them that not only could I help lead Aelawyn to more prosperous times, but that I wanted to be one of them, not just a Queen seated above them on a throne. It was the main reason I refused to wear my crown as I arrived in the town. When that crown was given to me by my father long ago, it was my royal birthright and the people of Aelawyn had no say in the matter. However, times had changed. If I were to wear it again, it would be because the people wanted it.

"I'll simply state my case and leave the rest to them." Hayden and I had discussed it many times at night around the campfires. He said that the only thing I could do was tell the truth and wait for them to either accept or reject it and me, which was their right. I just hoped they could see beyond the past and my father's sins. I hoped they were able to see me as an individual, instead of being an extension of him.

Trevor slowed his pace. "Today will be difficult. Our plan is to travel into the village as commoners, ask the people to gather, and then you'll only have a few minutes to 'state your case', as you said. We can't linger or cause too much of a scene, or we risk being seen by Tierney's soldiers."

The sky lightened from sapphire to cerulean, and I noticed he was wearing the clothing of a commoner. "Where did you get those clothes?" I asked, recognizing them.

"Asher loaned them to me," he answered, pulling the shirt away from his chest like it was too dirty to touch his skin.

After a few more steps I saw seven horses standing in a clearing, surrounded by pale blue fog. The mist was so dense, it appeared that their bodies were submerged and their heads were the only thing above water. The tension in the air was almost as thick as the mist surrounding us, dangerous and foreboding.

King Yurak inclined his head in greeting as we approached. "We'll ride through the forest and enter the village from the woods. Four of our men will accompany us for protection. The plan is to gather as many people as we can and allow you to speak with them, Princess."

I nodded, unable to dislodge the boulder stuck in my throat. His eyes scanned my head, disappointment spreading across his features when he didn't see my crown. I wasn't sure what the big deal was about my crown when we were supposed to be trying to blend in. Unless...

"Is this a trap?" I asked suspiciously.

Yurak's hands fell from the saddle of his horse and he turned to face me. "Pardon me?"

"Trevor, and now you, have pushed the issue about me wearing my crown, when yours are conspicuously missing from your heads. You told me that we needed to blend in, but if I wear my crown, blending in is exactly what I *won't* be able to do. Is this a trap?" I enunciated. "Are you trying to make me stand out somehow?"

Yurak's eyes darkened a shade before a mask of cool confidence replaced the look. "It's been three years since the villagers last saw you. In that time, you've transitioned from a child into a woman. I thought some proof might be in order. Even if you didn't wear it, I hoped you would at least bring it to prove your identity." He walked toward me and stopped, waiting a long moment before speaking again. "I mean you no harm, Carina."

The whole situation was making me paranoid. Maybe it was because they were royalty, and I didn't feel like I was anymore.

I looked at the King and Prince of Galder. They had something I didn't. There was something about Yurak and Trevor that made them kings, even though their borrowed clothing was stained and thread-bare at the knees and elbows. Even though their hair was mussed and they'd borrowed boots that were probably either too small or too large for their feet. There was something intangible, something that went beyond appearances. An air of superiority, a confident brow, or maybe the way they stood with pride, tall and authoritative. Whatever it was, it made me want to shrink and stand tall in front of them at the same time.

When King Yurak and his knights mounted their horses, Trevor turned to me. "May I help you onto your saddle?"

I nodded, easing my hand across her mane and asking her under my breath if she could take me to the village. The mare answered by brushing her head against my hand.

Having borrowed a pair of breeches from Matthew's sack of clothing, I swung my leg across the saddle, looking down to see the shocked expression on Trevor's face.

"I'm afraid of horses and not a skilled rider," I explained. "If I sit side-saddle, I *will* fall off. This is the safest way." Besides that, in the breeches I was fully covered; even though the look in his eyes made me feel anything but.

He strode to his horse, swung into the saddle with practiced ease, and trotted up beside me. Once we were mounted, Yurak instructed his men to surround us. It was a short ride. We entered the village just before dawn, secured our horses, and then Yurak and his men began knocking on doors, spreading the word that there would be a village meeting in front of the bakery in half an hour.

Answering their doors, the occupants of house after house promised to attend. While we waited, Trevor never left my side. He was quiet and pensive.

My ribs quivered uncontrollably. My knees threatened to buckle. *What was I going to say to them?* I wondered, panic making my thoughts race. Would we get caught by the Tierney guards? Would they see everyone gathering in the middle of town and come to investigate?

Trevor walked next to me through the village streets, watching the flurry of activity. When I tried to visit one home by myself, he pulled me back into the center of the street. "I'd like to help," I answered, surprised by his reaction.

"We can't risk your safety," he replied tersely.

"I'm not in danger here."

"You can't be too careful," he murmured, brushing an errant strand of hair from my eye, untangling it from my lashes. "I will keep you safe, Carina. Whether you realize it or not, you *are* in danger. You have been since the day Tierney cut your family down, and you will be as long as

296

Stefan lives. Unfortunately, he isn't your only threat. There are those who were grievously injured by your father, as well as those who would seek revenge simply because they can."

I folded my arms, irritated. "I won't be kept in a gilded cage again, Trevor. I won't be a puppet. If that's what you and your father want, you need to tell me now."

"That's not what we want at all!" he protested. "We don't have any nefarious intentions," he said, his eyes blazing with a fervor I didn't understand. "Anything you do, it will be *your* doing. As princess or queen, should the people accept you, you can rule as you please. But I cannot personally bear the thought of something happening to you while you are in my care."

I suddenly noticed the villagers beginning to emerge from their homes. They made their way to the bakery and a small crowd began to form, murmuring softly among themselves. Their eyes were wary with fear, and several people scanned my face, their brows creased as if trying to search their memories for a familiar face.

Would anyone remember me? Father rarely let us leave the castle, but when I was a child, I remembered attending a fall festival once. Rich, jewel-colored leaves rained down as the minstrels played. Ivy and I danced in the grass. Even the guards who watched us, men who were always serious and stern, fought back smiles.

Trevor nudged me. "Where were you just now? You looked happy."

"I was lost in a memory. A rare, happy one."

He shifted on his feet, looking down at them and then back up at me. "I hope you make many more of them, Carina."

Yurak waved us over. "It's time for you to speak, Carina."

I looked from the King to his son. Trevor nodded once. With that subtle but sure movement, he silently told me I was ready for this; that I could lay out my heart and see if they chose to trust me or push me away.

CHAPTER THIRTY-FIVE

ELLA

I stepped into the center of the crowd.

They would have to make a decision. Did they want me to lead them? Did they want me, and Galder, to help them?

"What's the meaning of this?" someone called out anxiously.

I cleared my throat, wiping sweat-covered hands down my dingy skirt. "My name is Carina."

Murmuring and gasps filled the air. "A few years ago," I continued, "I lived in the castle of Aelawyn and wore a crown on my head. I was your princess. But my father wasn't a good man. He wasn't a good King."

The crowd drew closer. Some stared, while others scowled. "I came to help you. I know what King Stefan of Tierney has done, and I know they control the castle as I speak. My question to you good people is simple: Do you want Prince Carden of Tierney as your King?"

A resounding *No!* came from the people.

"Then would you consider letting me be your princess again?"

"You're naught but a child!" a woman's voice rose shrilly above the others.

I turned and met her eyes, weary and cool, as gray as the sky before a spring storm. "I'm the same age as Prince Carden, madam."

"Your father was a monster!" a male shouted.

My eyes found the man who shouted those words. "You're right; he was. I suffered in his household. But I am *not* my father. I'm here to offer you another way. If you support me, the King of Galder has pledged a portion of his army to fight alongside you against Tierney."

"Galder?" the word seemed to fall from the lips of most villagers. Galder was not only respected, but feared. The strength of their army was known the world over. Because of their armies, their lands and people prospered. With Galder backing them up, they knew they stood a chance at finally winning a battle.

"I don't want to rule the same way my father did; safe in his castle while his people toiled. Since the first attack three years ago, I've lived in Tierney with a family of farmers. I know the value of hard work, and I want to work with you and transform Aelawyn into the kingdom she deserves to be." Emotion threatened to overwhelm me, but I continued, "I never expected to come back to this place. But a few short weeks ago, the Galderians found me in Tierney, told me what happened, and offered their support to keep Stefan from expanding his empire."

"What's in it for Galder, eh?" someone shouted. By this time, the sky had lightened and the Galderian knights were visibly on edge.

"We don't like the thought of being cut off from the other kingdoms, and that is exactly what Stefan will do, given the opportunity," King Yurak said, stepping forward and removing the ragged garment he'd borrowed to reveal a fine purple tunic embroidered with the Galderian crest.

A collective silence descended.

An elderly woman, whose back was hunched from both age and years of hard work, stepped forward and grabbed my hands. "You have my support, Princess Carina. I would rather give you a chance than have a foreign king shoved down my throat." Her hands shook as she smiled up at me with a toothless smile.

"Thank you," I whispered to her gratefully. My eyes welled with tears as I gave her a shaky smile.

The rest of the villagers agreed with the woman. Aye's came from every direction.

"There's just one problem, Princess," a man shouted from the bakery's door.

"What's that?" I asked.

"Tierney's guards are already in the castle."

King Yurak smiled. "Leave them to us. If you support Princess Carina, Galder will rid Aelawyn of that vermin. And I assure you, our Kingdom will always be a strong ally."

Another man stepped forward, stroking a long, wiry beard. "We have no army. What you see is all that's left now. If Galder fights with us against Tierney and then leaves, Stefan could just wait you out, come back and attack us again, and we'd all be slaughtered for our troubles."

Yurak shook his head. "I would not leave you unguarded. A portion of our army will remain until such time as you can assemble your own. It will take years, but some of my men will stay. They can help train soldiers. There will also be people from other kingdoms who will want to start new lives in Aelawyn once stability has been established. We will carry word to the northern lands."

As the small crowd gave its blessing, my heart broke. This tiny group of people were all that had survived both battles, but they'd fought anyway. "We'll fight with you, Princess, and with Galder!" someone called out. I was relieved and frightened at the thought.

Yurak explained to the crowd that we would leave to plan the castle attack, but in the meantime the people needed to lay low, go about their days as usual, and that soon, they would be called on for help. He warned them that Tierney would come for a fight, and soon. The villagers agreed to do as he asked. The men removed their hats and inclined their heads toward us respectfully, and the women thanked us as we left the village to retrieve our horses. The heavy mill stone that had hung around my neck for so long felt like it had been cut free.

ASHER

Millie's tone was frantic. She quietly begged her mother, father, and brother to come deeper into the forest with her. She said the forest where we were camped wasn't safe.

"Why would we leave? Ella will be back soon, and we can all make our way to the castle. We stick together as a family, Millicent," her mother chastised. "Stop being ridiculous."

"She's *not* our blood! No matter how you try to force it, she isn't family. We don't owe her anything," Millie said, her tone louder, but still controlled.

Father shot me a questioning look. I answered with a shrug.

"Fine. If you won't come with me, if you prefer Ella over your own flesh and blood, I'll go by myself," she said, storming into the woods in a huff.

"What has gotten into her?" Jewel asked Hayden.

He shook his head, watching Millie jog away. "I have no idea."

Suddenly, a loud battle cry came from the other side of camp, and before we knew it, all hell had broken loose. Soldiers, wearing the dark armor of Tierney, attacked so quickly we barely had time to arm and defend ourselves.

I rushed Jewel to the wagon and told her to crawl under it. Jewel's hand was shaking as I helped her crouch down.

"Matthew ran into the woods to warn Millie. He doesn't have a sword!" she said urgently.

"I'll find him," I whispered. "Stay out of sight." I looked to the left, seeing my father parrying the blow of a man twice his size, and my father was not a small man. I rushed to help, plunging my sword into the man's heart from behind. The squelching sound made my stomach turn. I jerked the blade back out, catching on bone and flesh.

It was one thing to practice sword fighting, but quite another to kill a human being.

"Behind you!" Father yelled.

I turned just in time to bury my blade in the neck of the attacker behind me. Warm blood sprayed over my face and clothes. I felt the blood and understood what was happening, but my mind seemed detached from it all.

"Asher? Are you alright?" Father yelled. I watched the man fall limply to the ground. Father shook me, turning me to face him. "It's them or us, son."

He was right.

It was them.

Hayden let out a bellow. He was fighting one man as another closed in to help his countryman. "It's them!" I yelled. "I'll help Hayden. Find Matthew and Millie. They went that way."

ELLA

The ride back through the forest was easier in the morning sunlight. Most of the fog that blanketed the land that morning had burned away, only wisps hanging over the fields now. I could almost see them evaporate little by little.

As the sound of heavy hooves pounding the earth came from up ahead, the four knights surrounded us in a tight formation. Trevor's eyes met mine, silently reminding me of the promise he'd made. He drew his sword. The horses were on edge, high-stepping to the side. I gripped the reins tightly, fearing I was about to be thrown.

Asher's dark hair rose and fell as his stallion slowed to a stop in front of us. His dark blue eyes were wide as he took me in. "There's been an attack," he breathlessly told the King.

The guards opened their stance to allow him to come near. He was panting, out of breath, and his hair was coated in sweat and... was that blood on his head and neck?

"You're hurt!" I exclaimed.

"There's been an attack. Your family and mine weren't injured. They're fine. Scared, but fine." He turned to Yurak. "A few of your men didn't make it. We were outnumbered, Your Highness."

Asher quickly spoke about the ambush from a small, efficient force from Tierney. "We managed to capture one. He's being questioned as we speak."

"Guards from the castle?" Trevor asked.

Asher shook his head. "No, these men came directly from Tierney ahead of Carden and his knights. Somehow they were tipped off about our location, and that you would be absent this morning, that our numbers would be fewer. They were looking for Ella," he said fiercely.

"We have a traitor among us." Spittle flew from between Yurak's bared teeth.

Asher flashed me a look of sympathy, warning, or both.

"What is it?" I asked, trembling.

"It was Millie."

When he said her name, I felt like I'd been punched in the gut. "No."

He nodded, biting one side of his lower lip. "She left camp just before Tierney attacked. She kept trying to get your family to go into the woods with her, but when they refused to leave camp without you, she left alone. After the attack, she was questioned by Galderian guards and admitted to helping Carden."

Yurak eased his horse around so he could look at me. "You don't want to know what I would do with a traitor, Princess, but you can handle your cousin's punishment. How you deal with her is your decision, and the first as interim Queen."

With those words, we silently rode back to camp.

"Are you sure no one was hurt?" I asked Asher as we rode.

305

He repeated that none of my family or his had been hurt. I believed him, but I still needed to see them myself. I squeezed the reins so hard they cut into my flesh, but I couldn't relax my grip. It was the only thing keeping me from falling off the horse and from falling apart altogether.

Dark plumes of smoke poured into the air from the direction of camp. I couldn't help the gasp that fell from my lips. Galderian soldiers were cleaning their wounds and the blood of the dead from their bodies. A man raised his arm to greet us. It was bandaged tightly; bright red blood seeping through the pale fabric. Another wiped his brow, inclining his head as we rode past. Relief lay in his dark brown eyes. *It's over*, they seemed to say.

I pulled back on the reins, dismounted, and ran when I saw my family. Crashing into Jewel, her whole body was already heaving with sobs. "I'm so glad you're okay," I told her. When I opened my pinched eyes, I saw Hayden and Matthew waiting just behind her. I let her go and threw my arms around them next. Looking heavenward, I thanked God for not taking them away and pressed my palms into my eyes to stave the tears that would not stop falling.

Matthew stood proudly, pinching his lips as he swiped away tears to hide what I'm sure he thought was weakness. The faces of my family were tight with worry. Nathaniel and Asher drew in close to our circle.

"What will become of Millicent?" Jewel whispered, her voice as wobbly as my bones.

"Where is she?"

"Over there," Jewel replied shakily as she pointed to a large sycamore. Millie sat beneath it, arms wrapped tightly around her stomach. The four fallen Galderian soldiers lay in front of her. If it was true, if she did betray our party – her

306

own *family* – she deserved to stare at those men. She was directly responsible for their deaths.

"I want to talk to her." I started walking, and when everyone started to follow, I stopped. "Alone, please."

I hoped Asher was wrong, that she didn't have a hand in any of this. Millie's wrists were bound with rope. Her hair, coated with sweat, hung limply from her head. She kept her shoulders back defiantly, watching as I approached.

She gave me a satisfied smile. She was proud of her actions. I wondered if she would be as proud of mine.

My fists tightened into rocks and my veins pumped fire through my body. "Did you help them?" I demanded.

The sound of her teeth grinding against one another filled the space between us. She sat there unflinchingly, refusing to answer.

"Do you have any idea what you've done?" I gestured to the men who lay dead a few feet away. "Look at them."

Millie refused.

"*Look* at them, Millie. Look at their bodies! This isn't a game! You had a hand in their deaths!"

She finally tore her eyes from me and glanced at the four slain men.

"They will never get to go home, Millie. They'll never hold their children, never see their grandchildren. Their families will mourn them. But if that wasn't enough... *your* family could have been killed. *Your* father. *Your* mother. *Your* brother. They could have been *killed*. Did you ever stop to think about that?"

She pursed her lips tightly together, a petulant child to the last.

"Answer me," I said sternly.

"Or what? You'll have them manhandle me again? Am I supposed to bow down before you now, just because you claim to be royalty?" she screeched, trying to push farther against the tree.

"No, but I'll throttle you like I should've done years ago if you don't open that fat trap of a mouth you have! I know how much you like to brag; how you like to make yourself feel special. Higher than everyone else. You like to drag anyone weaker than you through the mud. But this isn't the village, Millie, and this isn't a game. These are peoples' lives…the lives of your family—whom I know you love, even if you pretend you don't care. That was why you tried to get them to leave camp with you. You didn't want them in harm's way. How did it make you feel when they wouldn't listen?"

"Betrayed," she bit out. "All because they wanted to wait for YOU!"

"Why did you do it? What did Tierney offer you?" I asked, waiting as patiently as I could for an answer.

"Prince Carden already knew you were plotting against him. He didn't tell me who you really were, but at the ball, he asked me to keep an eye on you. So I did. When I learned about your lies, I sent word to the castle, and when we left for Aelawyn, I left a trail of fabric through the woods for his men to follow." She scoffed, "If anyone endangered our family, it was you, with your lies and tricks. This morning, while everyone watched you ride off with the King and Prince of Galder, I met their scout in the woods and told them you'd be gone. They were supposed to attack *your* party, not ours," she answered with a shrug. "Tierney is my home, and you took it away from me, just like you took my family. They like you better, even though *I'm* their flesh and blood. But you know what, Ella? You're nothing! Not a princess, and certainly not a queen. And I will do everything in my power to keep you from reclaiming that throne."

"Then you leave me very few options, Millie."

I knew it. Something in the back of my mind kept telling me she was going along with the change of plans far too quietly when Hayden first told her about my true identity and that we were leaving. She was too complacent. Too nice. Almost sisterly. Time and time again, she'd made it clear that I would never be that to her. And like a fool, this time I hoped she was actually giving me a chance. But despite everything in our past, I never would have expected she'd be capable of this.

I kept picturing Matthew laying among the fallen, staring hollowly into the heavens.

"What's going to happen to me?" she finally asked petulantly.

"I haven't decided yet, but know that it's *my* decision, Millie." I turned my back on her and began to walk back toward my family.

"Tell me!" she demanded.

I didn't owe her any explanations. Those days were done. I squared my shoulders and walked away, leaving her shrieking from the tree line; the hulking knights guarding her movements, but otherwise ignoring her. I needed time to think clearly about her punishment. Right now, I wanted her torn limb from limb.

I walked toward Jewel, saddened by the hopeful look in her eyes. "She'll go with us under guard, bound and as a prisoner of Aelawyn," I informed her. "King Yurak left it up to me to decide her punishment. If he had it his way, she'd already be dead. I won't have her killed, but I can't let her go. I can't risk that she won't lead them to us again—or worse. I hope you understand."

She began crying, but finally mumbled, "I do."

Hayden squeezed Jewel to his side. "That's more than fair," he answered.

It crushed me to see them so broken. However, Millie was stubborn to a fault, and I wasn't sure she wouldn't try to sabotage us again if left to her own devices. And if she did, I wouldn't be able to keep Yurak from executing her on the spot.

Fear and gratefulness fought for dominance over Hayden's features. This was a position I never imagined I'd be in, and I'm sure he felt the same. "More than fair," he repeated to himself quietly.

I wasn't sure there was any fairness left in the world.

CHAPTER THIRTY-SIX

ELLA

ing Yurak called for everyone to gather around. When we'd formed a circle around him, he began to speak. "We make for the castle now. The captured Tierney soldier admitted that little more than a dozen men guard the castle. They were given orders to attack Carina's party and then bolster the force left at the castle. I know you're tired. I know some of you are injured, but if we don't seize the castle now, we won't have another chance. Carden cannot be far off. Remove the armor from the Tierney soldiers and don it, men. We will attempt to fool them and enter the gate, posing as their own reinforcements."

Orders received, his men began removing the armor from the Tierney's dead.

Jewel brought me a long shirt made of knitted metal called chain mail. "The armor is too big, but you should wear one of these, at least." She gathered the clinking fabric as best she could and slipped it over my head. It was heavier than it looked. She wrapped her arms around me and whispered, "Matthew and I will guard Millie. What she did was wrong, but she's my daughter and…"

"I know," I said, hugging her.

She whispered in my ear, "Stay close to Asher. He'll keep you safe. He killed more of the Tierney men than any of the Galderian knights did." She pulled away, motioning to a large pile of bodies, clad in dark, Tierney armor.

"Asher did that?" I whispered.

A deep voice came from behind. "Some of it."

He stood behind me, already wearing the dark armor of Tierney, holding a sword he may have had a hand in making.

Jewel slipped away, giving us privacy. Asher looked dangerous and enormous in the armor that fit him like a second skin, perfectly molded to his body and impenetrable. His eyes were wary.

"Thank you for protecting them."

He stepped closer. "I'd do anything for you, Ella."

"I know. I'd do anything for you, too."

He nodded his head once and then brushed his thumb across the metal chains on my arm. He frowned, adding, "This isn't enough protection."

"I can't wear the armor, Asher. It's too big."

"You aren't fighting," he asserted. "You need to hide. In case there's another sneak attack."

"Asher, I'm not going to hide. If I want this Kingdom, I have to fight for it."

"Look, I know you've been practicing with a sword, but this isn't practice. If you want to take your Kingdom, you need to use this," he whispered, placing a kiss on my mouth. "And this," he said, kissing my head. "Let *us* fight for you." Asher smiled. "I'm not saying you can't fight if you need to defend yourself. You can, and you should. Here – I have something for you," he finally said.

"I hope you never have to use it, but just in case…" He held out a small, silver dagger with a hilt encrusted with vines that crept up the blade. I pressed the pad of my finger against the sharp tip, stopping before it broke the skin. "It's deadly, but also light."

"Thank you, Asher." I marveled at the artistry of it, instantly recognizing it was forged by his own hands.

He handed me a leather belt with a sheath that perfectly fit the blade he'd forged. I cinched it around my waist and pushed the dagger into the leather, where it lay in wait.

"If you're in a situation where you need to defend yourself, please don't hesitate. You *live*. Understood?"

I nodded. I would fight. I would live or die trying, scratching and clawing to survive. "How did you find time to make this?" I swallowed the knot in my throat.

"When we were cleaning up the forge, packing our tools, I made it for you. We had to look busy, but I knew you needed a blade of your own. I… I know it's just a dagger, and that Trevor can give you pearls and rubies and all sorts of riches…"

"I don't want any of that. I never have. And a gift of pearls wouldn't mean anything, coming from Trevor. He probably has a treasury full, ready to lavish on any young woman who catches his eye. But you *made* this. With your bare hands, by the sweat of your brow, and you… the design. It's ivy." As comprehension dawned, my fingers trembled on the handle.

"This means more to me than any fine jewelry, Asher. You made it with your heart."

"My heart is yours," he breathed, and I pulled him close and kissed him, forgetting everything around us.

Nathaniel called for his son. "We're always getting interrupted," Asher said with a smile, before rushing to help his father.

It was an awful thing to strip the dead of their armor and clothing, but we wanted to live. We wanted to win this battle and take the castle before Carden got there and the Tierney force grew too big for us to fight. The dark armor was the disguise the Galderians needed to get inside the gate. Trevor helped Yurak don the metal of Tierney. His face and body were tense as he turned to face his men after a whispered moment with his son.

"Every able-bodied knight should climb into the back of a wagon. Our story is that we are the first wave, sent from Stefan to ward off an imminent attack from Galder. We'll tell them that the Galderian army will arrive by nightfall. I'll be honest with you...this may or may not work. If Tierney has already gotten word to the knights inside the castle, they'll expect us to try something. Our hope lies in these disguises. Pray we arrive first." He curled his lip at the sight of the armor he wore—the army of his enemy—and flexed his fingers around the hilt his sword. I recognized it as Nathaniel and Asher's design. "We need a man from Tierney to speak on our behalf. They'll recognize our accent."

Asher stepped forward. "I'll do it."

Pride and fear tore through my body.

Yurak thanked him and raised his sword solemnly. "Our brothers did not die in vain. We take their strength and honor with us!" he shouted, pointing in the direction of the castle of Aelawyn and taking off at a gallop. Trevor rode at his father's side, his eyes burning into mine as they led the column of Galderian knights away from camp.

Asher raised my hand to his lips, placing a soft kiss on it, and then mounted a horse. "My father and Hayden will keep you safe," he promised.

As he rode away, I paced back and forth, unable to stand still. I didn't want to stay behind if he had to fight. Jewel stayed by Millie's side protectively, and I noticed she'd taken one of the slain soldiers' swords.

We helped move the knights too injured to fight into the woods beyond the camp, and then hid in case Carden and his men were close, and until Yurak sent word.

But there was little fighting to be had. The Tierney soldier was right. The castle was largely unguarded, and those who had been charged with keeping hold of the imposing structure were eager for reinforcements. Too eager. They opened the gates at the first glint of the Tierney suits of armor, allowing the disguised Galderians inside.

Walking through the castle gate after so long was surreal. The ghosts of the past were alive and well in this place. Everything was the same; the thatched steel of the portcullis, the thick, stone walls that were only slightly more weathered than when I left, the cobbled stone underfoot. But there were no proud red pennants flapping in the wind, no color or soul in this place. It was empty. A tomb.

I found the twin windows that marked my room and Ivy's and imagined her body rocking in the stiff breeze on a rope of white, knotted sheets. I closed my eyes, trying to shut out the memories of my old family. Most of my new family was with me. Hayden and Matthew walked on either side of me, but Jewel had stayed with Millie and her guards.

Trevor hovered nearby, speaking with Nathaniel about the swords he'd made them. They were light and easy to wield, and Trevor wanted more of them forged as soon as possible.

Asher's hand clasped my elbow. Could he feel me shaking? It was midday in summer, but I still felt cold. Could it really have been so easy to reclaim, or did a hidden danger lie in wait for us?

King Yurak waited just outside the entrance. With leaden feet, I climbed the stairs, Asher with me every step of the way. I didn't miss the flash of irritation in the King's eyes when he noticed Asher's hand on my arm and him by my side.

His eyes flicked toward Trevor, who gave Nathaniel an apologetic smile and left their conversation. Trevor jogged ahead, standing beside his father. His eyes met mine and he nodded resolutely, as if this were right, fair, and all was well in the world. But I knew that taking the castle was the easy part. Yurak's plan worked, and we got lucky and beat Carden to the gate. A shiver crawled up my spine. Rivers of blood would run through Aelawyn again. The real war hadn't even started.

Soon, Tierney's forces would march with Prince Carden up to the wall, where they would try to either break or breach it. No one in the village or castle was safe until they were defeated or driven away.

When I reached the King and Prince, I inclined my head. "Sire, if Tierney draws near, the lives of the villagers are in jeopardy," I observed.

Yurak smiled. "Then, by all means, Princess Carina. Invite them to take refuge within your walls."

I turned to Asher, who didn't even need me to ask. "I'll see them to safety," he volunteered.

"Have them herd what livestock they can into the castle yard. Tierney will slaughter them to starve us out," Yurak added with a knowing gleam in his eye. I wondered what atrocities he'd witnessed during his reign, and how many he'd inflicted on his enemies.

Nathaniel jogged down the stairs with his son. They retraced their steps back across the cobbled stone path that had been soaked with the blood of my people years ago, and through the raised portcullis.

Yurak looked at the stone wall, probably searching for weak areas. "Now that we have control of the castle, Carden will likely rest his men. We have time to prepare."

Trevor cleared his throat. "Princess Carina," he said, offering his hand.

Accepting his hand, I let him pull me to the top step and through the doors. My family stayed outside, discussing how to prepare for the onslaught we were facing.

The castle looked different. Or maybe I was the one who had changed, and the castle was exactly as it had always been.

Empty.

Cold.

Unwelcoming.

I felt like a stranger. Because I'd become one.

This wasn't my home.

Windows let in the warmth and sunlight, but it wasn't enough to rid the shadowy chill that danced in the corners and hallways, and in the dark places that lay behind the walls, the ones I knew by heart.

I stepped away from Trevor, turning in a circle. The last time I walked these floors, I had to be careful not to step on bodies or blood. I remembered Piers calling for someone to find a cloak for me, his lip curled in disgust. The Tierney knights had respectfully closed the eyes of their dead brothers, leaving coins atop their lids.

But we left them there to rot on the floor.

I walked up the staircase, my feet finding the way to my old room. The door to my chamber sat crooked on the hinges, and it groaned as I pushed it open and stepped inside. The room smelled musty, and a thick coating of dust had settled on top of everything.

The bed was still made. I looked at the window seat and made my way to it. At one time, this seat was my favorite place in the world. Outside, people from the village were leaving the village, carrying what they could. Sheep and goats, pigs and horses were all being herded toward the gate. Asher and Nathaniel were spreading the word quickly.

Directly below the window, there were no blood stains on the stones. Someone had scrubbed them away, removed the dead, and then buried or burned the mass of bodies. Not for the first time, I wondered when Ivy had jumped. I didn't remember hearing anyone scream from the street below. If she jumped before the attack took place, someone would have seen her. Why did she do it after the fighting started?

My chest hurt. I walked out of my chamber and into the room beside it. Ivy's room was cold, like her spirit still lingered. The doors of her wardrobe were still wide open, just as I'd left them after taking her shoes. I tore a few of her dresses from their hangers and brought them to my nose. They didn't smell like her anymore.

Her bed was bare. The noose she'd made still lay on the floor just in front of the window, the folds of fabric coated in a heavy layer of dust. Covering my mouth, I walked over to the fabric and fell to my knees. Tears welled and fell quickly as I clutched the soft linen circle to my chest. "Why?" I asked, sobbing.

Why didn't someone take this and burn it?
Why did she leave me?
How could she do such a thing?
I needed her. I loved her so much.

And now any time I thought of her, it wasn't her smile or her laughter I imagined. It was the way she lay dead on this floor. Sobs wracked my body and I couldn't catch my breath.

Ivy was gone. I knew that. She'd been dead for years, but it didn't hit me until that moment; the permanence and heaviness of her loss. How desperate she must have been, and how she never burdened me with her fears. She kept them all bottled up inside until she couldn't take it anymore.

The last time I saw her alive, she hugged me so tight and said she was sorry. She apologized for what she knew she was about to do.

I jumped when someone put their arms around me. Trevor tried to comfort me, but there was no comfort to be found in this room. There was no comfort in this place.

I pushed him away and scrambled to my feet, rushing from the room and down the steps. I raced past King Yurak, who stopped his conversation with the knights of Galder as I flew through the foyer toward the throne room.

"Ella?" Matthew yelled, jogging behind me. Hayden called out, too.

I shoved the golden double doors, the force causing them to hit the walls behind them, wobbling on their golden hinges. Gold. Aelawyn had gold. Father thought everything we owned had to be made out of it. This room was a prime example. The walls, the columns, the sconces… All of this gold, yet Father was no more than a petty thief.

He only knew how to take. He gave his people scraps, but kept the best for himself. His throne sat at the front of the room. It was the only thing in the room that wasn't gilded. The dark wood stood proudly on the dais, like it was waiting for him to sit down again.

Never once did he say that he loved me or Ivy, because he didn't. The punishments he meted out were cruel and barbaric. I brushed away an angry, burning tear and marched to the platform toward that God-awful pile of wood, my fists curling.

All this time, I thought my mother hated me. I thought she'd have stood at Father's side while he slit my throat if I stood up to him. I thought she'd watch from behind his shoulder as I bled out on the floor in front of King and country, my lifeblood dripping from my father's blade, from his hand.

They told me she was the one who arranged for me to marry Yurak Trevor. Where was that kindness when we were children? Where was that mother when Ivy and I were beaten and made to crawl over the stone for hours until our knees were raw and bloody, and then forced to clean up the stains we left behind? We were so small, too small to have to endure someone like our father. And even if Mother tried to help me in the end, it wasn't enough.

We were *her children*, and she stood back and let him break us.

He broke us. He broke our spirits, and at times our bones.

The healers he sent to hide what he'd done, to clean us up and take away the pain, couldn't take away the memories.

With a rage-filled cry, I overturned the throne, pieces of the wood splintering and breaking apart. *Oh, how the mighty have fallen!* It lay in a pile at the bottom of the steps, all except one small piece that had broken off. It lay at my feet. I picked it up and took a deep breath.

320

I threw the final piece of the throne – of my father's legacy – on the floor, straightened my spine, and looked toward where my family, Yurak, and Trevor were gathered, mouths agape, by the double doors. "We have firewood, if anyone needs it."

With heavy legs, I walked down the stairs, across the room and out the door, making my way back into the fresh air and sunshine, taking deep breaths. It was over. My past was over.

It was time to claim my future.

As the villagers entered the gate, I thanked them for coming, welcomed them into the castle, and told them to make themselves comfortable.

Hayden came over and clapped me on the shoulder. "I'm proud of you."

I wasn't sure why. I completely melted down in front of everyone—including the King of Galder. Within minutes, I went from mourning my sister to damning my father. My past had completely overwhelmed me. When my lip began to quiver, he hugged my shoulder and said those four words again.

"I'm proud of you. You'll be a wonderful Queen because you care for your people." We quietly watched the villagers bustling around the courtyard for a few moments, and then Hayden continued. "Jewel is with Millie. She doesn't want to leave her alone. But Matthew and I will make sure that everyone gets settled inside the castle."

In just hours, everyone from the village was safely inside the castle walls. Two familiar figures walked toward the castle. Asher and Nathaniel. Their gaits were identical and unmistakable.

"That's everyone," Nathaniel said.

"Close the portcullis!" I shouted to the guard atop the wall.

The pointed steel teeth slammed into the earth, a dusty plume rising around them. I prayed they were strong enough to withstand the battle that was coming. I prayed we were, too.

CHAPTER THIRTY-SEVEN

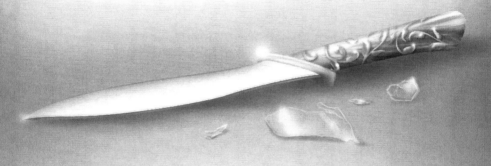

ELLA

The Galderian soldiers sat in clusters all around the castle yard, some sharpening their swords and knives. Others simply sat and hung their heads. They could only wait and prepare as best they could for the onslaught they knew was coming soon.

The villagers had brought in what food they could carry, and the yard was filled with livestock. Matthew helped lead the horses and cattle to the stables, and the goats and lambs, pigs and chickens were herded around to the back of the castle where there was plenty of space and grass. Soft bleating and whickering filled the air.

That was why I was outside. I needed fresh air. Time to breathe for a moment.

The gardens were in poor shape. Someone had planted, but never tended them. Hayden went right to work, taking what could be eaten and clearing the weeds around the rest. I knew he was worried about Millie and when he worried, he had to keep his hands busy. I was worried, too. When I bent to join him, Trevor caught my arm and pulled me aside. "A princess does not soil her hands and clothes with manual labor," he chastised. "You forget your place."

I gritted my teeth. "And you're forgetting yours."

His face relaxed. "All I meant was that you don't have to do this anymore."

"Believe it or not, Trevor, but I love gardening. It keeps me calm and busy." I wiped my hand on my overdress, his eyes following the smear of earth left in its wake. "And while I'm here to help Aelawyn as their Princess, I need to feel normal, too. This is normal for me, Trevor."

"You can't honestly believe you can have it both ways, do you? You can't be both commoner *and* Queen."

I wiped the sweat from my brow. "That's the thing. I *am* both. I'm the product of two worlds that should never have overlapped, but did. If the people want me, *this* is what they'll get." I didn't need to remind him that this was what *he* would get as well. He wanted me to squeeze into a gown, place a pretty crown on my head, and do nothing more than smile and wave.

"Then be willing to bend a little," he pleaded. "If you don't bend, I'm afraid you will break, or that someone will break you before you can begin to live the life you wish for." With those words, he shoved his hands in his pockets and casually strolled back toward the castle, his hair glistening

324

in the sun. I wondered if he knew firsthand what it felt like to be broken; if he might also be wearing a mask.

When he was gone, Hayden gave me a nod of approval. "You handled him well. I wanted to throttle him."

I smiled and reached for a small shovel. "Eventually, they'll have to accept—"

"Princess Carina, an army approaches! Come inside!" someone shouted.

My stomach dropped. I met Hayden's eyes. "Make sure they're safe!" I yelled.

"Go. I'll get Matthew. Jewel and Millie are fine."

I ran around the castle, squeezing and pushing through the crowd who was desperate to know which approached—their saving grace, or their damnation. Because if Tierney had beat the forces of Galder to the castle, we wouldn't stand a chance.

Asher found me and our sweat-slickened hands locked together.

King Yurak stood atop the wall, a spyglass at his eye. The last rays of daylight shone bright over Aelawyn. The brightness made it difficult to see the color of the flags they'd raised. Yurak squinted. They were still too far away. He couldn't tell which army it was, only that it was formidable; a glittering swarm of metal and man overtook the land. At last the King handed the glass to his knight, turned to face us, and gave a relieved smile. "Praise God. It is Galder."

If this was only a portion of their men, Galder's army must be enormous. A single rider approached with a raised flag, but he wasn't far ahead of the men behind him. Yurak took his glass back again, alarm crossing his features. He noticed the same thing we all did. They weren't trotting toward the castle; beast and man alike were running. When the shouts of the front rider came close, we could finally make out his words.

"Tierney is upon us! Open the gates!"

King Yurak briefly hesitated, training his spyglass on the rider again. Asher whispered in my ear, "He's making sure it's his men, and not Tierney using the same trick we used to take this castle."

I turned to him, mouth agape. "Everyone needs to get inside!" I screamed. "If Tierney's army is right behind them, the fighting could spill through the gate before we can close it."

Yurak heard me and called to his soldiers. "Women and children inside! Everyone else: Arm yourselves!"

Women kissed their husbands who shoved them into the crowd trying to get into the castle, sharing glances they hoped wouldn't be their last. Children cried, clutching their mothers' thighs as they left their fathers behind. The air was thick with fear.

These people had already lost so much, and now they were risking everything again. The King thought Carden would rest his men before the attack and assumed they would attack at dawn. He said we had time to prepare. He was wrong.

Yurak's men scurried to find their armor and weapons. Shouts and cries came from all angles. Asher's hand tightened on my arm as the last of the women and children made their way up the steps.

"Go inside with them," he pleaded.

Matthew jogged to us, carrying a helmet and breastplate he'd found. "Can you help me get this on?" he asked hurriedly.

Asher helped him into it, stepping back when he heard Jewel's cry. She rushed down the stairs. "What are you doing? You can't fight, Matthew! You'll be killed! Ella, come inside!"

326

"I'll be right behind you," I lied. She gave me a look that said she saw right through it.

"Matthew, come with me!" She reached out for him, but he moved out of her reach.

"I can fight, Mother!" he argued, muttering a curse that made her stop in her tracks. He pulled the helmet onto his head.

"Jewel, go," Asher begged. "I'll stay right beside him."

She shifted her weight, torn between protecting her children.

"Go check on Millie, Mum. No one's down there. She'll be scared. I'll stay with Asher, I swear," Matthew yelled.

With that, she finally went inside.

The Smith's wagon sat on the cobbled stones. Asher ran to it and rifled around in the back, finding Matthew and himself a sword. Matthew ran to get it and quickly helped Asher back into the armor he'd worn that morning.

I instantly noticed it was the wrong color. It was the dark metal of Tierney. "What if they don't know it's you?" I cried.

"Don't worry about me, Ella. I'll be fine." He kissed me fast, but let his hand linger on the small of my back, staring into my eyes like he had so many things to say, but didn't know where to start. It felt too final. Like he was saying goodbye just in case.

"Asher—"

"RUN!" he screamed, dragging me toward the door just as the portcullis was raised. Men on horseback poured through the open gate. Matthew ran to help with their horses.

The Galderian army was not only renowned for their skills with a blade, their archers were rumored to be the deadliest in all the kingdoms. Their archers took to the wall overhead.

327

In gleaming, unscratched armor, Trevor appeared in front of me and Asher. "What are you doing out here? Are you insane? Get inside the castle!" he seethed at me before baring his teeth to Asher. "She'll be their first target!"

He positioned himself between me and Asher, grabbing hold of my upper arms. "Carina, we cannot be distracted while we fight because we're concerned for your safety. Your safety is paramount. If you want to help, find everything you can that will burn and toss it out the windows. We need wood, fabric—anything that will hold a flame. And we need it now."

"I'll help," I said to Trevor, but not before throwing my arms around Asher, whispering in his ear, "Be safe. Come back to me."

"I promise. I'm going to find my father, Hayden, and Matthew. We'll stay together."

As promised, I went to every room. "Throw anything that will burn out the windows—furniture, tapestries, drapes, bedding. Everything!" I cried to the assembled women and children. Together, we ransacked the rooms and before long, debris was piled high beneath the window.

Soldiers and villagers on the ground bundled what debris they could into tight balls. As a great trebuchet was pulled into the castle yard, rumbling and rattling over the cobblestones, the portcullis slammed closed behind it.

"Ready yourselves!" Yurak screamed above the commotion.

But could anyone ever truly be ready for war?

CHAPTER THIRTY-EIGHT

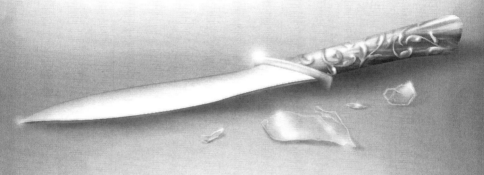

ELLA

My flesh crawled with every scream, every cry that rose to the windows. The archers were able to hold off Tierney's forces for a while, but the number of soldiers they sent was overwhelming. The trebuchet hurled our makeshift balls of burning debris with practiced precision. They exploded into Tierney's army, but the hordes kept coming. Like an unrelenting, dark wave upon a sandy shore, their army weathered our strength and diminished our hope.

Explosions rocked the castle, mortar sprinkling from between the great stones with each blast. No one was allowed near the windows. We huddled in the corners of the rooms.

Millie was locked the dungeon by herself. With every able body needed for the battle, the guards locked all the cells and doors and left her behind to join the fight. Jewel was distraught. She hadn't been able to find anyone to unlock the doors to the dungeon, and she wanted to be with Millie. More than that, she needed to know her husband and son were alive.

Instead, she and I sat beside each other, wincing with every blast, praying every scream wasn't from someone we loved. Asher had promised he would make it, but could anyone really keep a promise like that?

Minutes felt like hours, and hours like days. The fighting lasted well into the night, and when Tierney's soldiers finally lifted great ladders, some of their men were able to slip over the wall. They were met with swords, fury, and the unflinching will of a people who weren't willing to give even an inch of their freedom away. Not again.

Inside, thick smoke wafted in from the windows. The sound of exhaustion and desperate groans filled the air as hour after hour, the battle raged. For hours the panicked, terrified shrieks of the dying intermingled with the silence of the dead.

But at dawn, everything went quiet. And it stayed that way.

I remembered back when Tierney attacked the first time. I was trapped in my room, forced to endure the sounds of battle by myself, when all of a sudden, it went quiet. My fingers began to shake with the memory, fearing a repeat of those moments. *Had we lost?*

The women and children around me watched as I stood and walked over to my window and looked down into the courtyard. King Yurak's face was smeared with soot, sweat, and blood. He raised an arm and bellowed, "Princess Carina, the Kingdom of Aelawyn is victorious."

We won.

I let out the breath it felt like I'd been holding since the battle began and gave him a smile of thanks.

Tierney lost the battle.

It was over. It was finally over. I blinked away tears and walked from room to room, sharing the good news. Then, together, we unbarred the castle door and stepped into the morning sunlight. We survived. Because the people were strong and brave, and because Galder fought with us, we won.

In that moment, I saw why my mother had loved Yurak at one time. He was strong-willed, a true leader, and his men were well-trained and cared for. Standing beside his father, Trevor waved. I waved back, but my eyes restlessly searched the grounds for three other men. Where was Asher? Where were Hayden and Nathaniel?

My eyes flicked back to Trevor, whose smile had evaporated.

"Ella!" a familiar voice called from somewhere in the castle.

"Asher?" My heart thundered as my feet carried me toward him.

Jewel and I ran inside. Asher was walking down the staircase. "I've been looking for you. Oof!"

I leapt into his arms, nearly toppling him over, but he just laughed. "Where are Hayden, Matthew, and your father?"

"Around back near the gardens. They're fine, just exhausted and badly in need of a drink."

Jewel left us, running to the back of the castle.

"Everyone's okay? No one was hurt?"

He shook his head. "Matthew fought well. He knew some dirty tricks. I wonder who taught him those..."

I smiled.

"He threw dirt into the eyes of one of the men who came after him. Then he ran him through."

Pride for him surged through me, but also fear. He was only fourteen. While I knew what it felt like to *see* death at that age, I didn't know what it felt like to *cause* a death.

"He's okay," Asher said, stroking my hair as he held me. I didn't ever want to let go of him. "Do you want to see him?"

"Yes."

"Well then, you have to let go."

"But I don't want to," I said, laughing.

He smiled and kissed my hair. "Neither do I."

It took several days for those who fought to regain their strength, but when they were rested, we made a feast fit for our warriors out of beef and lamb. And while the entire village and all of Galder's men ate and celebrated the victory, King Yurak pledged that his army would stay for a time to make sure King Stefan didn't try to attack again.

Thankfully, they didn't return.

Weeks later, half the Galderian force was dismissed by its King and given leave to travel home. Yurak asked Nathaniel and Asher to make all sorts of weaponry for the people of Aelawyn.

"The armory is empty, and the people need weapons to defend themselves with. My men will train anyone willing to learn to fight, with sword, bow, or hands," Yurak pledged. "Men, women, and children can begin learning right away. We'll need every person who is able."

I knew the men who were ordered to stay in Aelawyn couldn't stay here forever. They had families and lives in Galder. We needed to learn how to protect ourselves.

He kept his word, and for weeks his men worked with the villagers. They trained for endurance, accuracy with a bow, and learned to fight with wooden swords. The trainees never complained or quit, because they'd seen the ravages of war firsthand. They knew how taxing it was on a person. The exhaustion and pain. They knew the cost of not being stronger than the enemy they faced. They'd already buried their friends, family members, and neighbors. Aelawyn was free. Now they had to fight to stay that way.

Once the dust settled and a new sense of peace and normalcy descended over the kingdom, King Yurak and Prince Trevor invited me to dine with them privately. I knew what they wanted. They wanted me to uphold my end of the bargain. There were conditions and expectations that were still required of me.

During dinner, Yurak was gentle but firm. I calmly sipped from my goblet as he lectured me. "Since the battle, you've been busy. You've walked around the castle talking with the villagers, dressing as they dress, digging in the dirt."

My eyes snapped to Trevor, but he refused to look up from his plate.

"However, now your people need you to lead. They don't need a friend or an equal; they need strength. They need to look at you and know you can and will do what's best for them. Now is the time to set yourself apart from them. Have your own throne constructed, and dress like the Queen they need. They've given you the crown and castle; now, you need to focus on helping them repair the damage."

Throughout Yurak's speech, Trevor remained quiet. He wouldn't even meet my eyes, a look of guilt visible on his face.

His father continued, "The damage Tierney caused is superficial. Buildings can be rebuilt. Lives can be mourned.

But the damage your father caused was deep. It'll take a long time to repair the broken relationships with the northern kingdoms, but it can be done, and *you* have to be the one to do it. Stop wearing dirty overdresses," he chastised. "Wear a gown. Wear your crown. You're not a farmer anymore. You are Ella Carina, Princess and soon to be Queen of Aelawyn. Let your people know what kind of Queen you'll be. Right now, they're hopeful. Don't disappoint them by putting your own wants in front of their needs."

He was right. I hated it, but he was right. The people *did* need a ruler, and for the time being, that was me. "I'll do my best to be what they need," I finally said, properly chastened. "There is a slight problem, though. I no longer own any fine dresses."

Yurak was prepared for everything. "A caravan with everything you will need, as well as supplies for the castle, should arrive on the morrow."

The meat in my mouth suddenly felt too chewy and would not break down. I swallowed it along with my pride. "Thank you for your generosity," I said quietly, remembering my manners. "We will reimburse Galder for whatever provisions you provide."

"With what?" Yurak asked, a confident smile on his lips.

I wiped it away with a single statement. "Tierney never robbed the treasury. Aelawyn is not destitute, and neither am I."

He opened his mouth, but no words came out.

"I'll forever be grateful for what you've done for Aelawyn, King Yurak, but I will pay for anything you give us."

I wiped my mouth and tossed the napkin over my plate, unable to stomach another bite with them. "If you'll excuse me." The legs of my chair scraped loudly against the stone. I didn't bother to push it back in. And I didn't look back.

The caravan from Galder arrived the following day with seed, food, fine bolts of fabric, and—true to his word—dresses that had somehow been made to fit me perfectly. I left my chamber in a whisper-soft pink gown with sheer fabric skirts that grazed the floor as I walked down the hall. Jewel had arranged my hair, and instead of a crown, a braid encircled my head. Yurak wanted me to look the part of Princess, but my crown no longer fit. And before I put it on, I wanted to see Asher. I needed him to know that no matter what I wore, how I looked, or how properly I spoke, my heart still belonged to him.

I walked out of the castle and down to the forge within the castle yard, searching for Asher's familiar face. My eyes zeroed in on him like a magnet. Waves of heat rippled the air around him. When he looked up, his eyes dragged slowly down the length of me and then back up. A lazy smile formed on his face as he wiped the sweat from his brow with a rag and walked out of the building and into the sunlight.

"You look beautiful," he breathed against my lips before kissing them.

"Thank you. I've missed you."

Nathaniel continued to pound on a red-hot piece of metal, but raised his hammer to say hello before beating at the glowing chunk again, a smile tugging at his lips. Asher had turned to see the exchange and glanced back at me. "We've been busy."

"I know, and I can't thank you enough."

He smiled, looking me over again.

I grabbed the fabric of my skirts, feeling shy. "Yurak said I needed to look the part of a princess, but I feel silly."

He shook his head. "You shouldn't. This is what you were born for, Ella. This is who you were meant to be."

But it wasn't. "I wasn't meant for this; I was crafted entirely for you, Asher Smith, and you were created solely for me."

A grin, brilliant as the sun above, stretched over his soot-smeared face. My fingers itched to touch him, but when I lifted my hand to do exactly that, he stopped me. "Don't. You'll get dirty. We can't have that, now can we?"

I supposed not. Lowering my hand, I told him, "I miss you."

"I miss you, too. We've been working from dusk till dawn. It's an enormous undertaking to arm an entire Kingdom—even a small one. We found Aelawyn's armory, but it was empty. Either the weapons are being stored somewhere else, or Stefan's men took them. Yurak is having his men look everywhere just in case." He squinted up at the sun, no doubt checking the time.

"I'm not sure where all the weapons went," I answered lamely. It was a strange puzzle. Tierney didn't take them when they took me away, but maybe they came back and took them later. Or maybe the men stationed here to hold the castle for Carden hid them somewhere. It was pure dumb luck that they didn't find the treasury itself while they were stationed here. Otherwise, we'd have nothing.

My father's personal treasury was located in a hidden room, and he and all those who knew of the secret room died along with him when Tierney attacked. The only times I was allowed inside the treasury were the times when my head outgrew my crown and a new one was made. My mother would lead me to the dark room, quietly place it on my head, and then send me back to my chamber.

"At least you get to do something useful," I said grumpily. "I've been attending meetings about strategy now that the Kingdom is secure. Yurak wants to invite the northern Kingdoms to visit so he can introduce me and try to secure their alliances."

Asher reached out to touch an errant strand of hair that escaped my braid, but stopped himself. "You can touch me, Asher."

"I don't want to get soot on you. I'm a mess."

I didn't care. "Can I see you later?"

"Carina?" a voice called out. Trevor strolled over to us. "My father would like to speak with you."

Of course he would. That was all he had time for right now. I plastered a dutiful smile on my face and replied, "Certainly."

Asher ticked his head toward Trevor. "Duty calls."

It looked like I wouldn't see Asher that night, after all. Our time together had been reduced to brief moments stolen between responsibilities; responsibilities that weighed heavily on both of us. All we had time for were rushed kisses and trying to divulge all we could to each other in the shortest time possible, because someone was always coming to get me for one ridiculous reason or another.

"This will pass," he'd say, gently kissing my forehead. "Things are just getting settled."

How much longer until they were entirely settled? I was so tired of everything pulling us apart, when all we wanted was to be together.

CHAPTER THIRTY-NINE

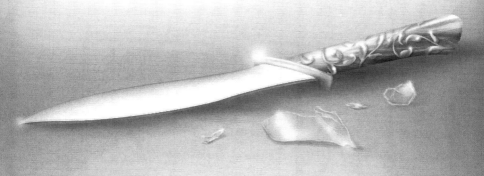

ELLA

Messengers had been dispatched to each of the three northern Kingdoms. I'd written long letters informing them that I was now Princess. I also warned them about King Stefan, and invited them to send representatives to the castle to discuss trade. Everyone loved gold, and Aelawyn's hills had plenty to offer. I thought the three Kingdoms would be excited to start fresh.

I was naive. Only one replied.

The Kingdom of Waverly, a peninsula surrounded on three sides by the sea, sent word that a representative would travel to Aelawyn before the end of summer, which was still a few weeks away. But long before we expected them, Prince Orad and two knights arrived.

Weary from having traveled so far, they were ready for their rooms, a meal, and a bath upon their arrival. The castle stirred to life, a beehive of anxious energy, readying things for our guests. The day passed in such a flurry, I didn't catch my breath until Yurak insisted that I stop fussing about and go dress for dinner.

I didn't know what to say to Prince Orad to convince him of my intentions. I would have to ask him to trust me, before I gave him a reason to. He didn't know me. But he knew my father. The only sliver of hope lay in the fact that he came. He answered my letter when no one else would.

Yurak kept insisting that I be assigned a proper lady-in-waiting instead of continuing to rely on Jewel. He'd given his subjects the option to travel to Aelawyn and start lives here. Some took him up on the offer, and our village's population had doubled in size almost overnight. Several of the Galderian women were given jobs in the castle.

He wanted one of the Galderians to assist me, but so far, I'd been able to hold him off. Jewel was indispensable to me, always there to help me dress. If he replaced her, I'd never see her. If she wasn't with me, she was in the dungeon, sitting with Millie.

"How's Millie?" I asked as she tightened the laces on the corset we were trying to get on.

Her hands stilled, like they did every time I mentioned her. Only my family and Asher knew, but I visited Millie in the dungeon several times a week. It was dank and stank of mildew and mold, but I tried to make sure she was treated well. She had warm blankets and a new feather mattress, and Jewel even brought in a few of her things from home. It didn't matter how many times I visited or what I brought her, she refused to speak to me, turning her head and pointedly ignoring my questions.

Jewel wanted me to set her free. She'd asked more than once. But I couldn't. Yurak might take both of our heads if I did. The only thing I could promise was that once he left and returned to Galder, I would let her go. But she would never be allowed to leave Aelawyn.

She knew too much.

And there was a chance that Stefan would have her killed—either to hurt me, or because she'd been helping Carden and the two of them failed to stop us.

Jewel finished tying the laces and walked to the wardrobe to retrieve my gown. "Millie is reading the books you sent. They keep her mind busy," she finally answered.

"Does she need anything else?"

"Not that I can think of."

With the corseted underdress laced, I glanced in the mirror. It was like I was looking at a new person. My waist was small, and the shape of the gown plumped my breasts. Earlier that day, I'd snuck away into the treasury and retrieved one of my mother's crowns. Yurak wanted me to look like a Queen? My mother's crown would do exactly that.

"Does Matthew like it here?" I asked, trying to lighten the somber mood.

She smiled over my shoulder in the mirror, the tension in her shoulders melting away. "He's very happy. He's always loved animals, and now he has so many to tend to, he'll never get bored."

Matthew leapt at the opportunity to work in the stables and with the castle's livestock, and boasted that he was the only nearly-fifteen year old able to handle the work.

Jewel held the dark gown out for me and I dove into it, the silken panels gliding over my skin in feather soft layers.

As she buttoned the pearl buttons at the back of the gown, I straightened the layers of my skirts.

"You are all grown up," she said in a cracking voice, before clearing her throat and speaking again. Millie and I were the same age, and I could tell she was thinking of her now. "Hayden wanted me to give you this," she said quietly. She held out a small, golden band. "I know you have plenty of gold, and jewelry much finer than this, but this ring was my mother's. She had two. When Millie... Well, one day, I'll give the other to her. But we wanted you to have one of them."

Tears clogged my throat and welled in my eyes as I picked up the tiny circle from the center of her palm and pushed it onto my finger. "Thank you," I said softly. "You don't know how much this means to me."

She hugged me to her, saying, "I think I do. I can't imagine the strength it takes to walk through your past every day. It must be hard to live with all those ghosts, Ella."

God, it was. It was so hard.

We clung to each other for a long moment, each taking a deep breath. "Everything's going to be okay, Jewel. I promise."

She pursed her lips together and nodded emphatically. "I know it will. In time. It's just hard." Jewel sniffled and reached into the small chest of drawers to retrieve my mother's crown—my crown. "And now, the most important item you'll wear this evening."

The gold settled heavily onto my head, reminding me of the responsibility that rested on my shoulders. "This isn't the most important thing," I said with a watery smile, staring at the gold band she'd given me.

Jewel held my upper arms in her hands, giving a gentle squeeze. "Ella, wearing this won't be easy, but I'm proud of you for putting away what *you* want, for what the people of Aelawyn need. They need *you*, Ella. Yurak is a good man, but he's stern and unforgiving. Who knows…perhaps years of being King does that to a person. But after so many years of harsh rule and uncertainty, these people need a soft hand. They need *your* hand." Jewel squeezed me once more and stepped back; the motherly smile that stretched over her face filled with equal parts pride and heartbreak. "They're expecting you, Princess," she said.

"I hope I don't disappoint them," I choked out.

She brushed a strand of hair behind my ear. "Meet your heart's expectations first. Don't lose yourself in trying to play a part. If you stay true to you, you'll never disappoint anyone. It simply isn't possible, because your heart is good. *You* are good. Just make sure you stay that way."

I hugged her tight and promised to do just that.

When I stepped out of my room and into the hallway, she hovered by the door. "I'll clean up in here and help you later tonight," she promised. "You'd never get out of that corset alive without my help!" she said with a wink.

I smiled and thanked her, and then tried to calm the trembling of my knees. Prince Trevor and King Yurak were waiting for me at the bottom of the staircase, their backs to me. When they heard the swishing of my skirts, Yurak turned, nodded sagely, and bent to whisper something into his son's ear. Trevor turned around and his eyes caught on my crown, and then the gown I wore. He tugged on his collar and then schooled his features, clasping his hands behind his back with a regal air.

The dress Yurak had commissioned for me was delicate but sturdy. The corset's boning was made of steel, an effective cage. My lungs couldn't fully expand. The material was the color of the midnight sky, a blue so deep it was nearly black, a color you could look at for hours and never see all the shades inside. The stitches were made with golden thread, accenting my crown.

My lips were sticky from the cherry balm Jewel applied, the cloying scent teasing my nose. My stomach turned somersaults. I felt fake, like a little girl wearing her mother's clothes to dress up in. And given the gravity of the situation and what was at stake—the opportunity to forge a new relationship with Waverly—I prayed Orad wouldn't see right through me.

When I reached the bottom step, Trevor was there, his eyes catching on my shoes; Ivy's slippers, made of glass. It felt right to have a piece of her with me. After all this time, I finally forgave her and came to peace with the fact that I'd never fully understand her mindset. She must have been very sad, lonely, and desperate, and made the irreversible decision to leave the only way she knew how, as selfish as it was. She was gone, and there was nothing I could do to bring her back. The only thing I could do was move forward, carry her memory in my heart, and live the best life I could in her honor.

"You look stunning," Trevor said with an unabashed smile.

I swallowed quickly before answering him with a simple, "Thank you."

As much as I looked the part of a Princess, he looked the part of a Prince. Dressed in black pants and a tunic to match, he wore a satin sash across his chest, the deep plum purple of Galder.

Having spent time with him and his father, I knew he would be a great King one day. Between the two of them, they never stopped thinking and strategizing. They talked about everything, from the simple layout of the village and how best to help the people rebuild the homes and shops that were torched, to the intricacies of historic relations with the northern Kingdoms and how best to draw them into an alliance with Aelawyn.

All day long, they argued about the best way to approach Prince Orad about trade. Their plan was to show the Kingdom of Waverly what Aelawyn could offer once she stood tall and proud again. To the west, in the mountains, Aelawyn had seams of gold that stretched through the rock. They'd once been mined. They could be mined again.

Trevor tucked my hand into the crook of his elbow. Yurak strolled with us, a crown of thick silver sitting on his brow, inlaid with jewels that looked like sea water. Not quite blue and not quite green, but a delicate mixture of both. Trevor's crown was a shorter, smaller version of the same.

The King of Galder introduced me to the Prince of Waverly. "Princess Carina, allow me to present Prince Orad."

Prince Orad bowed and reached for my hand, pressing a cool kiss to the back of it. "It is a pleasure to visit Aelawyn once again, Princess. Thank you for extending the kind invitation. My King and Queen, Rauld and Illiana, send their regards and are most eager to heal the relationship between our countries."

With a head of hair the colors of salt and steel, rich, dark skin, and caramel-colored eyes, Orad was beautiful. And while his mouth said his King and Queen were eager to repair what had been lost between our kingdoms, his eyes said it was my father who severed it, and he was charged with finding out if I was just like him.

"Thank you for accepting our invitation," I said cordially. "It's a pleasure to have you visit. How long will you be staying with us?"

"Only a fortnight, I'm afraid. Fall is coming quickly, and we're preparing for a harsh winter. Traveling by sea in this weather is unforgiving in the north."

Yurak led us to a rectangular table. When King Yurak asked if I'd like to be seated at the head, I declined, claiming the seat beside Orad instead. "I hope you don't mind," I whispered. "We'll never get the chance to talk if we're so far away."

For the first time since we met, Orad smiled.

Over steaming trenchers filled with delicious meat, vegetables, broth and bread, we spoke of mundane things, everyone sizing each other up. Orad's men sat to his right, Yurak sat opposite him, and Trevor sat beside me at my left.

When Orad asked about my upbringing, I answered his questions honestly. When he asked me to elaborate on my answers, I did unflinchingly, leaving nothing out. I asked him questions, and Trevor and Yurak weighed in with their own tales from Galder. By the end of the night, everyone was smiling, the atmosphere had thinned, and the tension had eased. It felt like the beginning of something great for Aelawyn.

When the goblets were empty, King Yurak saw Prince Orad and his men to their rooms. Trevor and I stood near the table watching them leave.

"That went better than I expected," he said, giving a great sigh.

"It did," I agreed. I actually thought it was fun!

"May I see you to your room?" he asked gallantly.

"I'm pretty sure I know where it is," I teased.

I took his arm as we left the Great Hall, excited that I'd soon be out of this gown. As we turned the corner, I almost smacked into someone.

Blue eyes locked onto mine. Asher sputtered an apology, quickly taking in the dress, the hand wrapped around Trevor's arm, and the golden crown atop my head. "I'm so sorry, Ella," he stammered, standing up straighter. "I didn't mean to—"

"*Princess* Carina," Trevor corrected in a snappish tone.

Hurt flashed in his eyes, but he recovered quickly. "Princess Carina. Pardon me." Before I could stop him, he shoved past Trevor and down the hallway to the back of the castle.

"Why did you do that?" I all but yelled, jerking my arm away from Trevor.

"He had no right to address you so informally, especially while you're wearing the crown. If Orad had seen it..." he said, shaking his head. "You are no longer the friend of your subjects, Carina. You are their leader, their Princess. You and they should both know and respect it." The muscle in his jaw ticked twice.

"We both know Asher isn't just 'one of my subjects'," I chided. "He doesn't have to address me formally."

"He should," Trevor bit back at me. "*Princess* shouldn't be a word he's ashamed to use. And he needs to stop calling you Ella. Your people know you as Carina." He paced back and forth. "Does he know how lucky he is? Does he let you know how blessed he is for every moment he spends with you?"

"What we say and do in our time together is none of your business, but you've certainly become an expert in interrupting us whenever we're together!" My voice rose with each word. "You had no right to speak to him that way!" I fumed.

"I want you to reconsider," he said calmly and carefully.

"Reconsider what?" I asked, my head ticking back. My crown wobbled.

"Our betrothal. I want you to consider honoring it."

"No," I said coolly, giving him a levelling glare. I turned and walked away, careful of my steps. The last thing I wanted was to shatter Ivy's shoes.

I found Asher outside at the forge, a cool wind whipping around the pair of us. "You keep saying he doesn't want you. Was that proof enough?" he asked, gesturing toward the castle.

"I'm sorry," I answered, my cheeks coloring.

"He's been after you since he first stepped foot in Tierney. You were his, and then you were taken away. Now he wants you back."

"He asked me to reconsider our betrothal," I admitted.

Every muscle in his body tensed and he paused, catching his bottom lip in his teeth. "And will you?" he asked cautiously.

"Of course not!" I exclaimed indignantly, throwing my hands in the air. "I'll say it one more time – he's not the one I care about."

"It isn't about whether you care about him, it's about marrying someone who is your equal in every way. He can stand beside you while you wear that crown, while you host other Kingdoms and talk about trade alliances. But me..." He gave a sigh and looked down at the ground. "Ella, I don't know any of those things. I can't offer you anything but metal."

"I don't care about him, Asher, and I don't care about what he wants or thinks he's entitled to. *He* can't compete with *you*. Not when it comes to my heart. Do you think I have any idea what they're talking about during all these meetings and dinners? Most of the time I don't have a clue! My father didn't let me attend anything having to do with the Kingdom's affairs. I was locked in my room day and night. The only people I ever saw were servants. Wearing a crown doesn't give me all the knowledge I need to be a good ruler. I'm learning, too."

I took a few steps and stood before him, staring until his eyes finally rose to meet mine. "I'm not Princess material, Asher. I'm not sure I ever was. This crown sits on my head simply because of my birth, and I can't control it any more than I can the wind. I can't control Trevor's feelings any more than I can my heart...and my heart belongs to *you*. I can't say it any clearer than that. But if this isn't the life you want, I underst—"

He kissed me then, his large hands gripping my waist and tugging me to him, holding me there. This time, he poured everything he had into wordlessly telling me he was mine. Crown and titles and all the things that stood between us be damned.

The kiss was filled with longing, apologies, promises, and all the things we'd left unsaid since the battle took place. It was long and languorous, and when we finally parted, we were both gasping for air. And then he kissed me again. And again.

We spent the next hour reveling in the feel of one another. He backed me into the forge and lifted me onto one of the work tables, settling between my legs, and I urged him even closer with my heels and tugged at his shoulders with my hands, raking fingernails through his hair until deep rumbling groans emerged from his chest.

The coals in the forge still glowed a vibrant orange, the flame inside them ebbing and flowing. In that moment, I knew exactly how they felt. Cooled by forces beyond their control, yet wanting nothing more than to burn.

Finally, Asher lay his forehead on mine and wrapped his arms around my back. "You should go. Or I should go... before we don't want to."

"Too late," I said, trying to quiet my thundering heart.

"For me, too," he said against the column of my neck.

"Don't let them tear us apart," I pleaded. "Don't give up on me just because of a silly crown. I'm still me," I whispered, staring down at our joined hands.

"I know. I'm just worried I'm not good enough for you."

"There's no way in this world you could ever be anything other than perfect for me, Asher Smith. I'm afraid *I'm* not what you want, that I can't be what you need. I want you to feel comfortable with me, no matter how I look, what I wear, or who is around me. I love you."

He breathed a sigh of relief. "I love you, too."

He pressed a soft, lingering kiss to my lips. When he repeated the phrase, my heart caught the words and locked them away. She hoarded any part of Asher she could, and I couldn't blame her for being greedy. Our time together was always rushed, but we burned brighter than stars when we collided. It was for those times that I lived and breathed. It was only when I was with Asher that I felt alive.

CHAPTER FORTY

ELLA

The hours I spent with Prince Orad, Yurak, and Trevor were long, but fruitful. Trevor was incredibly smooth. If something happened to Yurak, there was no doubt in my mind that he could lead his kingdom and do a very good job at it. In fact, I believe it was his pointed arguments that made Orad consider our offers at all.

At the end of the first week of his visit, a tentative trade agreement was made, although Orad refused to fully align with us against Tierney until we proved that we were trustworthy. "Trust is earned, not freely given," he said with a glint in his eye. That being said, I didn't think it would take many months of trade for us to prove our reliability.

One afternoon, I invited Orad on a tour through the village so he could see the reconstruction. I wanted him to see our devastation. He hadn't mentioned the status of his country's relationship with Tierney or breaking ties with them. I thought he might want to consider it after seeing the damage they so willfully inflicted on a defenseless nation.

The sound of felled trees echoed through the village. So did the sound of hammering. Everyone worked, carrying material where it was needed, hammering planks into place, or mixing mortar. The framework of several buildings stood proudly with new skeletons made of fresh oak and pine. But mostly they were made of hope. It was the only thing that kept us moving forward.

While Orad's men chatted with the baker about having to rebuild his shop from the ground up, it left me and the Prince alone for a moment. "You're in love with the smith's son," he said casually.

"I am," I replied confidently. I wasn't sure how he knew, but I wasn't going to lie about it.

"It vexes Yurak to no end," he said with a smile tugging at the corner of his mouth.

"He wants me to marry Trevor," I confided. "When we were younger, we were betrothed." Orad's eyes glittered with that information, his head tilting to the side as if to say, *Oh, really?* Obviously Yurak hadn't let that fact spill from his lips.

"You don't want to be Queen," he observed, strolling forward, hands clasped behind his back.

In all honestly, no, I didn't, but I didn't want to upset the fragile friendship between our kingdoms, either. Instead, I answered, "I want stability. I want what's best for this

352

Kingdom, and for the people of Aelawyn to be safe, and right now they aren't."

He chuckled. "You may not want to be Queen, but you play the part well. To be completely honest, when I realized who your father was, I considered rescinding our reply and staying home. But I'm glad I came. It's refreshing to see someone so young trying to right the wrongs of the past."

"Thank you," I answered, pleased with his candor.

He chuckled. "I believe our kingdoms will be great friends as long as you're in power. You're young, and one of the blessings of youth is that you have plenty of time to make difficult decisions, even about ruling a Kingdom. Maybe you'll grow into the crown, even learn to enjoy it."

We walked peacefully together for a while, watching the buzz of activity around us. I was proud of these people – my people.

"This walk was a good idea. Thank you for inviting me to see your village. They're resilience is inspiring."

I smiled, looking all around me. It really was.

"And just so you know, I'll speak to my parents about what I've seen. The Kingdom of Waverly doesn't trade or align with those who attack neighboring Kingdoms without cause."

Feeling a great sense of satisfaction in our budding friendship, we strolled back to the castle together, soaking in the sunlight.

In the castle yard, a few Galderian knights had set up targets and were showing some young men and women how to shoot a bow and arrow. Orad's eyes lit up. He excused himself and offered to teach them how he'd learned to shoot.

I made my way to the forge. I knew Nathaniel and Asher would be busy, but I needed to see him.

Asher dropped what he was doing and all but ran to me, lifting me into his arms and twirling me around. I giggled until he eased my feet to the ground again. "It's so good to see your face," he said wistfully.

I saw him last night and again very early this morning, but he sounded as desperate as I felt. Nathaniel chuckled from behind us, muttering something about *kids* and *young love.*

Asher's lips found mine for a brief moment. Too brief. "Can you meet me after dinner tonight?" There was longing in his voice. The butterflies in my stomach awakened and began to flutter their wings.

"Of course. I'll be here as early as I can."

He nodded. "I'll be here waiting. I have something to tell you."

"What is it?" I asked, trying to guess at the excitement dancing in his blue eyes.

"Tonight I'll explain everything. I promise."

Nodding, I affirmed, "Tonight."

Jewel helped me dress. The emerald green satin was begging to be stained with strong, soot-covered hands. However, the time spent at dinner passed excruciatingly slow.

Trevor acted like he wanted to be anywhere but here. He gulped goblet after goblet of wine, refusing to engage in any of the table conversation. There was a dangerous glint in his eyes, one I hadn't seen before. Prince Orad noticed, too. He glanced from me to Trevor and back, his eyes glittering with the question I didn't have an answer to. King Yurak tried to act as though he was oblivious to his son's strange behavior, but I knew better.

After most of the dinner had passed in awkward silence, Prince Orad cleared his throat. "Difficult day, Prince Trevor?"

"One might say that," Trevor answered, his eyes glassy and his face flushed and red.

"I think it's best that you retire, Trevor. Get some rest," Yurak told his son. His tone left no room for argument.

In answer, Trevor drained his goblet and slammed it down on the table, the sound startling me. Trevor pinned me with a look that was nothing short of pure fury. Orad tensed to my right, grasping the arms of his seat and rising slightly when Trevor stood up. He left the room without a word, his footsteps echoing down the hall. Thankful that I wasn't betrothed or married to him and his temper, I sipped my water and gave Prince Orad a smile of thanks as he relaxed in his chair.

I replayed the evening over and over in my mind. No one said anything to offend Trevor over dinner, but maybe something had happened beforehand.

When Orad finally excused himself from the table, I did the same and practically ran outside to see Asher. I wanted to hear his news! He was waiting at the forge, leaning against one of the work tables, thick arms crossed over his chest.

Gathering my skirts, I ran down the steps. He met me at the bottom and caught me in his arms, twirling me around. "What is it?" I asked excitedly.

"What?" he asked like he didn't know what I was talking about.

I swatted him playfully. "Tell me your news."

"Father and I... are going to build a forge in the village. He'll continue to work here in the castle yard and take on two apprentices, while I run the village forge and take an apprentice of my own."

My heart sang for him. "Asher, that's wonderful!"

He smiled, scrubbing the back of his neck. "I hope I can teach. I've never taught anyone before."

"You'll be amazing," I told him, hugging him tight, breathing onto his neck.

His smile fell away. "It means I may not get to see you as often."

"That's not true! We'll just have to make time. We had to in the village, and we'll have to now. It won't be any different."

He squeezed me. "I'll mark the trees to be felled tomorrow. Then we'll cut them into beams and drag them back to the site of the new forge."

"Where will it be?"

"Just down from the bakery, along the same road. We'll be closer to the forest so the constant smoke won't bother anyone." Excitedly, he told me his plans for the building. It would be bigger than their forge in Tierney, wider, with more surfaces to work on. Prince Orad of Waverly had already agreed to trade with them. They would deliver a large anvil to Asher in exchange for a thousand sharpened arrow tips. I listened as he told me how fast and easy those could be made. It would be the first thing he would teach his apprentice, an apprentice he'd already chosen.

This was his dream come to life.

When I pulled away, I couldn't help but smile, tears welling in my eyes. "I'm so happy for you, Asher."

He used his thumbs to brush away the tears and kissed me soundly on the lips. "It's a start," he said quietly. "It's a good start."

TREVOR

At dinner, she kept glancing at the door. I wasn't even sure she was conscious of it; her obvious need for him. I told Father what happened with them in the hallway and he snapped at me. Apparently, I wasn't trying hard enough to win her affections.

But how could I possibly compete when Asher Smith was waiting to pounce just outside? Every time she heard a hammer fall, she would think of him. When I posed that exact question to Father, he simply answered that he would get rid of him.

I knew when I saw her eagerness to leave dinner that he wouldn't be able to get rid of Asher so easily. She loved him, peasant-born though he was, and there was nothing we could do to keep her from it.

Father all but threw me from the room, but I was finished anyway. I couldn't stomach food any more than I could the thought of her in Asher's arms.

CHAPTER FORTY-ONE

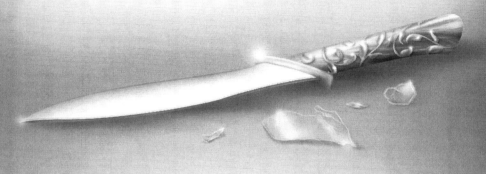

ELLA

Three days passed before I could slip away to see Asher. Hoping I could catch him, I stopped by the forge. Nathaniel confirmed that he was likely in the village, still hammering away. The three-walled structure of his very own forge was nearly built, and I couldn't wait to see it. Asher was so adept at creating things, I had no doubt his workshop would be functional and sound, but I bet it would also be beautiful. I'd written him a few letters, but they sat in my room on my desk. I needed to talk to him, to feel his arms around me. As I was rushing toward the gates, Trevor called out to me.

"Carina?"

"Yes?" Stopping at the gate, I pinched my eyes shut. *Please let him go away.*

"It's sundown. Where are you going?" he asked.

"Into the village."

"Let me escort you. It isn't safe for you to go alone."

"It's perfectly safe, Trevor. I appreciate your concern, but I'm capable of walking into the village alone." And I was going to see Asher, whom Trevor absolutely did *not* want to see.

"Please?" he begged. "I won't get in your way. I'll just see you there and busy myself until you're ready to leave, assuming you *will* be leaving Asher this evening," he added with a smirk.

My cheeks heated at the insinuation. "I just want to see how his forge is coming along." Miffed, I could tell he wasn't giving up or going away. He was coming with me. Deciding not to let him ruin my evening, we walked around the castle to the gate. Trevor asked the soldier stationed at the top to raise it for us, and we strolled down the dusty road toward the village.

Candles and lamps lit the windows of the houses. It looked like most of the shops were almost rebuilt and would be reopening soon. It was amazing how much could be done when everyone worked together. Soon, the wounds Aelawyn bore would be covered with fresh skin.

"You're quiet," Trevor said, his hazel eyes flaring with mischief.

"I was just looking at all the work they've done."

He nodded because he'd been taking it all in, too. "They've been busy, and it won't be long until they're finished, settled, and thriving. My father thought it would take years, but it seems like the people are eager for things to return to normal." There was that word again. *Normal.* At this pace,

I wondered how long they would still need me, and if they really did at all.

What the Kingdom really needed was people; in particular, more soldiers training to fight. The villagers were learning, but we didn't have enough people to stop another attack. The Galderian soldiers were still teaching those who could learn, but with so few people, if we were attacked, we'd be easily overpowered.

"We've been stuck inside all week. Do you find it stifling?" he asked. "Never being outdoors, I mean. For years, you were outside every day. All day, I assume, in the fields."

"I was, and yes, it's hard for me to be cooped up inside all day."

Trevor had kept his distance since the night his father asked him to leave the table at dinner. He was cordial, but hadn't tried to talk to me until now. This walk seemed like his attempt at an apology.

"Do you wish you'd never left?" he asked, his feet stopping.

I stopped, too. Looking up at him, I told him the truth. "Some days I wish you hadn't come to Tierney. Other days, I'm grateful for it."

"I understand. We upended your life. I'm sure you had future plans with Asher."

"Nothing was planned, but we were moving forward. Here, everything is stalled... indefinitely. What about you?" I asked, attempting to change the subject. "One day, you'll be the King of Galder. Are you looking forward to it?"

He smiled tightly. "The feeling vacillates. Some days I'm suffocated by it, while others, I look forward to taking the reins. It shifts almost daily," he admitted, glancing over at me.

I knew the feeling.

361

"You'd be good at it," I told him. "I sit in the room with you and I'm in awe. You understand everything your father does, but you bring new ideas, fresh ones, to the table as well. You'll be a wonderful king one day."

"I want to be; I suppose I'm just nervous. It's a huge honor to be responsible for the welfare of others. Every move determines their fates and futures, and while some decisions can be made and unmade, the people's lives hang in the balance. Make a wrong move, and the Kingdom suffers."

"I haven't seen you make a wrong move yet," I told him honestly.

"Thank you. You truly don't want to be Queen?" he asked curiously, watching me from the corner of his eye.

"No, I don't."

"Because of Asher? Is he the only reason?" he asked. Our footsteps were slow as we talked, but it was the most honest conversation he and I had ever had. Maybe we had more in common than we thought.

The bakery was just ahead, which meant Asher's forge wasn't far. "No, he's not the only reason," I admitted. "I just don't think I want this life. No one is honest. Everyone seems to be playing a game, always positioning themselves, negotiating, backstabbing. I don't play them as well as you and your father, and I'm not interested in developing those skills. I just want to live a simple life and be happy."

His smile faded away. "I wouldn't know what that felt like."

"You could make a different choice," I offered, knowing he wouldn't.

"I can't. My father is depending on me, and then Galder will depend on me to lead. It's what I was born for, and what I've been groomed for since birth." The sadness in his voice matched the feeling in my heart.

 362

"For someone whose feelings on the subject vacillate, you seem confident. But me? I feel…trapped," I admitted quietly. "I knew I would marry well, but my sister was firstborn. If anyone should have been Queen of any Kingdom, it should have been her. I guess I didn't give it much thought after all that happened here. When I left, I left that life behind me. But now, I'm back and I just don't fit this world anymore."

He nudged me with his elbow. "Do you think we're meant to be one thing or the other? A young woman much wiser than I once told me that it is quite possible to be both Queen and commoner."

I laughed out loud. "That would require getting your hands dirty, and a young Prince once told me that was against the rules. I can't imagine you approving of a Queen with dirty cuticles."

"Firstly, most royal hands are soiled with worse things than dirt. And secondly, I owe you many apologies, it would seem. I'm sorry for how I acted at dinner the other night. I was having a bad day," he said quietly, nodding ahead. "The forge looks empty. Perhaps he's having dinner."

From the sounds of it, a lively crowd was gathered inside a building just across the small road. Through the window, we saw people dining and laughing as musicians played in a tiny corner of the room. I couldn't help the smile that spread across my lips. The smell of cooked meat wafted through the air as the door was pushed open by someone leaving.

"I'll wait out here. Please don't rush," Trevor said companionably. "Enjoy what time you have with him."

I nodded, making my way toward the door. Glancing through the window again, the faces of the people inside became clearer. I found Asher's dark hair immediately. He was seated at a table, and he wasn't alone. A beautiful girl with long, blonde hair and a heart-shaped face sat at his side. As they laughed, I realized I hadn't seen Asher that happy in... Well, I wasn't sure I'd ever seen him so happy. Swallowing hard, I stepped away from the building and back into the shadows.

"Was he there?" Trevor asked innocently.

I walked toward him. "It's getting late. We should get back."

My heart was cracking and crumbling to pieces, based on the scene I just witnessed inside. I'm sure he wasn't seeing the girl. Probably. He wouldn't do that to me. Would he? I wasn't jealous of her, necessarily; I was jealous of their smiles and laughter and the light-heartedness they shared. It was something he and I didn't have anymore.

We didn't have time to talk, laugh, or smile; to just be us, Asher and Ella. All because I had to be Princess Carina. I felt the first stirring of hatred for the princess I had to be.

Trevor hesitated, his brows furrowed. I waved for him to come on, but he walked away from me, toward the window to see what upset me. My heart dropped when he looked inside and his shoulders tensed. When he turned back around and walked slowly toward me, pity shone on his face—pity I didn't need or want. "I'm sure it isn't what it looks like. They just seem to be friends," he said gently.

"I know." I choked on the bitter words, rubbing a hand across my face. In any event, I couldn't stay there. When I started to walk back the way we came, Trevor fell into step beside me. Neither of us spoke until we approached the castle gate once more.

Trevor stopped and grabbed my arm, halting me. "I'm sorry."

"You have no reason to be," I answered flatly.

The muscle in his jaw ticked. "I mean for the other night at dinner. I was angry and had no right to be. The same way I'm angry now and have no right to be."

"Why were you angry?" I watched as he took a deep breath and blew it out.

He released my arm and put his hands on his hips. "Because you kept looking at the door," he said simply.

"The door...?" I asked, confused.

He nodded. "You kept looking at the door, and I knew. I knew you wanted to be with him – or anywhere but where you were. I've seen people who wanted to leave dinner simply to escape the monotonous conversation. I've seen those who are exhausted and want nothing more than to go lie down. But you wanted *him*. You just wanted to be with Asher, and it killed me to know that you were going to walk out of that room and straight into his arms. It hurts me that you're hurting right now, all because of him."

I took a step back. "He didn't hurt me this evening. Our circumstances did."

"But don't you see?" he pleaded, stepping closer. "Your circumstances will not change. Not for a very long time, Carina. *This* is how you will have Asher: from a distance. Close, but never close enough. You will love him, but never be able to *be* with him. And I don't think you will ever be happy living your life with the few stolen moments each of you can spare."

"That's where you're wrong, Trevor. I *can* be happy with whatever we have, and I know he can be happy with them until I'm able to step down," I argued.

"There *is* no stepping down, Carina! My father wants you to be Queen. The coronation ceremony is already being planned, he simply hasn't told you yet. And once you're crowned, and we leave this place, you will be all alone. Your people will have no one else to depend on," he growled. Schooling his features, his eyes begged me to listen. "If you want Asher to be happy, you need to let him go. If *you* want to be happy, you need someone who will share the life you were born to lead."

I turned away from him. "No," I whispered, fearing the truth in his words.

His finger swept my skin from the bend of my neck to my shoulder blade, back and forth as he quietly whispered, "It's true. You need someone who can shoulder your burdens; someone who knows how to navigate the world you live in. It's different from the world Asher lives in; not better or worse, but different all the same. If I am destined to be trapped in this life, I would rather be trapped with you than with anyone else on this earth. One day you will have to open your eyes and see the truth, Carina. I'll be here when you do."

My voice broke. "I don't want you to be."

He sighed, his warm breath fanning my neck. "I know."

CHAPTER FORTY-TWO

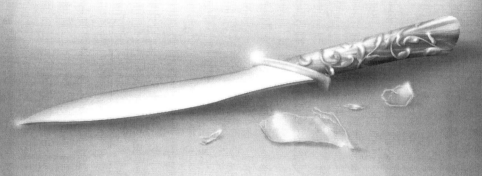

ELLA

The following morning, there was a knock at my chamber door. I opened it, expecting Jewel, and found a young boy standing there with a large bouquet of flowers. He gave me a toothless grin. "These are for you."

I crouched down to meet his eyes, smiling back at him. His rust-colored hair was a bit too long and his pants too short, but he didn't care. I took the flowers from his hands. "Thank you for these." I sniffed them and held them out for him to smell.

He sneezed and wiped his nose on his sleeve. "They aren't from me, Princess," he said, his cheeks turning bright red.

He twisted one leg back and forth, tucking his arms behind his back bashfully.

"Who are they from?" *Maybe Asher missed me more than he seemed to last night.*

The boy glanced up at me. "They're from Prince Trevor. He gave me two coins to bring them up to you." The boy grinned as he stuffed his hands in his pockets, and I heard the coins clink against one another as he toyed with them.

Determined not to show my disappointment in the name of the sender, I curved my finger, motioning him forward, and reached out to hug him. He squeezed me fast and stepped back.

"If you see Prince Trevor, please thank him for me." As soon as he was dismissed, he bolted.

The heavy door was almost closed when Jewel pushed it open from outside. "Ella?"

"Good morning, Jewel," I said, pulling her in for a much-needed hug.

She chuckled. "Well, you're certainly cheerful this morning!" Her eyes caught the flowers in my hand. "But I suppose such lovely flowers will do that to a girl. Are they from Asher?"

"No, a little boy brought them to me." It was technically true, and to be honest, I didn't want her to know they came from Trevor. I didn't want her to know what he said to me or how I didn't sleep a wink last night, wondering if he was right about Asher and whether his life would really be happier and better without me.

Was I being selfish to ask him to wait for me? After he established his new life in the village, would he even want to?

"That was awfully nice of him. How sweet! On the way here, a small boy tried to run me over."

"Probably him," I laughed.

"I'll find something to put them in. But for now, Prince Trevor has requested that you dress comfortably and join him for a morning horseback ride."

A horseback ride? To spend the morning outside instead of cooped up in the castle? That sounded amazing.

"No meetings today?"

"Not that I've heard. Prince Orad is leaving on the morrow, and there will be a feast to send him off tonight," she said. "But for today, take advantage of the fresh air. The Galderians may not be able to take a breath again for a while." She winked and walked over to my wardrobe. "Dress or trousers?"

"Trousers, please."

She tsked playfully, but brought out a pair of pants, boots, and a tunic that the tailor had made to fit me. I hadn't had an excuse to wear them until now. The fabric hugged my body scandalously compared to what I normally wore but would be much easier to ride in than a skirt or dress. I could bend and move and still be covered modestly.

"I see you every day, but it's always so rushed. We never have time together now," I told her wistfully.

Jewel gave a small smile as she helped me into my tunic, careful not to mess my hair. "I know. Hayden and Matthew miss you, too. Maybe we could have supper together one day."

The Galderians controlled most of my time now, and I wasn't sure it would be possible, but I'd try. "That would be wonderful," I answered brightly. "I'll see what I can do."

Jewel looked me over and clucked her tongue. "I'm not sure I should let you out of this room in that outfit."

It was tight, but functional, and I couldn't help but laugh at her motherly tone. She gathered the flowers in her hands. "I'll find something to put these in."

"Thank you, Jewel." I hoped she knew how much I appreciated her help. Just that small amount of contact seemed to get me through the day.

Today would be different. No posturing. No worries about Tierney, and how no one had heard from them since victory was claimed, or how the three men we sent to gather information on King Stefan and his plans never returned.

Matthew was in the stables, and somehow, he'd grown taller since I saw him a week ago.

"Matthew!" I cried out.

My brother looked up and did a double-take. "Ella?"

"How are you?" I grinned, throwing my arms around him. He returned the hug.

"I've been great! Thanks for giving me this job," he gushed. "I really love working with the animals. I was expecting you to be wearing some enormous gown, and thought I'd have to figure out how to maneuver you onto the saddle."

His teasing grin was all it took for my own to form. "I won't test you today. If I'm riding, I'm riding my way."

"That outfit will do it." He nodded, averting his eyes. He acted as if what I wore was indecent. I didn't understand what the big deal was. It wasn't any different than what he was wearing. I was completely covered.

"Is Trevor already inside?"

"He is. Your horse is ready. I saddled a steady mare for you. She's old but gentle, and she minds."

It was hard to believe this was the grown up version of the eleven-year-old boy who taught me how to gather eggs. The same boy who welcomed me with no conditions or expectations whatsoever, who was just happy I was there. "Thank you."

Matthew shrugged. "It was nothing. Enjoy your ride."

370

Enjoy your escape, he meant. I planned to. I walked into the shadows of the stable. Trevor was waiting at the far end with the reins of his horse in one hand and mine in another. His eyes widened as I approached.

"Good morning!" I greeted him. "Thank you for inviting me." He wore a similar, though less form-fitting outfit, but also a sword and daggers. "Are we riding into battle?" I joked, although the dagger Asher made me was on my hip.

Trevor smirked. "One can never be too careful."

"Thank you for the flowers, Trevor. It was a nice surprise."

"You're welcome. And thank you for joining me this morning. I thought you might need some practice with horseback riding. The day we rode into the village, you looked terrified."

Trevor had only seen me on a horse once, but he was right. I *was* scared. I needed more confidence on horseback, and there was only one way to get comfortable.

The feeling of warm air and the wind on my face was heaven. We rode out of the gates, through the village—where Asher was again absent from his forge—and into the forest beyond, following well-trodden trails that snaked between and over the hills. The woods were quiet, and we took a long time exploring them.

Along the way, Trevor showed me how to use the reins to guide the horse. I was getting better by the minute. The rich scents of decaying leaves swirled around us as we slowed to a walk. Trevor gestured ahead of us.

"There's a creek just up ahead. The horses need water."

We needed to go back to the castle soon, but I didn't want the morning to end. Trevor kept his distance when I told him I could dismount on my own and led his horse to a small brook. The horses drank, blinking away the gnats flying around their eyes. Trevor brushed his hand across his horse's back. "Thank you for riding with me."

"Thank you for inviting me."

"I was hoping you wouldn't turn me down, given what happened last night." He pinched his mouth together before adding softly, "I know you were hurt. I know he hurt you."

Swallowing the lump that immediately formed and clogged my throat, I turned my attention to my horse, raking my fingers through her mane.

"I hate seeing sadness in your eyes, Carina."

My fingers curled into the horse's mane as I held in a breath, praying he wouldn't come closer. When the moment passed and he kept his distance, I mustered the strength to speak. "Why do you insist on calling me Carina when everyone else calls me Ella?"

"It's how the people knew you, and it seems to fit. It's as lovely as you are."

I wished he would stop saying things like that. "We should go back."

When the horses finished drinking, we carved a pathway back through the forest toward the village, passing Asher's forge. He was nowhere to be seen. He was probably still in the woods, felling trees. Once the walls were up, he would need to build work tables and other things. I tried to push the disappointment out of my mind as Trevor and I guided our horses back to the stable where Matthew was waiting. Trevor graciously excused himself, claiming he needed to attend to an important matter.

"Do you need me?" I asked.

He hesitated. "No, stay and visit with Matthew."

372

He didn't have to tell me twice. Matthew and I sat in the barn on a wooden bench and he asked me all about being a Princess. I asked him about his day, what he had to do every day at the stables, and how he liked Aelawyn. He told me he liked living in the castle.

"We won't live there forever, though," he was quick to add.

"Why not?"

"Because soon you'll be Queen, and we'll still be peasants. Nothing can change that," he said. "I just hope I'll still get to work with the animals when you run us out of here."

"That would never happen, Matthew! You know me better than that. I might have to wear silly dresses, but I'm still the same Ella you knew." I gave him a hug and asked him to walk me back to the castle. I saw Trevor leaning against a hay-filled wagon watching us, his arms casually crossed over his chest. An easy smile was stretched over his lips, and I realized I'd never seen him look like he was having an ounce of fun.

"Mum said you want to have dinner with us soon," Matthew mentioned.

"I do." I chanced a glance at Trevor, who gave a small nod. It was a good idea, his eyes said. "I'll see if we can this week. I'm sorry I've been so busy," I said, feeling guilty.

Matthew smiled and ticked his head toward the castle. "Don't worry about it. You have a pretty big responsibility."

"I'll see you soon. I promise." I hugged him, taking comfort in his familiarity, and left Matthew to his chores.

Trevor walked with me, bumping into my shoulder on purpose. "I see now that we've monopolized every moment of your free time, and your family has suffered for it. I'll make sure Father knows that you need time with them."

"I'll tell him myself, thank you," I quipped playfully.

Trevor winked. "You'll make a fine Queen."

ASHER

Jerard was in the woods with me just beyond the forge when two riders approached. We made our way out of the forest, but not quickly enough. The only thing I saw was their backs, but I could tell in an instant that one of them was Ella. The other was Trevor, his golden hair gleaming in the sunlight. They paused briefly at the forge, and then took off toward the castle.

"Who was that?" Jerard asked, catching his breath. We'd been working from sunup to sundown for days. Last night was the first real, warm supper either of us had eaten in a week. We ate with our new neighbors and with Jerard's wife, Sarah, who'd out-eaten both of us. She was eating for herself and the babe in her belly.

Though it was nice to do something other than work, I missed Ella. She would have loved the music, we would've danced, and I would've made sure she had fun. Every time I saw her, it was like another small part of her had been chipped away. Yurak was carving her out to be exactly what he wanted, what he thought she should be.

The thought of the Galderians trying to change her into one of their own made my blood boil.

I cursed. *I can't believe she was just here and I missed her! Maybe I can catch up.*

"I need to run to the castle," I said suddenly. "Can you handle things here for a while?"

"Aye, after I get some water, that is," Jerard said with a tired smile. Sweat parted the sand-colored strands of his hair. He and I both needed to wash up. "Go. Get your

374

princess," Jerard said knowingly. "I can't wait to meet her," he yelled. I was already running.

By the time I reached the castle, the gate was closed. I called to the guard on the tower above.

"What's your name?" he asked, annoyed, his eyes raking down my filth-covered clothes.

"Asher Smith."

"State your business."

"I need to speak to Princess Carina," I yelled up to him.

"The Princess is busy at the moment. You'll have to come back later." If the Galderian soldier had been in front of me, I would have strangled him.

"I need to see her. Please."

He shook his head, chuckled, and mumbled something to his friend before turning his back to me.

I slammed my palm into the portcullis. "I'll be back!" I shouted.

CHAPTER FORTY-THREE

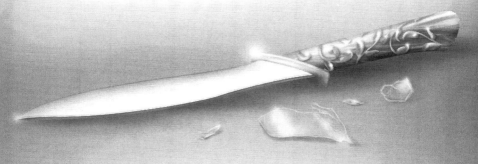

ELLA

That night, a feast was held in honor of Prince Orad and his men to commemorate their departure tomorrow. We packed food for them to take along their journey north.

The remaining Galderian knights joined us. Even with the room being half full, the Great Hall felt empty. I wanted to fill it with all of Aelawyn's people again. I wanted them all to come here, like they did when we celebrated the victory over Tierney. They should feel welcome in the castle – their castle.

"You wear a wistful smile," Orad commented quietly, wiping his mouth on a napkin.

"I was thinking about the future."

"Then I am glad you wore such hope on your face. Without hope, there is no possibility for prosperity."

He was right. I watched as a slow smile spread over his lips.

"Would you like to dance, Princess?" he asked.

I accepted, and he took my hand and led me to the open floor in front of the musicians. At the end of the dance, Orad bowed as I curtseyed. "Yurak said that you will be crowned soon. Since the journey is so long, we won't be able to send a party to attend your coronation; but know that you have my support should you require it. Simply send word, and it will be answered."

I swallowed. "Thank you. You have no idea how much that means to me."

He chuckled. "You will be a fine Queen. Right now I know your heart is torn, but you'll do what's right in the end."

As he led me back to our seats, I felt lighter than I had in weeks. Maybe he was right.

The music and wine flowed into the late hours of the night. Everyone was happy to celebrate our new friendship with Waverly. The next morning, Orad and his men left at daybreak. Yurak, Trevor, and I saw him and his men through the gate and watched as their horses kicked up dust in a path that carved toward the village.

With Prince Orad gone, the castle seemed to take a weary breath. Their party was small, but the servants had to work day and night to see to their needs. King Yurak didn't even argue when I told him I'd like to dine with my family.

Jewel, Hayden, Matthew, and I enjoyed a private dinner. Conversation was stilted at first; awkward, when it had once been the easiest thing in the world. Things were different between us.

And then there was Millie. She was present at the table, even though she wasn't there.

Taking a sip of wine, I announced, "I'd like to help you in the gardens tomorrow, Hayden."

He stopped chewing and looked at me curiously. His fiery hair was turning silver. "Why?" he asked.

Jewel swatted his shoulder and he gave her a mean look. "What was that for?" he growled.

"She wants to help. Don't ask why – just tell her what time to be in the gardens," she chastised playfully.

"Fine – I rise at dawn. You can come down when you're able." He shot another hateful look in Jewel's direction, mostly in jest. I half expected him to stick his tongue out at her.

"Dawn it is," I replied.

With the tension finally broken, Matthew felt comfortable enough to tell us all about his day. He'd helped one of the goats give birth, and the umbilical cord had become wound around the baby's neck. He saved her. "That's not the best part of my day, though. It's nice that we're actually having dinner as a family again—*this once*," he punctuated.

"I don't want it to be just *this once*, Matthew. I don't think one meal a week with family is too much to ask. Don't you agree, Jewel?"

She smiled. "I certainly do."

There was a sadness in her eyes. They kept drifting to the empty chair.

Hayden cleared his throat. "This veal is delicious."

Jewel took a sip of her wine and offered a small smile. "How is Asher?"

379

I felt my shoulders slump. "I don't know. I've been to his forge several times, but he's never there."

"He's been awfully busy lately, but I'll ask Nathaniel if there's a good time to catch him," Hayden said with a wink.

"Thanks."

The following morning, I woke before dawn, squeezed into the plainest dress in my wardrobe, and made my way to the gardens outside. Hayden was already there, looking over the neat rows of vegetables.

"Good morning!" I said cheerfully.

He turned and smiled, offering his own greeting. "Jewel will be along shortly. She visits Millie in the mornings."

"Do you visit her?" I asked.

"Evenings." He walked with his hands clasped behind his back. "I like to visit her in the evenings because it gives her a visitor to look forward to at dawn and dusk. Matthew tries to take her food midday."

"I visit, but she won't speak."

"I imagine she's afraid and ashamed. In time, she'll come around."

He crouched down to pull some weeds, so I went to the next row and helped. It dawned on me that Jewel had said the same thing to me several years ago. When Piers dropped me on their doorstep, we took my gown to the shop to exchange it for plainer dresses. Millie was upset, and Jewel told me Millie would come around in time. The Farmers always had hope that she would somehow grow up, learn to accept things, and stop causing trouble. I believed she could, too. She just had to see that she was wrong, and want to change for herself.

"Nathaniel says Asher's been very busy with the new forge," Hayden added conversationally. "He's not seen much of him lately. But when he sees him, he'll ask about the best time to catch him."

"Hmm," I huffed, expressing my disbelief. Surely he wasn't too busy to see his own *father*. They were close. Hayden glanced up and gave me a pointed look, reminding me that until last night, I'd been too busy for my own family as well. Properly chastened, my hands returned to the earth, plucking the dirty little weeds trying to rob the crops of water.

"How long do you think it'll be before someone comes looking for you?" Hayden chuckled, standing up straight and stretching his back.

"Taking bets?"

He grinned. "Absolutely."

"Half an hour?"

He shook his head. "Two minutes."

"I hope you enjoy losing, Uncle, because it's dawn and most of the castle is just waking up. They'll need time to figure out that I'm not in my chamber."

Hayden walked to a small wagon at the end of the row and grabbed a hoe. A moment later, the door nearest us swung open and Jewel appeared. "Ella, Trevor is looking for you. Hurry, before he sees you kneeling in the mud."

Glancing at Hayden, he smiled in victory. I pursed my lips together at his smugness, squinting my eyes at him. "You may have won this time…"

"Ay, and if you want to be bested again, you know where to find me. Now, run along before Jewel has a conniption fit," he said merrily, shooing me away.

"Hurry." Jewel waved me forward. "Trevor said King Yurak wants to see you."

381

Of course, he did.

I followed Jewel to my chamber and let her scrub the dirt from my fingers, grinning as the mud clouded the bowl of crystal clear water. It reminded me of home.

She grumbled the entire time. "I knew this would happen. It was a bad idea. This isn't coming out from under your nails. The King will notice, and then he'll ask you what you've been doing, and you'll have to tell him."

"So, I'll tell him."

She paused in her ministrations and raised an eyebrow. "You think he'll be happy that you were pulling weeds in the gardens?"

He wouldn't be happy, but for a few moments, I had been, and it was totally worth it, my face said back to her.

She resumed her scrubbing in earnest. "Honestly, Jewel, my hands are clean now! Probably cleaner than they've ever been before."

I pulled off the dress I was wearing and she helped me into another, more ornate one—one that the King had brought from Galder and would no doubt approve of seeing me in. She let loose a groan when she noticed the state of my hair. "Sit and I'll fix it."

With a long, dark braid hanging down my spine and my mother's crown atop my head, I made my way to the great hall where Yurak and Trevor were breaking their fast. The soldiers positioned outside the hall pushed the doors open for me.

Yurak waited patiently while I was seated. "Good morning," I greeted them both. I immediately saw that Trevor was *not* happy. Neither was Yurak. Surely this wasn't because I was gardening!

"Carina, there is something I'd like to discuss with you," Yurak began.

382

I swallowed the knot forming in my throat. *He saw me in the garden.*

"Of course."

"The people of Aelawyn are rebuilding. You've seen the progress they've made."

I had, and it was magnificent. A simple nod was my reply.

"They need a Queen, not a Princess. They need leadership, and I'm afraid I cannot stay here indefinitely to guide you. I would like to proceed with your coronation, and I would like you to consider allowing Trevor to stay here indefinitely. He's been at my side since infancy, and I feel confident that he can answer any questions you might have and guide you along the way."

This is too fast. It's all happening too fast! Just then, a plate appeared in front of me, piled with steaming food, and it gave me a moment to compose my thoughts. Thanking the woman who brought it, I took a sip of hot cider. The sweet drink warmed my belly from the inside out.

The only two words I could muster were, "How soon?"

"One month from today. I will send messengers to all the Kingdoms, with the exception of Tierney, of course."

One month?

"This will require great devotion on your part, not only in becoming Queen, but in dedicating yourself to learning how to rule before the title is bestowed upon you. I know you weren't privy to the way your father handled things, and honestly, it's almost a blessing that you weren't. We can show you the *proper* way to run a kingdom."

"The proper way?"

"Yes; meaning how to conduct the business of the Kingdom so that she prospers," he replied tersely, his fingers tightening on the edge of the table.

383

I didn't want to be Queen. I just wanted Aelawyn to be safe. I knew I could lead her, but leading as Queen would be a very different experience than it was as a Princess. It would be more official, not to mention permanent.

"I see the worry on your face," Yurak said. "But you agreed that if we helped you reclaim your Kingdom, if Galder defended her, that you would take the crown and throne back. I expect you to remain true to your word."

"Yes," I choked out. "I will. It's just very sudden."

He shook his head. "I've given you plenty of time to adjust to your new life, Carina. I know you are young and untested, but it's time for you to step forward; to leave my shadow and make your own."

Quiet until then, Trevor finally spoke. "I'll stay by your side."

If his father weren't there, I would have asked him *why*. Why not return to his home and country? Why stay to help when I was clearly an ungrateful wretch who didn't *deserve* the title of Queen any more than I wanted it?

The longing in his eyes answered my unspoken questions and I quickly looked away, unable to stomach what I saw. I'd seen the same look in Asher's so many times before.

His father's gruff voice gave me reason to look away. "I also want you to reconsider honoring your betrothal."

My lips parted.

"Before you speak, please listen," he said, leaning forward. "It's what your mother wanted. This is her letter." He slid a yellowed piece of parchment across the table toward me. Only the oily, red, circular stain of my mother's wax seal remained at the fold. "You may have it, but please take my request—and hers—seriously. She wanted what was best for you. She had no say in Ivy's betrothal, but she orchestrated yours despite the danger she would face from your father should he learn of her involvement. Your circumstances may have changed, but the marriage is still what's best for you. She wanted someone who would be strong enough to stand beside you, who wouldn't let you drown in a world of darkness. My son is that man. He is your match in every respect. I've watched the pair of you, and I know you have become friends. Over time, you could become so much more. I see the potential that in your youth, you do not see."

My fingers lifted the delicate paper. "May I be excused?"

When Yurak nodded, I pushed my chair back and walked from the room, not daring to look at Trevor. Somehow, I held the tears in until I was in the hallway.

ASHER

I returned to the castle gate the next morning, slipping in alongside a wagon they'd granted entrance to, and headed to the forge to speak with my father. He greeted me with a smile and a clap on the shoulder, asking me questions about the new forge, my apprentice, and the general state of things in the village. I answered each one before asking my own.

"Have you seen Ella?"

"Aye," he answered. "She asked about you. She's been to see you several times, but hasn't found you at the forge."

"I've been in the forest more than the forge lately."

He nodded, crossing his arms over his chest and leaning against the work table. "Have you tried the castle yet?"

"No, I came here straight away."

He nudged me with his arm. "Well then, what are you waiting for?"

I smiled and gave him a quick hug before jogging toward the back door of the castle and slipping inside the shadows. The cooks squawked when I ran through their kitchen, but at least I made it inside. I wasn't quite sure where she'd be.

Rounding a blind corner, I ran headlong into someone. I looked up, expecting to see Ella, since it seemed we were always running into each other. But it wasn't Ella I saw. As we both stumbled back from the contact, I grabbed my forehead as he adjusted his crown. His eyes narrowed at the sight of me.

"Asher Smith?" he asked.

"Yes, Your Highness."

"Come with me. We have a rather delicate matter to discuss." His guards saw that I turned and followed as he instructed, closing in around us and herding me into a room behind the King.

He walked to the window and threw open the curtains that blocked out the sun. Dust motes danced in the beams of sunlight among the books that lined every wall. The library of Aelawyn's castle was vast.

"You're probably wondering what I would possibly need to discuss with you, so I won't waste your time or mine. I appreciated you fighting alongside my men. It showed bravery and highlighted your skill with a blade."

"Thank you, Majesty."

His mouth pursed together before he spoke again. "Ella Carina will be crowned Queen of Aelawyn in one month's time."

My Ella would be Queen so soon? The knowledge was like a punch to the gut.

"I thought it only fitting to tell you that she has also agreed to honor her betrothal and marry my son. I'm aware of the relationship you had with her, and I know she still

386

harbors feelings for you, though they have waned of late. Your presence in the castle or on the grounds will cause her great difficulty fulfilling her obligations; therefore, you are to remain in the village. See to your work. Enjoy your new forge and find another woman with which to build a life." He paused for a moment, and then continued in a voice laced with poison. "However, if you step foot inside the castle gates again, I'll have you flogged. If you reach out to Carina via letter, I'll have your father flogged. If you interfere in any way with this marriage before it takes place, I'll have you and your father put to death. Am I clear?" His hazel eyes were cold despite their color. He was serious.

"Yes, Sire." I had to admit, he was crystal clear. I gritted my teeth as he told his men to escort me to the gate—away from Ella.

CHAPTER FORTY-FOUR

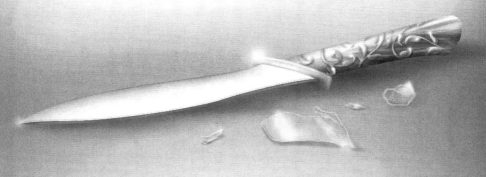

ELLA

tay still!" the Galderian dressmaker barked. When I left Yurak and Trevor behind after breakfast and returned to my room, she was waiting. I made the mistake of referring to her as a seamstress. She took great offense to that title, and had been making my life hell ever since. She was a hateful woman, angry that the King made her leave home for something as simple as a coronation gown. She'd grumbled the phrase repeatedly and stuck me with more than a few pins. When she jabbed me again, I almost kicked her.

"I'm not a pin cushion!" I fumed. But the witch only grinned. She actually grinned.

My mother's letter waited on my desk as the woman measured my waist again, watching as her assistants brought in bolt after bolt of fabric, all of it in varying shades of white.

As the fitting dragged on, she clucked her tongue in dissatisfaction at every decision I made. About the length of the gown, the shape of it, the way the sleeves and back would be buttoned. "More work for me," she said with a huff. But when I asked for her suggestions, she refused to give them.

"Your collarbones are delicate. Would you like the neckline to show them?" she asked, tucking her silver hair back into a scrap of cloth tied around it.

"That would be lovely, thank you."

She scowled at my smile, but I didn't let it waver. I would kill her with kindness.

Right about that time, Jewel knocked and entered. When she saw me standing on the large wooden block, scraps of fabric being woven and pinned around me, she clasped her hands over her mouth. Her eyes filled with tears. "Oh, my."

With hesitant steps, she made her way toward me. I stepped off the block and hugged her tightly as she cried. She was happy for me, but I knew her thoughts went to Millie. "It won't be long now, Jewel."

"I know," she cried into my ear.

The dressmaker summoned me back to the block, harping that I was wasting her precious time—time she would need every second of to make this monstrosity of a gown before the coronation. There would be fittings – many fittings – in my future, she promised with a scowl. Jewel stayed with me, watching as the woman and her assistants buzzed around the room. When they finally left, taking all their bolts, sheers, needles, and measurements with them, I breathed a sigh of relief and sat down beside her.

"Is it true?" she asked.

"I have one month." *Of freedom*. Hearing the words come from my own mouth didn't make them feel any more real.

"And you're going to marry the Prince of Galder?" she said quietly.

I turned to her, shocked. "Who told you that?"

"King Yurak proclaimed it this morning in the village square."

"That snake!" I hissed and jumped to my feet. "I never agreed to that." Pacing the room, I couldn't help but think of Asher. What if he had heard his lies? "I need to find Asher, but first I need to make it clear to the King that I am *not* marrying his son."

Jewel stared at me, her eyes wary.

"What is it?" I asked apprehensively.

"King Yurak gave Hayden and our family a large farm outside of the village, on an enormous piece of land," Jewel said, obviously conflicted. "The Lord who used to own it was slain when Tierney attacked the castle. Along with the land, there's also a large house. It's three times the size of our old home, and he's giving us more livestock than we know what to do with."

My heart filled my throat. I was so happy for them and yet, I was losing them at the same time. "When did he give it to you?"

"A few hours ago. Hayden and I just returned; we took Matthew to look at it before we accepted. It's more than we ever hoped for, but…"

"But it's what you've always dreamed of," I finished for her. She nodded. "It is."

"You'll take Millie with you."

Jewel stiffened. "In a month, we will, if you'll allow it."

"I'll allow it now."

"Ella, I don't—"

I stood up, my hands shaking with rage. I wanted to throttle someone. "No, *now*. If he wants me to act like a Queen, then by God, I will. Millie will go home with you now. I won't have her hidden beneath this castle rotting away while you both work your fingers to the bone."

If no one was here to watch over Millie, he could do whatever he wanted with her. I wouldn't stand for that.

She grabbed my hands, steadying them. "If you're certain..."

"I am," I said confidently. "When do you leave?" I didn't want her to go.

"Hayden is gathering our things now. There's so much to be done! I still want to stay and help you, and I promise to come as often as I can."

I shook my head. "Don't worry about me. There are plenty of people in this castle to help, and you'll need to get your new house in order."

"You'll be a wonderful queen, Ella. Just be you, not what you think Yurak wants."

"That's the problem. He seems to think he owns my every decision, and it's my own fault for letting him lead for so long. I should have sat on the throne from the very beginning, but I was too busy running from it."

She hugged me and whispered in my ear. "I'll tell Asher it isn't true. We'll stop at his forge on the way."

"Thank you, but I'm not sure it matters at this point. I think Asher's already decided I'm not worth the trouble the crown causes."

She shook her head. "He can't have changed his mind. The way he looked at you..."

"Things change. People change." My words may have been hollow, but my heart was cracking open, spilling all the regret and shame I held in. I'd let him slip right through my fingers.

She tried to tell me that Hayden looked at her the same way, to ease my aching heart in the way only a mother could. The least I could do was ease hers by returning her daughter to her. "I'll make sure Millie is ready," I vowed. "Go help Hayden and Matthew. I'll bring her to you."

She swallowed, her wary eyes saying she wasn't sure I should do this, and mine assuring her I would be fine. As she slipped out the door, I took a steadying breath. I glanced at the letter that sat on my desk, still unread. It would have to wait. I made my way down the hallways and staircases, slipping inside the iron door that led to the damp dungeon below.

The guards let me pass without questioning why I was there.

Millie sat on her cot with her legs pulled to her chest, shivering.

"Millie."

She turned her head, looked at me for a brief moment, and then faced the wall again.

"Guard!" I yelled. They were just down the hall. Footsteps approached quickly, and the sound of jangling keys filled the air. Millie watched as I held my hand out. "Give me the key that unlocks this door."

He opened his mouth and shut it. "Princess, with all due respect…"

"Now," I demanded.

"I have orders not to release this prisoner," he argued, anxiously scrubbing at his forehead.

"Your new order is to give me the proper key. *I* will release her."

The guard shuffled through the keys, pulling a long, iron one from the ring. "King Yurak'll have my head for this," he muttered.

"I promise he won't," I assured him, taking the proffered key and twisting it in the lock. The mechanism disengaged and the door swung open with a screech. "Millicent, come with me. You're going home."

"My home is in Tierney," she bit out.

"No it isn't, but if you'd like to join your family in their *new* home, this is your chance. It may be your only opportunity, so I suggest you take it."

Her eyes raked over my fine clothes, all the way up to my crown. In the end, she stood, her legs shaking under her weight. She'd been fed twice daily, but her body had atrophied in the dungeons from a lack of movement. She shot me a threatening look, one fierce enough to have the guard grab hold of the hilt of his sword. I held my hand out to him, stopping his approach.

However misguided her decisions were, Millie fought fearlessly for what she wanted. I envied her for that.

"They're waiting near the gardens," I told her.

Millie nodded once and followed me out of the darkness, up the steps, and through the back entrance where Hayden, Jewel, and Matthew rushed to her side. She squinted. I wasn't sure if the sunlight hurt them so bad they watered, or if she had somehow grown a heart while she was locked away.

My eyes welled, too. Jewel motioned me forward to join the family in celebrating, but I shook my head slightly. She pinched her eyes closed and hugged Millicent tightly. "You should go now," I instructed them. "I'll see you to the gate."

Hayden turned to hug me. "Thank you, Ella. Please come find us as soon as you are able."

"I will," I promised. And I would make good on that promise. Family dinners once a week would become tradition. I swore it to myself and then to them.

Matthew hugged me quickly, brushing his tears away as he headed for Hayden's horse, Brutus. He took the reins and patted the strong column of his neck.

Jewel crushed me against her chest. "Thank you," she cried. "I promise she won't cause any more trouble."

"I won't be lenient if there is a next time."

Millie shot a scathing look in my direction.

I walked alongside them to the gate and ordered the soldier to lift the portcullis and let them through. *When did we start keeping it clamped shut during the daytime?* The villagers weren't able to access the castle. This had to stop. I lingered, watching until they were out of sight. My heart ached to go with them. I'd lost contact with Asher, and now my family was leaving, too. I knew this would happen, but I didn't expect it so soon.

"Carina?" I closed my eyes against his voice, and then turned and walked back toward the gardens, hoping he wouldn't follow, but knowing he would.

When Trevor fell into step beside me, I stopped and turned to him. "How could you let your father lie like that?"

He opened his mouth to protest, but I cut him off. "No!" I shouted. "Not another lie, Trevor."

"I didn't know. I just heard myself. That's why I came to find you. I knew you would be upset." He grasped my upper arm, but I jerked away.

"Of course, I'm upset! I never agreed to marry you Trevor, and you know it."

"You only agreed to read your mother's letter, I know. And while I hope you change your mind, if friendship is all you'll accept from me, I'll gladly give it. I didn't know he would make a false announcement. I swear it."

"I just released Millicent from the dungeon. Did you know your father gave my family an enormous plot of land, including a house and livestock, outside the village?"

"I didn't," he said. There was no lie in his eyes.

I felt so isolated and alone. "I already miss them so much," I admitted, my lip wobbling uncontrollably. He pulled me into his arms and held me as I cried.

"I'm sorry," he said quietly against my hair.

ASHER

When the Farmers pulled up outside the forge in their wagon, I knew something was wrong. "Is she alright?" I shouted, rushing toward them. I was startled when I saw Millicent sitting beside Matthew in the back of the wagon. She pinned me with a look so evil, it gave me pause.

Jewel jumped down to meet me. "Ella is fine. We've just been given a wonderful gift."

Matthew jumped down from the back of the wagon and prattled on about the size of the house, the fields they would have, and most of all, the animals they'd been given. It was more than generous and would make their dreams come true, but it came at a steep price. It meant Ella would be left behind. King Yurak was systematically separating her from everyone she loved.

Worry hung heavily on Hayden's brow. "Ella asked us to stop by. She's come into the village a few times to see you, but hasn't been able to catch you."

"The last time I went to see her, the King threatened to remove my head if I stepped back inside the gate."

His eyes widened. "What about Nathaniel?"

"He's of use to the King at this point, so he should be fine in the forge. For now," I added. "I'm worried about her. First me, and now all of you. He's taking away anyone who means anything to her."

Jewel worried her hands. "She said to tell you not to listen to the gossip spreading round that she'll be marrying Prince Trevor."

"Is that what they're saying?" That would *not* happen. She couldn't marry him.

Hayden crossed his arms over his chest and sighed. "What do we do?"

"I'm not really sure, but I'm thinking it over."

"Well, when you figure it out, come and get me. Don't lose your mind, or you may lose your head. We can talk it over together. Okay?"

I nodded. "Okay."

The man made me shake on it, sealing the bargain with my word and his.

CHAPTER FORTY-FIVE

ELLA

I grabbed my mother's letter and walked to the window seat, curling my legs up on the plush, new cushion. On the street below, the people of Aelawyn enjoyed their lives. Small children petted bleating lambs. A man with a large bag on his shoulder passed by, teasing the children that the lamb would bite. Women walked together toward their chores with smiles on their faces.

Their laughter was genuine. They were free and happy.

In the sunlight beaming in through the window, in her slanted and elegant handwriting, I read the words of my mother, addressed to Yurak of Galder...

Word may have reached you by now that our eldest daughter Ivy has been betrothed to Prince Enik of Halron. While the marriage will be advantageous to Aelawyn in both gold and alliance, I fear for her. Since the announcement, she has withdrawn into herself. Though circumstance dictates that I cannot be the mother my daughters require, and though I cannot alter Ivy's future, there is a chance that I can perhaps influence the future of my youngest daughter, Ella Carina.

If your son has not yet been betrothed, perhaps you might consider Carina as his match. She is kind, intelligent, and quiet. Though she is young, I know in my heart that she has the potential to do great things and be a formidable Queen to any Kingdom who is fortunate enough to have her.

I pray this letter finds you well.

Eternally yours,
Ariona

Queen of Aelawyn

It was a plea; a desperate attempt to steer my life in a pleasant direction, when Ivy's was already lost. If she'd somehow arranged Ivy's betrothal, or if she'd been brave enough to stand up to our father...

No, she would have been slaughtered, leaving us completely at his mercy. She did all she could by becoming as invisible and unassuming as possible, and then risked everything when she put the quill to parchment on my behalf. A silent plea, sent by trusted messengers to the only man she ever loved and who loved her in return.

My heart ached for her.

For my sister.

Even for Yurak.

He tried to help, offered an unbelievable amount of gold to ensure my betrothal to his son, and she was still killed for standing beside the King and throne she hated. She died trying to help me escape into a new and better life.

I needed to see my family, to see Asher. Tucking the letter between the delicate pages of a favorite book, I made my way to the gate. "Open, please," I shouted to the guard atop the wall, shielding my eyes with my hand against the bright midday sun.

"I'm afraid I can't do that, Princess."

"And why is that?"

"The King ordered the gate to be sealed until further notice." The man was simply following orders, but it didn't stop me from bristling.

I narrowed my eyes at him. "We'll see about that."

"I'm sorry, Highness. There is nothing I can do. It's a matter of safety."

Safety? I rushed up the main steps and threw open the door, searching out Yurak and finding Trevor instead.

"Where are you going in such a rush?" he said teasingly, before his smile faded away once he took in the rage that contorted my face.

"Why is the gate closed?" I demanded.

He blinked once and led me by the elbow to a nearby room, where he shut and locked the door. It was a closet, full of brooms, mops, and pails. "We didn't want to alarm everyone just yet," he whispered. "Right now, the best of Aelawyn's soldiers are in the village, keeping watch, and the remaining soldiers from Galder are guarding the castle." He paused a moment, choosing his words. "One of our messengers was dispatched to Galder yesterday on business my father needed to attend to. His horse brought him back to the castle, decapitated, with a Tierney tunic stretched over his torso."

I swallowed the shock. "They aren't going to accept that they lost."

He shook his head slowly. "It doesn't appear that way. So, until we assess the threat, Father asked the gates to remain closed except for certain times when people may enter and exit. Those times will vary daily, so they cannot be predicted. The nobility and royalty will not be allowed to venture outside the castle grounds until we can ensure that it is safe to do so."

"Of course, but we need to tell the villagers."

"Father has already taken care of it," he replied.

My fists balled. *He should have let me speak with them!* I survived with them. They chose *me* to lead them.

Soon. Within the month, Yurak would return to Galder.

I know in my heart that she has the potential to do great things and be a formidable Queen to any Kingdom who is fortunate enough to have her.

My mother was wrong about a great many things, but I prayed she was right about me.

ASHER

Father arrived at sundown, his wagon full of all the things we'd brought from home. The castle forge had been emptied and dumped hastily into the back of his wagon. Our horse had been hitched in the same fashion.

The look on his face was one of rage, and I knew that though my father was a gentle man, he'd been pushed too far. "The King had me escorted from the grounds like a common criminal!" he bellowed. "After all we did for him – for Aelawyn – he had his men toss my things into the wagon like rubbish and take me to the wall, while everyone watched and wondered what I had done. I didn't do anything but work my hide off for him!" he sputtered.

Ella's family. Me. Father. She was inside the castle and completely, utterly alone.

How could she not see it?

Father wagged a finger in my face knowingly. "Now, don't you get upset at her. There's talk in the castle that there's been an incident involving Tierney. She's safe, but they aren't going to open that gate for a long time. She's probably holed up in her chamber at this point and doesn't know they threw me out, too."

His words didn't help, but while Father paced, I patted the horse's neck and tried to calm down. The animal's knowing eyes peered up at me.

I wasn't angry with Ella; I was angry with Yurak and his son. Unloading my father's tools into the new forge, I considered trying to dispatch a letter to Ella. But then I remembered Yurak's chilling words; the way he threatened my father. I couldn't put his life in danger.

I wasn't supposed to initiate any further contact with Ella Carina. That was his command.

That didn't mean she couldn't reach out to me, though. She would find a way.

ELLA

The following days were spent inside my chamber, walking the hallways, or walking the grounds. Trevor was a constant shadow any time I left my bedroom. He tried to lift my spirits by telling jokes and stories about his childhood, but my thoughts and worries were with my family and Asher. Were they safe? I sent word for them days ago, letting them know they were welcome any time and that I wanted them to come to the castle and stay until things settled down with Tierney, but my letters went unanswered.

I went to talk to Nathaniel but the forge was empty. *He left without saying goodbye?* He probably heard about the messenger and wanted to make sure Asher was safe.

Trevor was walking beside me when someone sounded a horn, followed by shouts coming from the front of the castle. A soldier ran toward us, shouting, "Get inside! Now!" He rushed us toward a side entrance and shoved us inside the stone walls. Once we were safe, the man raced back through the door and Trevor bolted it from the inside.

"What if someone else needs to get in?" I cried, my hands shaking.

"They'll have to find another way," Trevor said calmly. He laced his fingers through mine and added, "Come with me."

I followed him up a winding stairwell that led into one of the towers and into a room I hadn't entered in years. There was a large bed with messy covers, a wardrobe, and a desk covered with parchment, quills, and ink. There were unlit candles on every surface.

He pulled me to the window. "We'll be safe here, and this way we can still see what's happening."

This was *his* room. And as uncomfortable as that thought made me, I needed to know what was going on outside. A single rider on a horse approached the gate, wearing Tierney black, weary in the saddle and sagging to the side.

"Is it another one of our messengers?" I asked.

404

"I don't know…It could be a trick, a diversion," he said quietly. "There could be a larger force hidden and waiting to strike once the gate is up."

"Has Galder been attacked? How do you know this?" I asked, shocked.

"No, it hasn't, but my father studied military strategy with his generals. His knowledge is vast, and fortunately he insisted I attend all of his meetings."

The rider approached the gate, clinging desperately to the neck of his horse. When he tried to raise his arms, he nearly fell off. The soldiers on top of the wall trained their arrows on him, waiting on the command to kill.

"He's trying to surrender! What are they doing?" I asked quietly.

"First, they'll make sure he's not a danger—that he isn't armed, and then they'll take him to the dungeon." He said it as if it were an everyday occurrence; so nonchalantly, I couldn't help but stare at him.

"I want to be there," I said suddenly.

He turned his head to face me. "What?" he asked incredulously.

"I want to be there when they speak to him."

He shook his head. "I'm afraid that's not possible—"

Enough of this. "I'm afraid it is. I insist."

Gathering my skirts, I left his chamber and made my way down the spiraling stairs while Trevor followed me, begging me not to do this, telling me it was dangerous.

"My father will be furious!"

"Let him be. I've had enough! If he ever wants to leave and go back home to Galder, he needs to step aside and let *me* wear the crown."

He let loose an exasperated growl. "You have no experience with these matters!"

I stopped suddenly and he almost bowled me over, but I wheeled around and stuck my finger in his face. "Then *this* is the perfect opportunity to gain some."

He pursed his lips tightly and I turned on my heel, making him run to catch up to me once more.

People were running through the hallways and corridors every which way, fleeing and taking cover where they thought was the safest. Terror shone in their eyes and desperation fueled their steps, but I walked to the front doors of the castle and told the soldiers to open them. The two men glanced at each other, uncertain. "NOW!" I roared.

The Galderian knights surrounded the man. They hauled him off the horse and patted him down. The man was unarmed. King Yurak suddenly appeared behind us.

"Why aren't you in your chambers?" he seethed, baring his teeth at his son.

"Because *I* demanded to see and know what was going on inside my Kingdom!" I replied haughtily.

Yurak was opening his mouth to reply, when one of his knights called to him. "Your Highness, you're not going to believe this."

"Is it safe to approach?" he yelled back.

"It is. Our scout just returned. The forest is clear."

To Yurak's chagrin, all three of us made our way toward the stranger. His head lolled forward as the knights held him upright. He couldn't have stood without their help.

Yurak stepped in front of the man, two of his knights moving to flank him on both sides. Four more flanked me and his son.

"What is your name and purpose here?" Yurak demanded.

The man strained to lift his head, beads of sweat coating his brow. His eyes were swollen and purple, and his cheek was sliced open and oozing blood. His lip was split. There were bruises on every inch of him. Panting with every word, he said, "My name is Prince Carden of Tierney. I ask for mercy and asylum."

CHAPTER FORTY-SIX

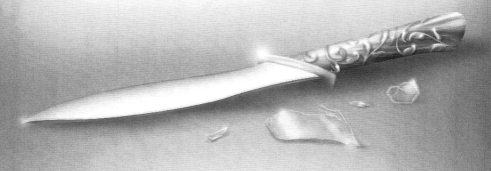

ELLA

arden opened his eyes. I studied his features; his black hair, his dark brown eyes, and the fire that was somehow still alive in them. Carden's jaw ticked, as if to say I had no right to scrutinize him, had no right to pity him. It was hard not to in that moment, even if he was the boy who tried to take my kingdom. The boy whose father I hated nearly as much as my own. I made my face as neutral and cold as possible.

"What happened to you?" I asked, stepping forward to position myself beside King Yurak.

"It seems," he took a deep breath, coughing up a stream of blood that splattered just short of my gown, "that my father favors my brother William at the moment."

"How do we know this isn't a trick?" Trevor said. "Your father is a viper. How do we know this isn't a trick to get you close to Carina, close enough to strike?"

"Please," he mumbled, his head sagging once more. "Put me in the dungeons. Lock me in the darkest hole you have and keep me under guard. Just help me. I'm dying."

A red stain blossomed on his shirt, proving his words. "He's wounded. Take him to the dungeon, but have a healer sent to him immediately," I demanded.

Yurak turned and quirked a brow as the knights did as they were told. "If he dies, it'll give Tierney a justified reason to attack," I said brusquely. "I won't have it. We'll help him, get answers, and figure out what to do with the Prince *after* we have all the information."

Surprisingly, Yurak flashed a small smile of approval. "Very well, Highness."

I should have felt warm from the compliment. I should have been glowing as a result of his praise. But all it did was leave me feeling as heavy as the crown perched on my head.

I followed Carden to the dungeon, ensuring that the guards who carried him treated him with respect and dignity.

"No one is to further injure this man. Is that understood? If I hear of it, you'll never see your homes or families again." It was a harsh threat, but a necessary one.

"Yes, Your Highness," the four knights muttered.

"Have guards watch him day and night, and give them the same instruction and warning. You're still needed along the gate in case this was just a diversionary tactic."

Another assent from the men and I chanced a glance at Carden, who was laying prostrate on a hay-covered cot, one

410

arm slung over his forehead and the other clutching the wound on his ribs. The cell smelled of urine and mold. It was dark and humid, definitely not a room fit for a prince. But he was the son of my enemy and, to be fair, he had requested that we place him in the darkest hole we had. This was it.

The day after Carden showed up at the gate, Tierney sent two scouts into the forest and our men sent a message back with them, one Stefan wouldn't soon forget. I shuddered to think about the brutality of it, but violence was the only language Stefan spoke now. Tierney would know that Aelawyn was standing stronger than ever before. We weren't afraid to defend our borders and people, and they would be wise to stay off our lands.

The gate remained closed, and soldiers and spies were positioned throughout the forests on all sides of Aelawyn.

I wrote and dispatched two more messages; one to my family, and one to Asher and his father, letting them know that I couldn't leave to visit them. I asked them to come stay at the castle and hoped they would reply in person, sooner rather than later. This time, instead of asking a soldier to deliver the letters, I asked one of the men from the village who was being trained by them. He spent his days in the castle, but lived in the village and returned to his home every night. He promised to personally deliver the message to the Smiths. In my letter, I asked Asher to take my family's letter to them. It was my fervent hope that they would all come and stay here until Stefan backed down.

I had a feeling he knew Carden was here.

With only one week left until the coronation ball, we'd only received replies from the Kingdoms of Roane and Halron, stating their parties would attend. Their responses were unexpected, given that they both ignored our first invitation. Everyone was working hard to prepare, both for the event itself, and to host two of the northern Kingdoms.

I was nervous. Would Roane send Isabel to visit Aelawyn and would she by chance bump into Asher. Stamping down the jealousy that reared its head, I tried to focus.

As soon as we could, we would send a shipment of gold to Orad. In exchange, he would send linen, oil, and iron. But while tensions were still escalating with Tierney, we couldn't risk sending anyone into the mountains until it was safe. I hoped that the Kingdoms of Roane and Halron would consider trading with us as well.

For three days, I endured the distasteful dressmaker and her entourage. At the end of each day, the dress got bigger; more yards of pristine white fabric layered one on top of the other, more lace, and more pearls. What started out as a choppy, barely sewn mess, was metamorphizing before my very eyes.

Yurak had gotten nowhere with Prince Carden. The young man was tight-lipped to a fault, and he was dangerously testing Yurak's patience—patience that was thinned to the breaking point. This morning was no different. When Trevor asked his father if he'd gleaned any information from the Prince of Tierney, he exploded, slamming his fist on the table.

"He refuses to speak, and *I* refuse to allow him to remain silent! I know you ordered that he be treated well, Carina, but if he continues to refuse—"

"I'll talk to him," I interrupted.

The King became deathly quiet at my words.

"Maybe she should," Trevor said in support.

Exasperated, Yurak said, "Well it certainly couldn't hurt. You'll go with her," Yurak said to his son.

He could go to the dungeon with me, but I wanted to talk to Carden alone. I had a feeling that whatever he had to say, he intended to say it to me alone.

With the fabric of my skirts gathered in my hands, I made my way down the dingy steps, each one bringing me closer to Carden. Why would he choose to come here, of all places? And what happened to make his father turn on him? What did he do?

The guards at both sets of the two locked doors let us pass through, but I stopped before we got to Carden's cell. "Trevor," I said quietly. "I need to speak with him alone."

He opened his mouth to argue about it, but I held up my hand. "He hasn't spoken with your father for a reason. I'll wager to say he won't open up if you're here."

"He might not talk to you, either," he argued, jaw ticking.

"I have to try."

Gritting his teeth, he finally agreed. "Fine, but I'll be close by; able to reach you if he so much as twitches a finger through the bars."

"Thank you."

He inclined his head. "It is always a pleasure to stand at your side, Carina."

I took a deep breath and left Trevor standing between the shadows and flickering torchlight. Two men stood guard outside his cell, looking bored. I dismissed them. I looked into the dim space and saw Carden lying down on his cot.

"How are you feeling?" I asked carefully.

He winced as he sat up. "Well enough, Princess. I suppose I should thank you for sending the healer and not leaving me to die and rot down here." The Prince's face was pale and gaunt. Dark circles hung heavily beneath his eyes. But the swelling and bruises had started to fade away, and the laceration had healed into a thin line.

"If you want to thank me, you can give me the answers I need."

He let out a groan. "I was wondering how long it would take before Yurak sent you. Or did they just now loosen your leash enough so you could visit?"

"I came because I wanted to."

He stood and stretched, wincing and clutching his ribs beneath the white shirt that was far too large for him. "What would you like to know, Princess?"

"Why did you come *here*, of all places, to seek asylum?" If he was going to talk, that was the first thing I needed to know.

"Because you're here," he said simply. "I knew that if anyone in this land would understand my circumstances, it would be you."

"You were within an inch of death when you showed up," I prompted.

He smiled slightly. "And you had me healed." He paused, and I could tell he was carefully choosing his words. "Father was angry when my men and I returned home after having lost the battle for this castle. He made us train for hours and hours every day, until my men were bone-weary and exhausted. Most of them could barely lift their swords. So, when he ordered me to lead my men back to Aelawyn's gates and fight again, I refused. He called me a traitor and ordered my own men to kill me. Then, he threatened to kill anyone who refused, and promised to slaughter their families as well."

"He's out of his mind," I exclaimed, horrified.

"He is," Carden nodded. "And my men could see it. They knew he would make good on his threats if they didn't do what he asked. I tried to get away, but was barely out of the castle when they caught up to me. Had I not stumbled to the stables and my horse in time..." He shook his head, his lips pinched bitterly.

"How do I know this isn't all a lie? A ruse to get close to me, to gain my trust, and then kill me?"

He smiled wistfully. "You don't."

"That leaves you in a bad position," I said quietly.

He let out a pent-up breath. "I suppose it does. But you showed me mercy when I needed it, so I'll stay here as long as you allow it."

"What if I decide to send you away? If I have you escorted back to the Tierney border?"

He shook his head. "I wouldn't make it a mile within my borders before someone slaughtered me. If that's your plan, Carina. I beg you to end my life here. Don't send me back there. I don't want to die at the hands of my own men, and by extension, my father or brother."

"Thank you for your honesty," I said, moved by his candor. "But why wouldn't you speak with Yurak or the knights?"

He snorted in an unprincely manner and rested his forehead on the bars. "I wanted to speak with the *ruler* of Aelawyn, not a King from Galder pretending to hold two thrones. Besides, if Yurak had his way, I'd already be dead. I wanted to thank you in person for saving my life."

I stared at him. Would Yurak have killed him?

"You don't believe me about Yurak?" he said shrewdly, sensing my hesitation. "Galder is known the world over for their strictness and obedience to archaic laws. Trust me, Princess. If you weren't here, Yurak would have let his true colors show already." He winked at me, and then in a whisper added, "All Kings are tyrants. Be a good Queen."

"Does that mean you would've been a tyrant?"

He pushed off the bars, and as he walked back into the darkness and sank onto his cot once more, he responded with one word. "Absolutely."

ASHER

Trevor was the one who asked Father to vacate the forge. His excuse? His father had already sent for a smith from Galder to fill the position, and he was expected any day. Galderian soldiers helped him load his wagon, and then escorted him from the castle yard.

Father hadn't seen Ella in weeks, not since she came to him asking when the best time would be to catch me at the forge. When I told him about the threats from King Yurak, Father's fists tightened into stone. He forbade me from going anywhere near the castle grounds, but said he would think of a way to draw Ella into the village when it was safe again.

Prince Carden had ridden up to the castle gate, bloodied and half-dead, and since then the gate had remained shut. No one was allowed in or out, even those who worked in the castle but lived in the village.

In just a few short days, the gates would open again. This time, for Ella's coronation. If the rumors were true, right after she and Trevor were married, she would be crowned Queen of Aelawyn. Parties from the northern Kingdoms of Halron and Roane would be arriving any day.

I shuddered to think that Isabel might be among them. I didn't want her venom to reach Ella.

Everyone in the village seemed to be focused on the happy couple. I overheard snatches of conversation from the women on their way through the shops; wondering aloud what her gown would look like and what shoes she would wear. However, I already knew which ones would be on her feet. *"What a handsome young couple they will make!"* and *"How strong and fearless they will be together!"* was all I heard. I couldn't find enough metal to pound the frustration away.

If she really went through with this and married Trevor, it would be his ring on her finger, not mine. She had the strength to stand up to Yurak and release Millie; surely, she wouldn't let them force her to marry someone I knew she didn't love.

I'd been hired to make iron fencing for a home being repaired in the countryside, and lately it had consumed my days and nights. Thank goodness Father and Jerard were here. We certainly had our work cut out for us, but we worked well as a trio.

Jerard, who was quickly catching on to blacksmithing and my moods, knew something was off. He'd been tiptoeing around the forge all morning, avoiding anything that would get in my way. "Are you okay?" he finally asked.

"No." I shoved a cooling piece of iron into the fire and tugged off my gloves. "I can't stand by and watch her marry someone else!" I fumed.

"Do you think she will?"

Scraping a hand over my face, I gave him the only answer I had. "I don't know."

He clapped me on the back. "Then stop her."

"How?"

"The gates'll be open for the coronation. Sneak in and find her. Tell her how you feel."

I blew out a breath. I knew it couldn't possibly be that easy, but I would blend in better with a large crowd. It would at least give me a chance.

"I'm going to make her a ring," I vowed.

"That's the spirit! You just need to make sure you don't get caught before you find her." He looked around at the villagers rushing this way and that, checking for someone who might be close enough to eavesdrop. "I know a way in," he whispered. "A secret way. But you can't tell anyone that it was me who told you, and you can't go until the day of the coronation. With the gates open, they won't be watching the secret entrance. All eyes will be on the future Queen and the main gate to make sure Tierney doesn't attack while the gate's up. It will still be tricky, since the guards and knights will be on high alert, so we'll need to blend in. I'll work on that."

"How—"

He held up a hand, closing his eyes. "It's really better if you don't ask questions. Just leave it to me."

CHAPTER FORTY-SEVEN

ELLA

The evening before my coronation, there was a knock at my door. I prayed it wasn't Trevor or his father, and hoped it would finally be someone I loved, even while knowing it probably wasn't. I felt nauseous. This day had come too fast. "Who is it?"

"It's Nettle, Highness."

Nettle was my new lady-in-waiting, and had been with me since Jewel left. She was sweet and patient, but she wasn't Jewel, and Nettle's presence made Jewel's absence even more profound. "Come in."

She was from Galder, with the tell-tale Galderian coloring of fair hair the color of sunlight and crystal blue eyes. She was a year older than I, shy and soft spoken. As she closed the door gently behind her, she turned and looked up at me from beneath her lashes. "Are you feeling any better?" she asked.

I felt awful, but troubling her with my problems wouldn't help anything. "I am," I lied.

She glanced over at the chamber pot that reeked of vomit. "I brought a new one. It's just outside."

As she retrieved it, I fought another bout of nausea. "I don't know what I'll do tomorrow if I can't hold down my food."

Her eyes widened. "Perhaps you shouldn't eat, Highness."

I looked out the window. "No, maybe I shouldn't." My voice sounded as far away as Asher's forge. It might as well have been in another kingdom, because even though he was just down the road, I couldn't reach him.

Nettle continued to busy herself, saying, "All the preparations have been made. The seamstress will arrive in the morning to help you dress, and there is a woman from Galder here to style your hair. Your new crown arrived this morning, but King Yurak said you weren't supposed to see it until the ceremony. He wants it to be a surprise."

"That's fine." I couldn't care less about what the crown looked like, anyway.

"You seem...upset," Nettle said carefully, sensing my mood.

When she walked over to me, I gestured for her to sit down next to me. "Do you ever feel trapped?" I asked.

She toyed with a stray thread on her skirt. "Sometimes, Your Highness."

I stared at her. "Of course, you do. I'm sure you didn't have your heart set on being assigned to empty my chamber pot and help me get dressed each day."

420

Her eyes widened and I could see the fear shining in them. "I do love helping you, Highness. Please don't think I'm ungrateful!" she stammered.

"I don't think that at all, but I understand." I drew my knees to my body and laid my chin on them. "I feel trapped, too."

The question of *Why?* was written all over her face. "I had dreams for my life that didn't include ruling a kingdom, and all the problems that come with it."

"And what of your marriage to Prince Trevor, Highness? Are you happy with him as your husband and King?" The question was as innocent as she was, but it tore through me like a sword through flesh, burning and slicing through parts of me I didn't know could bleed.

"I'm *not* marrying Prince Trevor tomorrow, the next day, or any day in the future," I asserted. "My heart belongs to someone else."

She cocked her head to the side, confused. "But preparations have already been—"

"I know," I interrupted. "But hear this…there will be no marriage tomorrow."

ASHER

Jerard somehow managed to procure two Galderian guard uniforms. I didn't ask how. "Are you sure you want to go with me? You know what Yurak said would happen." If we were caught, he would face the same punishment I would.

"I'm sure," was all he said.

That settled, we walked through the village and into the woods before changing into the uniforms, and then made our way around to the back area of the castle where there was a small trap door in the forest floor, covered with leaves and brush. Jerard crouched down and pried it open, glancing up at me with a grin.

"Afraid of the dark, Asher?"

"Not a chance."

He opened the door and walked down an earthen ramp that led into a tunnel. I followed behind, closing the door behind us.

The dark corridor obviously hadn't been used in a long time. Jerard held his hand out to tear through the cobwebs. Another ramp led us to a second door, but when he tried to open it, it didn't budge. He put his back to it and pushed with his legs. With a shudder and a groan, it broke free. Dirt rained down around him.

We waited a few moments to make sure no one heard us. A few minutes passed with no movement, and he asked, "Should we go for it?"

Suddenly, I didn't think this was such a good idea. I had a bad feeling.

Jerard eased the door slightly open with the top of his head and tips of his fingers, glancing around furtively. "All clear," he whispered back to me.

With those words, the muscles of my stomach finally relaxed and I released a pent-up breath. He shoved the door aside and climbed up and into the sunlight. I followed behind, blinded for a second, and that was when someone grabbed my tunic, gathering it at the base of my neck and throwing me to the ground. My eyes met Jerard's wide ones.

"What have we here?" a deep voice rumbled as a man crouched down to get a look at us.

My lungs constricted in fear. My first thought was Ella. My second and third were of my father and Jerard's wife and unborn child.

ELLA

"The corset needs to be cinched tighter. Hold in your breath," grouched the dressmaker. I sucked in a harsh breath as her assistants worked the laces on my corset. Again. My ribs were being crushed. She was doing this on purpose. I'd been her personal pin cushion since she came to Aelawyn, and now she was trying to break my bones. The pressure in my face and head built until I couldn't stand it. When I didn't think I could last one more minute without letting out my breath, she clapped.

"There!" she said smugly. "It's perfect."

I could breathe—with difficulty. While I tried to get used to breathing without moving my ribcage, the seamstress barked at her assistants to bring the gown. It hung on the wardrobe door across the room and was so voluminous, it took three women to keep all the layers of fabric from dragging across the stone floor. With my arms together overhead, I dove into the gown and eased my arms into the lace sleeves. With the fastening of each button, it became clear the woman was very good at what she did. The dress fit every inch of me perfectly; form-fitting from neck to waist, and then cascading to the floor in layer after beautiful layer of feather-light tiers.

The fabric was white, but the hue had a delicate, pale blue tint to it. "The color suits you," Nettle said quietly as the other women buzzed around pinning and hand-sewing the hem.

"Thank you," I answered. I ran my hand down the fabric of my stomach. It *was* magnificent, but I was scared out of my mind.

And alone.

The dressmaker, a woman who still refused to give me her name, glanced up from where she crouched in front of me. "Where are the shoes you'll wear today? This might be the right length if you're wearing tall heels."

I asked Nettle to retrieve the glass slippers from my wardrobe. She returned quickly, gently placing them before me. It wasn't until I eased my feet into the shoes that reality hit me.

My sister should have been there wearing her shoes. She should be the one crowned Queen of Aelawyn, yet there I was, wearing the dress that should have been hers, my feet in her shoes. Soon, I would wear her crown. I would stand alone and hope the people couldn't see how badly my knees shook; how I wanted to turn, hold up all the delicate layers of my dress, and run away to a soot-covered forge.

No further alterations were needed. With Ivy's shoes, the dress was the perfect length. The dressmaker and her assistants quickly gathered their things and left the room without another word or a backwards glance. Nettle stood quietly against the wall, worrying her hands.

"Can I get you anything?" she asked hesitantly.

"No." I attempted to smile but failed miserably. "Would you give me a few moments alone?"

She nodded her head. "I'll be outside if you need me."

"Thank you."

After she pulled the door closed behind her, I stood there and listened to all the sounds drifting in through the

424

window. As the guards announced the opening of the gate, a crowd of villagers poured in, the din of their chatter filtering up to me. A little girl sat above the crowd on her father's shoulders as he walked across the cobblestones. Women chatted merrily, wearing their best dresses and skirts and braids in their hair. Where were Asher and Nathaniel? Where was my family?

I searched for Asher in the sea of people, needing to see him. With nothing more than a single nod of his head, he could calm me down and tell me everything would be okay, letting me know this wasn't a colossal mistake.

My door opened, the hinges creaking. I hastily wiped my tears away before turning to find Trevor standing in the doorway.

"Trevor, I wasn't expecting anyone." I tried to compose myself and give him a smile, but the tears would not stop.

"I'm sorry." He took several long strides across the room and stopped just before reaching me. At first I thought he was just sorry I was crying, but then he took a deep breath and exhaled loudly. Again, he repeated the words. "I'm sorry."

"For what?"

"I've been such a fool, Carina. I'm sorry for having any part in my father's manipulative games, for not being strong enough to stand up to him and tell him no, for not respecting what you wanted and trying to make you love me, and most of all for hurting you." His hazel eyes bore into mine.

I shook my head. "You haven't hurt me."

"Haven't I? My father believes we're getting married in just a few minutes, and I let him believe you wanted to go through with it. I was afraid to disappoint him, and because I was a coward, I've hurt my only friend."

My mouth gaped open in shock as he continued his confession. There was a sheen of sweat on his forehead.

425

"I thought you told him I didn't want to marry you! You *promised* to tell him!"

"I should have, and I was wrong to not honor that promise. But I want to be honest to you from here on out. You are my friend, and I owe at least that much to you." A pained look crossed his face. "I vow to make things right. I will tell my father that we will not be married and I'll stand by your side whether you want to accept the crown or not, but there's something I have to tell you that's much more pressing, Carina."

"What is it?" I asked tremulously, afraid of what I might hear.

"Asher is in the yard."

My breath whooshed out, but I immediately set to action, gathering my skirts. "I need to see him."

He caught my arm. "You need to listen to me first. Father devised a plan. He thought if we got him and his family away from you, we might be able to persuade you to go through with this marriage, to accept this life—this crown—you didn't want. I gave the order for Nathaniel to leave, and then Father had Asher removed from the castle and told him that if he stepped foot back inside the gate, he would…" Trevor pursed his lips and looked out the window.

He was here. Asher was inside the gate… My stomach dropped. "He would *what?*" I asked, stepping in the direction he was looking and forcing him to meet my eyes.

"God, you are a vision," he breathed, moving toward me. His pained eyes raked over my face, framed by ringlets that were pinned into place, my neck, my gown.

"What did your father tell Asher?" I prompted him again.

"He told him he would have him and his father executed if he came near you again, or even attempted to contact you."

His words were like a dagger, and for a moment my heart stuttered. I splayed my hand over my stomach.

That was why Asher disappeared, and why his father was gone, too.

He reached out, trying to comfort me, but I knocked his hand away angrily.

"I just learned about my father's threat, and I came straight to you."

"If Asher's in the yard, he's in danger!" I yelled.

He straightened the lapels on his dark jacket, uncomfortable and fidgety. "We've grown close in the past several weeks. We've become friends."

"We have." *What did* that *have to do with anything?*

Trevor knelt on one knee and looked up at me, taking my hand in his. "I know I'm not the man you want to see before you, but if you accept me as your husband, I vow to protect you and all you love for as long as I live—even Asher Smith." He cleared his throat, a pained look stretching across his face. "You can still see him. You can still love him and be my wife. But I can't offer my help if you don't accept me."

I didn't *want* his help! "Why would I need your help?" I asked, irritated.

He hung his head.

He isn't hurt, is he? I couldn't control my breaths, and suddenly my restricted ribcage was bursting, straining against the fierce bones of the corset. My head felt light, too light, and the room began to spin. *He came back and Yurak found him...*

"You're father has him. Doesn't he?" I stepped back from him. "No. Not Asher," I gasped.

"He and another man snuck into the castle yard wearing tunics that belonged to Galderian soldiers. The tunics had been reported stolen."

I shook my head, tears filling my eyes.

"Let me help you," he implored again. His body moved toward mine as he stretched his hand out.

Fearing I had no other choice, I said, "You can help me if you want—as my friend. But I will never marry you. Whether you stand up to your father or not is your choice, but I won't betray my heart just so you can keep your father's approval," I replied with a shaking voice. And then I ran, past him and out the door, shocking Nettle as I rushed past her.

I'd asked the dressmaker to make a long pocket in the side of the gown. My ivy-handled dagger was inside. I would use it if I had to. I would defend Asher's life with my own, even against the King of Galder. *Please don't let it be too late.*

Trevor shouted for me to wait, but I couldn't. I wouldn't.

"Where is he?" I yelled over my shoulder.

"He was outside, in the side yard, but I don't know where he is now."

Oh, God. I rushed through the hallways, drawing gasps from everyone I passed. People pressed their backs against the wall as I bellowed for them to move, to get out of the way.

I ran, my glass shoes clinking perilously on the stone floor with each step. The front doors were open, and the people of Aelawyn were already gathered.

Down the hall, I saw a guard standing at a door that led to the far side of the castle. We never had guards stationed there. Suddenly I knew where Asher was. I ran, my dress billowing behind me like a cape on a windswept moor. "Open this door!" I demanded.

He hesitated, shifting on his feet. "I can't," he answered anxiously.

"Open this door right now!"

"You don't want to go out there, Princess."

428

"Yes, I do!"

I heard sounds of a scuffle beyond the heavy wooden door. "Asher!" I shrilled as the guard fumbled for his key. "Hurry up! Open this door or I'll have your head mounted on my wall!" I cried, pounding the door with the heel of my palm.

As the lock disengaged, the guard's icy blue eyes met mine with a silent warning. Trevor stood behind me, his lips set in a straight, thin line. He held the door open as I rushed outside, where a crowd of knights hovered in a circle.

As I ran down the steps, I tripped and almost fell over. My foot crumbled beneath me. No, my foot wasn't broken; my shoe was. The heel of my right shoe had shattered, leaving shards of glass underfoot. Toeing the broken shoe off and then the whole, matching one, I pushed toward the group of Galderian knights, shoving them out of my way. "Move!"

In the center of them, two men were on their knees. The stones all around them were splattered with blood. "Asher?" I cried, recognizing him in an instant and reaching out for him, falling to my knees. Blood trickled from cuts above his brow. His eyes were blackened and swollen, and his nose was badly broken. His tunic had been torn away, and the parts of his torso I could see were bloodied and bruised.

The man with him was in even worse shape, clutching his ribs and panting as he used his free hand to stanch the river of blood that poured from a gash on his head.

"Don't touch him." The order came from behind as Yurak approached.

The people of Aelawyn surrounded us, drawn to the commotion like moths to a flame. But I didn't care. *Let them see.*

I spun around to look at the imperious King of Galder. "You had no right!" I sputtered.

"I had *every* right!" his voice thundered.

Trevor moved, positioning himself between his father and me, and then he drew his sword on his father. He held the tip of his blade was inches from the King's throat. The crowd let out a collective gasp. "You will stand there and you will listen to every word that comes out of her mouth, and you will not speak until she is ready for you to speak. For once in your life, listen!" he roared at the King. "I've done everything you've ever told me to. But what you've been doing is wrong. *This* is wrong, and I won't continue to stand by and let you hurt Ella or those she loves anymore."

Yurak's face turned bright red. The vein in his forehead began to throb. His expression was nothing short of murderous and it was aimed at Trevor, me, and Asher.

Despite the shape he was in, Asher tried to push himself up to his feet. Unable to stand, he crawled forward to put himself in front of me, every inch of him seething at Yurak. Yurak—whose own men shrank from him. Carden's words came back to me: *All Kings are tyrants. Be a good Queen.*

"Get behind me," Asher panted, his teeth grinding together.

But I would not cower. I refused to yield. For the first time in my life, I would stand in front of a King and cut him down.

This was him.

The true Yurak, hiding dark deeds beneath a majestic surface.

The King. The one whose words were beyond reproach.

The one whose orders were obeyed and who wouldn't tolerate insolence.

The one who threatened Asher's life and drove away everyone I loved.

My father tried to break me with threats and violence. Yurak tried to break me with mind games and manipulation.

One was just as bad as the other, but neither would be tolerated. Not anymore.

"She's young and naïve. She doesn't know what's best for her life." Yurak addressed Trevor as if I wasn't there at all. Enough of this.

"I'm not marrying your son."

"Didn't you read your mother's letter?" he snarled. "She wanted you to have a better life! My son can give that to you. A match with him will ensure that your mother's last wish comes true."

"I don't love your son, Yurak, and he wouldn't be happy if we were wed. Don't you see that? How is what you're doing to keep me and Asher apart, any different from the way my father tore you and my mother apart? How?"

The truth of my words seemed to smack him in the face. I could see his angry features soften, his thin lips relax as he considered the true meaning of my words.

"As a child I lived in fear, terrified that I would make my father angry and he would have me killed on the spot. He almost did—twice. But what scared me the most was the thought that he would hurt my sister or my mother. So one day, I stopped fighting back. I let him break my spirit, and sometimes my bones. I was incapacitated by fear, too afraid to ever tell him no, but I won't make that mistake again."

I pulled myself up to my full height, feeling more confident with each word I spoke. "No. I will not marry your son, Yurak. I refuse to subject myself or him to a loveless marriage. I respect him enough as a friend to want better than that for him." I glanced at Trevor, who pinched his lips together and nodded his head in thanks. Taking a deep breath, I took a tentative step toward the King.

"You've helped me, and this Kingdom, so much," I said, softer now. "You knew my mother long before I was born, and believe me when I say that I would've loved to have met the woman you knew. But growing up, I didn't know her," I said softly. "And, though I'm thankful that you both intervened on my behalf, and wanted more for me than my father had planned, circumstances changed. I changed.

"I won't marry your son, and I won't allow you to hurt *any* of my people for the sake of furthering your own agenda." A hard look crossed my features and my voice was deadly as I added, "And you won't touch another hair on the head of the man I *do* love," and motioned toward Asher.

Yurak raked shaky hands through his hair and muttered a curse. "You're young; you don't know any better. I am sorry you had a horrific childhood, Carina. I'm sorry I wasn't able to help you then, but I'm trying to help you now. I am trying to make you a good Queen. To that end, sometimes a leader must sacrifice what they *want* for what their people *need*."

"People keep telling me that, and I've told myself those same words. But the truth is that I only have one life to live, and only one opportunity to live it the way I want. I may be young, but I'm not a fool. Your days of manipulating me are over. You helped my Kingdom when she needed it, and I will be forever grateful. But that doesn't mean I'm your puppet, or that I'll blindly do anything you ask."

Yurak swallowed, the thick apple bobbing in his neck. Trevor offered a hand to Asher, helping him stand. He swayed on his feet, but his friend was upright behind him, still holding his head wound.

"If this is what being a Queen is all about – I want no part of it."

"This is your birthright!" Yurak argued. "You gave your word! You promised that if Galder fought with Aelawyn, you would assume the throne!"

432

"Some promises are meant to be broken, Yurak, and this is one of them; especially when I know I'm not the best choice for this Kingdom. I can't do this. This is *not* the life I choose. I choose rags over riches, and I choose Asher Smith. If he'll still have me."

A squeeze of his hand and a raspy, "Yes," were all I needed.

Trevor lowered his sword, noddingonce to me.

"And who will lead your people?" Yurak asked dismissively, sweeping his hand across all of Aelawyn, the square bursting with people who'd witnessed our spectacle. "You're just going to leave them? Go live on a farm?"

I almost laughed.

Yes! I wanted to shout. I wanted to leave and live on a farm and dig in the dirt and kiss Asher's lips whenever I wanted.

"Perhaps Trevor would consider staying," I suggested. "If the people will have him, he could govern Aelawyn until the village is fully rebuilt. He can keep building up the army, and when he needs to leave to lead his people in Galder, a new ruler can be chosen. They chose someone to lead them before. They can choose again."

Trevor clutched his chest, shocked at the suggestion. "Why me?"

"Because you're willing to lead and not follow. You came to me and did what was right, even though you knew it would go against your father's wishes. And even though it went against your own. Today, by coming to me, you chose to be your own man instead of your father's shadow."

I turned to Yurak and to the people behind him. "And he's ready. He's so ready for this. He's smart – he was the one who made the trade deal with Waverly! He knows the best way to defend this Kingdom because you taught him well. He knows how to run it, and he'll do an amazing job, whereas I know nothing about any of this. In my ignorance, I could ruin everything we're trying to rebuild. This isn't a chance the people should be willing to take. They need someone who can lead the second they sit on the throne, and that someone isn't me."

I shook my head and looked at Trevor. "I've sat with you in all the meetings. You speak with Kings as though you're their equal because you are. You aren't intimidated. You're a master at military strategy. I know how you led during the battle. If you follow your heart, like you just did here today, you'll be a great leader."

Asher wouldn't be alive if Trevor hadn't been brave enough to defy his father and come to me today. I knew it must have been difficult for him to do, because I knew what it was like to try to please a parent who had ridiculously high expectations. I knew what it was like to be denied the thing you wanted most. At first I was angry when he came into my room and told me about Asher, but he *did* tell me. He came to me and told me before his father's men killed them. The only reason I got to them in time was because Trevor had a conscience. Trevor had a heart; a heart that loved me, and loved the thought of ruling, even though it scared him. He could rule Aelawyn for a few years and help them get back onto their feet, and it would prepare him for ruling Galder one day. He was what Aelawyn needed, not me.

Yurak assessed his son. "He is a better man than I," he said quietly.

"Yes, he is," I agreed.

Asher squeezed my hand, looking at me through swollen lids.

"I need to get a few things from my chamber," I said definitively. Just then, Nathaniel and Hayden pushed their way to the front of the crowd, helping Asher and his friend.

"I'm okay," Asher told them. He limped toward me and took my hand.

The moment of truth came as we walked around the King of Galder, and I wondered if he would allow me to pass. His body tensed, but he didn't stop our passage. However, Trevor jogged alongside us until we stopped, and asked a final question. "Will you stay in Aelawyn?"

"I'm not sure yet."

He shook Asher's hand. "Take care of her."

"I will," Asher replied.

Yurak watched us walk away through the sea of people— my people. Their quiet murmurs of encouragement were more than welcome as we walked up the castle steps hand in hand, a commoner and the former princess who wanted to be his. Asher paused on the staircase to collect the glass slipper that was still whole. When he placed it in my free hand, I smiled and cried and thanked him. I still had a piece of my sister. In my hand and in my heart, she was with me.

A woman with long, blonde hair and a heart-shaped face, the same woman I saw sitting with Asher through the window of the tavern, ran to his friend and threw her arms around him. Her belly was swollen and as she cried and kissed him, her hands couldn't stop touching him.

"My apprentice Jerard and his wife. She's expecting," he said, following my eyes. I had been so foolish.

"Come upstairs with me?" I asked.

We rushed to my room, where Nettle was already waiting inside with a large sack ready for me. I stuffed some clothing, shoes, the crown I wore as a child, my mother's crown, and Ivy's shoe into the sack. Asher carried the bag as we made our way down the steps, despite my protests.

"You'll break your neck if you trip on those skirts," he teased. "You should've put on some boots."

I smiled. "A princess doesn't wear boots."

"Thank god you're not one anymore," he teased. At the bottom of the staircase, he kissed my lips and we walked out of the castle and through the crowd, together at long last.

As we left the castle of the Kingdom of Aelawyn, my family and his walked alongside us. I could finally breathe—or at least I would be able to, as soon as I got this corset off.

Jewel insisted he go straight to the healer, and I didn't have the heart to tell her that the whole village was probably back in the castle yard.

"Is anything broken?" I asked him quietly.

"My pride and my nose, maybe a couple of ribs. But they'll be fine."

Hayden quietly walked between Matthew and Nathaniel.

Millie grumbled about how stupid I was to give up the crown, castle, and Kingdom, but Jewel and Hayden shushed her.

TREVOR

What I loved most about Ella Carina of Aelawyn was that she was unafraid of following her heart. She walked fearlessly beside Asher, his blood all over her white gown, clasping his hand as they walked through the people and then the gates, her head held high. She wasn't wearing a crown, but she might as well have been.

She never told me about her childhood, or just how brutal her father had been, but she survived it despite him. I silently applauded Tierney for having cut him down before he could trample the spirit that now blazed triumphantly inside her. She thought she was broken, but she was the strongest kind of broken I'd ever seen.

Though it hurt to watch her leave, a seed of hope sprang up in my heart. She trusted me. She told me I was ready, and in my heart I knew I was. She called me a good man, and my father agreed. And I promised to be her friend. Friends helped one another, and she asked me to help her. I would lead Aelawyn. For her. Because it was right, and because she deserved to have the kind of life she wanted. I just hoped I could be a good leader until another could take my place. I hoped I could be the man Ella confidently said I was.

Clasping my hands in front of me, I kept my head high as well, my shoulders pressed back. When the former Princess, and almost Queen, of Aelawyn disappeared from sight, the people turned to me.

It was time for me to step forward and guide them.

"I know you were expecting a coronation today, and perhaps a wedding, but it seems fate had other plans. I would be proud to accept the Princess's recommendation if you'll have me."

The people assented, ayes rising in the air. I wasn't sure if it was due to shock or the fact that they had little choice in the matter, but the die had been cast either way.

"Well since that's settled, let's not let this beautiful day go to waste!" I said laughingly. "Please join us inside the castle for a feast, and let us celebrate new beginnings together."

My father gave a slight nod and followed me inside the castle and into the Great hall. When we first found Ella in Tierney, my father told me that if I successfully wooed her, our union would make both kingdoms prosper. It would allow him to keep his promise to her mother, one he desperately wanted to keep.

I didn't expect her to steal my heart in the process.

There was a place deep inside my chest that ached, and I knew that no matter how much time passed, it would always be there. It ached for the absence of her in my life, for I knew she would not return. It ached for the tattered dreams of what I'd once hoped would be a future with Ella Carina of Aelawyn.

And that ache wouldn't leave my chest for a very long time.

CHAPTER FORTY-EIGHT

ASHER

She walked toward me, a basket on her arm and a smile on her face. I wiped the sweat from my brow and the soot from my skin before making my way toward her with a newfound spring in my step. Grabbing her waist as she collided with me, I lifted and spun her around in the air, making her giggle. She loved that.

"Don't spill our supper, Mr. Smith," she teased. *Mr. Smith.* The small band of steel felt red-hot in my pocket. I wanted to call her *Mrs.* and make her mine for good.

She and I were living in her parent's large estate home, but in our spare time, our fathers and her brother were helping me fell trees for a home of our own. She just didn't know it yet.

I brushed a strand of hair from her face and swatted her backside when she turned to unfold the picnic blanket. She smiled over her shoulder and then arranged the food and ale, and just like our first picnic lunch, we sat together, close but not close enough. I noticed the slice of cake she'd brought for us. She baked one every few days since we'd left the castle, counting them as she made them with tiny tick marks on a paper she pinned to the wall. When I asked her why she was counting, she grinned and said she wanted to make it to a thousand.

"Are you happy?" I asked abruptly.

The corners of her lips turned upward. "Of course. Aren't you?"

"I am happier than I've ever been in my life. There's only one thing that could possibly make me happier."

Her face scrunched in confusion. "What's that?"

I reached into my pocket and pulled out the folded note.

> *My Ella,*
> *Will you marry me?*
>
> > *Yours forever,*
> > *Asher*

She covered her mouth with her hand, dropping the note into her lap. In my pocket, my fingers found the second ring I'd made her. The first had been lost when the guards found me and Jerard sneaking into the castle yard on coronation day.

I held the small band out for her.

 440

"I know it isn't gold, but I made it for you. If you would be my wife, Ella Carina, there isn't a day that would go by where I wouldn't thank God above for sending you to me. There isn't anything I wouldn't do for you, Ella. I love you so much it hurts sometimes."

She settled in my lap with her arms around my neck. "Love should never hurt, Asher Smith. Would it ease the pain if I said yes?"

"It would definitely help..." I grinned. "*Mrs.* Smith."

When her lips pressed against mine, she melted into me and I into her. We paused long enough for me to slip the ring onto her finger before resuming our kiss. The pain of the squeezing of my heart was immediately forgotten, but my love for her only continued to flourish.

CHAPTER FORTY-NINE

Once upon a time, in a land not so far away, there was a kingdom ruled by a generous and kind Prince from another land. He saw that the Kingdom prospered under his rule. When several peaceful years passed and a young man, not from noble but of peasant blood, gained the favor of his people, the Prince placed a crown upon the young man's head and declared him King of Aelawyn.

King Matthew Farmer was just and kind, and despite the long hours spent indoors making sure that all was well with his people, he often took walks to the stables to see to the horses and livestock. He rode through the village that continued to thrive, just to see that his people were happy on his way to his family's country home.

His mother and father hosted supper every Sunday afternoon, and he never allowed himself to miss the weekly event. There, his sister Millie, her husband, and their three children—all with hair like fire—would hug and wrestle him as if he weren't King at all. There, his father would clap him on the shoulder and his mother would pull him in for a hug. And he would see his cousin, who wasn't really related by blood at all, but who was as a sister to him as well. Ella and Asher and their twin sons, with the dark brown hair of their mother and deep blue eyes of their father, would often join in the fray.

His family ignored his finery, and for a few blissful hours he would step into peasant clothes and go outside to play with the children. One day, he hoped to meet a girl who stole his heart away and have children of his own.

He hoped.

He dreamed.

Aelawyn prospered.

Once upon a time, all was right in the world. All because one girl was brave enough to follow her heart, trading riches for rags. And because a charming young man ignored both to become Prince of her heart.

And the two of them lived happily ever after.

ACKNOWLEDGEMENTS

Riches to Rags was a labor of love and wouldn't have been published without the hard work and help of some very special people.

To my hubby and our kids, thank you for being so supportive, even when I had to work late into the night.

To my mom, thanks for always helping me with the plots to my stories.

Thanks to all my family and friends who ask about and support my dream.

To my beta-readers: Melanie Deem, Cristie Alleman and Ashley Cestra, thank you for helping make it better.

Thanks to Stacy Sanford. She worked tirelessly to slay the editing on this book and without her wit and wisdom, I'd be lost.

Thanks to Melissa Stevens, who drew the cover and interior illustrations. Thank you for bringing Ella's world to life.

To Kelly Risser, who helped me with the back cover copy on this book, I appreciate you so much.

The world is a better place because we can lose ourselves in our imaginations for a little bit. Thanks to every reader who picks this, or any of my books up and gets lost. I appreciate you so much.

And thanks to God for his many blessings in my life.

ABOUT THE AUTHOR

Award-winning author Casey L. Bond lives in Milton, West Virginia with her husband and their two amazing daughters. She loves to read almost as much as she loves to write, letting the voices in her head spill onto the blank page.

Check out the Riches to Rags landing page on her website and see a map of the kingdoms mentioned in the book!

www.authorcaseybond.com

CONNECT ON SOCIAL MEDIA

Facebook: www.facebook.com/authorcaseybond

Twitter & Instagram: @authorcaseybond

RELEASING IN 2018

A retelling of sleeping beauty unlike any you've read before.

Get ready, witches.

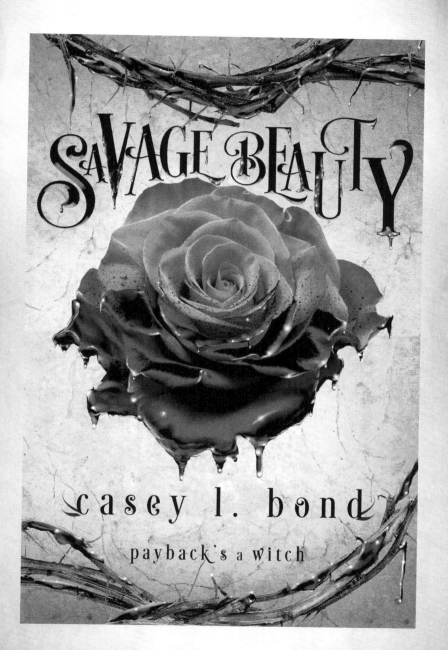

SAVAGE BEAUTY

casey l. bond

payback's a witch